Society

# GAIL
# WHITIKER

MILLS
BOON

Published in Great Britain 2014
by Mills & Boon, an imprint of Harlequin (UK) Limited,
Eton House, 18-24 Paradise Road, Richmond, Surrey, TW9 1SR

REVENGE IN REGENCY SOCIETY
© 2014 Harlequin Books S.A.

*Brushed by Scandal* © 2011 Gail Whitiker
*Courting Miss Vallois* © 2010 Gail Whitiker

ISBN: 978-0-263-25016-9

052-0715

Harlequin (UK) policy is to use papers that are natural, renewable and recyclable products and made from wood grown in sustainable forests. The logging and manufacturing processes conform to the legal environmental regulations of the country of origin.

Printed and bound
by CPI Group (UK) Ltd, Croydon, CR0 4YY

**Gail Whitiker** was born on the west coast of Wales and moved to Canada at an early age. Though she grew up reading everything from John Wyndham to Victoria Holt, frequent trips back to Wales inspired a fascination with castles and history, so it wasn't surprising that her first published book would be set in Regency England. Now an award-winning author of both historical and contemporary novels, Gail lives on Vancouver Island, where she continues to indulge her fascination with the past, as well as enjoying travel, music and spectacular scenery. Visit Gail at www.gailwhitiker.com.

# Brushed by Scandal

GAIL WHITIKER

To Mum and Dad, who continue to be an ongoing source of love and support in so many areas of my life. Thank you for always being there.

And to my good friend Lynne Rattray, who inspires me with her *joie de vivre* and her unflagging sense of humour.

# Chapter One

It was a perfect night for sin. The mid-May evening was deliciously warm, the air sweet with the fragrance of rosewater and violets, and the attention of one hundred and forty-nine of the guests moving slowly through the overheated rooms of Lord and Lady Montby's palatial London house was focused on anything *but* the young lady slipping furtively through the French doors and onto the dimly lit balcony beyond.

Fortunately, as the attention of the one hundred and fiftieth guest had been fixed on that silly young woman for some time, the chances of *her* making a clean escape were never very good. Over the course of the evening, Lady Annabelle Durst had watched the exchange of smiles and glances passing between Miss Mercy Banks and a certain red-coated officer, and, given that the gentleman had recently left the room by the same doors through which Miss Banks now passed, Anna had no doubt that a clandestine rendezvous was planned. A rendezvous that could only end in disaster for one or both of them.

'Mrs Wicks, would you please excuse me,' Anna said quietly. 'I've just seen someone I really must speak with.'

'Why, of course, Lady Annabelle, and I do apologise for having taken up so much of your time, but I really didn't know who else to turn to. Cynthia simply refuses to listen and I was at my wits' end, wondering what to do next.'

'I understand perfectly,' Anna said, endeavouring to keep one eye on the French doors. 'Cynthia has always been the most stubborn of your daughters and if you force her to spend a month in Scotland with her grandmother while her sisters are allowed to go to Bath, she *will* rebel. However, I believe the compromise I've suggested should help to alleviate the tension and make everyone feel better.'

'I don't mind saying it's made *me* feel a great deal better,' Mrs Wicks murmured. 'You're an uncommonly wise young woman for your age, Lady Annabelle. Your father must be very proud.'

Aware that her father would have been a great deal more proud had he been sending word of her upcoming engagement to *The Times*, Anna simply inclined her head and moved on. There was no point in telling Mrs Wicks that her unwed state was an ongoing source of consternation to her father or that he had offered to settle not only a handsome dowry, but one of his smaller, unentailed estates on her the moment she announced her engagement. Why bother when there was absolutely no one in her life for whom she felt even the slightest attraction?

As for being deemed a very wise young woman, Anna supposed it could have been worse. She might have been called studious or obliging—agreeable, even—none of which truly described her character. Yes, it was true, she had been dispensing an inordinate amount of advice to wilful young ladies and their frustrated mothers of late, but what was she to do when they kept coming to her for answers? Their problems were relatively easy to understand and comparatively simple to fix, even if the parties involved thought otherwise.

As to the hapless Miss Banks, that was clearly a situation Anna was going to have to deal with personally if she hoped to ward off imminent disaster.

The balcony, illuminated by multiple strands of brightly coloured lanterns strung from one end to the other, ran almost the entire length of the house, but one glance in either direction was enough to show Anna that her quarry had already vanished into the gardens. Foolish girl. Did she really believe that the gardens were empty? That no one else had sought privacy in the shadowy follies and Grecian temples sprinkled throughout the trees?

Obviously not or she wouldn't have allowed herself to be led astray—and Anna had no doubt the girl *had* been led. Mercy Banks was as green as a leprechaun's jacket. Barely seventeen, she was in London for her first Season, so it was only to be expected that, upon meeting a young man who looked at her as though she were Aphrodite reincarnated, she would mistake attraction for something deeper.

Anna had been seventeen once, too. She remembered all too well the excitement of looking up to find a handsome gentleman watching her; the exhilaration of his hand casually brushing hers when they drew close enough to converse, followed by the warmth of his breath as he leaned in close to whisper a compliment.

Oh, yes, she knew well the lure of those forbidden bowers. But *because* she had been prevented from making a mistake by someone who had noticed her infatuation and taken the time to intervene, Anna now recognised the importance in doing the same for others. Unfortunately, as she walked down the stone steps and into the garden proper, she realised she was not the only one intent on locating the wayward Miss Banks. Marching with grim resolve along the gravel path ahead of her was the young lady's mother, determined to find her errant daughter before some dreadful misfortune could befall her.

Obviously, more desperate measures were now called for.

'Mrs Banks,' Anna called in a pleasant but carrying voice. 'What a pleasure to see you again.'

Mrs Banks, a small, rotund lady wearing a dark green gown and a headband adorned with flowers and fruits of an exotic hue, paused to glance over her shoulder; upon seeing Anna, she stopped, her expression of concern changing to one of pleasure. 'Why, Lady Annabelle, how nice to see you again. It must be nearly a month since we last had an opportunity to chat. Lady Falconer's musicale, wasn't it?'

Anna inclined her head. 'I do believe it was.'

'I thought so. Dreadful soprano. I vow my ears rang most painfully for the rest of the night,' Mrs Banks said with a frown. 'But what are you doing out here all on your own?'

'The house was so warm, I thought to enjoy a quiet stroll through the gardens,' Anna said, keeping her voice light and her words casual. 'But where is Mr Banks this evening? I take it he did come with you.'

'Oh, yes, albeit reluctantly. He's not much into these society affairs, but I told him we must make an effort if we hope to settle Mercy in an advantageous marriage.' Mrs Banks sighed. 'For his sake, I hope she finds a husband sooner rather than later. He's that anxious to get back home.'

'I'm sure it will be sooner,' Anna said, heart jumping as she caught sight of a red coat just beyond Mrs Banks's right shoulder. 'But I wonder, Mrs Banks, if you've seen the new fountain Lady Montby recently had installed over by the reflecting pool? It really is quite spectacular.'

'I'm sure it is, but at the moment, I am more concerned with finding Mercy.'

'Really?' Anna affected a look of confusion. 'I am quite sure I saw her inside the house.'

'You did? Where?'

'Heading in the direction of the music room.'

Mrs Banks rolled her eyes, but Anna noticed a definite softening in the lines of tension around her mouth. 'I might have known. Someone told Mercy that Lady Montby had recently acquired a new pianoforte and naturally she was anxious to see it. The child is quite musically gifted,' her mother confided proudly. 'And while I take care not to compliment her too much, I am hopeful it will help in the quest to find her the right kind of husband.'

'I'm sure she will do you both proud,' Anna said, slipping her arm through the older woman's and turning her around. 'But as long as we're heading back inside, why don't we take a peek at the fountain? It will only take a moment, and then you can carry on and look for your daughter.'

Obviously deciding it was a good idea, Mrs Banks made no demur as Anna led her in the direction of the fountain, which was indeed a spectacular affair, and which, more importantly, was located at the opposite end of the garden from where Anna suspected Mercy and her officer were hiding. Once there, she introduced Mrs Banks to Mrs Wicks, who immediately launched into a diatribe about the difficulties of presenting ungrateful daughters to society, whereupon Mrs Banks said how thankful she was that she only had one daughter to marry off, rather than three.

Anna left the two women happily commiserating with one another and quickly retraced her steps. She was almost at the far end of the path when Miss Banks stepped out, her cheeks flushed, her blue eyes wide with apprehension. 'Lady Annabelle!'

'Miss Banks. Enjoying a few minutes *alone* in the garden?' she asked pointedly.

'Yes! That is…no. That is…oh dear.' The girl looked up and the expression on Anna's face turned her cheeks an even brighter shade of red. 'Please tell me Mama didn't know where I was.'

'She did not, but only because I suggested you were still inside the house,' Anna said. 'If she had caught you and your young man out here together, the consequences would have been dire!'

The girl's pretty face fell. 'I know. And I promise I won't do it again. It's just that…'

When she broke off blushing, Anna prayed the silly girl hadn't done anything irredeemably stupid. 'It's just that what?'

Mercy sighed. 'He said it would be all right. He told me… he loved me.'

Of course he had, Anna thought drily. Was a declaration of love not the most common justification for inappropriate behaviour on a young man's part? 'Then I take leave to tell you that he had a very poor way of showing it. Has he secured your father's permission to speak to you?'

Miss Banks looked even more miserable. 'We have not even been formally introduced. We first saw one another in Hyde Park a week ago, then again at a masquerade two nights past.'

'At which time he suggested a rendezvous for this evening,' Anna surmised.

The girl nodded.

'Then you must not see him again until a formal intro-duction has been made. Whatever his feelings, asking you to meet him alone in a secluded garden demonstrates the worst kind of judgement,' Anna said firmly. 'He must seek a proper introduction and when the time comes to speak of his intentions, he must approach your father and ask permission to call upon you. Please believe me when I say that what he did tonight was *not* an indication of love, Miss Banks, no matter how much you would like to believe otherwise.'

The young girl bit her lip. 'No, I don't suppose it was. But I did so want to see him again…even if only for a few minutes.'

'A few minutes are more than enough to ruin a lifetime,' Anna said more gently. 'You must guard your reputation as fiercely as you would your most precious possession, because right now, it *is* your most precious possession. Once lost it can never be regained and no one will suffer more for its absence than you. So, no matter what *any* gentleman says to you, or how sweetly he says it, do not let yourself be tempted into such an indiscretion again.'

'Yes, Lady Annabelle.'

Anna could see from the expression on Mercy's face that she had learned her lesson and that the episode would not be repeated. Nor did Anna expect that it would. It wasn't that Mercy was bad. She was simply young and impetuous, as were so many girls her age.

As Anna herself had once been.

'And now, we shall return to the house and you will find your mother and endeavour to set her mind at rest,' she said, leading Mercy back along the gravel path. 'As for your young man, you are not to look for him again, and, if he seeks you out, you are to tell him you will not speak to him until the two of you have been properly introduced…which I shall endeavour to do later this evening.'

Miss Banks gasped. 'You would do that for me?'

'I would, but only if you give me your promise that you will never see…' Anna paused. 'What is the officer's name?'

'Lieutenant Giles Blokker.'

'Fine. That you will not see Lieutenant Blokker again without suitable chaperonage. I may not be around to save you the next time.'

'You have my promise, Lady Annabelle. And thank you!
Thank you so very much!'

Upon returning to the ballroom, Miss Banks did exactly as
she had been told. When Lieutenant Blokker tried to approach
her, she treated him to a look that would have done her crusty
old grandmother proud and then went in search of her mother.
The young man looked understandably crushed, but Anna
hoped it had taught him a lesson. If he truly cared for Miss
Banks, he would do whatever was necessary in order to further the connection in the manner of which society approved.
If not, he wasn't worth having in the first place.

'Do you attempt to save them all from themselves?' asked
an amused masculine voice close to her ear. 'Or only the ones
who don't know any better?'

Anna turned her head and found herself looking into the
face of a stranger. A very handsome stranger, but a stranger
none the less. 'Were you speaking to me, sir?'

'I was. And pray forgive my boldness, but I happened to be
in the garden when you came upon the young lady, and such
was my timing that I was privy to most of your conversation
with her just now. She is indeed fortunate to have you as her
champion.'

His voice was velvet over steel. Resonant, powerful, the
kind of voice that held audiences spellbound and sent impres-
sionable young women swooning. Anna could imagine him
reciting Shakespeare on the stage at Drury Lane, or reading
love sonnets by Bryon or Wordsworth, those low, sensual
tones sparking desire in any young woman's breast.

But was their meeting now entirely coincidental? While
she thought him too old for Miss Banks and too casual in
his addresses to her, the fact he had been in the garden at
the same time as they had, and that he just happened to be
standing next to her now, left her wondering.

'I only attempt to save the ones I deem worthy of saving,' she replied carefully. 'The rest I leave to their own devices.'

'Just as well,' the gentleman said. 'Most people sin for the fun of it and wouldn't welcome your intervention, no matter how well intentioned. Unlike Miss Banks, whose romantic heart would likely have got the better of her had you not stepped in to save the day.'

Anna caught an undertone of amusement in his voice and, despite her natural inclination to be wary, found herself smiling back at him. He was certainly an attractive man. His face was long rather than square, his jaw angular, his cheekbones high and well formed. Intelligence gleamed in the depths of those clear grey eyes and his lips, curved upwards in a smile, were firm and disturbingly sensual. His clothes were expensive, his linen impeccable, and while his hair shone black in the light of a thousand candles, the tiny lines at the corners of his eyes put him closer to thirty than twenty.

No, he definitely wasn't after Miss Mercy Banks, Anna decided. He could have eaten the silly little chit for dinner and still gone away hungry. But neither was this a casual conversation, of that she was sure. 'I am undecided as to whether I should be flattered by your comments or offended by them,' she said. 'I had no idea my actions were being so closely observed.'

'A gentleman should never make his attentions too obvious, Lady Annabelle. I pride myself on my ability to observe without *being* observed—a quality necessary to those who involve themselves in the convoluted lives of others. Wouldn't you agree?'

Anna's eyes widened. So, he knew who she was and what she was about. That alone should have put her on her guard, yet all it did was make her more curious. She liked a man who didn't play games; Lord knew, London society was all too full of them. 'I fear you have the advantage of me, sir.

You obviously know a great deal more about me than I do about you.'

'Only because you are more visible in society,' he murmured. 'And as much as I regret the inequity of the situation, we both know it would be ill-mannered of me to introduce myself, so I shall wait for the thing to be done properly as you have so kindly offered to do for Miss Banks.'

His words abruptly called to mind the promise Anna had made earlier and her brows knit in consternation. 'An offer made impetuously at best, I fear. Apart from the officer's name, I know nothing about the man and have no idea if he is even *worthy* of an introduction.'

'Then allow me to set your mind at rest. I happen to know that Lieutenant Giles Blokker is an amiable young man who, despite having behaved with the decorum of a rambunctious puppy, is an excellent catch. His father is Major Sir Gordon Blokker, who distinguished himself with Wellington on the Peninsula, and his mother is the former Lady Margaret Sissely. The boy was educated at Eton, went on to read English and history at Oxford, and, as his father's only son, he is heir to a considerable estate. More importantly, I believe he is the kind of man of whom both Miss Banks's mother and father would approve.'

Surprised by the extent of the man's knowledge and by his willingness to share it, Anna inclined her head. 'I am grateful for your recommendation, sir. How fortunate that you are so well acquainted with the officer.'

'In fact, we've never met. But one hears a great many things during the course of one's social day, and if I feel it is information that may be of use to someone else, I am happy to pass it along. I trust that, in this instance, it serves you well. Good evening, Lady Annabelle.'

With that, he bowed and walked away, leaving Anna with a host of unanswered questions tumbling around in her brain.

Who was he, and why did his sudden appearance at her side not seem as coincidental as he might like her to believe? By telling her all he had about Lieutenant Blokker, he'd put her in the enviable position of being able to make the promised introduction, aware that not only might she be introducing Miss Banks to her future husband, but that he was a gentleman worthy of the role. Had he known more about the predicament in which she'd landed herself than he had chosen to let on?

Not surprisingly, Anna found herself watching the handsome stranger as he moved around the room. She noticed that he did not linger with any one person or group for any length of time, but that his gaze touched on every person there, his expression unreadable as he took note of who they spoke to and with whom they danced. Even when he stopped to speak to an upright older gentleman who was clearly intent on engaging him in a serious conversation, his eyes continued in their restless study. Was he was a private investigator of some kind? He looked too aristocratic for such an occupation, but then, perhaps a man who didn't *look* the part was *exactly* the sort of man who should be doing that kind of work.

He'd certainly made an impression on her. For once she'd actually *enjoyed* having a conversation with a gentleman newly met at a society function. Normally, she was quick to wish them over, knowing all too well what they were really all about.

*Is this someone with whom I have anything in common? Do I feel a connection strong enough to spend the rest of my life with him? And, of course, what do we each stand to gain by aligning our families in marriage?*

They were all questions Anna had asked herself in the past. And with that one unfortunate exception where the marriage *would* have been a disaster, the answers were always the same.

No, not likely, and nothing.

But this gentleman intrigued her. She found herself watching for him in the crowd, curious to see how he acted with other people, anxious to catch just one more glimpse of him. Wanting to know if he might be looking back at her.

And when he did and Anna felt her gaze trapped in the soft silver glow of his eyes, she knew it was too late to look away. She had carelessly exposed herself, allowing her interest in, and her curiosity about, a stranger to be revealed. Was it any wonder that when he tipped his head and slowly began to smile, she felt the heat rise in her cheeks and the breath catch in her throat?

Goodness, who would have thought that with just one look, he could make her feel as awkward as a schoolgirl, as young and as gauche as Miss Mercy Banks. Surely as a mature woman of twenty-four, she knew better than to encourage the attentions of a man she'd only just met...

Anna dipped her head and boldly returned his smile. No, clearly she did not. But as she opened her fan and reluctantly turned away, the knowledge that a handsome man whose name she didn't know still had the power to make her blush was more than enough to keep the smile on her face for the rest of the evening.

'Parker, have you heard anything I've said?' Colonel Tanner demanded in a harsh whisper.

'Every word, Colonel.' Sir Barrington Parker's expression didn't change, though he was careful to pull his gaze from the face of the exquisite young woman who had just smiled at him across the room. No small feat for a man who appreciated beauty as much as he did. 'You wish me to investigate the disappearance of your mistress—'

'I never said she was my mistress!' the older man blustered.

'There was no need. Avoiding my eyes while you described her told me all I needed to know,' Barrington said smoothly. 'She is approximately twenty years old, slim, with dark brown hair and rather startling green eyes. The last time you saw her she was wearing a pale blue gown with a white shawl and a bonnet with either blue or black ribbons.'

The older man grunted. 'Apologies. Just don't like blathering on to a man who doesn't appear to be listening.'

'I wouldn't accomplish much if I didn't listen, Colonel,' Barrington said, though in truth he hadn't been paying as much attention as he should. Through the mirror on the wall behind Tanner, he had been watching Lady Annabelle Durst attempt to play matchmaker. She had waited until Lieutenant Giles Blokker was in the midst of a small group of people with whom she was obviously acquainted and had sought the necessary introduction. Then, as the other couples had drifted away, she had engaged Lieutenant Blokker in conversation, no doubt with the intent of bringing Miss Banks's name into the discussion.

At that point, Barrington had seen a look of cautious optimism appear on Blokker's face, followed moments later by one of genuine happiness. When Lady Annabelle turned and started in the direction of Miss Banks and her mother, the young pup had fallen into step behind her, clearly delighted that he was on his way to being formally introduced to the young lady who had captured his heart.

'Where did you last see Miss Paisley, Colonel?' Barrington asked, reluctantly dragging his attention back to the matter at hand.

'Hogarth Road. I keep a house there. Nothing elaborate, you understand,' the Colonel said gruffly. 'Just a place for friends to use when they come up to London.'

Barrington nodded. He knew exactly what the house was

used for and it certainly wasn't the convenience of friends. 'I shall make enquiries. Where can I reach you?'

'Best send a note round the club. Wouldn't do to have anything come to the house.'

Barrington inclined his head. Though most wives knew about their husbands' affairs, none wanted proof of them showing up at their front doors. 'As you wish.'

'Look here, Parker, it's not what you think,' the Colonel said, clearing his throat. 'Eliza's not like the rest of them. She worked as a lady's maid in a respectable establishment until the eldest son took a fancy to her. When she was turned off without references, one thing led to another until she ended up in a brothel. That's where I met her,' he said, again not meeting Barrington's eyes. 'She told me her story and naturally I felt sorry for her, so I asked her if she'd like to come and work for me. I knew Constance was looking for a new maid and I thought it might be a way of getting Eliza back into respectable employment.'

Barrington's smile was purposely bland. 'And did your wife agree to take Miss Paisley on?'

'She did, but it wasn't long before she realised there was something going on and I had to let Eliza go,' the Colonel said regretfully. 'Felt so damned guilty, I offered to put her up at the house on Hogarth Road until she was able to find something else.'

With the small stipulation, Barrington surmised, that she become his mistress while she was there. A gentleman's altruism only extended so far. 'It would seem Miss Paisley has much to be grateful to you for, Colonel.'

'I thought so, which was why I was so surprised when she left without telling me,' the Colonel said. 'Bit concerned, if you know what I mean.'

Barrington did know and he wasn't surprised. Tanner was a decent chap, somewhere in his mid-fifties, with four married children and eight grandchildren. His wife had been in poor health for the last five years and, though he was devoted to her in every other way, her ill health had prevented them from enjoying a normal marital relationship. So he had turned, as so many men did, to the ranks of the *demi-monde* and there he had encountered Miss Elizabeth Paisley, the young woman for whom he had developed an unfortunate affection. Now she was missing and the Colonel was worried about her.

Probably with good reason, Barrington thought as he shook the man's hand and walked away. It was a simple fact that women of Miss Paisley's ilk were concerned with one thing and one thing only. Survival. It wasn't easy making a living on the streets of London. A woman never knew if the man who pulled her into a darkened alley and threw up her skirts was going to be a paying customer or the last man she ever saw alive. Being a prostitute was not without its risks. But being the mistress of a wealthy man took away those risks and gave a woman security. It put a roof over her head and kept food on her table. So why would someone like Miss Paisley walk away from all that if she'd had any other choice?

It was a question Barrington couldn't answer. And as he prepared to leave Lady Montby's reception—after deciding it was best that he not stop to engage the delightful Lady Annabelle in conversation again—he realised it was one that would trouble him until he did. To that end, he made a mental note to ask his secretary to make some initial enquiries into Elizabeth Paisley's whereabouts. Sam Jenkins had been with Barrington long enough to know what kind of questions to ask and who to ask them of. Then, depending on what he turned up, Barrington would either call upon one of his extensive network to continue the investigation or delve into the matter himself.

He wasn't sure why, but as he climbed into his carriage for the short ride home, he had a feeling there was more to the disappearance of Miss Elizabeth Paisley than met the eye.

# Chapter Two

Anna pulled her dapple-grey mare to a halt by the base of a large oak and waited for Lady Lydia Winston to catch up with her. The two had made a point of riding together on Tuesday and Thursday mornings, and these rousing canters had become one of the highlights of Anna's week. Lady Lydia, daughter of the Marquess of Bailley, was by far one of the most amusing and interesting people Anna had ever met.

'Goodness!' Lydia said as she drew her spirited Arabian bay level with Anna's mare. 'I was sure I had you at the big tree, but you sprinted past me as though I was standing still!'

'I suspect Danby put oats in Ophelia's bucket this morning.' Anna reached down to give the mare's glossy neck an affectionate pat. 'She's not usually that quick off the mark.'

'Nevertheless, I had enough of a lead that it shouldn't have made a difference. Tarik isn't used to being left behind.' Lydia's ready smile flashed. 'I won't be so easily fooled the next time.'

Anna laughed, pleased that her little mare had done so well. She nudged her to a leisurely walk, content to enjoy the glorious morning sunshine and the relative emptiness of the park. During the fashionable hour, the avenue they were now travelling would be crowded with elegant carriages and their equally elegant passengers, but at this time of day it was the perfect place to enjoy a brisk canter.

'By the by, have you heard the news?' Lydia enquired.

'That depends. All I heard at Lady Montby's reception last week was that Cynthia Wicks had threatened to run away if her mother forced her to spend a month with her grandmother in Scotland.'

'Good Lord, so would I,' Lydia declared. 'Lady Shallerton is a cold fish with whom I wouldn't wish to spend an hour, let alone a month. But it wasn't Miss Wick's escapades I was referring to. It was the Baroness Julia von Brohm's.'

'Baroness von Brohm,' Anna repeated slowly. 'Should I know her?'

'La, Anna, where have you been? It is all about town that the Viennese baroness has come to London to find a new husband.'

'Why? What happened to her old one?'

'He died. Almost two years ago now, leaving her a very lonely but extremely wealthy young widow. Apparently, he showered her with the most glorious jewellery and she was heartbroken when he died. Not because he gave her jewellery,' Lydia was quick to say, 'but because they were genuinely in love. But she is finished with her mourning now and has come to London to start a new life. I understand she's taken a very fine house in Mayfair and is in the process of redecorating it from top to bottom.'

'I'm surprised she would have chosen to leave Vienna at such a time,' Anna remarked. 'One would think she would prefer to stay with her family and friends.'

'Friends I'm sure she has, but again, rumour has it that her only brother moved to America when she was quite young and hasn't been heard from since. And both of her parents are dead.'

'How tragic. What about her late husband's family?' Anna asked.

'Apparently, they were never close. Difficulties with the mother-in-law, from what I hear.'

'So Vienna is full of unhappy memories and the arms of her family hold no welcome. No wonder she decided to come to London,' Anna said. 'Has she any close friends here?'

'I don't believe so. Society is wildly curious about her, of course, but it hasn't exactly thrown open its doors in welcome.'

'Then we must be the first to do so,' Anna said without hesitation. 'I suspect once people see the daughters of the Marquess of Bailley and the Earl of Cambermere welcoming her, the rest of the doors will open soon enough. All it takes,' she added with a knowing smile, 'is that first little push.'

Barrington's sword flashed once, cutting a smooth silver arc through the air and echoing down the length of the long gallery. Metal slid along metal as the two men moved through the orchestrated dance of extend, lunge, parry and retreat, and while concentration was etched on the faces of both men, only Barrington's brow was dry. He feinted to the left, drawing his brother-in-law's blade wide and ultimately opening him up to defeat.

'Damn it!' Tom Danvers snapped as the point of Barrington's sword flicked his chest for the fifth time. 'You've beaten me again!'

'And I will continue to do so if you do not apply yourself more keenly to the sport,' Barrington said, drawing back. 'You won't stand a chance if you keep both feet firmly planted on the ground, Tom. You need to keep moving. Dance on the balls of your feet.'

'Oh, yes, that's easy for you to say,' the other man complained good-naturedly. 'I've three stone and five years on you and it's not so easy being nimble when you've more weight below your waist than above it!'

Barrington laughed. 'Then tell that pompous French chef of yours to start preparing less fattening meals.'

'What? And have him quit because *I* had the audacity to tell him what to cook! Jenny would have my head. Monsieur Etienne is the finest French chef in London!' Tom exclaimed.

'Be that as it may, he is not doing *you* any favours by serving all those heavy sauces and rich desserts,' Barrington pointed out. 'If you wish to be quicker on your feet, the weight will have to come off. In fact, I have a solution.'

'I'm not sure I wish to hear it,' Tom muttered.

'Of course you do. I shall take Monsieur Etienne off your hands for a few weeks and you can have Mrs Buckers. I guarantee your clothes will fit better after only three days.'

'Perhaps, but I won't care because Jenny will have left me.'

Barrington clapped his brother-in-law on the back. 'A man must sacrifice for his sport. Ah, there you are, Sam. Has my two o'clock appointment arrived?'

'Not yet, Sir Barrington,' the secretary said, 'but another gentleman has and is asking to see you. I put him in your study.'

Barrington nodded. A visitor in his study meant one of his network had come in with information. Friends he welcomed in the gold salon. Any one else was made to wait in the hall until he had ascertained the nature of their business. He did not purport to be a private investigator, but, because of his past successes, there were those who sought him out regardless.

'Thank you, Sam. Tell the gentleman I shall be there directly.' He turned to smile at his brother-in-law. 'Sorry to cut it short, Tom...'

'No need to apologise. You're a busy man, and, in truth, I've taken all the humiliation I can for one day,' Tom said good-naturedly. 'Before I go, however, Jenny wanted me to find out if you were available for dinner one night this week. She misses you dreadfully and even young George was heard to say it has been a great deal too long since his Uncle Barr came to play with him.'

Barrington's pleasure was unfeigned. 'Tell my sister I shall make a point of coming one evening this week, and then inform my nephew that I shall be sure to arrive early enough to play two games of hide and seek with him.'

'He will not sleep for the knowledge,' Tom said, starting for the door. 'By the by, I should warn you that you won't be the only guest.'

Barrington groaned. 'Don't tell me Jenny's matchmaking again?'

'I'm afraid so.'

'Who is it this time?' He sighed.

'Lady Alice Stokes.'

Barrington dug into his memory. 'Lady Alice—?'

'Stokes. Eldest daughter of the Earl of Grummond,' Tom supplied helpfully. 'Beautiful, cultured and an heiress in her own right. Jenny thinks she would be perfect for you.'

'That's what she said about the last three ladies she introduced me to and they were all unmitigated disasters.'

'True, but at least you wouldn't have to worry about Lady Alice marrying you for your money. Or for your title,' Tom pointed out.

True enough, Barrington conceded. An earl's daughter could do much better than a baronet, and if she had her own money, his wouldn't be as much of an attraction. 'Very well, you may tell my sister I shall come on Friday. That should give her ample time to put everything in place.'

'You're a brick, Barrington,' Tom said in relief. 'I was afraid you'd bow out if I told you the truth, but I didn't like the idea of you being caught off guard.'

'Rest assured, I shall be the perfect guest,' Barrington said. 'And you need not fear retribution from my sister. I shall act suitably surprised when the beautiful Lady Alice and I are introduced.'

'You are a gentleman in every sense of the word.'

'Just don't let me hear any mention of the words *engagement* or *marriage* or I shall be forced to renege on my promise,' he warned.

Tom grinned. 'I shall do my utmost to make sure you do not.'

They parted on the best of terms; Tom to return to his happy home, Barrington to return to his study to find out what new information had come to light. While there might be more comfort in the former, he was not of a mind to complicate his life by taking a wife. Investigating the underhanded dealings of others was hardly conducive to forming intimate relations with gently reared young ladies. It was neither the occupation of a gentleman nor what he'd planned on doing when he'd returned to London after his father's death.

However, when an unfortunate set of circumstances involving two of his father's friends and a large sum of money had forced him into the role, Barrington had discovered a unique talent for uncovering the hidden bits of information others could not. His carefully cultivated network of acquaintances, many of whom held positions of power and even more who held positions of knowledge, made it easy for him to find out what he needed to know and, over time, he had established himself as a man who was able to find solutions for people's problems.

Naturally, as word of his reputation had spread, so had his list of enemies, many of them the very men he had helped to expose. Beneath society's elegant and sophisticated façade lurked a far more dangerous element—one comprised of men to whom honour and truth meant nothing. Men who were motivated by greed and who routinely committed crimes against their fellow man.

Hence Barrington's wish to remain single. While he could be reasonably assured of his own safety, he knew that if his enemies tried to get to him through the woman he loved, he would have no choice but to comply with their demands. The unscrupulous did not trouble themselves with morals when it came to getting what they wanted.

That's why he had taken to avoiding situations that might place him in such an awkward situation. He existed on the fringes of society, close enough to be aware of what was going on, but far enough away that he wasn't seen as potential husband material. So far it had worked out well, much to the annoyance of his happily married sister. He was able to assist the people who came to him with problems, while avoiding the complications that came with marriage.

Now, as he headed to his study, Barrington wondered which of the sins was about to be revealed and who would be thrown out of Eden as a result. Paradise was sometimes a very difficult place in which to live.

'Ah, Richard,' he said, opening the door to see his good friend, Lord Richard Crew, standing at the far end of the room, his attention focused on a particularly fine painting by

Stubbs that covered a large part of the end wall. 'Still hoping I'll sell it to you?'

'Hope has nothing to do with it,' Crew murmured. 'Eventually, I'll name a price you won't be able to refuse.'

'Don't be too sure. I've rejected every offer you've put forward so far.'

'Fine. I'll make you another before I leave today.'

Barrington smiled as he moved towards his desk. Lord Richard Crew was an ardent lover of horse flesh and owned more paintings by Stubbs, Tillemans and Seymour than any other gentleman in London. Quietly picking them up as they came available for sale, he had amassed an impressive collection—with the exception of *Whistlejacket*, a magnificent painting of a prancing Arabian thoroughbred commissioned by the Marquess of Rockingham and acknowledged by many to be one of Stubbs's finest. *That* was the piece of work currently hanging in Barrington's study, and the fact that he owned the *one* painting his friend wanted more than any other was a constant source of amusement to him and an ongoing source of irritation to Crew.

'Did it ever occur to you,' Barrington asked now, 'that money doesn't enter into it?'

'Not for a moment,' Crew said, finally turning away from the canvas. 'Every man has his price and it's only a matter of time until I find yours. But rest assured, I *will* find it. And I know exactly where I'm going to put *Whistlejacket* once I finally wrest it from your iron grip.'

Barrington smiled. 'And where might that be?'

'In my study, opposite my desk. That way I'll see it when I'm working.'

'I would have thought you'd want it in your bedroom.' Barrington moved to the credenza and poured brandy into two glasses. 'That way, you'd see it most of the time.'

'True, but I would only be paying it half as much attention.' Crew's smile widened into a grin. 'After all, there are so many *other* pleasurable things to occupy oneself with in the bedroom, wouldn't you agree?'

The question was rhetorical. Lord Richard Crew's reputation as a lady's man was honestly come by because, in point of fact, Crew adored women. He had ever since a buxom dairy maid had introduced him to the pleasures of Venus in the loft of his father's barn, followed in quick succession by three of the housemaids, two of the village shop girls, and a married woman Crew had steadfastly refused to name.

As he'd grown into a man, his appreciation for the fairer sex had not waned, but out of respect for his parents, he'd left off tupping the household servants and moved on to ballet dancers and actresses. He had steadfastly avoided marriage and refused to trifle with virgins or débutantes, saying it was a matter of pride that he had never deflowered an innocent or given false hope to a well-born lady. And once it became known that he preferred his women uncomplicated and experienced, the list of married ladies willing to accommodate his voracious appetite grew.

Hence Barrington's surprise when, during the investigation of the Marchioness of Yew's infidelity, he'd learned that his good friend was finally in honest pursuit of the lady's very respectable and exceedingly lovely nineteen-year-old daughter, Rebecca.

'Sexual conquests aside, dare I hope you've come with news about the identity of Lady Yew's alleged lover?' Barrington enquired.

'Nothing alleged about it.' Crew strolled towards the desk and picked up a glass in his long, slender fingers. 'I happened to be in the lady's house on the occasion of the young man's last visit and saw them acting very lover-like towards one another.'

'How convenient. Were you there in hopes of seeing the lovely Lady Rebecca or to question the mother?'

'Most definitely the former.' Crew raised the glass to his nose and sniffed appreciatively. 'Unlike our young Romeo, I have no interest in romancing ladies over the age of thirty. The bloom has long since gone from that rose.'

'But with maturity comes experience,' Barrington said, reaching for his own glass. 'A gently reared miss of nineteen will know nothing of that.'

'Fortunately, I am more than willing to teach her all she needs to know.' Crew swallowed a mouthful of brandy, pausing a moment to savour its flavour before sinking into a chair and resting his booted feet on the edge of the desk. 'However, returning to the matter at hand, the gentleman in question is not our typical Lothario. I've never heard his name mentioned in association with lady *or* ladybird; in truth, I'd never heard of *him* until his arrival in London just over a month ago. So the fact he has chosen to dally with a marquess's wife is somewhat unusual.'

'Are you sure they *are* lovers?'

Crew shrugged. 'Lady Rebecca confided her belief that they are. She told me she's seen the gentleman enter her mother's private quarters on more than one occasion, and, as I was leaving, I saw them myself going upstairs together hand in hand.'

'Damning evidence indeed,' Barrington said. 'And reckless behaviour for a man newly arrived in London. Does he suffer from a case of misplaced affection or unbridled lust?'

'Knowing the marchioness, I suspect the latter,' Crew said in a dry voice. 'It's well known she favours younger men because her husband is a crusty old stick twenty-five years older than she is.'

'Still, she has charmed a legion of men both younger *and* older than herself, and, up to this point, her husband has always been willing to turn a blind eye,' Barrington said. 'For whatever reason, he is not inclined to do so this time.'

Crew shrugged. 'Perhaps he fears a genuine attachment. It's all very well for a woman to take a lover to her bed, but it is extremely bad taste to fall in love with him. People have been known to do abysmally stupid things in the name of love.'

'Too true. So, who is the poor boy Lord Yew is going to flay?'

'His full name is Peregrine Tipton Rand.'

'Good Lord. *Peregrine Tipton*?'

'A trifle whimsical, I admit, but he's a country lad visiting London for the first time. Apparently, his father owns a farm in Devon. Rand's the oldest of four brothers and sisters but he hasn't shown much interest in taking over from his father. Seems he's more interested in books than in bovines, so when the mother died, the father shipped him up here to stay with his godfather in the hopes of the boy acquiring some town polish. Unfortunately, all he acquired was an affection for Lady Yew.'

Barrington frowned. 'How did a country boy come to be introduced to a marchioness?'

'Through the auspices of Lord Hayle, Viscount Hayle.'

'Hayle?' Barrington's eyebrows rose in surprise. The beautiful Lady Annabelle's *brother*? 'I wouldn't have thought the Earl of Cambermere's heir the type to associate with a country gentleman of no consequence.'

'I dare say you're right, but as it happens, he has no choice.

Rand is *staying* with the family. Cambermere is the man reputed to be his godfather.'

'Reputed?'

'There are those who say the lad bears a stronger resemblance to the earl than might be expected.'

'Ah, I see.' Barrington rapped his fingers on the desk. 'Wrong side of the blanket.'

'Possible, though no one's come right out and said it.'

'Of course not. Cambermere's a powerful man. If he did father an illegitimate child years ago and now chooses to have the boy come live with him, no one's going to tell him he can't. Especially given that his own wife died last year.'

'But there are other children living in the house,' Crew pointed out. 'Legitimate children who won't take kindly to their father foisting one of his by-blows on them.'

Especially the son and heir, Barrington reflected grimly. Viscount Hayle was not the kind of man to suffer such a slight to his family name. If he came to suspect the true nature of Rand's paternity, he could make things very difficult for all concerned. So difficult, in fact, that Rand might hightail it back to the country, and that was something Barrington had to avoid. He needed to find out as much as possible about the young man *before* news of his liaison with Lady Yew went public—because there was no doubt in Barrington's mind that it would. The marchioness wasn't known for being discreet. Her list of lovers was a popular topic of conversation at parties, and the fact that *this* time, her husband had chosen to make an example of the young man would definitely make for scintillating conversation over wine and cards.

'You've gone quiet,' Crew said. 'Mulling over how best to break the news to dear Peregrine's unsuspecting family?'

'As a matter of fact, I was.' Barrington got to his feet and walked slowly towards the long window. 'I met Lady

Annabelle Durst at Lady Montby's reception the other week.'

'Ah, the beautiful Anna,' Crew murmured appreciatively. 'Truly one of society's diamonds. I cannot imagine why she's still single.'

Barrington snorted. 'Likely because she's too busy trying to prevent silly young women from ruining themselves.'

'An admirable undertaking, though knowing how many silly young women there are in London, I don't imagine it leaves much time for looking after her own future.'

'Virtually none,' Barrington said, his thoughts returning to the lady whose existence he had first learned about during an investigation he'd undertaken the previous year. It had not involved Lady Annabelle directly, but had focused instead on the uncle of one of the girls she had been trying to help. As a result of that investigation, however, Barrington had become familiar with her name and with her propensity for helping naïve young girls navigate their way through the choppy waters of first love.

Always from a distance, of course. Given his own self-imposed boundaries, Barrington knew better than to risk getting too close to her, but he was strongly aware of her appeal and smart enough to know that she could be dangerous for that reason alone. He'd met a lot of women in his life, but there was something about Lady Annabelle Durst that set her apart from all the rest. Something rare. Something precious. Something indefinable…

'Well, if you're going to sit there all afternoon and stare into space, I'm leaving.' Crew drained his glass and set it on the desk. 'I am expected for tea with Lady Yew and her daughter; if you have nothing more to tell me, I may as well be on my way.'

'Fine. But while you're sipping tea and whispering endearments in Lady Rebecca's ear, see if you can find out anything else about her mother's relationship with Rand,' Barrington said. 'The more I know about the situation, the better off I'll be when it comes time to confront him with it.'

Crew unhurriedly rose. 'I'll ask, but, given the extent of the marquess's displeasure, I doubt you'll hear Rebecca *or* her mother mention the name Peregrine Rand with favour again.'

Anna was reading Shakespeare when the door to the drawing room opened. Leaving Hamlet on the page, she looked up to see their butler standing in the doorway. 'Yes, Milford?'

'Excuse me, my lady, but a gentleman has called and is asking to see Mr Rand.'

Anna glanced at the clock on the mantel. Half past eight. Somewhat late for a social call. 'Did you tell him Mr Rand was from home?'

'I did, but he said it was a matter of some urgency and wondered if you knew what time he might be home.'

'Lord knows, I certainly don't.' With a sigh, Anna set her book aside. 'Did the gentleman leave his card?'

Milford bowed and silently proffered the tray. Anna took the card and read the name. *Sir Barrington Parker.* How strange. She knew the man by reputation rather than by sight. A wealthy baronet with an impressive home, he was, by all accounts, a cultured, educated and exceedingly charming man who was also reputed to be one of London's finest swordsmen. The story went that he'd spent several years in Paris training under a legendary French master; when his father's death had compelled him to return to England, Sir Barrington had been besieged by the pinks of society asking him to teach them his skills. With very few exceptions, he had refused every request.

Why, then, would he be here now, asking after a man with whom he was unlikely to have even the slightest acquaintance? 'Ask him to come in, Milford. Then inform my father that we have a visitor.'

The butler bowed. 'Very good, my lady.'

The wait was not long. Moments later, the door opened again and Milford announced, 'Sir Barrington Parker.'

Anna rose as the butler withdrew, but the moment the baronet arrived she stopped dead, totally unprepared for the sight of the man standing in her doorway. *'You!'*

'Good evening, Lady Annabelle.' Sir Barrington Parker strolled into the room, as impeccably turned out as he had been the night of Lady Montby's reception. His dark jacket fit superbly across a pair of broad shoulders, his buff-coloured breeches outlined strong, muscular thighs and his cravat was simply yet elegantly tied. 'I told you an occasion would present itself whereby our introduction could be made in a more acceptable manner.'

'You did indeed,' Anna said, struggling to recover from her surprise. She'd thought about him several times since meeting him at Lady Montby's, and, while she'd found him a powerful presence there, he was, in the small confines of the drawing room, even more compelling. 'I simply did not think it would be in my own home or that the illustrious Sir Barrington Parker would turn out to be the gentleman with whom I exchanged opinions the other night.'

'Illustrious?' His beautiful mouth lifted in a disturbingly sensual smile. 'I fear you are confusing me with someone else.'

'On the contrary, rumour has it that you are an excellent fencer and an unparalleled shot. *And* that you've uncovered more than your fair share of secrets about those who move in the upper reaches of society.'

His smile was indulgent, much like that of a teacher addressing an errant pupil. 'You and I both know how foolish it is to put stock in rumours, Lady Annabelle. One never knows how or why they start and most often they are proven to be wrong.'

'Do you deny that it was you who exposed Lord Bosker as an embezzler?' Anna said. 'Or that you just *happened* upon that letter naming his fine, upstanding cousin, Mr Teetham, as his accomplice?'

'I tend to think the timing was, for the most part, coincidental,' Sir Barrington said, careful to avoid a direct answer. 'Their crimes would have come to light soon enough. They grew careless, too confident in their own ability to deceive.'

'But *you* were the one who drew attention to what they were doing,' Anna persisted. 'Had you not, they would most likely have continued in their games and who knows what other crimes they would have perpetrated. But forgive my manners, Sir Barrington. Pray be seated.'

'Thank you. And while your confidence in my ability is flattering, I should tell you it is entirely misplaced.' He glanced at the chairs arranged in front of the fireplace and settled into the wingback chair opposite the one upon which her book lay open. 'There were other people involved in their arrest and to a far greater extent than myself. But, as we are talking about other people's affairs, how did matters proceed between Miss Banks and Lieutenant Blokker after you and I parted company the other night?'

Surprised he would even remember the conversation, Anna managed a smile. 'Remarkably well, all things considered. Lieutenant Blokker turned out to be a delightful young man and I realized, after speaking with him, that while the manner of his approach to Miss Banks left much to be desired, his intentions were strictly honourable.'

'Ah yes, the ill-fated rendezvous in the garden,' Sir Barrington mused. 'Not the best thought out of plans, but thanks to you no harm came of it.'

'And thanks to you, the two are now formally introduced and eager to begin a courtship,' Anna said. 'But I don't suppose Miss Banks's romantic escapades have anything to do with your reason for being here this evening.'

'Regrettably, they do not. I was actually hoping to speak to your house guest, Mr Rand, but I understand he is from home.'

'Yes, he is.' Anna gazed at him, surprised to feel her heart beating a little faster than usual. Obviously she wasn't used to being alone with such a disturbingly handsome man. 'I wasn't aware the two of you were acquainted.'

His dark brows arched ever so slightly. 'Are you acquainted with *all* of Mr Rand's friends and associates, Lady Annabelle?'

'As a matter of fact, I am. Peregrine has only recently come to stay with us, and, given how anxious my father was that he become known in society, I took the liberty of including him in all of *my* social activities,' Anna said. 'That being the case, I think I can safely say that I *do* know with whom he is and is not acquainted. I have never heard him speak of you.'

Briefly, the gentleman smiled, but while it softened the lines of his face, it did nothing to lessen the intensity of the expression in his eyes. 'I am not acquainted with Mr Rand, Lady Annabelle, nor is he with me,' he said quietly. 'I've come here at the behest of another, on a matter of extreme urgency to both.'

'An urgent matter?'

'Yes. One I would prefer to discuss in private with the gentleman. Or, failing that, with your father, if he is at home.'

'He is, Sir Barrington,' Lord Cambermere said, walking into the room. 'But if Edward has done something that warrants discussion—'

'It is not Edward Sir Barrington wishes to speak to you about, Papa,' Anna said calmly. 'It is Peregrine. And there is no point in my giving you privacy since we both know Peregrine will tell me everything the three of you say the moment Sir Barrington leaves.'

'He may not wish to tell you this,' Sir Barrington said, slowly getting to his feet. 'And I would prefer to speak to you about it in private, my Lord.'

Cambermere frowned. He was a tall, solidly built man with warm brown eyes, a ruddy complexion and dark hair that was just beginning to show signs of grey at the temples. His clothes were more suited to a country gentleman than a man about town, but now that his year of mourning was over, Anna was hopeful he might once again take up an interest in socialising, and, by necessity, his appearance.

'Yes, I'm sure you would,' the earl said. 'But I have no doubt Anna speaks the truth about the boy's repeating everything we say. He's my godson, you see, and the two have become as thick as thieves in the short time they've been together. I'm surprised he's gone out without her tonight. Still, he's a quiet enough lad. I can't imagine him doing anything that would be inappropriate for Anna to hear about.'

Anna could tell from the look on the baronet's face that he was less than pleased with her father's decision. Equally aware that trying to force the earl into a private interview was not the conduct of a gentleman, Sir Barrington merely shrugged those broad shoulders and said, 'Very well, though you may wish to change your mind once I begin to relate the details of the situation. You see, not long ago, a titled gentleman came to see me with regards to a personal matter concerning his wife.'

'His wife?' The earl looked decidedly confused. 'What has this to do with Peregrine?'

'The gentleman suspected his wife of having an affair,' Sir Barrington continued. 'Naturally, he asked me to make enquiries as discreetly as possible and to keep the results similarly confidential. He knew I'd had some success in this area and I agreed to look into the matter for him and see what I could learn. Now, having discovered the identity of the gentleman, I felt it behoved me to hear his side of the story. That's why I'm here. I regret to inform you, Lord Cambermere,' Sir Barrington said quietly, 'that the gentleman guilty of having an affair with the wife of a highly placed nobleman is none other than your godson, Mr Peregrine Rand.'

# Chapter Three

'**P**eregrine!' Anna said on a gas. 'You think *Peregrine* is having an affair with a married woman? But that's impossible!'

'The facts would indicate otherwise,' Sir Barrington said. 'But perhaps you would care to explain why you believe it to be so unlikely?'

'Because he isn't the type to get involved in something like that. In fact, I don't think he's ever even been involved with a woman. He is…a student of history,' Anna said, needing to make him understand why his accusation was so totally misplaced. 'Old bones and ancient ruins hold far more appeal for Peregrine than would the charms of the most practised seductress.'

At that, Sir Barrington's mouth lifted in a smile. 'I doubt Lord Yew would appreciate his wife being referred to as a practised seductress, but—'

'Lord Yew!' Cambermere interrupted. 'Dear God, don't tell me you're talking about the marchioness?'

'I am.'

'Damn!' The earl muttered something under his breath,

then abruptly turned to his daughter. 'I think under the circumstances it would be best if Sir Barrington and I were to continue this conversation in private, Anna. There's nothing here you need to be involved with.'

'But why not? I already know the worst,' Anna said. 'And I stand by my claim that Peregrine is innocent of the charge.'

'Unfortunately, I have evidence to the contrary,' Sir Barrington put in. 'And I do not intend to reveal *that* in front of you, no matter what your father says.'

'Of course not,' Cambermere mumbled. 'Not fit for a lady's ears, I'm sure. But I will have the details of it before the lad comes home.'

'But, Papa—'

'No, my dear. Sir Barrington and I will discuss this alone,' her father said firmly. 'When Peregrine gets home, have Milford send him straight to my study. And you are *not* to speak with him beforehand.'

Anna said nothing as the two men left the room because, in truth, she didn't know what *to* say. Peregrine involved in a scandalous affair with a married marchioness? Impossible! Even if he were to lift his head out of his books long enough to look at a woman, it certainly wouldn't be to one married to another man. He had a stronger moral code than that, of that she was sure.

And yet Sir Barrington Parker claimed to have proof of the affair. What kind of proof could he have, and how had Peregrine come to be accused of this wretched undertaking in the first place? Had Lord Yew a grudge against him? Perhaps as the result of a card game or a wager? Had they had words over some political issue, or a difference of opinion over the current government's handling of some matter of concern to both of them?

There had to be *something*. Anna refused to believe that

Peregrine would ever stoop to something as shoddy as an affair. He might have been raised in the country, but everything about his behaviour thus far convinced her that his parents had instilled good moral values in him.

Why should that change simply because he was visiting London for the first time?

'And you are quite sure of your facts?' Cambermere said unhappily.

'Quite.' Barrington walked unhurriedly around the earl's study. It was a comfortable room—masculine yet not oppressively so, with large leather chairs, several glass-fronted bookcases and a large mahogany desk, the surface of which was covered with papers and estate ledgers. Tall windows bracketed a portrait of the fifth Earl of Cambermere, the present earl's father, and on the wall opposite hung one of a lady Barrington suspected of being the late Lady Cambermere.

Obviously, the earl liked looking at his wife's portrait. Perhaps she'd spent time with him here, keeping him company while he worked on the complexities of estate business. Certainly there was evidence of a woman's touch in the room: the brass candlesticks on the side table; the throw cushions that picked up the dark blue of the curtains; the warmth of the Axminster carpet. All the small, homely things that turned a house into a home. All the things his own house was so noticeably lacking.

'I never lay charges without being sure, my Lord,' Barrington said. 'It wastes time and inflicts unnecessary pain on the innocent. Mr Rand's activities were confirmed by a family member who saw the two enter Lady Yew's chamber and by a friend of mine who happened to be in the house at the same time as Rand. He was quite specific about the details of Mr Rand's visit, right up until the time he and the lady went upstairs arm in arm.' Barrington turned to face the older man. 'And regardless of whether or not what took place upstairs was of an intimate nature, you know as well as I do that his being alone with the marchioness is more than enough to convict him.'

'Damn!' the earl swore again. 'I never expected behaviour like this from Peregrine. Edward's always been one for the ladies. God knows how many have lost their hearts to him. But he's a good-looking lad and as charming as they come.'

'Has he shown no interest in marrying?'

'No, and at almost twenty-six, he's of an age where that's exactly what he *should* be turning his mind to,' the earl said testily. 'I've told him as much, but he doesn't pay heed to me. Says he'll marry when he's good and ready and not a moment before.'

'So he likes to play the field,' Barrington said.

'Always has. But Rand isn't inclined that way. In the time he's been here, I don't think I've ever heard him *talk* about a woman, let alone embroil himself in a sordid affair with one. My daughter was right in that regard.'

Barrington didn't bother to offer a reply. Family dynamics were neither of importance nor of interest to him. Emotion had to be kept separate from fact or everything risked drowning in sentimentality. Some might consider him cold for harbouring such a belief, but as far as he was concerned, it was the only way to do business. 'My Lord, I trust you appreciate the gravity of the situation,' he said bluntly. 'Lord Yew is understandably angry that his wife entered into an intimate relationship with another man; while it is correct to say that the lady is equally to blame, it is the gentleman the marquess intends to punish.'

'Of course,' Cambermere agreed. 'Men are always at fault in these situations. Well, what do you propose we do about it?'

Barrington was about to answer when the door to the room burst open and Lady Annabelle swept in, all blazing eyes and righteous indignation. 'Forgive me, Papa, but I simply *cannot* stand by and allow Sir Barrington's accusation to go unchallenged. Peregrine would *never* do something like this. It runs contrary to everything he stands for—which leads me to believe that it must be Sir Barrington's information that is in error.'

Barrington stared at the woman standing just inside the door, aware that she truly was magnificent. The candlelight deepened her hair to a rich, burnished gold and, in the dim light, her eyes shone a clear, deep blue. She was like a golden lioness protecting her cub. He almost hated having to be the one to prove her wrong. 'I have someone ready to swear that Mr Rand spent time alone with the marchioness in her private rooms, Lady Annabelle,' he said quietly. 'I need not tell you how damaging such a disclosure would be.'

He saw her eyes widen and knew that she did indeed appreciate the gravity of what he'd just said. But it was equally clear that she still didn't believe him. 'How do you know your witness was telling the truth, Sir Barrington? You have only his word that what he claims to have happened really did. I know Peregrine and I can assure you that he is not the type of man—'

'Anna, please,' her father interrupted. 'If Sir Barrington says he has proof of Peregrine's guilt, we must believe him.'

'But why? If he only took the time to speak with Peregrine, he would know that what he is suggesting is quite impossible.'

Cambermere sighed. 'You must forgive my daughter, Sir Barrington. She has grown uncommonly fond of my godson in the short time he's been here and is clearly reluctant to hear ill spoken of him.'

'I understand,' Barrington said, wondering if the closeness between the lady and Mr Rand had anything to do with the fact that they might well *be* brother and sister. 'Is Mr Rand spending the rest of the Season with you?'

The earl nodded. 'That was the plan. His father and I are... old friends. We were...at school together,' he said, glancing at a file on his desk. 'Haven't seen him in years, of course, but I was at his wedding and agreed to stand as godfather to his firstborn.' He turned towards the window, his face half in shadow. 'A few months ago, I received a letter from him, telling me that his wife had died and asking if I'd be willing to take Peregrine for a few months. Show him the sights of London, that sort of thing.'

'And you agreed.'

'I thought it the right thing to do.' The earl swallowed hard, his voice when he spoke gruff. 'He is my godson, after all.'

Barrington nodded, not sure whether it was grief or regret that shadowed the earl's voice. 'Are *you* aware of the company your godson keeps, Lord Cambermere?'

'Can't say that I am. His interests run vastly different to mine. He doesn't ride, he prefers not to hunt and I don't believe he's all that partial to moving in society. As my daughter said, he would rather spend his evenings with a book.'

*Or in the marchioness's bed.* 'Do you know where he is this evening?' Barrington enquired.

He saw the look that passed between Cambermere and his daughter, but wasn't surprised when the earl said, 'No. As I said, I don't make a study of the boy's comings and goings.'

'Yet you said Lady Annabelle usually goes with him to social engagements.'

'Yes.'

'Then why is she not with him tonight?' Barrington asked.

Barrington glanced at Lady Annabelle as he waited for a response. What little he knew of her encouraged him to believe that she would give him an honest answer. But when he saw her colour rise and her golden brows knit together, he suspected she already had. 'I see.'

'No, you don't see!' Lady Annabelle said quickly. 'Peregrine didn't ask me to accompany him because he was going to visit someone with whom he was already acquainted. It wasn't necessary that I go along.'

'Were you not surprised that you did not also receive an invitation to the reception?'

'Not at all. There are often events to which I am invited that other members of my family are not,' she explained. 'We may move in the same circles, Sir Barrington, but we do not have all the same friends.'

Barrington knew there was nothing to be gained in challenging the remark. Lady Annabelle was trying to defend Mr Rand—and failing badly in the attempt. 'Lord Cambermere,' he said finally, 'my client has made it clear that he intends to make an example of the man involved with his wife. However, for the sake of you and your family, I would prefer to see this matter settled quietly and with as little scandal as possible. If I could get Lord Yew to agree to it, would Mr Rand be willing to break off his association with Lady Yew and swear that he would never see her again? Perhaps be willing to write a letter to that effect?'

Cambermere nodded. 'I don't see why he would not—'

'But why *should* he write such a letter, Papa!' Lady Annabelle demanded. 'If he has done nothing wrong, surely there is no—!'

'*Enough*, Anna! If you cannot keep silent, I *will* ask you to leave,' her father said, displaying signs of impatience for the first time that evening. 'I don't know if you appreciate how serious a matter this is. In years gone by, Peregrine would have been called out for such an offence. In fact, I'm sure the thought crossed Yew's mind. He is not a man to be trifled with.'

'But you are condemning him without trial,' she persisted. 'Pronouncing him guilty without even giving him a chance to prove his innocence. All on the strength of *this* man's say so!' she added, her voice suddenly growing cold.

Barrington's eyes narrowed. So, the fair Lady Annabelle would defend her visitor to the last, blindly ignoring the evidence that he had put forward. Pity. While her loyalty did her credit, all it meant was that the outcome of the situation would be that much more painful for her in the end.

'If I may suggest,' he said slowly, 'I am well aware of how shocking this must sound and agree that Mr Rand must have his hearing and be given a chance to explain. But I do have an appointment with Lord Yew tomorrow afternoon and he will be looking for answers. So I would ask that you speak to Mr Rand as soon as possible and get back to me at the earliest opportunity.'

'I shall speak to him the moment he returns home this evening,' the earl said, 'and send word to you first thing in the morning.'

'Thank you. You have my card.' Barrington glanced at Annabelle, but wasn't surprised that she refused to meet his eyes. 'I regret, Lady Annabelle, that our introduction should have taken this form. It is not how I wished we might have started out.'

'Nor I, Sir Barrington.' She did look at him then and Barrington saw how deeply she was torn. 'If you knew Peregrine as I do, you would understand why I say that he is incapable of such a deceit.'

'Sadly, it is not possible for me to be intimately acquainted with everyone I am asked to investigate. Nor would it do me any good to encourage that kind of relationship. I must judge what I see without emotion clouding my vision. I trust the word of those who provide me with information and trust my own skills when it comes to assessing the value of what they've told me. I have no reason to doubt the source of this particular piece of information.'

'Yet who is to say that your source is any more honest than Peregrine?' she parried. 'He is as much a stranger to you as your source is to us. Does he even *know* Mr Rand?'

'By sight, and that is all that matters,' Barrington said. 'I deal in facts, Lady Annabelle. Not emotion. One dilutes the other to such an extent that the truth is often unrecognisable.'

She shook her head. 'I'm not sure I like your truths, Sir Barrington. You presume a great deal without being personally involved.'

'It is *because* I am not personally involved that I am able to reach the conclusions I do.'

'Then I sincerely hope that when we come to you with proof of Peregrine's innocence, you will offer him as sincere an apology as he deserves,' she said.

Barrington inclined his head. 'I will be happy to offer an apology if such is warranted. But if he is guilty, I expect the same courtesy from you. I'm good at what I do, Lady Annabelle—and I haven't been wrong yet.'

Her chin rose and he saw a flash of defiance in her eyes. 'There is a first time for everything, Sir Barrington. And in this instance, I will enjoy being the one who points it out to you.'

Barrington stared down at her, aware that while she frustrated him to the point of distraction, she also aroused in him feelings of an entirely different nature. In fact, he was finding it harder and harder to look at her and not imagine how she would feel in his arms. How the softness of her body would fit into the hard angles of his and how sweet the taste of her lips would be.

And that was the problem. While he admired her more than any woman he'd ever met, the fact that he wanted her in his bed was an unforeseen and unwelcome complication.

'I expect time will provide the answer to that,' he said, offering her a bow. 'My lord,' he said, turning to her father, 'I look forward to your visit on the morrow.'

'I will be there, Sir Barrington.' The earl's face was set in grim lines. 'Of that you can be sure.'

In the weighted silence that followed, Anna restlessly began to pace.

'You don't like Sir Barrington,' her father said flatly.

'It is not so much the man I dislike as his attitude,' Anna muttered, her eyes on the faded pattern of the carpet. 'I am as deeply convinced of his error as he is of mine, yet he is intractable.'

'And you are not?' her father retorted. When she said nothing, he continued, 'What of his claim that he has never been wrong?'

'A man may make whatever claim he likes, but we have only his word that it is the truth. And regardless of what he says, I will *not* believe Peregrine guilty of this.' Anna stopped and looked at her father. 'You know what kind of man he is, Papa. You've spent time with him. Talked with him at length.'

'Yes, I have, but women can make fools of us all. And sometimes circumstances compel us to do things…to *be* things…we would not normally do or be,' her father said.

Anna shook her head. 'That may hold true for some men, but *not* Peregrine. He is a good and honest man. I would stake everything I own on that.'

'Then I would advise you to be careful, my dear. Sometimes what we believe in our hearts is as far from the truth as it is possible to be. And that which we say will *never* happen, happens with alarming regularity.'

'You're speaking in generalities,' Anna said. 'I'm talking about Peregrine, and I know him a damned sight better than—'

'Annabelle!'

Anna sighed. 'A great deal better than does Sir Barrington Parker. Besides, if Lady Yew *is* having an affair, it is only what her husband deserves, cold, unfeeling man that he is.'

'Nevertheless, she is his wife and it is her duty to remain faithful to him,' the earl said.

'Even though he has kept a score of mistresses since the day they were married?'

The earl's face flushed. 'You should not be speaking of such things!'

'Why not? It isn't as though Lord Yew makes an effort to conceal his activities. He is constantly seen at the theatre with one or other of his mistresses. I'm surprised he hasn't invited them home to dine—'

'Enough! I will not hear you speak of such things, Anna,' the earl said harshly. 'Go back to the drawing room and continue with your needlework. I shall deal with Peregrine when he comes home and then we will settle this matter once and for all!'

It was well past midnight by the time Peregrine finally came home. Lying awake in bed, Anna heard the front door open, followed by the sound of muffled conversation. No doubt Milford telling Peregrine that the earl wished to see him. She heard footsteps, the sound of another door opening and closing, and then silence.

How long would the interview take? Would her father give

Peregrine a chance to explain himself? Or would he assume, as Sir Barrington had, that Peregrine was guilty and demand that he make amends at once?

It did not make for pleasant contemplation and, irrationally, Anna wished it had been anyone *but* Sir Barrington Parker who had brought forward the accusation. Because despite what she'd said to him tonight, she *was* attracted to him, more than to any man she'd ever met. She felt surprisingly at ease in his company, even though the sight of him set her pulse racing and her thoughts whirling. She enjoyed his sense of humour, admired his intellect and sensed that beneath that cool and controlled exterior beat the heart of a strong and passionate man.

But how could she be attracted to *any* man who wilfully intended to persecute a man whom she considered as practically a member of her family? Their formal introduction had been made as the result of his coming here to investigate Peregrine's behaviour. An *erroneous* investigation, Anna assured herself. Because if she allowed herself to believe that Peregrine would indulge in such a pastime, it could only mean that she didn't know him as well as she'd thought—and she liked to believe that being able to read people on an intuitive level was something she did well.

It was what enabled her to offer advice to confused young women who came to her, and to their equally confused mothers. By cutting through the layers of emotion, she was able to see down to the bones of the situation. And yet, was that not the very justification Sir Barrington Parker had used for his conduct tonight?

'...*I deal in facts, Lady Annabelle. Not emotion. One dilutes the other to such a degree that the truth is often unrecognisable...*'

Perhaps, but in this case, emotion was all Anna had to go on. Emotion and trust. She had to believe in the integrity of

her family and all they stood for. For where would she be—
indeed, where would *any* of them be—if she could not?

Anna awoke to the first rays of sunshine slanting in
through her bedroom window and realised that she had fallen
asleep without ever having heard Peregrine come upstairs.
Bother! Now she had no way of knowing what the result of
his conversation with her father had been. Nor could she just
barge into Peregrine's room and ask him. He might be her
father's godson, but he was still a young, single male and it
would be inappropriate for her to go to his room alone, even
under circumstances like these.

With that in mind, Anna quickly rang for her maid and set
about getting dressed. Peregrine was normally an early riser,
but if she could catch him before he set off, she might have
a chance of finding out what she needed to know. Unfortunately, though she hurried her maid through her preparations,
it wasn't timely enough. By the time she reached Peregrine's
room and knocked on the door, there was no answer and she
could hear nothing from inside. He must have already gone
down for breakfast. Perhaps he'd passed a poor night after
the interview with her father.

Given how angry her father had been, Anna knew that to
be a definite possibility.

In the breakfast room, however, she was disappointed to
find only her brother seated at the long table. Edward looked
up at her entrance, his greeting somewhat reserved. 'Good
morning, Anna.'

Anna inclined her head as she made her way to the sideboard. 'Edward.' Though only two years separated them in
age, they had never enjoyed a close relationship. Edward
tended to belittle her efforts at helping others, while she
couldn't understand his cavalier treatment of friends and
servants alike. She had once seen him cut a good friend

dead when word of the fellow's marriage to a lady of lesser standing had reached him, saying that anyone who associated with rubbish was like to be tainted by the smell. And when his valet had come down with a fever, Edward had dismissed him, saying he couldn't abide to be in the same house as a sick man. Her father had offered to reassign the poor man to the stable, but not surprisingly, the valet had chosen to leave.

Now, as Anna helped herself to a slice of ham, a piece of toast and a boiled egg, she was thankful the rest of the staff were in such excellent health. 'Have you seen Peregrine this morning?' she asked, sitting down across from her brother.

Edward didn't look up from his newspaper. 'No.'

'What about Papa?'

'Out.' He turned the smoothly ironed page. 'Said he would be back in an hour.' He glanced at the clock. 'That was half an hour ago.'

So, her father had already left to meet with Sir Barrington Parker. That meant she *had* to speak to Peregrine as soon as possible. But where was he? And if he'd gone out, when might he be back? If she could talk to him, find out what had really happened, she might be able to speak to Sir Barrington on his behalf.

Leaving her plate untouched, she got up and headed for the door.

'What, no breakfast?' Edward enquired. 'Cook will be displeased.'

'I haven't time. I have to find Peregrine.'

'He's probably still in his room,' Edward said, turning another page. 'I understand he was drinking quite heavily at the Grundings' soirée last night.'

Anna stilled. 'Where did you hear that?'

'From someone who was there.' He finally looked up and smiled. 'It seems our country guest is finding London very much to his liking.'

Pursing her lips, Anna left the room. Edward hadn't meant the remark kindly. For whatever reason, he'd taken an instant dislike to Peregrine and had taken to making snide comments about his appearance, his manner of dress, even his accent. Anna had taken him to task about it several times, but it hadn't made any difference. The sniping continued and Edward made no attempt to hide his feelings when Peregrine was around.

Fortunately, Peregrine knew how Edward felt about him, but he refused to make an issue of it, saying it likely stemmed from the difference in their upbringings. Edward had been raised in a nobleman's house and was heir to an earldom, whereas Peregrine had been raised on a farm with parents who, though comfortable, were neither titled nor gentry.

Still, he was a guest in their home and he deserved better. Anna liked him very much. Despite his obvious lack of sophistication, he was good natured and quick to laugh and didn't belittle her efforts the way Edward did. He admired her for caring enough about the welfare of others to get involved and he also liked many of the same things she did, so they frequently found themselves laughing together at the various social events they went to.

Edward, on the other hand, was never to be found in the same room as Peregrine. Supremely conscious of his own position in society, he sought the company of those equal to him or blessed with a higher status. If there was a snob in the Durst family, it was definitely her brother.

Reaching Peregrine's door, Anna raised her hand and knocked. 'Peregrine?' When she heard no response, she waited a moment and then tentatively pushed it open.

He wasn't there. Worse, his bed hadn't been slept in.

Anna felt a knot form in the pit of her stomach. *Where had he spent the night and where was he now?* Equally important, what kind of mood was he in? Peregrine was an uncommonly sensitive man. If her father had falsely accused him of having an affair with Lady Yew, Peregrine might well have left the house angry and embarrassed that his godfather would believe such shameful lies about him. But where could he have gone?

There was only one way to find out. Heading to her bedroom, Anna fetched her bonnet and gloves. Returning to the hall, she rang for Milford and asked to be told where Sir Barrington Parker lived.

'Lady Annabelle Durst, Sir Barrington,' Sam said quietly.

Barrington looked up from the deed of land he had been perusing and saw the lady standing in his doorway. She looked like a breath of summer in a gown of pale yellow silk trimmed with deeper yellow ribbons, an elegant wide-brimmed bonnet perched atop her golden hair. Her lips were a soft dusky rose, but her blue eyes appeared unusually bright against the pallor of her skin. She was distraught and, recognising that, he rose at once. 'Lady Annabelle.'

'I hope my timing is not inconvenient, Sir Barrington.'

'Not at all. Pray come in. Bring your maid, if you wish.'

'No, I would rather speak to you privately.' Lady Annabelle waved the girl into a chair outside his study. 'I cannot bear not knowing.'

So, it was curiosity that had compelled her to come. Obviously, she hadn't spoken to her father yet. Barrington indicated the high-back chair in front of the fireplace. 'Won't you sit down?'

She did not. Visibly upset, she began to pace. Barrington understood the compulsion. He had been a pacer once himself. 'May I ring for tea?'

'Thank you.' This time, she did look at him. 'That would be most welcome.'

He glanced at Sam, who nodded and quietly withdrew.

For a moment Barrington said nothing, more interested in studying her than he was in initiating a conversation. She was as beautiful as ever, but this morning she looked to be drawn as tight as a finely strung bow. He had a feeling that if he pulled too hard, she would snap. 'What did you wish to ask me, Lady Annabelle?' he said softly.

Her head turned towards him, her blue eyes filled with misgivings. 'Have you seen my father this morning?'

'I have.'

'And? Did he speak to you about Peregrine?'

Barrington nodded, aware that he was far more in control of his emotions than she was of hers. 'Are you sure you won't sit down?'

'Please…just tell me,' she implored. 'I wanted to ask Peregrine myself, but he wasn't in his room this morning; by the looks of his bed, he hadn't slept there at all.'

'I suspect he did not,' Barrington agreed. 'Lord Cambermere informed me that after his conversation with Mr Rand last night, the young man left the house without any indication as to where he was going or when he might return. Apparently he was in a state of considerable distress.'

He saw her eyes briefly close. 'Did he admit to…what you accused him of?'

Barrington wished he could have said otherwise, but he wouldn't lie. Not even when he knew the boy had. 'No.'

With a soft cry, Lady Annabelle sank into a chair. 'I knew it! I *knew* he was innocent.' When Barrington made no response, she raised her head, her eyes narrowing at the expression on his face. 'You don't believe him.'

'It takes more than a man *saying* he didn't do something for me to believe him innocent when the evidence speaks so clearly of his guilt.'

'But why would he lie?' she protested.

Barrington gave a non-committal shrug. 'Why does anyone

lie? To protect themselves or to protect someone else. I'm sure you've had dealings with young women who told you one thing, yet did another.'

'Yes, because they had no wish for their misdemeanours to become public.'

'Exactly. Mr Rand is likely embarrassed by what he's done and hopes to convince others that he is not at fault.'

He saw her stiffen. 'Peregrine has *never* lied to me.'

'Perhaps there has not been enough at stake for him to do so,' Barrington said quietly. 'Now there is.'

The door opened again and Sam walked in, carrying a silver tea service. At a nod from his employer, he set the tray on the small table beside the desk and then quietly withdrew. Barrington crossed to the table and picked up the milk jug. 'Milk and sugar?'

'Just milk, thank you.'

He poured a drop into one of the cups, then filled both cups with hot tea. Accepting hers, Lady Annabelle said, 'I still think you're wrong, Sir Barrington. If Peregrine said he is not involved with Lady Yew, he is not. Why can you not accept that as truth?'

'Because the rest of his behaviour leads me to believe otherwise. How do you explain the fact that he chose not to stay home last night?'

'I suspect he was deeply embarrassed by my father believing him capable of such reprehensible conduct. Would *you* not wish to avoid someone who had accused you of doing something you had not?'

'Maybe. But I also like to think I would be mature enough to admit my mistakes, if I were so foolish as to make them.'

'And I repeat, I do not believe Peregrine has made a mistake.'

He heard the quiet certainty in her voice and was moved to

smile. He, too, had once been so trusting; so willing to believe in the goodness of others. When had he lost that *naïveté*?

'The attraction between a man and a woman is one of the most powerful forces on earth, Lady Annabelle,' he said. 'You have no idea how many crimes are committed, and how many lies are told, in the name of that attraction.'

'Not perhaps as well as you do,' Lady Annabelle agreed, 'but we are talking about Peregrine's character and of that I believe I *can* speak with authority. If he told my father he is not having an affair with Lady Yew, he is not.'

'Then it would seem we have reached an impasse,' Barrington said. 'There is nothing more to say.'

She looked somewhat taken aback by his easy acceptance of her statement, but, equally willing to accept it at face value, she finished her tea and then set the china cup and saucer back on the table. 'What will you tell Lord Yew?'

'I don't know,' Barrington said honestly. 'But I have between now and two o'clock to work it out.'

'Then I shall leave you to your deliberations.' She stood up and offered him her hand. 'Thank you for seeing me, Sir Barrington.'

'My pleasure.' Barrington felt the softness of the glove in his hand, the slenderness of the fingers within. 'I'm sorry that circumstances are such that you leave believing the worst of me. Again.'

'Actually, I don't. We each have our own ways of involving ourselves in other people's lives, Sir Barrington,' Lady Annabelle said. 'I tend to think the best and assume people innocent until proven guilty, whereas you believe the exact opposite.'

'Not at all. I simply strive to uncover the truth,' Barrington said. 'That is why people come to me. And experience has taught me that if the truth is not immediately discernible, it *will* come out in the end.'

'Then at least you and I are able to part knowing that the truth of *this* matter has already been established,' she replied. 'Goodbye, Sir Barrington.'

Barrington inclined his head, but said nothing as she left the room. He stood by his desk until he heard the sound of the front door close before letting his head fall back and breathing a long, deep sigh.

So, the lovely Anna thought the matter closed. Wrong. Peregrine Rand *was* guilty. The fact he had chosen not to *confess* his sin meant absolutely nothing. In his heart, he knew what he'd done and, if Peregrine was as noble as Lady Annabelle made him out to be, guilt would eat away at him until he had no choice but to make a clean breast of it. Either way, the young man was doomed to failure.

As it seemed was he, Barrington reflected, when it came to securing the good opinion of the lovely Lady Annabelle Durst. If it turned out that his accusations were correct and Rand was guilty of having an affair with Lady Yew, she would resent him for having proven her wrong. On the other hand, if Rand was telling the truth, she would resent him for having doubted his integrity in the first place. In short, they had reached a stalemate. And contrary to what either of them might wish to believe, in a situation like this, there was simply no way one or the other of them was going to win.

# Chapter Four

Anna finally caught up with Peregrine later that afternoon. She had been resting in her room, nursing the megrim she'd had for the better part of the day, when she heard the heavy thump of footsteps in the hall and realised he was finally home. Pushing the lavender eye pads aside, she quickly got up and went to the door. 'Peregrine!'

He clearly wasn't in the mood for conversation. Dressed in boots, hacking jacket and breeches, he didn't stop when she hailed him and was almost at the bottom of the stairs before she finally caught up with him. 'Peregrine, wait! I need to talk to you.'

'I haven't time.' His voice was unusually brusque. 'I'm going riding with friends and I'm already late.'

'Then you'll just have to be a few minutes later,' Anna said, putting her hand on his arm and turning him around. 'Where were you last night? I was worried about you.'

'You had no reason to be. I simply went out.'

'But not until *after* you spoke to Papa. Why did you leave again? And why didn't you come home?'

He flicked the hard leather crop against the top of his

boot. 'I lost track of time. When I realised how late it was, I decided it was best I just stay out.'

'Why? Because of something Papa said?'

Peregrine was a good-looking young man with a shock of thick, black hair, deep brown eyes and a wide, generous mouth. A mouth that suddenly narrowed in anger. 'I don't care to talk about it.'

'But you don't have a choice, Peregrine. There's a rumour going around town that you are having an affair with Lady Yew,' Anna said, needing him to understand the gravity of the situation. '*I* know it isn't true, but you can't simply pretend the rumour doesn't exist.'

'As a matter of fact, I can. I told your father as much when he questioned me about it last night and I certainly don't intend to stand here and justify my behaviour to you!'

Stung by the vehemence of his reply, Anna said, 'I'm not asking for justification. I just told you I don't believe what people are saying. But a meeting is being held this afternoon between Lord Yew and the man he asked to investigate his wife's infidelity and your name is going to come up—'

'Damn it, Anna, did I not just say that I don't want to talk about it?'

'But you must! Your reputation as a gentleman is at stake, don't you understand?'

'What I understand is that a man's private business is not his own,' he snapped. 'Do you know why I jumped at the chance to come to London? Because I was tired of having to listen to my father's sanctimonious preaching. Of being told what I could and could not do. I thought that by coming here, I would finally be able to lead my own life. Yet now I find that every move I make is watched and criticised by people I don't know, and that even you and your father have no qualms about intruding into something that is none of your business.'

'None of our business?' Anna repeated in astonishment. 'How can you say that? You are my father's godson. We *care* about you.'

He had the grace to look embarrassed. 'I'm not saying you don't.'

'Then why are you being so defensive? I know you didn't have an affair with Lady Yew,' Anna said. 'For one thing, she's already married. For another, she must be at least fifteen years older than you.'

'Since when did either of those things matter to the fine, upstanding members of society?' Peregrine shot back. 'Half of London seems to be involved with people other than their wives or husbands. Why should Susan and I be any different?'

*'Susan?'* Anna interrupted, shocked. 'You call her *Susan*?'

'Yes.' He raised his chin in defiance. 'What else would one call a good friend?'

'Given that she happens to be someone else's *wife*, I would have thought Lady Yew the more appropriate form of address,' Anna said, concern lending an edge to her voice.

'You're being stuffy, Anna. I didn't do anything wrong,' Peregrine said. 'She gave me leave to speak to her in such a manner.'

'Really? And what else did she give you leave to do?'

The tips of Peregrine's ears flamed red. 'Nothing.' But when he refused to meet her eyes and began fidgeting with his crop, Anna knew he was lying to her—and she felt the foundations of her world tremble.

So, it *was* all a lie. Peregrine *was* involved with Lady Yew. Worse, he was *in love* with her. He'd given himself away when he'd spoken her name. His mouth had quivered and his eyes had softened, the way a person's always did when they referred to the man or the woman they cared about deeply.

And she, stupidly, had believed him. She had defended him to both her father *and* to Sir Barrington Parker, a man she had charged with making a false accusation, when all the while it was Peregrine who had been telling lies.

Needing to regain a measure of calm, Anna turned her back on him, clenching her fists at her side. 'Since you obviously did not see fit to inform my father of the truth last night, I will have it now,' she said, fighting to keep her voice steady. *'Are* you having an affair with the Marchioness of Yew?'

'Anna, *please!'*

'Don't Anna me! I want the truth, Peregrine. People's reputations are at stake here. Mine included.'

'Nonsense! This doesn't concern you!'

She whirled to face him. 'Of course it concerns me! I spoke up on your behalf,' she cried. 'I defended you to someone who was ready to think the worst of you. And I refused to believe them when they told me what you were supposedly guilty of.'

Footsteps on the stairs alerted Anna to the fact that they were standing in a place where anyone might hear them, prompting her to grab Peregrine's arm and pull him into the drawing room. 'Furthermore,' she said, closing the door behind them, 'I assured Father and this...other gentleman that you couldn't possibly have been guilty of having an affair with Lady Yew because you didn't even *know* her.'

'But I did know her,' Peregrine admitted.

'How? *I* didn't introduce the two of you.'

'No. Edward did.'

'Edward?' Anna repeated, confused. 'But...when were the two of you ever at a society function together?'

'It wasn't at a society function we met.' Peregrine ran his fingers through his hair, hopelessly dishevelling it. 'Edward had been on at me, saying that if I had any hopes of becoming a gentleman, I needed to educate myself in gentlemanly ways.

That meant knowing how to shoot, how to ride and how to fence. Since I'm already a good rider and I can handle a gun, that only left fencing, a sport to which I've had absolutely no exposure. Edward offered to take me to Angelo's and I met the Marquess of Yew there.'

'That doesn't explain how you met his wife,' Anna pointed out.

'She was waiting for him outside in their carriage,' Peregrine said. 'Edward pointed her out to me when we arrived. When I commented on how beautiful she was, he kindly offered to introduce us.'

*Kindly?* Anna doubted her brother had *ever* had a kind thought in his head when it came to Peregrine. 'All right, so you were introduced. If you knew Lady Yew was married, why did you pursue her?'

'Because on the way home after the match, Edward told me about their marriage. He said it was a loveless union and that Lady Yew was desperately unhappy because Yew paraded his mistresses right under her nose and didn't give a damn as to what she thought.'

'Be that as it may, she *is* his wife and you were wrong to interfere.'

'But she doesn't *love* him!' Peregrine said, his voice rising. 'She told me that what she feels for me is the most wonderful, the most exciting feeling she's ever experienced, and that when we finally are able to be together—'

*'Together?'* Anna interrupted incredulously. 'Are you telling me that Lady Yew said she was going to *leave* her husband?'

'Not in so many words, but—'

'Don't play games with me, Peregrine. Did she or did she not *say* that she was going to leave her husband?'

'Not exactly, but—'

'So she made you no promises that she would run away with you,' she said flatly.

'Well, no, but—'

'There are no buts, Peregrine. Lady Yew has been playing with you.'

'She wouldn't do that!' he said hotly. 'You don't understand how it is between us! She *loves* me!'

'Love? I doubt the woman knows the meaning of the word,' Anna said dismissively. 'In fact, I can give you the names of at least ten other young men with whom she claims to be in love. Men with whom she has flirted and danced and driven nearly insane with jealousy. It's what she does.'

'I don't believe you,' Peregrine said, stubbornly clinging to his beliefs. 'She said nothing to me about other men. And even if there were, it doesn't signify. What she felt for them could be nothing compared to what she feels for me. She said she's never met anyone like me before.'

Anna sat down, aware that Peregrine was no more educated in the ways of love than poor Mercy Banks. 'I'm sorry, Peregrine, but Lady Yew is *not* going to run away with you. Her husband is one of the richest men in England. He owns properties in four counties and his personal worth is staggering. As his wife, Lady Yew is one of the most influential women in society. If you think she would risk throwing that all away to run off with the penniless godson of the Earl of Cambermere, I would advise you to think again.'

'But Edward said—'

'I don't care what Edward said,' Anna said, though she damn well did care and she intended to talk to her brother at the first opportunity. 'Tradition is the foundation upon which society is built. Noble families marry into noble families, thereby ensuring that the tradition carries on. Casting discretion to the wind and haring off because you believe yourself in love with someone else's husband or wife is destructive to the fabric of society—and nobody knows that better than those who occupy its uppermost rungs. I'm sorry, Peregrine, but the kindest thing you can do for yourself is to get over this as quickly as possible and then move on with your life.'

Anna knew it was a sobering speech, but she also knew it was one Peregrine needed to hear. He had to understand that his hopes were futile, that whatever dreams he harboured were as insubstantial as fairy dust.

'But I *love* her,' he whispered, misery inflecting every word. 'How am I supposed to get over that? I've never felt this way about a woman before.'

'You get over it by waking up each day and telling yourself that she is married to a man who will *never* divorce her... even if she wished him to.'

Anna said the words as gently as she could, but she still saw Peregrine wince and felt her heart go out to him. It was never easy hearing that the person you loved didn't love you in return. In fact, finding out that you were little more than a source of amusement, whether it be for an hour or a day, or even a year, was the most devastating thing imaginable. It destroyed your confidence and tore at the very foundation of who you were.

Having been through it, Anna knew exactly how injurious it was to one's sense of well-being.

For a few minutes, Peregrine just sat there, his brow furrowed, his eyes bleak with despair as he struggled to come to terms with everything she had told him. It was hard waking up from a dream, but he had been indulging in an impossible fantasy; for his own good, Anna knew he had to come back to reality.

He finally stood up and slowly began to walk around the room. 'Part of my reason for staying out last night,' he said slowly, 'was because I was embarrassed. I never expected your father to find out what was going on. I thought it was just between Sus—between Lady Yew and myself.'

'Yes, I'm sure you did,' Anna said. 'But while London might seem like a big city, never forget that there are eyes and ears everywhere. When you play with fire, you will eventually get burned.'

'I know, but you never really believe that. It's as though you're living in a bubble. You can see out, but no one can see in. But, of course, everyone can.' Peregrine dropped his head and breathed a long, deep sigh. 'Your father thought it would be a good idea if I were to...write a letter to Lord Yew, apologising for my behaviour. He said that if I promised not to see Lady Yew again, it might...smooth things over with him.' He raised his head. 'Do you think he's right?'

Aware that it was Sir Barrington Parker who had suggested writing the letter, Anna simply inclined her head. 'I think the letter a good idea, yes. With luck, it will set the marquess's mind to rest and persuade him to let the matter go. Because if he takes it into his head to persecute you, Peregrine, there will be no future for you in London.'

Peregrine nodded, and for a full five minutes he was silent, reviewing his options. Then, as if realising he had none, he said finally, 'Very well. I shall write the letter. But I'll give it to you, rather than to your father. I don't think he ever wants to see me again.'

'Don't be a goose, of course he wants to see you.'

'You weren't there,' Peregrine said ruefully. 'You didn't see the look on his face. Why do you think I lied to him, Anna? God knows I didn't want to. But when I saw how disappointed he was at even having to *ask* me if I was involved with Lady Yew, I knew I couldn't tell him the truth. So I lied. That's why I couldn't stay here last night,' Peregrine admitted. 'I was too ashamed to sleep under the same roof as him. He's been so good to me. I couldn't bear to repay him like this.'

'Oh, Peregrine,' Anna whispered. 'If Father was disappointed, it was only because he cares about you and wants you to do well in London. He knows how harsh society can be towards those who flaunt its rules.'

'Then society is a hypocrite!' Peregrine cried. 'I'm not the only man involved with a married woman. There are countless other such affairs going on and everyone knows it!'

'Yes, and they are tolerated as long as they are conducted discreetly and with neither party voicing an objection,' Anna told him. 'But for whatever reason, Lord Yew has chosen to object to the liaison and, as a gentleman, you have no choice but to withdraw.'

The gravity of her words must have penetrated his romantic haze, because for the first time Peregrine seemed to appreciate the magnitude of what he had done. He glanced down at his boots, his mouth working. 'Very well. I shall go for my ride as planned and while I am out I shall think about what I wish to say. Then, I shall come back and write a letter of apology to Lord Yew.'

Anna did a quick mental calculation. Sir Barrington had said he was meeting with the marquess at two. There wasn't a hope Peregrine would be back from his ride in time to have the letter finished and delivered by then, which meant she had no choice but to send word to Sir Barrington herself.

'Peregrine. Have I your word that you will stop seeing Lady Yew, that you will say as much in your letter to Lord Yew?'

Peregrine frowned. 'Have I not just said I would?'

'Yes, but I need to be very clear as to your intentions.'

'From where I stand, I don't think I have any choice.'

'Fine. Then off you go on your ride,' Anna said. 'I'll see you at dinner.'

'Not tonight.' Peregrine got up and slowly walked towards the door. 'Edward said he would be dining at home this evening and I have no intention of sitting at the same table and letting him humiliate me any further in front of your father.'

'Why would he do that?'

'Because I was foolish enough to confide my feelings for Lady Yew to him.' Peregrine looked at her and sighed. 'He knew exactly how I felt—and he said nothing at all about it being a hopeless quest.'

Anna needed no further explanation. How could she explain that it was just her brother being himself? 'I'm sorry, Peregrine. Really, I am. And I know how hard it is not to be with the person you love, but there will be others. You have only to open your heart and let love find you.'

His mouth twisted. 'I've been open to love a long time, Anna, but this is the first time it's come anywhere close to finding me. Infatuation is one thing, but true love doesn't come along every day.'

No, it did not, Anna reflected as she sat down to write the letter to Sir Barrington. True love was elusive: as fragile as a sigh, as mysterious as the night. It inspired placid gentlemen to write romantic poetry and sensible young women to lose themselves in dreams. For those lucky enough to find it, love could be a life-altering experience.

But falling in love could also be a painful and humiliating experience, one that shattered a person's belief in their own self-worth and that was best forgotten as quickly as possible. Her brief, ill-fated liaison with the Honourable Anthony Colder was a prime example of that, as was poor Peregrine's misplaced affection for Lady Yew. If anyone needed proof of the *destructive* power of love, they need look no further than that.

Lady Annabelle's note arrived well in advance of Lord Yew's visit and while Barrington was relieved that a solution had been found, her words did not make him feel better. Not when he knew what it had cost her to write them.

Sir Barrington,
As time is of the essence and Mr Rand is otherwise occupied, I thought it best to send word of his intentions as quickly as possible. I have been informed that he is indeed guilty of having an affair with the lady in question; however, he has assured me that he intends to end the relationship and that he is willing to confirm the same in a letter addressed to her husband. I hope you will convey these sentiments to the gentleman and that he will find it a satisfactory resolution to the problem.

Neither my father nor Mr Rand has been made aware of this correspondence and I would prefer that it remain that way. As one who has been accused of 'involving herself in the convoluted lives of others', I think it the wisest course of action.

It was simply signed 'Annabelle Durst' in a clear and legible hand.

So, Mr Peregrine Rand had been unable to maintain his lies in the face of the lady's questioning. Good—because there was no doubt in Barrington's mind that Annabelle *had* questioned him. Profess to believe him she might, but she had still needed to hear from his own lips that he was innocent of the charge and that the rumours were not true.

How devastated she must have been to find out that they were…and how difficult for her to write this note. She had believed wholeheartedly in the young man's innocence, put trust in her intuition when it came to what he would and would not do—only to discover that her intuition was not strong enough to stand up against the wishes and desires of his own heart. Disillusionment was always a bitter pill to swallow.

He glanced again at the parchment in his hand. Closing his eyes, he raised it to his nose and gently inhaled. Yes, it was still there…a lingering trace of her fragrance, the scent sweet but sensually provocative. An echo of the lady herself. He set the parchment down and walked slowly towards the long window, his mind filled with thoughts of Anna.

It was a long time since a woman had affected him to this degree. Indeed, he wasn't sure one ever had. For the most part, he'd always believed aristocratic ladies to be like exotic birds: lovely to look at, but troublesome to own. They strutted around society's stage like the fragile, inconsequential creatures they were, generally offering nothing of substance beyond the ability to play the piano or paint pretty pictures. It was the reason he had found commitment so easy to avoid.

But Lady Annabelle was neither fragile nor inconsequential. She was intelligent. Passionate. The quintessential lady and beautiful beyond all. But beauty without soul had never appealed to him, and it was because she cared so much about other people that Barrington found himself so strongly attracted to her. She cared about Mercy Banks and the host of other silly young women who needed her help in extricating themselves from situations that could have ruined them. She cared about her country visitor, who might well be her half-brother, and about her father, who, with typical male arrogance, was ready to dismiss everything she said. Yes, admirable indeed was the Lady Annabelle Durst. A lady worth getting to know.

And yet, as a result of what had passed between them, Barrington doubted a deeper acquaintance was possible. In his hand, he held her acknowledgement that she had been wrong, and he right. That was the first strike against him. He had proven everything she had most desperately wanted not to believe. She had stood up for a man who hadn't deserved her loyalty, and she had been let down. Matters would never be easy between them now.

Still, now that he knew the truth about Rand, he would do everything he could to mitigate Lord Yew's anger and to settle the matter as humanely as possible. As for Rand, if he truly believed himself in love with Lady Yew, he was already suffering enough by having found out what she was really like. No point making it worse by dragging his name through the mud, and by association, the beautiful Lady Anna's.

The note Anna received from Sir Barrington later that afternoon was brief, but reassuring.

> Your note was well timed. I met with Lord Yew, and after being assured of Mr Rand's willingness to see the error of his ways, the marquess is willing to let the matter go. He will settle for a letter and a promise of restraint on Mr Rand's part and shall consider the matter closed. I have not written to your father. I leave it to you to inform him of the outcome, and Mr Rand.
> I remain,
> Your most humble servant
> B.

Anna folded the letter and tapped it against her chin. So, the matter was resolved. The Marquess of Yew had been informed as to the identity of the guilty party and had been willing to accept an olive branch in the form of a promise and a written apology. Sir Barrington had handled the matter admirably. As long as the marquess honoured his word, Peregrine would be free to go about London without the finger of blame being pointed at him at every turn.

Just as well, since Anna was quite sure he would have bolted had such been the case.

Unfortunately, as she set out for her afternoon visit to the Baroness von Brohm, Anna realised that the entire affair had left a bad taste in her mouth. Not only were her feelings towards Peregrine affected by what she had learned, but her brief acquaintance with Sir Barrington Parker had been tainted by the events they had both unwittingly been drawn into. She had insinuated that he hadn't known his business, accused him of misjudgement and gloated when she'd believed him wrong. She owed him an apology.

But was he the type of man to whom apologising was easy? She remembered the way he had teased her over her steadfast belief in Peregrine's innocence, mocking her belief in the man's inability to tell lies. Would he be condescending of her apology now? Had he been waiting for just such a moment to say, 'I told you so'? Anna hated to think of him as being deliberately cruel, but, not knowing the nature of the man, she had little else to go on.

She was not at all surprised that thoughts of him occupied her fully during the carriage ride to Mayfair.

Julia von Brohm was not what Anna had been expecting. Thinking to see a pale, unhappy woman in her mid-forties wearing the unrelieved black of a widow still in mourning for her husband, Anna was surprised to be greeted by a slender and very attractive woman of no more than thirty, garbed in a stunning gown of rich burgundy satin. Her honey-brown hair was arranged in a simple but elegant chignon at the nape of her neck, and her eyes were a clear, bright blue that appeared even brighter against the translucent whiteness of her skin.

'Lady Annabelle,' the baroness said, extending both hands in greeting. 'I cannot tell you how pleased I was to receive your note.'

'And likewise, how pleased I was to receive your acceptance,' Anna said. 'I regret that my good friend, Lady Lydia Winston, was unable to come, but her mother was taken to bed with a terrible head pain and required her assistance.'

The baroness's pretty face softened in sympathy. 'Poor lady. Having had a mother-in-law who suffered with megrims, I know the role a daughter must play. But I am so pleased that you were brave enough to come on your own.'

Anna tilted her head to one side. 'Brave?'

'Come now, Lady Annabella. You must surely have heard the rumours—that I am a lonely widow who cannot stop crying for her late husband. That I am a beautiful woman whose company must be endured, but not enjoyed.'

The smile came easily to Anna's lips. 'I knew you were a widow, Baroness, and I assumed that you would be lonely. But I certainly did not hear that you were dismal company or someone to be avoided. And even if I had, I would have come anyway and drawn my own conclusions.'

'I am very glad to hear it,' the baroness said in her charmingly accented voice. 'And I think that you and I are going to become good friends. Ah, Smith,' she said to the young maid who appeared in the doorway. 'We shall have tea and a plate of pastries. Cook would be most upset if we did not offer our guest a sampling of her wares.'

As the maid curtsied and withdrew, the baroness turned back to Anna. 'I hired most of the staff upon my arrival, but dear Frau Hildenbaum has been with my family since I was a girl. She insisted on coming to London with me and when she heard I was having an English lady to tea, she set to work. She has been baking since early this morning.'

'How delightful, for I confess to a definite weakness for pastries,' Anna said as she sat down on a comfortable sofa across from the baroness. The room was quite beautiful, the walls papered in pale blue and gold silk, the shades of which were reflected in the carpet and furnishings. An exquisite medieval tapestry was suspended from a brass rod between the two long windows that gave view over the square below, and numerous other works of art adorned the walls. The baroness either had exceptional taste or the good fortune to have ancestors who did.

Even more stunning was her jewellery. Anna's eyes were repeatedly drawn to the brooch pinned to the bodice of her gown. It was shaped like a flower, with a single piece of amber in the centre and with petals made up of diamonds and rubies.

'You are admiring my brooch?' the baroness asked during a lull in the conversation.

Anna looked up, embarrassed to have been caught staring. 'Yes. Forgive me, but it is so beautiful.'

'My late husband gave it to me for my twenty-first birthday.' The baroness's face glowed. 'Ulrich spent a lot of time travelling and often came home with little trinkets like this. He had exceptional taste.'

'Baroness—'

'Please, won't you call me Julia?' she interrupted gently. 'I have no wish to be so formal with you.'

'Then you must call me Anna. And I was about to say that your husband must have loved you very much to have given you such an exquisite gift.'

As soon as the words left her lips, Anna regretted having uttered them. She had no wish to invoke unhappy memories for Julia and she feared that mentioning her late husband in such a way might be all that was required to bring them on. But apart from a delicate flush, Julia remained admirably in control of her emotions. 'He did love me. Ours was a true love match. Not common in our world, I suppose, but I was more fortunate than most.'

'So it wasn't an arranged marriage.'

'Oh, yes, but Ulrich and I fell in love shortly after we were introduced. That probably sounds ridiculous, but it is the truth.'

'I think you were indeed incredibly fortunate,' Anna said. 'I know of so many marriages that are arranged for the benefit of the parties involved and end up being the most dismal of relationships. That is why I always prefer to see marriages based on love. Have you any children, Bar—Julia?'

Where the mention of her husband had not brought tears to her eyes, the mention of children did. 'Sadly, no. Ulrich and I were not able to conceive a child together. Perhaps if we'd had more time—'

When Julia broke off, Anna leaned over to place her hand over the other woman's. 'I am so sorry for your loss, Julia,' she said gently, 'but you are young enough to marry again and to bear many healthy children.'

Julia nodded, her eyes glistening with unshed tears. 'I would like to think so, but if the difficulty in conceiving lies with me, it will not matter who I marry. I know that will serve as a deterrent to certain gentlemen.'

'Only those looking to set up a nursery,' Anna said, seeing no point in not stating the obvious. 'If we are being practical, there are many older gentlemen who would be happy to offer you marriage without children being a condition.'

'You are kind to say so, Anna, but, in truth, I do not long for a husband. The memory of Ulrich is enough.'

'But memories won't keep you warm at night and you are far too beautiful to spend the rest of your life alone,' Anna pointed out. 'You must get out in society and start mingling again.'

'I would like that,' Julia admitted, 'but in the three weeks I've been here, I have not received a single invitation.'

'Then we must start the ball rolling.' Anna smiled, convinced more than ever that she had done the right thing in coming to visit the baroness. She pulled an invitation from her reticule and handed it to Julia. 'This is from the Countess of Bessmel. It is an invitation to a soirée at her home the evening after next.'

'An invitation!' Barely managing to conceal her delight, Julia broke the seal and unfolded the invitation. 'But we have never met.'

'I know, but I chanced to be at a breakfast with the countess the other morning and told her I intended paying a call on you. She said she was planning to do the same, but that the pain in her legs was preventing her from getting around. That's when she asked if I would be good enough to deliver the invitation to you and to say how much she hopes you will attend.'

Julia read the invitation again and her smile brightened immeasurably. 'This is...so very good of you, Anna. And of Lady Bessmel, of course. I will write at once to accept.'

'Excellent, because she is looking forward to meeting you,' Anna said. 'Lady Lydia will also be there, and with three such highly placed ladies at your side, you can be assured that the rest of society will take notice.'

Julia's smile was as radiant as the diamonds pinned to her breast. 'Thank you, Anna. I feel better simply for having met you. And perhaps before you leave, you would like to see some of my other jewellery? I can assure you that a few of the pieces make this brooch look quite plain.'

## Chapter Five

Though Barrington did not make a habit of attending all of the society functions to which he was invited, he recognised the wisdom of dropping in on certain, select events. Dark alleys and gentlemen's clubs were all very well, but he had learned long ago that most of the truly useful gossip was to be overheard in the drawings rooms and ballrooms of society. And given that Lady Bessmel was acknowledged to be one of the finest gossips in London, the thought of missing an event at her magnificent Park Lane mansion was tantamount to professional suicide. Now, as Barrington stood opposite the entrance to the grand ballroom, watching the parade of swirling dancers make their way around the room, he wondered how many darkly held secrets would be exposed tonight.

A quick sweep of the room revealed the usual attendees: blue-blooded aristocrats with their equally blue-blooded wives, a smattering of officers and politicians, some in the present government, some casualties of the last, as well as the miscellaneous collection of ladies and gentlemen who, though not titled, were well born enough to receive the much-coveted invitations. Colonel Tanner was standing at the far side of the room with his pale little wife, but, other than a brief nod in Barrington's direction, betrayed no sign of having seen him.

Barrington allowed his gaze to move on. He was used to being ignored by those for whom he worked, if one wished to call it that. It was a hazard—or a blessing—of the job, depending on how one looked at it.

Then, suddenly, there was a commotion as three ladies entered together. Lady Annabelle Durst, magnificent in lilac silk, Lady Lydia Winston, lovely in shimmering green, and a third, slightly older but equally striking woman with whom Barrington was not acquainted. She wore an elegant silver-grey gown, long white gloves and a diamond necklace that could have fed London's poor for a year. And when he heard whispers in the crowd and realised that most of Lady Bessmel's guests didn't know who the lady was, he put the pieces together. This must surely be the mysterious Baroness Julia von Brohm.

More importantly, however, it was also the first time he had seen Anna since the arrival of her note acknowledging Peregrine's guilt. How would she receive him? With haughty indifference or grudging acceptance?

Knowing that the question had to be asked, he crossed the room to where she stood and bowed in front of the three ladies. 'Good evening, Lady Lydia. Lady Annabelle.'

'Why, good evening, Sir Barrington,' Lady Lydia said with unaffected pleasure. 'How nice to see you again. I thought perhaps you had been in hiding, we have seen so little of you.'

'Alas, I have been kept busy with work,' Barrington said, conscious of Anna's eyes on him.

'Yes, so I understand,' Lady Lydia's eyes sparkled with mischief. 'I happened to bump into your sister at Hatchard's the other day. She said you haven't been round for a visit since the occasion of her last dinner party.'

Barrington's mouth twisted, remembering his less-than-memorable meeting with Lady Alice Stokes, a pleasant woman with whom he'd had absolutely nothing in common. 'I will go round and see Jenny this week. And apologise,' he added with a rueful smile. Then, bowing towards Anna, said, 'I trust all is well at home, Lady Annabelle?'

'Yes, thank you, Sir Barrington.' Her expression was tranquil, but Barrington thought he detected a quiver in her voice. Surely she wasn't nervous about seeing him again?

'And Mr Rand?' he asked.

'He is doing as well as can be expected, under the circumstances,' she said quietly. Her hair was drawn softly off her face and caught up with a cluster of deep pink roses. Barrington thought she had never looked lovelier. 'Are you acquainted with Baroness von Brohm?' she asked, adroitly changing the subject.

'I am not,' Barrington said, turning towards the third lady, who was watching him with undisguised interest. 'I was hoping I might prevail upon one of you to make the introduction?'

'With pleasure. Baroness, may I present Sir Barrington Parker,' Anna said smoothly. 'Sir Barrington—Baroness Julia von Brohm.'

The lady regally inclined her head. 'Sir Barrington.'

'Baroness.' Barrington bowed over her hand. 'I'm surprised it has taken this long for us to meet, given that word of your arrival has been swirling for weeks.'

'There has been a great deal to do and I have kept much to myself,' the baroness admitted. 'But Lady Annabelle felt it was time to make my appearance in society and I am grateful to her and Lady Bessmel for their kindness in making it happen.'

'We decided to take Julia under our wing,' Anna explained. 'I'm sure you won't find that surprising, given what you know of me.'

Barrington wasn't sure if she was taking him to task, but when he saw the twinkle in her eye, he allowed himself to hope that the remark intended nothing of the sort. 'Yet another convoluted life exercise?' he ventured.

He was relieved to see her smile, and for the first time since the arrival of her note, he felt himself breathe properly again.

'Ah, Parker, good evening,' Lord Cambermere said, joining them. 'Might have known I'd find you hoarding the three most beautiful women in the room.'

'On the contrary, having only just made the baroness's acquaintance, I cannot be accused of hoarding. Especially since the other two ladies are as well known to you as they are to me.'

'Julia, allow me to introduce my father, Lord Cambermere,' Anna said with a smile. 'Papa, Baroness von Brohm.'

The earl's gaze sharpened, a man appreciating the beauty of a woman. 'I had heard of your arrival, Baroness, and am compelled to say that Vienna's loss is our gain. I trust you are enjoying life in London?'

'To be honest, I have experienced very little of it, Lord Cambermere,' the baroness replied. 'As I told your daughter, I have been busy setting up my household. There has not been much time for sightseeing or socialising.'

'But now that Julia is finished with all that, I have assured her that we shall be seeing a great deal more of her in society,' Anna said. 'Tonight is her début, if you will.'

'And a splendid début it is,' the earl said quietly. 'Would you allow me to introduce you to a few of my friends, Baroness? Having seen me in conversation with you, they will not forgive me if I neglect to do so.'

Barrington saw the look of pleasure that warmed the baroness's face, but also noticed the look of startled surprise on Anna's. Obviously she wasn't used to her widowed father paying court to a beautiful woman, especially one who was also so recently widowed. But, true to form, she recovered with swiftness and grace. 'Yes, do go, Julia. Papa knows everyone and he is perfectly respectable. Just don't start him talking about horses.'

'Oh, but I love horses!' the Baroness was quick to say. 'My late husband's stable was one of the finest in Vienna.'

'Good Lord,' the earl said, leaning forwards. 'Never tell me that your late husband was Captain Baron Ulrich von Brohm?'

A soft gasp escaped the baroness. 'Yes. Did you know him?'

'I most certainly knew *of* him. I read several of his papers on early equine development and thought his ideas were nothing short of brilliant.' The earl offered the lady his arm. 'I would be honoured to have a chance to speak to you about him.'

As an opening gambit, it couldn't have been better. Barrington watched the baroness place her gloved hand on Cambermere's sleeve, aware that her eyes were bright with interest as they rested on his face. They were already talking about horses as he led her away, prompting Barrington to wonder how many of the earl's friends were likely to be introduced to the beautiful baroness that evening.

'I think you have a success on your hands, Anna,' Lady Lydia whispered. 'If everyone else is as taken with the baroness as your father, we will surely see her married before the end of the Season!'

Barrington tended to echo Lady Lydia's assessment, though he wondered how Anna felt at having her father's affection for the woman so bluntly stated. It wasn't always easy for daughters to accept a new woman into their father's life, especially daughters who still lived at home. The arrival of a stepmother could make their lives hellish. Still, given the friendship that seemed to exist between Anna and the baroness, Barrington doubted that would be the case here.

'Sir Barrington,' she said suddenly, breaking into his thoughts, 'I wonder if I might have a word with you? In private.'

He turned to find her sapphire gaze fixed on him. 'By all means.'

'Then I shall go and speak to Lady Bessmel,' Lady Lydia said promptly. 'She mentioned having received news of her son in Scotland and I have been longing to hear how Thomas goes on. I shall catch up with you later, Anna. Good evening, Sir Barrington.'

Barrington inclined his head, but he noticed that Anna waited until her friend was far enough away so as not to hear their conversation before turning to him and saying, 'I hoped I would have a chance to speak to you this evening, Sir Barrington. I'm sure we both recognise that I owe you an apology with regard to Peregrine.'

Barrington studied the face upturned to his, aware that it exposed far more than she realised. 'You owe me nothing, Lady Annabelle. I took no pleasure in being the bearer of bad news.'

'Nevertheless, I accused you of dealing in false information and that was a criticism of your professional conduct. For that, an apology must be offered.'

'*Must* be?' he repeated. 'Am I to conclude that you do not *wish* to apologise?'

Her gaze clouded over, a tiny frown appearing between her brows. 'Please don't misunderstand. If I appear reluctant to admit my error, it is only because it has caused me to question things about myself that I've not had reason to question before. I thought I knew Peregrine better than anyone. Certainly better than you. And I believed I was right in defending him when you first charged him with the affair. But, as it turns out, I really didn't know him at all. I was convinced he would never do something so foolish as to engage in an affair, yet that's exactly what he did.'

'But you and I both know that Mr Rand is not the first man to catch Lady Yew's eye, nor will he be the last,' Barrington said. 'She is the type of a woman who needs constant attention. Sadly, he is just the latest on a very long list of conquests.'

'I know, but that doesn't make it any better,' Anna said ruefully. 'And it certainly doesn't excuse what he did.'

'Love makes its own excuses. It has ever been thus.'

'Perhaps, but what disturbs me the most is that he truly *believed* she loved him.'

'He will get over it,' Barrington said with a smile. 'He is a young man and all young men must fall in love with at least one unsuitable woman in their life. It is a rite of passage. Useful in teaching us what to watch out for when we *do* finally go looking for a wife.'

Her smile was a reluctant twisting of her lips. 'I wish I could be as convinced of that as you, but when I see him suffering...'

'Women pine for love not found while men suffer from love already lost. It is our Achilles' heel, if you will. And for what it's worth, I suspect Rand was more in love with the idea of *being* in love than he was with the actual act of loving,' Barrington said, hoping to ease her guilt. 'By all accounts, he liked to read to her and she enjoyed listening to him.'

He saw a tiny smile lift the corners of her mouth. 'Peregrine has a lovely speaking voice. Not as mellifluous as yours, of course, but I expect he would have done well on the stage.'

*She liked his voice.* There was really no reason the compliment should have meant anything to him, but it did. Strange the things a man clung to. 'Regardless, I think it little more than a case of boyish infatuation. Lady Yew is a beautiful woman. She was probably flattered that a good-looking man so much younger than she would find her attractive and offered more encouragement than she should.'

'For all the good it did either of them,' Anna said with an edge to her voice. 'But I *am* sorry, Sir Barrington. You told me that collecting information was what you did and you obviously do it very well. I will not be so foolish as to doubt you again.'

Barrington inclined his head, wondering why he felt as though she was saying goodbye. 'With luck, there will be no occasion for us to find ourselves in a situation like this again.'

Then she smiled and, with her very next words, confirmed his suspicions. 'I suppose not. In fact, given what we know of each other, I doubt our paths will have any reason to cross again.'

As expected, the baroness's introduction to London society was a complete success and doors that had been closed to her in the past were suddenly thrown open with abandon. Society embraced her with the fervour of a shepherd welcoming home a long-lost lamb and gentlemen flocked to her side, eager to secure favour.

Because she was seen to be such good friends with Lady Bessmel and the daughters of the Earl of Cambermere and the Marquess of Bailley, her name constantly appeared high on the list of society events, both intimate and grand. Not surprisingly, Anna's brother and father were frequent visitors to Julia's afternoon salons, though the earl was very careful not to do anything that might result in scandal being attached to her name. He never stayed longer than was appropriate, or tried to take up too much of her time. But it was noted and remarked upon, after several society gatherings where both were in attendance, that the widowed Earl of Cambermere was evidencing a marked partiality for the company of the beautiful Baroness von Brohm.

Naturally, Julia was delighted with all the attention, but Anna noticed that she, too, was careful not to indicate a preference for any one gentleman over another, perhaps because she was still clinging to the memory of her late husband. But she was a gracious and entertaining guest, and though her list of contacts grew by the day, she never forgot that it was Anna's kindness that had originally launched her into society.

As such, she decided to hold a dinner party in Anna's honour, inviting, along with the rest of her family, twenty other guests including Lord and Lady Bessmel and Lady Lydia Winston. Knowing the company would be very smart, Anna decided to wear one of her newest gowns, an elegant creation in pale gold silk, a colour that was exceedingly flattering to her fair complexion. Her hair was arranged in a loose cluster of curls with a few wisps hanging free to frame her face. Elbow-length gloves, her mother's pearls and a light sweep of colour across her cheeks were all that were required to complete the ensemble.

Half an hour later, she stepped out of the carriage in front of Julia's house, with her father and Edward close behind. Both looked very elegant in their black-and-white evening attire, her father especially so. Peregrine, who was still reluctant to show his face in society, had decided to remain at home.

'Good thing, too,' Edward said in the disparaging tone he always used when Peregrine's name came up. 'No point the boy thinking he's entitled to move in good society when it's obvious he belongs in the country.' He plucked a strand of hair from the sleeve of his jacket. 'Besides, he'd likely just embarrass us in front of the baroness. He does, after all, have an eye for older women.'

'That was unkind,' Anna said flatly. 'You are as much to blame for Peregrine's fall from grace as he is.'

'I don't see how. I wasn't the one who jumped into bed with Lady Yew.'

'Don't be coarse, Edward, and please keep your voice down,' Anna said in a fierce whisper. 'You shouldn't have told him about the state of their marriage.'

'My dear Anna, there isn't a soul in London who doesn't know the state of the Yews' marriage,' Edward said blandly. 'Why should I have left Rand in ignorance? He would have found out sooner or later. And just because I told him Lady Yew was open to lovers didn't mean he had to go sniffing after her as though she were a bitch in season. And you needn't look at me like that,' he said when she turned a chilling glance on him. 'You're too old to pretend an ignorance of what goes on between a man and a woman. I know how besotted you were over Anthony Colder.'

Anna winced, the mere sound of the man's name causing her pain. 'I would thank you not to mention him in my presence again.'

'Why not? Surely you're not still pining over the fellow. He wasn't worth it, you know. The stories I could tell—'

'This conversation is over,' Anna said coldly. 'Please keep your opinions to yourself and refrain from making damaging comments about Peregrine in public, lest you find yourself defending rumours about your own less than sterling behaviour.'

'*My* behaviour?' Her brother's eyes widened in a credible imitation of innocence. 'What possible concern could you have about that?'

*Brushed by Scandal*

'I see no need to explain myself. We are both aware of your reputation with women.'

He slowly began to smile, clearly enjoying himself. 'And what have you heard about my reputation, pray tell?'

'Amongst other things, that you are fickle and heartless,' Anna said, boldly meeting his gaze. 'We've gone through three maids in the last year and I suspect your unwelcome attentions towards them had much to do with the reasons they all left. If you must indulge yourself, kindly do so in a manner that does not disrupt the household or result in frightened young girls being sent back to the country in tears.'

His eyes narrowed and for a long moment he stared at her in silence. 'Well, well, so the pretty bird has sharp talons,' he murmured finally. 'Who would have guessed?'

'Guessed what?' their father asked, joining them.

'Nothing.' Anna turned her back on Edward, shutting out his obnoxious comments and his condescending gaze. She knew he enjoyed goading her and most of the time she was able to rise above his petty teasing, to treat his remarks with the chilly disdain they deserved. But tonight he'd touched a nerve and, despite her best intentions, she had lashed out at him, a reaction she would no doubt come to regret. 'We should go in. I have no desire to keep the Baroness waiting.'

They were escorted by the butler into an elegant drawing room where most of the guests had already assembled. Anna saw Lydia talking to Lord and Lady Bessmel and smiled in acknowledgement of her friend's wave. She left her father and brother and went to join them.

'Good evening, Lord Bessmel, Lady Bessmel,' she greeted the older couple. 'And, Lydia, I'm so pleased to see you. How is your mother this evening?'

'Much better, thank heavens,' the girl said, clearly relieved. 'This last megrim has been very difficult for her, but the doctor gave her something that seems to be helping. But what an exquisite gown, Anna. Surely one of Madame Delors's?'

'I thought the occasion demanded something suitably festive.' Anna took a deep breath and glanced around the room. She had no idea if Sir Barrington had been invited, but she found herself looking for him regardless. 'Have you seen our hostess yet?'

'No, but I expect she will be down shortly.'

'Not the thing for a lady to be late for her own dinner party,' Lord Bessmel remarked.

'Patience, Harry,' Lady Bessmel said, patting her husband's arm. 'I'm sure the baroness is simply waiting for the right moment to make her appearance. Most Europeans have a flair for the dramatic. But what lovely pearls, Annabelle. Your mother's, if I'm not mistaken.'

'Yes,' Anna said, surprised that the countess would recognise them. 'How did you know?'

'I remember her wearing them. White or pink pearls are relatively common, but that shade of gold is quite rare.'

'They were a gift to her from Papa,' Anna said fondly. 'He always said Mama had the perfect complexion for them.'

'She did. Fortunately, so do you and they go perfectly with your gown, which I must tell you is absolutely exquisite. But look, I do believe the baroness comes.'

As expected, all eyes turned towards the door where the baroness, resplendent in sapphire satin, stood for a moment framed in the doorway. Her lovely face was wreathed in smiles, but Anna was quite sure it wasn't her smile or her gown that caused the collective gasp of astonishment that echoed around the room, but the magnificent diamond-and-sapphire necklace that was draped around her throat.

'Forgive me, dear friends, but a minor crisis upstairs

delayed my arrival,' she announced to her assembled guests. 'I trust you have been attended to in my absence.'

'We have been very well treated,' Lord Bessmel said as the baroness joined them. 'The important thing is that you are here now and looking quite spectacular, if you don't mind my saying so.'

'I don't mind you saying so at all, Lord Bessmel,' Julia said with a soft gurgle of laughter. 'In fact, I am convinced it is the one thing a lady *never* tires of hearing. Anna, my dear,' she said, pressing her cheek to Anna's. 'How beautiful you look tonight. You will most certainly rob the gentlemen of their senses. And, Lady Lydia, how delightful to see you again. I trust your mother is feeling better?'

'She is, Julia, thank you; she is so sorry she couldn't be here this evening. Unfortunately, noise tends to aggravate her condition.'

'I understand,' Julia said with a sympathetic nod. 'Megrims are such tiresome things. You are lucky not to be afflicted.'

'Good evening, Baroness.'

Julia turned and her smile brightened. 'Lord Cambermere, Lord Hayle, I am so pleased you were both able to attend.'

'An opportunity to spend time in the company of a beautiful woman should never be missed,' Cambermere said as he brushed his lips over her hand in a courtly, old-world gesture. 'And may I say you look magnificent this evening.'

A becoming flush rose in her cheeks. 'You are very kind to say so.'

'Kindness has nothing to do with it,' the earl assured her. 'I'm sure there isn't a gentleman in the room who doesn't agree with me.'

'Fortunately, most of them come with wives,' Edward cut in smoothly. 'Those of us who are single definitely have the advantage this evening.'

His smile was charismatic and his words flattering. Anna

saw her father's expression falter as Edward neatly inserted himself between them, but Julia's attention was already diverted, her head turned towards the door. 'And here is yet another handsome gentleman come to join our group. Good evening, Sir Barrington.'

Anna hadn't needed to hear Barrington's name to know that he was in the room. She'd felt the atmosphere change, a subtle quickening of interest as he crossed the floor like a sleek black panther moving through the forest. She saw heads turn, watched eyes widen and flirtatious smiles disappear behind discreetly raised fans. Obviously she wasn't the only one impressed by the width of his shoulders and the unfathomable depths of those cool grey eyes—

'Anna!'

Hearing Lydia's voice, Anna turned, but it wasn't until she saw the slight widening of her friend's eyes that she realised she had been staring. Botheration! The last thing she needed was Sir Barrington Parker mistakenly thinking she was interested in him. Or worse, infatuated by him.

Fortunately, the gentleman seemed completely unaware of her preoccupation, his attention now focused solely on his hostess. 'Good evening, Baroness,' he greeted her in that distinctively low, seductive voice. 'Forgive my late arrival. I was unavoidably detained.'

'You owe us no apologies, Sir Barrington,' Julia said easily. 'You are here now and that is all that matters. I believe you know everyone?'

Sir Barrington nodded, his gaze touching briefly on each of them as he paid his respects. Finally, he turned to Anna, his mouth curving in that maddeningly provocative smile. 'Lady Annabelle.'

'Sir Barrington,' she said, wishing she possessed even a fraction of his composure. 'We have not seen much of you this past while.'

'I was out of London for a few days on business, but made sure to return in time for this evening's gathering.'

'And for the fencing demonstration,' Lord Bessmel said with a wink.

Sir Barrington turned to stare at him. 'I beg your pardon?'

'The fencing demonstration. The one Lord Yew asked you to put on.'

'Forgive me, Lord Bessmel, but I am not aware I was giving a fencing demonstration. Where did you hear news of it?'

'From Lord Hadley,' the older man replied. 'He said he'd heard you speaking to Lord Yew, and that you had agreed to a series of open engagements at Angelo's.'

'Open engagements?' Anna repeated. 'What does that mean?'

'It means that every red-blooded male capable of lifting a sword will be there looking to take Parker on,' Bessmel explained with a smile. 'Should make for a damn good show!'

Anna glanced at Sir Barrington in bewilderment. Surely Lord Bessmel was mistaken. Sir Barrington Parker didn't give demonstrations. Everyone knew that. And if he did choose to spar, it would be with someone of his own choosing.

Could this be the Marquess of Yew's doing? she wondered. Had he demanded this of Sir Barrington as well as everything he had already asked of Peregrine? 'Is this true, Sir Barrington?' she asked in a low voice. 'Is this what you agreed to do?'

'Not exactly,' he murmured. 'What I agreed to was a private lesson with Yew's son, pointing out areas where he might improve. I certainly said nothing about a series of engagements with anyone who felt up to sparring with me.'

'But I fear that is what everyone is expecting,' Bessmel said, adding hesitantly, 'are you going to back out?'

'Surely it cannot be called backing out when one never agreed to it in the first place,' Lydia objected.

'I wouldn't have thought so,' Sir Barrington agreed, 'but I shall speak to Lord Yew about it when next I see him.' Then, seemingly unconcerned, he turned his attention to their hostess again. 'Baroness, that is an exceptionally beautiful necklace.'

'Why, thank you, Sir Barrington.' Julia caressed the deep blue stones with loving fingers. 'My late husband bought it for me. He knew my partiality for sapphires.'

'It is a remarkable piece of workmanship,' Cambermere agreed. 'I hope you keep it safely locked away.'

'I haven't thus far.' Julia's eyes widened. 'Is London such a dangerous place that one need fear being robbed in one's own home?'

'Not as a rule, but I regret to say there have been a series of jewel thefts in London of late,' Sir Barrington informed her. 'I understand Lord Houghton's home was broken into two nights ago and a number of valuable items taken.'

'You should be on guard yourself, Cambermere,' Bessmel said. 'I dare say your daughter's pearls are worth a pretty penny.'

'They are, but I suspect to Anna, like myself, their value is far more sentimental.' The earl turned to smile at her. 'My wife loved pearls. She always said they drew their warmth from the one who wore them. I gave her that necklace on our wedding day.'

'Was your wife born in June, my lord?' Julia enquired.

Cambermere looked surprised by the question. 'She was.'

'Then she was fortunate to be able to wear them without

tears. It is considered bad luck to give a bride pearls unless they are her birthstone.'

'Then you must also have been born in June, Lady Annabelle,' Sir Barrington said quietly, 'for the pearls to glow so richly against your skin.'

Anna felt her cheeks grow warm at the subtle caress in his voice. 'On the contrary, my birthday is in September.'

'Then, like the baroness, you should be wearing sapphires.'

'I say, Cambermere, these women could bankrupt us if they were of a mind to!' Lord Bessmel said with a hearty laugh. 'Now you will have to go out and buy your daughter a string of sapphires, just to appease the superstitious amongst us.'

'I think not,' Anna said quickly. 'Sapphires are beautiful stones, but, like Mama, I prefer the warmth of pearls.'

'I can understand why,' Sir Barrington said as the others turned away to chat amongst themselves. 'They are exceptional, as is the lady wearing them.'

Anna slowly raised her eyes to his face, aware of the fire in his eyes as his gaze lingered on her necklace. The low *décolleté* of the gown exposed far more skin than she was used to and she could almost feel the heat of his eyes burning her. When he finally raised his eyes to meet hers, the desire in them was plain. Was it any wonder her heart was beating double time?

Thankfully, Julia, catching the eye of her butler, said, 'Dear guests, shall we proceed to the dining room? I do believe dinner is served.'

# *Chapter Six*

At the conclusion of an exceptional meal, the baroness led the ladies into the drawing room, leaving the gentlemen to enjoy masculine conversation, good cigars and several fine bottles of port. Barrington, who enjoyed these sessions more for the information they provided than for the chance to socialise, accepted the offer of a light from Viscount Hayle, who settled into the chair next to his. Noticing the man's obvious boredom, Barrington said, 'Is the evening not to your liking, Hayle?'

Hayle slanted him a mocking glance. 'I get tired of listening to men like Bessmel and Richards bickering over political situations about which they know nothing. It's a waste of everyone's time and, frankly, I'd rather spend the night gambling or in the arms of a mistress.'

Barrington drew on his cigar, taking a moment to study the other man through the rising curl of smoke. 'I'm surprised Mr Rand didn't come with you tonight. I thought he usually accompanied your sister to these kinds of events.'

'He was invited but, thankfully, he declined,' Hayle said

tersely. 'It's bad enough having him around the house all the time, let alone being forced into society with him.'

'You do not care for Mr Rand?'

'Would you?' Hayle fired back.

Barrington was startled by the flash of raw emotion he saw in the other man's eyes and wondered if Hayle knew how much of himself he had given away. 'I'm not sure I know what you mean.'

'Then you're the only one who doesn't,' Hayle muttered. 'All you have to do is *look* at Rand to know he's no more my father's *godson* than he is the bloody Prince of Wales's.'

So, that was it. The son suspected the connection and wasn't in the least happy about it. Barrington tapped ash from the end of his cigar. 'I'd be lying if I said I hadn't heard rumours, but I don't believe anything's been substantiated.'

'Of course not. My father's the only one who can substantiate rumours like that and you can be damn sure he's not going to. Not now that he's met the baroness.' Hayle's eyes narrowed as he glared at his father sitting farther up the table. 'It's embarrassing the way he carries on with her. God knows, he's old enough to be her father.'

'I take it you do not care for the fact that the earl and the baroness seem to like one another?'

'I do not. It's unseemly the way he follows her around, hanging on every word she says. He might just as well come out and ask her to go to bed with him.'

Barrington reached for his glass of port, intrigued by the depth of vitriol pouring from the other man. 'I think you judge them too harshly. Your father is an amiable gentleman and the baroness is an exceedingly gracious woman. And as they are both widowed, why should they not enjoy one another's company?'

'There *is* a considerable difference in their ages.'

Barrington shrugged. 'The baroness can't be any more

than twenty-nine or thirty, and your father is, what...in his late forties? There are far wider gaps in age between husbands and wives in society.'

Hayle slowly began to smile. 'Yes. Like Lord Yew and his wife. But then, I suspect you already know all about that.'

Barrington inhaled deeply on his cigar. Hayle was bound to know about Peregrine's folly, but he was damned if he'd be the one to shed any light on the matter. When it came to secrets, he was as adept at keeping them as he was at prying them out of others.

Fortunately, Hayle didn't appear to be in need of an answer. 'How much do you think that sapphire necklace is worth?' he asked instead.

Barrington's shrug was carefully non-committal. 'I'm no expert, but, given the size and quality of the stones, I should think it considerable.'

'Enough to keep a man in brandy and cigars for the rest of his life, I'll wager.'

'Probably. How fortunate that you and I need not worry about such things.'

Hayle snorted. 'Speak for yourself.'

Barrington's gaze sharpened. 'You are your father's heir.'

'Oh, yes. But as he's still in his forties and hale and hearty, I'm not likely to inherit any time soon,' Hayle said sourly. 'So, what's your connection with the baroness?'

'We have no connection, *per se*,' Barrington said, aware that the man changed subjects more often than a lady changed her mind. 'We were introduced by your sister at Lady Bessmel's reception and have seen each other at a few society gatherings since, but nothing beyond that.' He gazed at the earl's son through a fine wisp of smoke. 'I understand it was your sister's idea to launch the baroness into society.'

'Of course it was. Anna loves to manage other people's lives. Personally, I think her time would be better spent smoothing her way into some man's bed,' Hayle said in a disagreeable tone, adding when he saw Barrington's stern look, '*After* she marries him, of course. Anna would never do anything as irresponsible as compromise herself. But it's long past time she was wed. Father's too soft. He won't force her into an arranged marriage, even though he knows it would be best for all concerned.'

'I'm sure your sister would have no problem finding a husband if that was something she truly wanted,' Barrington said, careful to keep the annoyance from his voice. 'She is an exceedingly beautiful woman.'

'But meddlesome and outspoken,' Hayle remarked. 'Men don't like that in a wife. They want quiet, biddable women who know their place. Anna is neither biddable nor accommodating, as I'm sure you know from the brief time you've spent with her. Mind, I've heard her mention *your* name more than once and that's saying something. Better watch yourself, Parker, or she'll have you in the parson's mousetrap before you can turn around.' He drained the contents of his glass, then signalled the waiter for a refill. 'So, I hear you're giving a fencing demonstration at Angelo's this week.'

Barrington's hand tightened on his glass. 'No. I am giving Lord Yew's son a lesson. In private.'

'I heard you were going to fight.'

'You heard wrong.'

'But why wouldn't you fight?' Hayle asked. 'You're reputed to be the finest swordsman in London. Why not show everyone that you are?'

'Because that's not what I do.'

'Then why are you giving Yew's boy a lesson?'

'I agreed to it as a favour to the marquess. I also happen to like Lord Gerald. He shows a great deal of promise with the foil and he is anxious to better himself.'

'Maybe, but you'll never make a fighter of him. He's too

soft,' Hayle said. 'He hasn't the heart for it. You'd do far better sparring with me. At least I'd give you a run for your money. So what do you say? Are you up for it?'

Barrington's expression was deceptively benign. He was used to cocky young men challenging him. At one time, he'd encouraged it, fond of pitting his skills against all comers. But that game had lost its appeal years ago.

He was about to say as much when the door to the dining room opened and one of the younger maids walked in. He hadn't noticed her earlier in the evening, which meant she likely hadn't been in the room. He would certainly have remembered her if she had. She was somewhere in her early twenties, with dark brown hair and rather startling green eyes—

Barrington stiffened. Green eyes and dark brown hair. Was it possible he'd found Colonel Tanner's elusive Miss Paisley? If so, he wasn't surprised that the Colonel had asked him to look for her. Though petite, she had a lush, curving figure that was nicely displayed in the black gown and white apron. Her face was heart shaped and delicate and she had a truly lovely smile. But equally aware of having drawn the attention of nearly every man in the room, her cheeks turned bright pink as she made her way towards the butler, who was standing in the corner overseeing the proceedings.

A whispered conversation followed, during which the butler's heavy eyebrows drew together in annoyance. Then, with a flick of his hand, he dismissed her.

As she headed back in their direction, Barrington noticed Hayle doing a leisurely appraisal of her charms. Then, slowly raising his glass, he watched her over the rim and when she was no more than five feet away, coughed. Not discreetly, as a gentleman might, but in a manner that was guaranteed to draw attention.

The girl glanced in their direction—and her step faltered.

Barrington heard her breath catch and saw her eyes widen as they met those of the man sitting next to him. Beside him, Hayle just smiled. Coldly. Like a spider watching a fly, knowing it was doomed.

The butler, noticing her standing in the middle of the room, said sharply, 'Be off with you, girl!'

She went, all but running to the door. Hayle turned away, seemingly uninterested. 'Bloody endless evening,' he muttered into his glass.

But the girl didn't leave. Barrington saw her hesitate by the door, saw her turn around to take one last look at Hayle, and the expression in her eyes said it all.

'Oh, I don't know,' Barrington remarked, drawing deeply on his cigar. 'Seems to me it's all in how you look at it.'

Anna was seated at the pianoforte playing an air by Bach when the drawing-room door opened and the gentlemen filed in. She knew the piece well enough not to be flustered by their arrival and kept on playing, watching with interest as they took their various seats and settled into conversation with the ladies. Her father stopped to chat with Lady Bessmel, but eventually ended up at Julia's side. His face was flushed and he was smiling. No doubt the result of an extra glass of port after dinner.

Edward spoke briefly to Lady Lydia Winston, but, judging from the expression on her face, the conversation was not at all to her liking. She stiffly got up and walked away. Edward just laughed.

'I was going to ask if I might turn the pages for you,' Sir Barrington said, quietly appearing at her side. 'But since it's obvious you play from memory, I doubt you are in need of my help.'

The glow of his smile warmed her. 'Nevertheless, it is kind of you to offer, Sir Barrington.'

'Kindness had nothing to do with it. I was looking for an excuse to talk to you.'

Anna was tempted to ask why he felt the need of an excuse, but the teasing quip died on her lips when she saw the way he was looking down at her. 'About something in particular?'

'Of course.' He stared a moment longer, before turning his attention back to the room.

Anna kept her eyes on the keyboard, waiting for her breathing to settle. Would it always be like this? Was she destined to feel this trembling excitement every time Barrington drew near? She certainly hoped not. It wouldn't bode well for their friendship if she did.

She cast a sideways glance at him and knew he was taking it all in. Making mental lists about the people and situations that intrigued him. Watching. Always watching.

'It must get tiresome,' she said at length. 'Always having to watch the behaviour of others.'

He turned back to smile at her, one eyebrow raised in amusement. 'That depends on your point of view. Some people spend their entire lives studying the behaviour of others. Wanting to know what their friends and acquaintances are doing. It's called being nosy and society suffers from it excessively.'

Her lips twitched. 'That's quite true, but what you do is entirely different.'

'Why would you say so?'

'Because you don't watch people with the intention of catching them doing something wrong. You watch with a view to catalogue it all for future reference. You notice who they speak to and who they ignore, if they drink too much or not at all, and if they dance with that person and not this one.'

'You make me sound rather devious,' he observed.

'No. Just observant. Something that probably serves you well given the nature of your...occupation.'

The piece of music came to an end and Anna rose to the polite applause of the guests. Miss Constantine was to play next, and as that young lady moved forwards to take her place at the piano, Anna dropped back and fell in beside Barrington.

'Did I detect a note of censure in your voice just then?' he asked as they slowly walked away from the instrument.

Did he? Anna didn't like to think she was revealing too much of herself, but with him, it wasn't always easy to know. 'I have the feeling, Sir Barrington, that one is never entirely safe around you. You see a great deal without ever giving the appearance of actually looking. That makes you dangerous.'

'Only to those with something to hide. The innocent have no reason to fear me.' His eyes found hers and held them captive. 'I trust *you* do not find me dangerous, Lady Annabelle?'

'Danger comes in many forms. I suspect knowing a man like you does not come without risks.'

'*Life* does not come without risks,' he said softly. 'But you're right. A man like myself is always more of a target, as are the people who associate with me.'

Thinking he was being overly dramatic, Anna smiled and said, 'In that case, you'd best warn Miss Erickson to keep her distance.'

'Miss Erickson?'

'Miss Sofia Erickson. I happen to know she is very fond of you.'

Barrington said, 'I'm not sure I know her.'

'Of course you do. Eldest daughter of Viscount Oswell and recently returned from visiting her aunt in Edinburgh. She made her come out this Season and has already been acknowledged as one of its greatest successes. She speaks French and Italian fluently, is an accomplished rider, and an exceptional singer.'

A smile ruffled his mouth. 'And have you had occasion to save the young lady from herself?'

'Good Lord, no.' The sensual curve of his lips brought a series of highly inappropriate thoughts to mind, but Anna forced herself to ignore them. 'She is one of the most intelligent young women I've ever met. She is mindful of the proprieties and quite capable of telling a gentleman to watch his manners if she feels he is out of line.'

'Tell me, how do you come to be so involved in the lives of all these young women?' Barrington asked curiously as they sat down together on the velvet settee. 'Surely your father would wish you to pay more attention to your own future than chasing around after everyone else's?'

Anna felt the familiar warmth creep into her cheeks—an annoyingly common occurrence since meeting this man. 'One can do both at the same time. Helping someone else navigate the path towards marriage does not mean I cannot walk the path myself.'

'But if you are too busy looking out for the welfare of others, how can you see to your own?'

'I hardly think I am doing one to the exclusion of the other,' Anna said defensively. 'Besides, what I do for these girls is important. All too often they find themselves swept up in the emotion of the moment and don't stop to think about the repercussions.'

'And so you step in,' he said softly. 'Like you did with Mercy Banks and Fiona Whitfield, and God knows how many others, in an attempt to save them from themselves.'

'It is all very well for you to mock me, Sir Barrington, but you cannot deny that—' Anna broke off to stare at him. 'How did you know I was involved with Fiona Whitfield?'

'Do you really need ask?'

'Yes, I fear I must. Fiona's mother and father were adamant that word of what happened to Fiona not leak out. I gave them my word that I would say nothing and, since the young man was sent abroad, I don't see how you could possibly be aware of what took place.'

'As it happens, I was making enquiries into the activities of Miss Whitfield's uncle,' Barrington told her. 'I learned of your association with the family at that time. And though I did not delve into the particulars of Miss Whitfield's situation, I did learn of *your* involvement with her whilst speaking to another family member.'

Anna gasped. 'Someone else knew what happened to Fiona?'

'I'm afraid so. But, like you, they were sworn to secrecy. And it worked out well enough in the end. She married Lord Priestley's son earlier this year and I understand they are very happy together.'

'Yes, thank goodness. It could have turned out so badly for her, and all because of that despicable man.' Anna sighed. 'It really isn't fair, you know. A man may tempt a woman with honeyed words and longing looks, yet *she* is the one who must behave with propriety at all times. If he manages to steal a kiss, he is not thought of any the less, whereas she is deemed to have loose morals.'

'Sadly, it has always been thus,' Barrington remarked. 'Society makes the rules and we must obey.'

'No. *Men* make the rules and then demand that women follow them. It is no wonder we sometimes falter.'

She saw the surprise in his face. 'Am I to assume from your comment, Lady Annabelle, that you yourself have faltered in the past?'

'That is none of your business!' she exclaimed.

'No, I don't suppose it is.' He laughed softly, the sound

sending shivers up her spine. 'But your reputation doesn't suggest a woman who would be easily led astray. I find my curiosity piqued at the thought of you having ever done anything wrong.'

'Then you will just have to live with piqued curiosity,' Anna said, abruptly standing up.

'Anna, wait, I meant no offence,' he said, likewise getting to his feet. 'If I've inadvertently touched a nerve, I apologise. It was never my intention to hurt you.'

Anna shook her head, too distracted by unpleasant memories of the past to notice his lapse into familiarity. 'And I did not mean to be abrupt, Sir Barrington, but I have no wish to talk about what happened in my past.'

'I understand. We've all made mistakes, some worse than others. But given your untarnished reputation and excellent standing in society, it's obvious your mistake, if that's what it was, did not serve as your undoing.'

'It could have,' Anna whispered, 'had a friend not come along when she had.'

And that was the tragic truth of her brief flirtation with the Honourable Anthony Colder. As a naïve seventeen-year-old, Anna had all but thrown herself at the god-like creature, believing the smiles he had bestowed upon her were the result of a genuine and mutual affection. Little had she known that his interest had more to do with her father being the Earl of Cambermere than it did with any charms she might possess herself. Anthony had been an avid social climber, as well as the most handsome man she had ever met. With those laughing blue eyes and a smile that set butterflies dancing in her stomach, she would have given him anything he'd asked for. And if he'd had his chance, he would have taken it.

Mrs Mary Fielding had known that, too. A twice-married woman wise to the ways of men like Anthony Colder, Mrs Fielding had seen the growing infatuation between the two young people and had guessed at its source, being more familiar with Anthony's background than most. She had known of his gambling debts, his easy way with women, and his devil-may-care attitude. And on that evening when Anthony, having drunk too much brandy and feeling far too sure of himself, had caught Anna alone in the gazebo by the lake and torn her gown in a boorish attempt at seduction, Mrs Fielding had appeared and promptly sent him packing. She had stayed with Anna until the worst of her grief had passed, and then, after drying Anna's tears, she had lent her a shawl to cover the tear and had sent her regrets back to their hostess, explaining that Lady Annabelle was unwell and that she was seeing her home in her own carriage.

It had been a painful lesson, but one Anna had learned well. She had gone home that evening and made no mention of the event to anyone. She regretted having told her parents and her brother of her affection for Anthony, but after that night she never mentioned his name again. Nor, thankfully, did she see him. Mrs Fielding informed her not long after that he had left the country.

Anna had never been so glad to see the back of anyone in her life. And though she thought it was impossible for her to blush any deeper, she was wrong. Even after all this time, her face burned at the memory of her stupid, stupid mistake…

'Tell me what happened, Lady Annabelle,' Barrington said in a low voice. 'Your secrets are safe with me. I know, better than most, the value of discretion.'

'Yes, I'm sure you do,' Anna said quietly. 'But the only way to completely ensure one's secrets is by keeping them entirely to oneself.'

'I'm sorry you cannot bring yourself to trust me.'

She looked up at him, surprised that he would mention trust in such a situation. 'I do not know you, Sir Barrington.

And the trust of which you speak is generally reserved for relationships between husbands and wives.'

'I've always thought that bonds of trust can exist between friends as well as lovers.'

'Perhaps, but it takes time to establish that kind of bond,' she said, sounding flustered even to her own ears. 'You are a single gentleman and I a single lady. It isn't the thing for us to...share secrets of an intimate nature. But if you were looking for a wife, you would do well to consider Miss Erickson. Apart from her many other attributes, she is a genuinely nice young woman.'

'What makes you think I'm looking for a wife?' he asked.

'Why would you not be? You just told me that we must abide by society's rules, and society dictates that men and women should marry. Is that not the purpose of these gatherings? To place one in the path of the other?'

'I suppose it is.' He hesitated a moment before adding, 'But I think it only right to tell you that Miss Erickson would not be of interest to me, even if I were of a mind to marry.'

If he were of a *mind* to marry? 'Are you telling me you intend to remain single?' Anna asked, eyebrows lifting in shock.

'That was my plan, yes.'

'But what of your obligation to your family?'

'I fear the task of continuing the Parker name will fall to a distant cousin with whom I am not acquainted,' Barrington said blandly. 'As to the obligation owed, I am more concerned with the welfare of the lady with whom I might wish to spend my life than I am to the furthering of my ancestral line.'

'Then I would have to say you are unique in your thinking,' Anna said. 'Most society gentlemen are concerned with their family name and marry to beget an heir.'

'Yes, but you should know by now that my life is not that

of a typical society gentleman. My reputation is such that people come to me when they wish to learn things about others. And because I ask questions people have no wish to be asked, I continuously put myself at risk.'

'Surely you exaggerate the danger.'

'I do not.' His smile held secrets she could not begin to imagine. 'The people I usually investigate are not the honourable men you meet in society, Lady Annabelle. They are scoundrels and blackmailers, men who operate beyond the boundaries of the law and who are completely without conscience. When I get too close, they get nervous. And when I convict them, they look for retribution.'

'But surely not of a life-threatening kind!'

He shrugged, as though trying to make light of it. 'There have been attempts on my life in the past and I have no reason to believe there will not be attempts in the future. The easiest way to ensure my silence is to eliminate the possibility of my saying anything at all. That said, I will not knowingly put anyone else in danger.'

'But if these men have issues with you, why should you fear for the safety of those close to you?'

'Because there *is* no better way to strike back at me than to hurt someone I care about.' They had walked, by tacit agreement, onto the balcony. Barrington rested his arms against the stone balustrade and stared down into the garden. 'And who could be dearer to me than the woman to whom I would give my name…and my heart.'

Anna felt her mouth go dry. Strange that the breeze should suddenly feel so cool. Was her body overly warm? They were standing quite close; close enough that she could feel the heat radiating from his body. 'So you would choose to live… without a woman to share your life,' she whispered, 'rather than expose your wife to possible harm?'

'In a heartbeat.' He turned his head so that his eyes bored

into hers. 'How could I say I loved someone if I didn't care about their safety? If the thought of something happening to them didn't tear me apart?'

Anna shivered. 'You could give up what you're doing. You are a gentleman. You have no need to work.'

'And what would I do with myself then?' He reached out and took her hand in his. 'I have servants to run my estate and stewards and secretaries to see to my affairs. But a man must have something of his own or what reason has he for getting up each day?'

As he spoke, his fingers caressed the palm of her hand, smoothing the tender skin at the base of her wrist. His touch was light, non-threatening—and it turned Anna's world upside down.

She closed her eyes, the sounds of the room beyond fading into the distance. She knew she should pull her hand free, but she was neither willing nor anxious to do so. His thumb was painting circles on her skin, lulling her with a touch.

'We get up because...that is what the world expects of us,' she said huskily. Dear Lord, what was he doing? Not content with massaging her palm and wrist, his thumb was continuing its treacherous voyage along the inside of her arm, causing disturbing quakes in her sanity. 'Surely there is...a kind of security, perhaps even of comfort, in the carrying out of our daily task?'

'Ah, but there are far sweeter pleasures to be enjoyed than that, my lady,' Barrington murmured as he brushed the back of his free hand against her cheek. 'The smoothness of a woman's skin, the softness of her hair.' He gently twined a lock around his finger and held it to his face, inhaling the delicate fragrance. 'Finer than silk and more precious than gold.' Then, releasing it, he gently grasped her chin between thumb and forefinger and tilted her face up. 'Last but not least, the sweetness of her lips...'

Anna had been kissed before…but never like this. Never by a man whose touch was enough to make her long to release her tenuous hold on respectability. His mouth moved over hers slowly, thoughtfully, shattering her resolve and filling her with a desperate need to be loved. Surely she deserved this. Surely, after everything she'd been through, she was entitled to some small measure of love and affection for herself?

As he deepened the kiss, Anna raised her arms, twining them around his neck, wanting to be close and then closer still. His tongue teased her lips apart and heat poured through her body, flowing like molten fire through her veins. She moaned, feeling desire rise and want settle low in her belly. Ah, the sweet, sweet pleasure…

But the pleasure was bittersweet. Even as his arms tightened around her, Anna knew it could come to nothing. Barrington had no intention of marrying. He'd just told her as much. And if he wasn't willing to offer marriage, what they were doing now was not only wrong, it was self-destructive. She wanted more from him. Much more than he was willing to give. And in the end, she would be the one who walked away with her heart in ruins. And therein lay the true sadness of the situation. The one man with whom she could have foreseen a future was the one man with whom it would never be.

'Stupid, stupid, *stupid*!' she whispered, breaking free of his arms.

'Anna, what's wrong?' he asked huskily.

'What's wrong? *I'm* wrong,' she whispered. '*This* is wrong. Because right now, I'm no better than the foolish young women whose reputations I fight to protect.'

'That's ridiculous!'

'Is it? You just told me you have no intention of marrying, yet I allowed myself to be held in your arms and kissed like any cheap whore. What is that if not the height of stupidity?'

Anna flung at him. 'At least Mercy Banks was hopeful of a marriage resulting from her liaison with Lieutenant Blokker! You've made it clear there is no such happy ending in sight.'

His face darkened, his breathing heavy and uneven. 'I said that because I don't want you harbouring false hope. But it doesn't change the way I feel about you.'

'And is that supposed to make me feel *better*? Am I supposed to be comforted by the knowledge that you desire me, yet have no intention of offering marriage?' Anna shook her head. 'There is a word for that kind of relationship, Sir Barrington, and it is not flattering.'

'It was never my intention to compromise you, Anna,' he said quietly. 'I care too much for you.'

'My name is Lady Annabelle. And if you care so much for me, leave me alone!'

Without waiting for his answer, Anna picked up her skirts and fled. Angry tears blurred her vision as she ran down the length of the balcony. *Idiot!* She'd made a fool of herself again, allowing herself to be held and kissed as though she were a naïve young schoolgirl. She, who prided herself on knowing all the games and all the excuses, had let herself be taken in. And by doing so, Barrington had undermined everything she believed in. When she had allowed him to kiss her, she had wanted to believe that it meant something. But it was obvious to anyone with an iota of sense that it meant absolutely nothing. Sophisticated Barrington might be, but he was still a man, and when it came right down to it, he wanted the same thing as every other man. Pleasure without commitment. Love without obligation. The very things she kept warning her young ladies to avoid.

The breeze came up and, once again, Anna felt chilled. She hadn't stopped to fetch her wrap before venturing outside, but neither was she about to run back into the drawing room now.

Observant eyes would see the evidence of her tears, recognise the flush in her cheeks and put their own interpretation on the events—and nothing on earth was going to persuade her to tell anyone what had really happened.

She glanced back over her shoulder, wondering if Barrington had followed her. She didn't know whether to be relieved or disappointed when she saw that he hadn't. All right, so she'd made a mistake. It wasn't the first time she'd done so, but at least this time she was old enough to recognise it for herself. Barrington had made his feelings for her clear. The episode would not be repeated. From now on, she would treat him exactly the same way he treated everyone else. Coolly. Professionally. Without emotion. He would never make her cry again.

It was a good ten minutes before Anna felt calm enough to venture back into the house. Not by the drawing room through which she'd left. That would be far too embarrassing, especially knowing that Barrington had gone back in only a short time ago. Instead, she walked to the end of the balcony and, finding another set of glass doors, tried the handle. Thankfully, it was unlocked and pushing it open, she walked into a small study—only to stop and gasp in shock.

Her brother and Julia's maid were standing by the door, locked together in a passionate embrace. *'Edward!'*

At once, the pair sprang apart, but it was too late to disguise what they had been doing. The maid's dark hair had come down around her shoulders, her gown was in disarray and her lips were red and swollen.

Embarrassed, Anna looked away. Obviously, her brother wasn't above seducing pretty housemaids, whether they be his own or someone else's. Refusing to meet his eyes, she murmured, 'Excuse me', and then immediately made her way to the door. Edward said nothing, but she heard his mocking laughter following her through the door. She supposed she shouldn't have been surprised. Her brother had once again proven himself the immoral creature she believed him to be.

*And what about you?* the little voice nagged. *Are you so much better? So much more virtuous?*

Anna felt her face burn with humiliation. No, perhaps she wasn't. She kept remembering the passionate encounter she'd just shared with Barrington, the shameless manner in which she had allowed him to kiss her. Oh, yes, she'd *let* him kiss her. She wasn't about to lay the blame for what had happened entirely at his door. He was gentleman enough that if she had asked him to stop, he would have—but she hadn't done that. She'd wanted to know how it would feel to kiss him. To watch his head bend slowly towards her, and to feel his mouth close intimately over hers.

It had been everything she'd expected—and more.

But Barrington was no more likely to become her husband than Julia's maid was to become Edward's wife. They had both been indulging in impossible fantasies.

*'Let he who is without sin cast the first stone...'*

A sobering thought. As Anna made her way back to the drawing room, she realised that the proverbial stone would never find its way to her hand.

# Chapter Seven

For the next few days, Barrington went around like a bear with a sore head. Unable to forget what had happened between Anna and himself at the baroness's dinner party, he was quick to anger and slow to unwind, because he knew he'd hurt her. And hurting her was the last thing he'd ever wanted to do.

He'd still been in the drawing room when Anna had finally returned, but she hadn't approached him again. She had remained coldly aloof, treating him as though he wasn't there. He wasn't surprised that she had left shortly after.

He'd left early as well, all pleasure in the evening gone. Upon returning home, he'd made for his study and downed a stiff glass of brandy, followed in quick succession by two more. But the potent liquor had done nothing to assuage his guilt, or to help him find escape in sleep. When the morning had come, he'd been as tired and as irritable as when he'd gone to bed.

Much as he was this morning, three days later, as he made his way to Angelo's Haymarket rooms for his ten o'clock appointment with the Marquess of Yew's son.

Barrington deeply regretted having made the appointment.

The last thing he felt like doing was teaching the finer points of fencing to the gangly nineteen-year-old son of a man he neither liked nor respected. However, he had given Yew his promise that he would show the boy a few things and he was a man who kept his word. All he could do now was hope the hour passed quickly and that he didn't do the boy an unintentional injury.

Unfortunately, Lord Bessmel was right when he'd said that word of the lesson—or demonstration—had spread. By the time Barrington arrived, the room was filled to overflowing with gentlemen of all ages, some carrying swords, some just there to observe. It was worse than he'd expected.

'Ah, Parker,' Lord Yew greeted him with a smile. 'Good to see you. Quite the turnout, eh? I vow you draw a larger crowd than Prinnie.'

'Perhaps because you put it about that this was to be a demonstration, rather than the private lesson we agreed to,' Barrington said.

'Really?' the marquess said lazily. 'I don't recall saying this was to be a lesson. But never mind, now you and Gerald have a suitable audience.'

'An audience that comes armed and ready to spar?'

The marquess smiled. 'You should be thanking me, Parker. You have your pick of opponents and since we both know there's not a man in the room who can best you, you're guaranteed to come out on top. Why not just have fun with it?'

'Because that's not what I do.' Barrington's jaw tightened. Unfortunately, they both knew this was something of a command performance. A 'small additional favour' in exchange for the marquess's silence over Peregrine Rand's affair with his wife. And while Barrington would normally have refused to play a part, all it took was the memory of the look on Anna's face when she had spoken of Rand's guilt to make him change his mind. He didn't particularly care about the other man's feelings, but he would have done almost anything to prevent hers being further injured.

'I've lived up to my side of the bargain, Yew. I trust you intend to do the same.'

'Are you questioning my integrity?' the marquess asked, peering down his long, patrician nose.

'No. But I know how angry you were with Rand and I don't want to think that all of this has been for naught.'

The marquess chuckled. 'I can assure you it has not. In point of fact, I wasn't really angry at all.'

Barrington's mouth tightened. 'I beg your pardon?'

The marquess's expression was remote as he gazed at the milling crowd. 'Rand is not the first man to make love to my wife, and, God knows, he won't be the last. Susan is voracious in that regard and while I enjoy sex as much as the next man, I am not inclined to engage in it as often as she might wish. So I turn a blind eye to her affairs. It flatters me to know that she is still beautiful enough to attract other men; it flatters her to know that she is desired by men younger than herself.'

No stranger to the unusual, Barrington was none the less bewildered by Yew's unexpected admission. 'Then why did you go to the trouble of persecuting him?'

The marquess's gaze narrowed. 'You really don't know?' When Barrington shook his head, Yew said in amusement, 'Because I was asked to.'

Having casually dropped his bomb, the marquess strolled away. Barrington, aware that the eyes of the room were on him, allowed nothing of his anger to show, knowing it would incite too many questions he wasn't prepared to answer. But he *was* angry. Furiously so. Someone had been playing with Peregrine Rand—and, by association, with him.

'Good m-morning, Sir B-Barrington,' Lord Gerald Fitzhenry said, coming up to him. 'It's v-very good of you to d-do this for me.'

Lord Yew's youngest son was a quiet, unassuming young man, who, though raised in an atmosphere of wealth and privilege, had managed to lose none of his good nature as a result. Perhaps the stutter kept him from becoming too arrogant, Barrington reflected. It wasn't a fashionable affectation, but a lifelong affliction, one the boy had desperately tried to overcome. But it was exacerbated by nerves and, given the unexpected turnout in the room, Barrington knew this morning's performance would be more difficult for Lord Gerald than usual. As such, he turned to face the lad with a reassuring smile. 'You show a great deal of promise, Lord Gerald. Perhaps I can point out a few things that will help you become an even better fencer.'

The boy's face shone. 'I would l-like that, very much.'

'Good. Then shall we take our positions?'

As Barrington led the way onto the floor, he was conscious of every eye in the room following him. He was acquainted with many of the gentlemen present and knew that some of them were decent fencers and were here for that reason alone. Having been taught by one of the finest swordsmen in France, Barrington possessed skills few others did and the chance to watch him spar today was an opportunity too good to miss.

But not all the gentlemen in the room had come simply to observe his technique. A movement at the far end of the room drew Barrington's attention. Looking up, he saw Hayle leaning against the wall, sword in hand. He had come to fight. He'd made that very clear.

Barrington had no intention of indulging him. Men like Hayle only wanted to prove their superiority over others. It was likely one of the reasons Hayle resented Rand's presence in the house. Though Rand offered no tangible threat, he was a competitor for the earl's attention, perhaps even for his affection. And if Hayle believed that Rand was his half-brother, he would naturally assume there was an affinity between his father and the other man he couldn't affect or control.

He wouldn't like that. Hayle needed to be seen as the only cock of the roost, and, so far, he had. Lord only knew what would happen if and when he found out otherwise.

An hour later, it was all over.

'You did well,' Barrington said, removing his mask and walking towards Lord Gerald. 'But you would do better if you kept your arm straight and the weight of your body on the front of your feet. You need to be able to move quickly around your opponent. Try to catch him off balance.'

'Yes, Sir B-Barrington,' said the grateful but sweating youth.

'And don't forget what I said about practising your double and triple feints. They'll stand you in good stead when you find yourself pushed to defend yourself. If you like, come round to the house and I'll lend you a couple of books that helped me when I was where you are.'

The boy's face shone as though he'd been given the keys to the kingdom. 'Thank you so much, Sir B-Barrington. I will t-try to d-do that.'

Barrington smiled and clapped the lad on the shoulder. He was glad now that he'd agreed to the lesson. Lord Gerald had turned out to be a surprisingly good swordsman and he was appreciative of the time he'd been given. He would benefit by what he'd learned today.

'Who's next then, Sir Barrington?' someone called out from the crowd.

Despite the cheers that greeted the man's words, Barrington shook his head. 'Sorry, gentlemen, the show's over. You can all go home now.'

Amidst the rumble of disappointment, another voice said,

'But this was to be a demonstration. Surely you wouldn't send everyone away without giving them what they really came here to see.'

Barrington's mouth compressed into a thin line. So, Hayle would challenge him publicly. A foolish thing to do. 'I'm sure there are others who would favour you with a match, Lord Hayle.'

'But it is with you I wish to engage, Sir Barrington,' Hayle said softly. 'Will you not stand and face me? I have been acknowledged a better than average fencer and would welcome an opportunity to go up against the best.'

Hearing the room suddenly fall silent, Barrington sighed. 'My purpose this morning was to instruct Lord Yew's son. It was not a general invitation to spar.'

'But surely there can be no harm in engaging in a friendly match,' Hayle said, advancing on to the floor. 'You are acknowledged the finest swordsman in England. Every one of us here could benefit by watching and learning, and I am willing to put myself forward as your student. If nothing else, I promise you a better match than the one you just concluded.'

'I was not engaged in a match,' Barrington reminded him. 'I was giving a lesson.'

'Then consider me your student and this an opportunity to improve *my* skills,' Hayle said with a grin.

Hearing murmurs in the crowd that were pushing for the match, Barrington sighed. Hayle obviously wasn't going to back down, especially if he felt he had the backing of his friends. And while he needed a lesson, Barrington knew it was in humility rather than sword play. 'Very well.' He walked back into the room and donned his mask. 'Prepare to engage.'

An excited murmur rolled through the crowd. Men who were halfway to the door quickly turned around and ran back into the room, aware that a far more entertaining show was about to get underway. Triumph and anticipation suffused Hayle's face as he stripped off his jacket and donned a mask.

In silence the two men made their way to the centre of the floor. After offering the traditional salute, they both took their opening stance.

It didn't take long for Barrington to assess his opponent's level of skill. Hayle was a showy fencer and quick on his feet, but there was no strategy to his play; at times, his technique was downright sloppy. Barrington easily scored five hits in a matter of minutes—and watched his opponent's face grow redder with each one.

'I think that's enough for one morning,' he said, starting to remove his mask.

'Stand your ground, sir!' Hayle shouted. '*I* will say when this is finished.' He took up his stance again. *'En guarde!'*

Barrington saw the anger in the other man's eyes and knew this could only end badly. He had no wish to humiliate Hayle in front of a room full of his friends and acquaintances, but neither was he about to throw the game in order to appease his vanity. 'Very well. We shall play one more bout and then call a halt. Does that meet with your approval?'

Hayle gave a terse nod and resumed his position.

The match recommenced. Barrington tried not to make the other man look bad, but the more desperate Hayle became, the more careless his play. He was caught flat footed several times and as the bout went on his moves became more and more erratic. After receiving his fourth hit, he shouted, 'Damn you, Parker!', then, abandoning sportsmanlike conduct altogether, he lunged, aiming the point of his sword directly at Barrington's throat.

Barrington heard the gasp from the crowd, but was already out of range. He stepped lithely to one side and quickly raised his own foil, deflecting the blow. Hayle spun around and was about to charge again when a voice rang out, 'Enough, Edward! Put down your sword! This engagement is at an end!'

The command vibrated with anger, but Hayle was oblivious, his attention riveted on his adversary. Barrington held his position, too, unwilling to trust his opponent. He risked a quick glance across the room and saw the Earl of Cambermere standing by the edge of the crowd. His face was red and he was shaking with barely suppressed fury. 'Did you not hear me, sir?' he called again. 'I said put down your sword!'

'I will not, sir!' His son's face was equally flushed. 'How dare you ask me to!'

'How dare *I*?' his father exploded, marching on to the floor. 'You impugn our family's honour by behaving in such a way and then have the audacity to question me? No, sir, I *will* not have it! If you cannot control your temper, find another sport in which to indulge.' He ripped the foil from his son's hand and threw it on the floor. 'This is a gentleman's game. You will apologise to Sir Barrington at once or I'll know the reason why!'

Barrington slowly lowered his sword, but remained in a ready position, prepared to fight if Hayle picked up his sword and re-engaged him. He had no idea what the man was going to do, but it was evident to everyone in the place that Hayle was beyond furious. In that moment, Barrington wasn't sure the man wouldn't turn on his own father and run him through.

Thankfully, the moment passed. As if realising he couldn't win and that his reputation would only suffer further by prolonging the encounter, Hayle took a step back, then bent to pick up his sword. 'I will not apologise to you this day or any other, Sir Barrington,' he said coldly. 'But I do regret that we were unable to finish our match. I look forward to the opportunity of doing so in the future.' Then, without so much as a second glance at his father, he snatched up his jacket and left.

Barely had the door closed before the level of conversation swelled to fill the silence. Barrington heard snippets of conversations, some questioning, many derogatory. Overall, none were particularly complimentary of Hayle's behaviour on the floor. Fencing was, after all, a gentleman's sport and what the audience had just witnessed was a display of anything but.

It was a few minutes before the earl was calm enough to speak. When he did, Barrington could see it was with considerable effort. 'Sir Barrington, pray accept my apologies on behalf of my son. His behaviour was unforgivable and I am truly sorry.'

'Apology accepted, but I suggest you do not take this too much to heart, Cambermere,' Barrington said. 'It is not uncommon for a young man to wish to win, especially in front of his peers.'

'If a man cannot win fairly or lose graciously, he should not play the game,' Cambermere snapped. 'I'm sorry you had to see that side of Edward's nature. He's always been a competitive lad, but of late, he has become even more so. I suspect it has much to do with Peregrine's arrival.' The earl sighed. 'They have not become the friends I'd hoped.'

'Was it realistic to believe they would?'

The earl glanced up, his sharp eyes meeting Barrington's. But Barrington's didn't waver, and, not surprisingly, the earl was the first to look away. 'Perhaps not. But they had to meet at some time.'

'Did they? I would have thought it possible for their paths never to have crossed. But it's a moot point now. You made the decision to invite Rand to London and must now deal with the consequences,' Barrington said.

'I know. But I was asked if I would have him,' the earl said quietly. 'And I wanted him to come.'

Used to gleaning meanings from things that were left unsaid, Barrington inclined his head. 'Then it really is none of anyone else's business.'

'Yet people choose to make it so,' Cambermere said fiercely.

Barrington's smile was tight. 'People like to pass judgement on matters that do not concern them. Some do it with the best of intentions, others do it without any care for the consequences at all. But as we said, the matter is private and one that concerns you and your family alone.'

Even has he said it, however, Barrington realised he had been given another glimpse into the complicated workings of Lord Cambermere's family, and it was evident from the morning's events that all was far from harmonious. There were simmering resentments, unsettled grievances, and barely restrained tempers. Instead of warming to the fact that his father had brought his godson to London, Hayle intended to do whatever he could to make Rand feel unwelcome—even to the point of humiliating him in front of his peers.

That much had become patently clear. As Barrington left the club and climbed into his carriage for the drive home, he *knew* who had asked the Marquess of Yew to make an example of Peregrine Rand. And, sadly, he also knew the reason why.

A full week passed during which Anna neither saw nor heard from Barrington. She told herself she didn't care, but as she lay awake in the dark hours of the night, she knew she was lying to herself. She *did* care. And it troubled her deeply that they had parted on such bad terms.

Try as she might, she couldn't forget the feeling of Barrington's arms closing warm and strong around her. She kept remembering the tenderness of his mouth as it moved with deliberate slowness over hers, sending shivers of delight up and down her spine.

It still made her quiver when she thought about it.

Still, longing for something you couldn't have was a complete waste of one's time, and there wasn't a doubt in Anna's mind that she would never have a life with Barrington. He'd made it perfectly clear that he had no intention of getting married, and it certainly wasn't her place to get him to change his mind. *She* was the foolish one if she thought there was any merit in that.

'Ah, Anna, there you are,' her father said, walking into the drawing room. 'Not going out this evening?'

'I'm not, but it would seem you are,' she said, rousing herself. 'Is that a new coat?'

To her amusement, her father's cheeks took on a ruddy hue. 'I decided it was time to spruce up my wardrobe. Doesn't do for a gentleman to let himself go and I haven't paid much attention to things like that since your mother died.' His voice softened. 'I had no reason to.'

'And have you a reason now?'

He glanced at her, suddenly looking boyish. 'Would it disturb you if I said I had?'

'Not at all. I like Julia very much.' Anna hesitated. 'I take it we are referring to Julia?'

'Of course!'

'Good. Then if she makes you happy, why should I object?'

'Oh, I don't know,' the earl grumbled. 'Some people say I'm past such things. That I'm too old for her. I am nearly twenty years her senior, after all.'

'If the lady does not mind, why should you? You don't

look your age, and she *is* past thirty, Papa. Old enough to make her own decisions.'

Her father glanced down at the floor. 'Your brother is not pleased by the association.'

Anna sighed. 'My brother is not pleased with anything at the moment so I shouldn't worry about it. Do what I do. Ignore him.'

'Can you not try to get along, Anna? He is your brother, after all.'

'Yes, he is, but I cannot bring myself to like the way he treats people; his attitude towards Peregrine is abysmal. He demonstrates a resentment that is neither warranted nor deserved. I've tried to tell him as much, but he refuses to listen.'

Her father looked as though he wanted to say something, but then he sighed, and shook his head. 'I blame myself for the distance between the two of you. Perhaps had I paid more attention to Edward when he was younger—'

'The fault is not yours, Papa,' Anna interrupted firmly. 'Edward has been given every opportunity to show himself the better man. He has wealth and position—there is absolutely no reason for him to be so harsh and judgemental towards others.'

'Perhaps he will change when he meets the right woman. It is my sincere wish that you both find suitable marriage partners and leave this house to start your own lives.' Her father regarded her hopefully. 'Is there no one for whom you feel even the slightest affection, my dear?'

Sadly, there was. But while Anna would have liked to give her father the reassurance he so desperately craved, there was no point in raising his hopes. Or hers. 'I fear not. But am I such a trouble to you that you would try to make me leave?'

'Far from it. You're a good girl, Anna. And though I don't

say it often, I am very proud of you. A week doesn't go by that some grateful mother doesn't tell me how helpful you've been in smoothing the troubled waters between her and her daughter. Most of them credit you with having saved their sanity!'

Surprised by the admission, Anna said, 'I can assure you they were exaggerating. None of the situations was that dire. It is simply easier for a stranger to see what needs to be done than someone who is intimately involved.'

'Nevertheless, they all told me how helpful you were and that I should be very proud to have such an admirable young woman for a daughter. And I told them all they were right.'

Her father was not normally an affectionate man, so when he suddenly bent down and pressed his lips to her forehead, Anna was deeply moved. 'Oh, Papa.' She got up and hugged him, aware that it had been a long time since she'd done so. If this was Julia's doing, she could only hope that the romance continued.

'Yes, well, I'd best be off,' the earl said gruffly. He stepped back and smoothed his jacket. 'Jul—that is, the baroness and I are having dinner together and then going on to the theatre.'

'Sounds lovely. Have a good time.'

'Yes, I expect we will.'

Anna smiled as she watched him go. It was strange to suddenly find herself in the role of the parent. She was well aware that she was the one who should have been going out for the evening and her father the one wishing her well. But there was only one man with whom Anna wished to spend time and the chances of that happening were getting slimmer all the time.

Troubled as he was by his feelings for Anna, Barrington knew he couldn't afford to ignore his other commissions. In particular, the locating of Miss Elizabeth Paisley. His belief that he'd found her at Baroness von Brohm's house had turned out to be false. He had gone back a few days later to question her, but the moment she'd walked into the drawing room, he'd known he was mistaken. The maid's name was Justine Smith, and though she was the right age, the right height, and had the right colour hair, her eyes were all wrong. Hers had actually been a pale misty blue where the Colonel had specifically told him that Elizabeth Paisley's were a deep, clear green. Barrington thought that in the candlelit room the night of the baroness's dinner party, he must have been mistaken when he'd thought the maid's eyes were green.

And so, at eleven o'clock that morning, Barrington resumed his investigation by visiting the premises of one Madame Delors, fashionable modiste. Dressmakers were privy to a great deal of gossip about wives and mistresses, and if someone had taken over the protection of Miss Elizabeth Paisley, there was a good chance Madame Delors would know about it.

Barrington stopped inside the door and glanced around the compact little shop. It was years since he'd had reason to frequent such an establishment, but it was evident they hadn't changed. Bolts of richly coloured fabric of every type and shade filled the shelves; dress patterns were tacked to the walls; and in the centre of the room stood a raised podium surrounded on three sides by mirrors.

'*Bonjour, monsieur,*' called a charmingly accented French voice. '*Puis-je vous aidez?*'

The owner of the establishment was small and compact, with dark inquisitive eyes and a head of flaming red hair that surely owed more to artifice than it did to nature. Still, it suited her well and Barrington doffed his hat. '*Bonjour, madame.* My name is Sir Barrington Parker. I would like to ask you a few questions, if you have a moment to spare.'

The woman's eyes narrowed, his comment obviously having put her on guard. 'What kind of questions, *monsieur*?'

'About a woman.' He purposely didn't use the term lady. 'One I believe you dressed in the not-too-distant past.'

'I dress many women, *monsieur*. You will 'ave to give me 'er name.'

'Miss Elizabeth Paisley. Petite, lovely, with dark brown hair and uncommonly pretty green eyes.'

The modiste evidenced neither surprise nor recognition. 'I do not think I know the lady.'

'Really? I was told you'd made clothes for her. Perhaps you dealt with the gentleman who bought them. A Colonel Tanner?'

Madame Delors obviously knew a thing or two about what one did and didn't say to gentlemen asking questions about other gentlemen's ladies. 'I 'ave many gentlemen coming to buy clothes for their ladies, *monsieur*. But they do not always give me the names of the ladies they are buying for.'

'No, I suppose not. And perhaps I should explain my interest in her.' Barrington walked farther into the store, cataloguing a thousand details in a single glance. 'Miss Paisley has recently come under my protection and it is my desire that she wear...a particular type of clothing when we are together. But because her taste and mine do not coincide, I am not willing to allow her to come in and order her own garments. Hence my reason for coming to see you today.'

'Ah, *je comprends*,' Madame Delors said. 'You would like me to make 'er a new wardrobe suitable only for you.'

'Precisely. Naturally, money is not a concern.'

'*D'accord*. What type of clothes do you wish to see 'er in, *monsieur*?'

'Intimate evening gowns, white and silver only, with simple but elegant lines. Semi-transparent. No heavy swatches of lace. No artificial birds or flowers. Nothing that will detract from the tantalising lines of her body.'

Madame Delors slowly began to smile. 'So the lady will not be wearing these gowns in public?'

'Definitely not,' Barrington said, resting both hands on the carved head of his ebony cane. 'They are for my eyes only. But I cannot tell you what size to make her garments because I do not have her measurements.'

Madame Delors smiled and nodded. 'I think I know the lady you speak of, *monsieur.*'

'Excellent. I trust it hasn't been too long since you last saw her? Women's figures do tend to change,' Barrington said, adding with a wink, 'a little more weight this week, a little less the following.'

Madame Delors's smile was reassuring. 'I saw 'er not all that long ago and 'er figure 'as not changed.'

'Good. Did she seem happy?'

The modiste gave a snort. 'The ladies come to me for clothes, *monsieur.* It is up to you gentlemen to make them 'appy!'

Barrington carefully hid a smile. Oh, yes, Madame Delors was definitely a shrewd business woman. He pulled three coins from his pocket. 'Do you happen to remember, on the occasion of her last visit,' he said, dropping one into her palm, 'if she collected the clothes herself or if you sent them somewhere else?'

The modiste's eyes locked on the shimmer of gold in her hand. 'I'm not sure…'

Barrington dropped another coin. 'Perhaps now?'

'The lady picked up the clothes,' the modiste said slowly, 'but I sent the bill to the gentleman.'

'To Colonel Tanner?'

When the modiste shook her head, Barrington dropped

the last of the coins into her palm. 'Then to whom did you send the bill?'

The modiste smiled and pocketed all three. 'Viscount Hayle.'

Anna was on her way to visit Julia when she remembered that Madame Delors had sent her a note asking her if she might be able to come in for a fitting. Anna had ordered two new morning dresses and a ball gown the previous week; although most fashionable modistes made house calls to their better clients, Madame Delors preferred to have her ladies come to her, saying it was easier to work in her showroom where she had everything necessary for making the required alternations.

Anna didn't mind. It was an excuse to get out of the house and it wasn't that much out of her way. But as she walked up to the front of the shop and went to open the door, it was suddenly opened from within and by none other than the man who had been uppermost in her mind for the last several days. 'Sir Barrington!'

'Good morning, Lady Annabelle. Lovely morning, isn't it?' He spoke without concern, as though it was the most natural thing in the world for her to find him coming out of a dressmaker's shop.

'Indeed. I feared it might come on to rain, but the skies have cleared up nicely.' Anna said, striving to match the casualness of his tone. There was only one reason a single gentleman frequented a shop like this, and it wasn't to keep abreast of the latest fashions. 'I've not seen much of you about town of late.'

'I have been otherwise occupied,' he said, drawing her aside as a mother and her three giggling daughters made to enter the shop. 'This is a very busy place.'

'Madame Delors is London's darling when it comes to

fashion,' Anna said. 'She boasts an illustrious clientele, most recently the Duchess of Briscombe.'

Barrington smiled. Given that Madame Delors also dressed the Duke of Briscombe's latest mistress, he knew better than to place too high a value on her level of exclusivity. 'Speaking of not being visible around town, how is Mr Rand going on?'

Anna sighed. 'Not at all well. He misses Lady Yew dreadfully; though I have told him she is not worthy of the heartache, I cannot dissuade him from his feelings.'

'Of course not. Love isn't logical,' Barrington said. 'It finds warmth in the most inhospitable of environments and draws comfort from the most uncomfortable of people. It demands neither explanation nor excuse. It is content merely to be.'

Anna stared at him in surprise. Such sentiments from a man like this? 'How is it you know so much about love, Sir Barrington, when, by your own admission, you have chosen to banish it from your life?'

'Who better than a man who has chosen to live without love when it comes to knowing how easily it takes root?' His grey eyes impaled her. 'I am not immune to the emotion, Lady Annabelle. I simply cannot give it a home. As I tried to explain to you the other night and failed so miserably.'

It was an olive branch, and Anna recognised it as such. But she knew she had to be cautious. The wounds from their last encounter were not yet healed. 'You didn't fail. It was simply not something I wished to hear. I do not believe any man or woman is truly happier spending their life alone.'

'It is not the natural order,' he agreed. 'God intended that man and woman should live together. It was the reason He gave them a home in Eden.'

'Until the serpent tempted Eve and they were cast out.'

Barrington smiled. 'As I recall, it was Adam's willingness

to eat the forbidden fruit that incurred God's wrath. Temptation has always been there. It is simply a man's ability to resist that sets him apart from others.'

'A philosopher,' Anna mused. 'I would not have thought it of you.'

'When you have learned as much about your fellow man as I have, you tend to become either jaded or philosophical. I choose the latter.'

Of course he would, Anna reflected, because he was that type of man. 'Well, I mustn't keep you here.' She gave him a falsely bright smile, aware that she was still no wiser as to why he was coming out of a busy modiste's shop now than she had been a few minutes earlier. 'I'm sure you have business elsewhere.'

'I do, my lady,' he murmured. 'But none, I can assure you, as pleasurable as this.'

As soon as she finished her business with Madame Delors, Anna headed for Julia's house and was pleasantly surprised to find Lady Lydia already there. She and Julia were partaking of tea and cakes and no doubt sharing the latest *on-dits* that were enlivening the drawing rooms of society. Her pleasure soon evaporated, however, when she discovered that it was not society's goings on that were keeping her two friends so occupied, but an unexpected crime.

'Your sapphire-and-diamond necklace has been *stolen*?' Anna said when Lydia informed her of it. 'But how? And when?'

'I have no idea how *or* when,' Julia admitted forlornly. 'I was dressing for the Buckerfields' reception last night and asked Smith to bring my jewellery case. When she did, I unlocked it to find the necklace gone.'

'But surely it has not been stolen,' Anna said. 'Perhaps just misplaced?'

Julia shook her head. 'I am very careful with my jewellery, Anna. I always take it off and put it immediately into the case. Then I lock it and put it away.'

'Is it possible someone took the key?'

'I keep the key on a ribbon around my neck. I only take it off to bathe and, sometimes, when I go to bed.'

'Have you questioned the servants about the matter?' Lydia asked. 'Your maid, for example. She would be in a perfect position to steal it.'

'I have spoken to all of them and to a person they denied knowing anything about it,' Julia said. 'And given how horrified they looked at the idea of something of mine being stolen, I can't imagine any of them actually *doing* it.'

'So what are you going to do?' Anna asked.

'I suppose I shall have to report it, but I don't like what I am going to have to tell whoever comes to take down the details.'

Lydia frowned. 'Why not?'

'Because the only people who knew about that necklace were the ones who came to my dinner party. I haven't worn it on any other occasion.' Julia bit her lip. 'What if one of my guests took it?'

'I don't believe that for a moment,' Anna said flatly. 'The people you invited were friends. They would never steal from you.'

'And if a thief did break into your house,' Lydia said, 'he would naturally go for the most valuable piece of jewellery he could find, don't you think?'

'So you believe this the work of a random criminal?' Julia asked doubtfully.

'I think it must have been,' Anna said. 'For one thing, what would any of your friends, or even other members of society, gain by taking the necklace? They would never be able to wear it in public.'

'But they could break it up and sell the stones individually,' Julia said. 'They might even be able to have some of the larger diamonds cut into smaller pieces.'

Anna didn't know what to say. It seemed impossible to imagine a thief breaking into Julia's house and stealing her favourite piece of jewellery, but it was even more incredible to think that someone she knew might have done it. 'I honestly don't know what to say, Julia,' she said at length. 'Other than that I am so very sorry this has happened.'

'Your father did warn me about keeping my jewels in a safe,' Julia said. 'But I truly did not think it would be necessary.'

'Have you hired any new servants?' Lydia asked. 'Or had people in the house who wouldn't normally be here. Chimney sweeps, for example, or trades people coming and going?'

'There have certainly been trades people in and out,' Julia admitted. 'The entire house is being redecorated and there has been a steady stream of paper hangers and plasterers coming through on a daily basis. But I instructed my maid to make sure they were never alone in my room and I have no reason to believe my orders were not followed. No, I shall have to hire a private investigator and ask him to look into it.'

'I say,' Lydia said, glancing at Anna. 'Why don't you get in touch with Sir Barrington Parker?'

'Sir Barrington?' Julia frowned. 'What would he know about matters like this?'

'You'd be surprised,' Anna murmured. 'However, he is very good at finding things out and I agree with Lydia that he is probably the best person to contact about this. He is nothing if not discreet.'

'Well, if you think that highly of him, I will certainly speak to him,' Julia said. 'I would very much like to have my necklace back. It has sentimental value far beyond any monetary value I could ever put upon it.'

'I don't think you will be disappointed with Sir Barrington's methods,' Lydia said, adding with a sly look at her friend, 'he has made quite an impression on Anna.'

'Lydia!'

But Julia was beaming. 'Has he really? How wonderful! I thought I detected something between the two of you at my dinner party, but when things became rather chilly later in the evening, I didn't want to appear rude by asking personal questions.'

'There is nothing between myself and Sir Barrington Parker,' Anna said quickly. 'I will not deny that he is…an attractive and engaging man—'

'Exceptionally so,' Lydia added.

'But we do not see eye to eye on several important matters and I doubt we will do so in the future,' Anna concluded. She reached for an iced *petit four*, hoping to distract the attention of the other two. 'However, I do stand by my assertion that he can be of help in this situation.'

Julia got up and crossed to the bell pull. 'Well, I am grateful for the recommendation, Anna, though I am sorry to hear there is nothing of a more romantic nature going on between the two of you. Sir Barrington really is such a handsome man. And that *voice*! I could listen to him all night. However, it is the heart that dictates these matters and, if you are not in love with him, there is nothing more to say. Ah, there you are, Smith. We'd like some fresh tea, please. This has gone cold.'

'Yes, ma'am.' The maid bobbed a curtsy, but something in the way she bent to pick up the tray drew Anna's attention. On her previous visits, the maid had served tea with both skill and efficiency. This time, however, she seemed slightly ill at ease. She also seemed thinner than she had on those earlier occasions, her black gown hanging loose around her shoulders. Anna thought it might have been a different girl, but upon closer inspection, she realised she was mistaken. The girl had the same heart-shaped face and the same dark brown hair pulled back in a tight chignon.

Perhaps she had things on her mind, Anna reflected as she reached for a macaroon. Servants had problems just like their employers. Maybe she'd recently fallen out with her gentleman friend, or a member of her family wasn't well. There were any number of reasons she might be looking poorly.

Still, it was none of her business, and as they waited for fresh tea to arrive, the conversation veered back to more congenial topics. Anna was simply thankful they had moved away from the subject of Sir Barrington Parker. His name was coming up far too often in conversation for her liking, and she wasn't at all happy at hearing that Julia thought there was something going on between them. She'd even been tempted to correct Julia's phrasing of her recommendation of Barrington, by saying it wasn't Sir Barrington of whom she thought so highly, but, rather, his skills as an investigator.

Unfortunately, that wasn't true either and when it came right down to it, Anna preferred not to lie to Julia. But she had to stand firm when it came to her feelings for him. She had to accept his reasons for keeping her at arm's length and move on. She had every intention of marrying one day; while she hoped it would be for love, she was intelligent enough to know that the luxury of feelings did not always accompany a proposal of marriage.

As to whether or not Sir Barrington Parker ever married, that was really no concern of hers.

## Chapter Eight

Barrington received a visit from Baroness von Brohm at half past ten the following morning. She was shown into the gold salon, whereupon she briefly told him about the theft of her necklace and of her sincere hopes for its recovery. He then asked a series of pointed questions, which she answered to the best of her ability. An hour later, he stood by the window and reviewed everything she had told him. He didn't have a lot to go on, but he had already concluded that there were four possible answers to the question of who might have stolen her necklace.

The first was that the jewel thief who had been plaguing London for the past three months had returned and struck again. He would have had a relatively easy time getting into the baroness's house. During his questioning, Barrington discovered that she often slept with her window open and that her bedroom was located at the rear of the house on the second floor, close to a small clump of trees. It was possible that someone had climbed a tree to the second floor, gained access through the open window and, after taking the baroness's necklace, had managed to escape the same way.

The stumbling block was that in order to get into the baroness's jewellery box, the thief would have had to get at the key the baroness kept on a ribbon around her throat. Barrington doubted any thief would have been able to remove the ribbon, steal the necklace, and make his escape, all without disturbing the baroness's slumber.

The second option was that a servant had taken it. This was certainly the more logical answer. The baroness employed a butler, a housekeeper, three maids, and a parlour maid, all of whom would have had access to her room at times when she was not present. But again, they would have needed the key to open the locked box, and, according to the baroness, the box showed no signs of a forced entry. It had been neatly opened and closed.

The third possibility was that a visitor to the house had taken the necklace. Barrington thought this the least likely of the four, but experience had taught him that it was often the *least* likely suspect who actually committed the crime. In this case, it meant that one of the many people who had paid calls on the baroness had gone up to her room and taken the necklace. But again, there was the matter of the key.

Which left the fourth and most likely possibility—that the baroness had simply misplaced the necklace. That kind of thing happened all the time. It explained why the jewellery case hadn't been tampered with and why the key hadn't gone missing. It also cleared any visitors to the house of the theft.

Unfortunately, the baroness had stated most emphatically that she had *not* misplaced the necklace and that she was in the habit of locking her jewellery away immediately after taking it off. The practice had been instilled in her by her late husband.

So where did that leave him? What was he missing with regard to the stolen necklace?

'Excuse me, Sir Barrington,' Sam said from the doorway. 'Lord Richard Crew is here.'

'Thank you, Sam. Be so good as to show him in.'

Barrington was relieved to have caught Crew at home. He'd sent a note to him immediately following the baroness's departure, but given his friend's sexual proclivities, one never knew where he was or what state he might be in. A fact confirmed when Crew walked into the room, looking slightly dishevelled and none too bright-eyed.

'You'd better have a damned good excuse for this, Parker,' he said testily. 'I was enjoying a rather delicious breakfast in bed when your note arrived.'

'Forgive me,' Barrington said, grinning, 'but I'm sure the lady won't mind drinking champagne alone.'

'Probably not, but I'm not sure I *want* her drinking it alone. I was rather enjoying what she was doing *before* your letter arrived, demanding that I present myself at your door.'

'It was not a demand. And I did say at *your* convenience.'

'Hah!' Crew said, collapsing into a chair. 'We both know that at *my* convenience really means at *yours*. So what was so urgent that it couldn't wait until later in the day?'

'Two things. I need you to make some discreet inquiries on behalf of a lady.'

'A lady?' He brightened. 'Always ready to be of service. Do I know her?'

'Baroness Julia von Brohm.'

'Ah, the merry widow. Yes, we were introduced at some gathering, though the name of my host and hostess escapes me at the moment. What has happened to the poor lady that she requires your services?'

'A rather magnificent sapphire-and-diamond necklace was stolen from her home a few days ago. I want you to keep your ear to the ground for any information that might come to light about it.'

'Do you think it's our jewel thief again?' Crew asked.

'It's possible, but I need to check out all avenues. I'll be questioning the baroness's staff over the next few days, but if someone's stolen the necklace with a view to selling it, you might catch wind of it before I do.'

'Wouldn't be the first time,' Crew agreed, putting his hands behind his head. 'I'll drop in at a few of the clubs and see if anyone's suddenly turned up flush.'

'You might want to check the hells as well. A necklace like that would go a long way towards settling a man's debts,' Barrington suggested.

'No doubt. What's the second request?'

Barrington opened the top drawer of the desk and took out an envelope. 'I need you to do some digging into an old family tree. The specifics are in the letter. Read it at your leisure—'

'But report back to you as soon as possible,' Crew said in a dry voice.

'Expedience is always the order of the day. By the by, how did your meeting go with the lovely Rebecca?' Barrington enquired as his friend got up to leave. 'Has she agreed to marry you yet?'

'No, though I expect an acceptance very soon. As I was leaving, Lady Yew brushed her hand against a rather sensitive part of my anatomy—and I'm quite sure it wasn't by accident.'

Barrington burst out laughing. 'I *beg* your pardon?'

'You needn't sound so shocked; I am more or less the right age; given that she is looking for a replacement for Peregrine Rand, she obviously thought to see if I was interested.'

'Even though you have been paying court to her daughter?'

'Perhaps she wants to bed me before her daughter gets the chance.' Crew's eyes flashed wickedly. 'Make sure I have all the necessary equipment.'

'As if your reputation would leave anyone in doubt,' Barrington said cynically. 'How did Lady Rebecca take to her mother's interest in you?'

Crew slowly began to smile. 'If I don't miss my guess, the next time I call, the dear girl will be pushing the butler aside in her haste to throw open the front door and give me her answer—which I have every expectation of being yes. After all, if she doesn't, she knows damn well whose bedroom I *could* be spending my nights in!'

Anna trotted Ophelia through Hyde Park, alert for the gentleman to whom she had sent a hastily scrawled note, asking that he meet her. It had been a bold gesture, and secretly she feared Barrington might soon tire of these imperious messages. But she had to know if Julia had been to see him and, if so, what he thought the chances of recovering the stolen necklace were. While she might not approve of or agree with his marital aspirations or lack thereof, Anna did believe that if anyone could find the missing necklace it was he.

Thankfully, he appeared within moments, sitting tall and easy in the saddle, his coat as black as that of the spirited thoroughbred he so easily controlled. His hands were strong and steady on the reins; in spite of her best intentions, Anna felt a quiver of anticipation at the thought of being close to him again. She'd told herself over and over that there was no hope of anything developing between them, but that didn't take away from the strength of her attraction for him. The way he looked at her, without the lewdness or speculation she saw so often in other men's eyes, made her feel as though she mattered, both as a woman and as a person. And the memory of the one kiss they had shared still caused her heart to quicken…

*She really had to get over this.* It was bad enough that thoughts of him kept filling her mind, but this silly racing of her pulse every time she saw him was ridiculous! It was imperative that she appear as cool as he was. As impervious to his charm as he so obviously was to hers.

He raised his hand and then put his horse to a brisk trot in her direction. Anna used the time to bring her breathing under control.

'Lady Annabelle,' he greeted her, drawing to a halt.

'Good afternoon, Sir Barrington. Thank you for agreeing to meet with me.'

'To quote your father, the opportunity to spend time with a beautiful woman should never be missed.'

And now she was blushing again. *So much for being impervious.* 'Forgive me for being so inquisitive, but I was anxious to know if Julia had been to see you?'

'As a matter of fact, we spent time together this morning.'

'And? Do you think you will be able to help her?'

'I will do what I can, of course, but there are many questions that need to be asked and several possible leads to follow. It will take time.'

'But there may not *be* that much time!' Anna cried. 'Given the size of the stones, Julia said the thief might decide to take the necklace apart, or to have the gems cut smaller.'

'That possibility does exist,' Barrington acknowledged. 'The jewels are too large to sell as they are, unless whoever took the necklace intends to sell it outside London. If they have contacts on the Continent, it could easily be sold intact in Paris or Brussels.'

Anna bit her lip. 'Julia will be heartbroken. That necklace means the world to her.'

'I know and am making inquiries. But whoever took the necklace isn't going to make it easy for us to find him.'

Anna ran her gloved hand over the smoothness of the mare's neck. 'Nevertheless, I'm glad you're involved. I know you'll find who did this and bring him or her to justice.'

He raised an eyebrow. 'Her?'

'Why not? Desperation knows no gender. A woman who needs money to feed her family is just as likely to steal as a man.'

'But it is more often a man who will take that kind of risk. A woman on her own is more likely to avail herself of…other avenues.'

'Such as prostitution?' she said quietly.

He met her regard evenly. 'Yes. Or, if she is attractive enough, becoming the mistress of a wealthy man. However, I would caution you not to let your thoughts dwell on this, Lady Annabelle. It will not result in the culprit being brought to justice any faster and will only serve to cause you needless worry. I will advise you of whatever results I am able to find as soon as I have them.'

'Thank you.' Anna wished she could think of something else to say, but she didn't know how or where to start. She usually found conversation so easy, but with him it was always a challenge. 'Well, I suppose I had best be—'

'Lady Annabelle!'

Hearing the shrill feminine hail, Anna turned to see a carriage approaching and smiled when she recognised the mother and daughter sitting within. 'Mrs Banks, Miss Banks, good afternoon,' she said.

'Lady Annabelle, I thought it was you and I simply had to come and tell you the news,' Mercy Banks said, jumping up as the carriage drew to a halt.

'Mercy, for goodness' sake, sit down!' her mother admonished. 'A lady does not bounce up and down like a hoyden!

You must forgive my daughter, Lady Annabelle. She has become quite uncontrollable of late.'

'Because I am so happy, Mama,' Miss Banks said, and though she promptly sat down, her joy could not be contained. 'I am to be married, Lady Annabelle, and it is all thanks to *you*!'

Aware of Barrington's eyes on her, Anna laughed and said, 'On the contrary, I think you played a considerable part in the production. I take it your intended is Lieutenant Blokker?'

'Of course.' Mercy's face assumed that dreamy aspect Anna had come to associate with young men and women in love. 'There could never be anyone else. He proposed to me at home in the garden yesterday and naturally I said yes.'

'Then I am very happy for you. When is the wedding to be?'

'The date has not yet been set,' Mrs Banks said proudly. 'We have been invited to dine with the young man's parents in Hanover Square to go over the details.'

'Hanover Square,' Barrington murmured so that only Anna could hear. 'Very nice.'

Anna only just refrained from rolling her eyes. 'Mrs Banks, Miss Banks, may I introduce Sir Barrington Parker.'

The gentleman gallantly doffed his beaver. 'Ladies.'

'Sir Barrington,' Mrs Banks said graciously. 'I believe I saw you in conversation with Lady Annabelle at Lady Montby's reception.'

'You did, though it was only in passing since we had not been formally introduced at that time,' Sir Barrington said smoothly. 'Unlike your daughter, I was not fortunate enough to have someone make the introduction for me.'

'Happily, it seems to have been made in the interim. And we will, of course, be sending Lady Annabelle an invitation. We are happy to see her bring an escort,' Mrs Banks said. 'I expect the affair to be quite grand.'

This time, Anna knew better than to look at the man beside her. 'Thank you, Mrs Banks. That would be very nice.'

'Well, we must be off. There is so much to do between now and the wedding, whenever it turns out to be. Good afternoon, Lady Annabelle, Sir Barrington.'

'Goodbye, dear Lady Annabelle!' Mercy called as the carriage pulled away. 'And thank you again!'

In the silence that followed, Anna heard Barrington chuckle—and felt her cheeks burn. 'I would have preferred that you not be a witness to that.'

'Why not? I found it highly diverting,' the odious man said. 'And you should be proud. You managed to get Miss Mercy Banks engaged, though in truth I'm not sure who is the more pleased: the mother or the daughter.'

'I venture to say they are equally delighted for entirely different reasons.'

'True. Hanover Square does have a very nice ring,' Barrington murmured. 'But I've no doubt it *will* be a splendid affair.' He turned to her and smiled. 'The wedding breakfast alone will be reason enough to attend.'

'Good. Since you *will* be attending, at least you can be assured of a good meal.'

'I beg your pardon?'

'Well, you didn't think I was going to this on my own, did you?' Anna enquired innocently. 'You are as much to blame for their engagement as I, so it seems only fair that you should accompany me to the celebration.'

It was an audacious statement and Anna held her breath as she waited for him to answer. What had got into her? A lady *never* asked a gentleman—it simply wasn't done. Fortunately, Barrington didn't seem to mind. Ever so slowly, he began to smile. 'It would be my honour to escort you, Lady Annabelle. Assuming, of course, that I am not engaged in resolving the convoluted lives of others on that particular day.'

Suppressing a ridiculous desire to laugh, Anna gathered the reins in her hands and lightly flicked her crop against the mare's withers. 'I trust, Sir Barrington, that on this most auspicious occasion, the convoluted lives of others will just have to go on without you.'

As well as involving Lord Richard Crew in the investigation of the baroness's necklace, Barrington made his own enquiries in a part of town the gentry seldom frequented. He wore clothes specifically chosen for the occasion: a hacking jacket a few years out of date, an old pair of topboots, scuffed and in need of a polish, and a beaver, too wide at the brim and looking decidedly worn. The effect was the appearance of a man down on his luck. One who was right at home with the patrons of the Rose and Thistle. Only the elegance of the ebony cane hinted at the presence of wealth, but Barrington wasn't about to venture into London's seedier neighbourhoods without it. The specially constructed walking stick had saved his life on more than one occasion.

He strolled into the inn at a few minutes past midnight and caught the eye of the landlord standing behind the bar. Jack Drummond nodded, drew two shots of whisky and, after a brief whisper in the barmaid's ear, led the way into a quiet back room. Barrington kept a watchful eye on the bar's patrons, but no one paid any attention to them as they passed. When they reached the small room at the end of the hall, Jack closed and locked the door behind them.

'Been a while, Sir Barrington,' the burly man said. He set the glasses down on a table and pulled up a couple of chairs. 'Everything all right with you?'

'Can't complain, Jack, can't complain.' Barrington leaned his cane against the back of the chair and sat down. 'You?'

'Never been better. Had a baby since last I saw yer and a

right little beauty she is. Don't know how with an ugly mug like me for a father.'

Barrington grinned. 'I suspect Molly had a lot to do with it. Is she well?'

'Aye, sir, she's fit as a fiddle.' Jack's face lit up like a child's on Christmas morning. 'Still happy to put up with me and that's saying something. Best day's work I ever did marrying that woman and it was only thanks to you I got the chance.'

Barrington shook his head. 'If you hadn't knocked the knife out of that Irishman's hand, I wouldn't be sitting here tonight.'

'And if *you* hadn't come running round that corner, shouting to wake the dead, that knife would have been buried in my chest clear up to the hilt.' Jack glanced at the ebony cane and smiled. 'Still carrying it, I see.'

'Never go out without it.' Barrington smiled. 'Some things are best not left to chance.'

'Can't argue with that. But you didn't come all the way down here to reminisce about the old days. What can I do for you?'

'I need you to keep an eye out,' Barrington said without preamble. 'A rather spectacular necklace was recently stolen from a lady's house and it's possible that over the next while, whispers about the necklace, or the necklace itself, may make its way into your inn. I want to know who's doing the talking and what they're saying.'

'I can do that,' Jack said with a nod. 'What kind of jewels are we talking about?'

'Sapphires and diamonds. Fairly large stones, so the thief may try to sell it by the piece. Or, if he leaves it whole, he may try to smuggle it out of the country. I'd appreciate you letting me know if you hear anything.'

'You've got my word on that, Sir Barrington,' Jack assured him.

Barrington pulled an envelope from his pocket. 'Use this if you think it will help. Otherwise, spend it on Molly and that new baby.'

Jack took the envelope, but didn't open it. 'You're a good man, Sir Barrington. I'll let you know if I hear anything. Chances are, if something that valuable's making its way around London, I'll hear about it sooner or later. Shall I contact you in the usual way?'

Barrington nodded as he tossed back his brandy. 'It's worked well in the past.' He stood up and held out his hand. 'Thanks, Jack.'

'A pleasure doing business, Sir Barrington,' Jack said, likewise getting to his feet. 'You can be sure if that necklace or any of its parts makes it down this neck of the woods, you'll be the first to know.'

Anna had intended to tell her father about Julia's necklace as soon as she'd heard about its theft, but one thing led to another and the days passed without her having a chance. Consequently, when she and her father finally sat together in the breakfast parlour a few days later, Anna wasn't surprised to find out that he already knew.

'Julia informed me of it over supper at the Hastings' last night,' the earl said, cutting into a slice of ham. 'Shocking turn of events. I told her to contact the authorities, but she informed me she had already engaged Sir Barrington Parker to look into the matter and that she'd done so on your recommendation.' He sent Anna a speculative glance. 'I thought you didn't like the man.'

'I do not like or dislike him. In truth, it was Lady Lydia's suggestion that Julia get in touch with him,' Anna said. 'I merely agreed that he would be a good choice because he was bound to be more discreet than most. He also seems to be privy to a great deal of information not known to the general public.'

'And how have *you* come to know that?'

Aware that her father was watching her a little too intently, Anna said casually, 'During my dealings with one of the young ladies whose life I was endeavouring to fix, I met Sir Barrington and he was able to provide me with information that was extremely valuable in securing the lady's happiness.'

'I see. So you've spent considerable time talking with him, then?'

'Not considerable, no.' Anna set her knife down. 'We met at Lady Montby's, spoke briefly at Julia's dinner party, then chanced to encounter one another in the park the other day.' She decided not to tell her father about the visit she had paid to the baronet's house over Peregrine's affair with Lady Yew. That would spark far too many awkward questions. 'It was then he informed me of his meeting with Julia.'

'I see.'

Anna sighed. 'Why is it gentlemen say that all the time, when I am quite convinced none of you see anything at all!'

'Oh, I don't know.' She was annoyed to see her father smile in that knowing kind of way. 'I think I'm beginning to see *some* things very clearly indeed.'

Disappointingly, very little information surfaced about the stolen necklace. London's underworld kept to itself, and those who were foolish enough to divulge what they knew suffered a noticeably shortened life. Consequently, neither Jack Drummond nor Lord Richard Crew were able to provide Barrington with the information he needed.

Closer to home, he questioned each member of the

baroness's personal staff, but turned up nothing of use. They were all extremely upset by the nature of the theft, but none were able to offer anything that pointed him in the right direction.

It was discouraging to say the least, but he still had one more avenue to explore. Knowing that gentlemen who imbibed too freely often tended to say far more than was wise, Barrington paid a late-night visit to one of his old haunts. The hell was known for high stakes' play and the young bucks who flocked to it were willing to risk all on the turn of a card.

Barrington knew many of them personally. Heirs to great estates who frittered away the years engaged in various debaucheries while waiting for their fathers to die. Restless second sons with little expectation of inheriting anything, but with allowances generous enough to allow them to gamble or drink their way into serious trouble. And the inevitable hangers-on. Those who clung to the coat-tails of the wealthy with either enough money or enough charm to make them tolerable.

Barrington knew them all. He had watched both his father and his grandfather drink themselves into oblivion and had sworn as a young man that he would never follow in their footsteps. As a result, for the first time in over two hundred years, the Parker name bore not a trace of scandal. And while his own line of work had not made him the most popular man in London, at least he knew he was doing what he could to make life better for those who were deserving of it.

*But at what cost to yourself?*

The question was unsettling. As was the fact that of late, he'd been asking it of himself more and more often. At one time, he had been able to ignore it because he had honestly believed there was nothing he would rather be doing, that there was no cost to exposing the dregs of London society.

But that wasn't true any more. His happiness was the cost. The warmth of a woman's love was the cost.

*Anna* was the cost—and the realisation hit him hard. Until recently, he hadn't allowed himself to say it. Even to think it. But ever since that night on the balcony, he realised that his feelings had begun to change. The idea of spending his life alone wasn't so appealing any more—and it was all because of Anna. He wanted to go to sleep with her curled up next to him, then to wake up and see her smiling at him. He wanted to lose himself in the lush warmth of her body and to experience the passion he knew he would find in her arms. Passion a few short minutes on a balcony had given him a tantalising glimpse of.

But, out of habit, he had put her off, telling her that he had no intention of marrying and using what he did as an excuse to keep her at a distance.

For the first time in his life, he wished he hadn't needed to.

Around one o'clock in the morning, after three hours of hard play, Barrington was getting ready to call it a night when one of the doxies came over to him and sat down in his lap. Her faded gown left little to the imagination and, as she draped her arm around his neck, Barrington was treated to a glimpse of full, rounded breasts and a long, slim neck. 'Sir Barrington Parker?' she whispered.

He looked up into a face that was still pretty and nodded. 'Yes.'

'Then somebody wants to see you.'

Surprised at not being propositioned, he said, 'What makes you think I want to see him?'

'Beats me, love, but he said he'd wait for you in the garden and not to be long about it. Said he had something to tell you.'

As she slowly straightened, she ran her hand up his chest, her fingers lingering for a moment at his throat. His shirt was open, his cravat long since having been shed. As she stroked the warm bare skin, she watched his face for signs that her attempts at seduction were succeeding. When she saw none, she sighed and moved away, obviously on the prowl for more lucrative business.

Barrington collected his winnings, picked up his cane and slowly got to his feet. It never paid to appear anxious in a place like this. Though most of the patrons were either drunk or unconscious, one never knew when watchful eyes might be following one's movements. Instead, he sauntered past the other tables, stopping to pretend an interest in one of the games, before heading towards the door.

The light grew dim as the corridor narrowed and the sounds of conversation and laughter faded away. Barrington concentrated on moving carefully now, senses alert for danger. Someone had gone to the trouble of following him here and of trying to make contact. He had no idea whether it was friend or foe, but experience had taught him well. The last thing he needed was an ambush by someone hiding in a darkened doorway.

Fortunately, no such attack came to pass and when he finally reached the unlocked back door, he stepped out into a small patch of heavily overgrown garden and looked around. For a moment, he saw nothing. Then, as his eyes adjusted to the gloom, he saw the faint outline of a man standing against the stone wall at the far end of the garden.

'Sir Barrington Parker?' The man's voice was coarse, the accent more north country than London.

'Yes.' Barrington slowly walked forwards. 'Who are you and how did you know to find me here?'

'Who I am doesn't matter. What I've got to say does. I understand you're looking for a necklace.'

Barrington stopped dead. So, the rats were finally making their way to the surface. He wished the light was such that he could put a face to the voice, but the man had positioned himself in such a way that his features remained in complete obscurity. 'What do you know about that?'

'Just what I was told to pass along.'

Barrington raised one eyebrow in surprise. So, the man was merely a conduit, a lackey of the person in possession of the necessary information. 'Does your master require payment for his information?'

'No. Said it was enough that the guilty party be exposed for what he'd done. A settling of an old score, if you will.'

Barrington smiled. A vendetta. How Italian. 'Very well,' he said slowly. 'What can you tell me?'

It took three minutes. Three minutes and Barrington had his name. A name he would have spent an eternity looking for and never found. After that, his informant slipped quietly into the night, the creaking of the back gate the only indication he'd ever been there.

Barrington stood alone in the silence of the neglected garden. He was used to hearing lies and rumours. Used to sifting through mounds of trivial information until he stumbled upon that one piece that might be of value. And he could honestly say there were only a handful of times in his entire life when he had truly been surprised by the nature of a revelation. This was one of those times.

But as he turned and slowly headed back into the house, he realised he wasn't only surprised, he was deeply apprehensive. The line he walked now was one of the finest he ever would. More than the reputation of a gentleman was at stake. Personal boundaries were about to be crossed. Feelings would be trammelled into the dust, beliefs battered, and impressions irrevocably altered.

He had the name of his thief. And, if his identity proved true, Barrington knew he risked losing everything that had come to matter in his life.

# Chapter Nine

Having just returned from a drive in the park, Anna was about to enter the house when she heard the clatter of carriage wheels in the street behind her. Aware that it was slowing down, she turned in time to see a matched pair of greys pulling an elegant black cabriolet draw to a halt in front of the house. Moments later, Sir Barrington stepped out, ebony cane in hand, his black beaver glistening in the afternoon sun.

'Sir Barrington,' Anna said, cursing the tiny catch in her voice. 'This is a surprise.'

He looked as startled as she, but there was something else in his expression she couldn't quite define. 'Lady Annabelle. I thought you would be out paying calls.'

'In fact, Lord Andrews has just returned me home from a drive in the park.'

'Andrews!' His countenance darkened. 'You allowed him to take you driving?'

'I did,' Anna said, caught off guard by the sudden intensity in his voice. 'He has been after me for weeks to allow him to show me his new pair of blacks, so when the weather turned fine this morning, I decided I would allow him to do so.'

'And did you enjoy your drive?'

Remembering several rather alarming moments when the horses had been going too fast for safety, Anna was tempted to tell him no, but pride demanded a different answer. 'It was…invigorating.'

He snorted. 'Invigorating. Andrews is a mediocre whip at best and notorious for buying troublesome animals. He has an inflated opinion of his ability to train them, so when a seller tells him a horse is bad tempered, Andrews tells them they're not using the right methods of control. But most of the time, he ends up selling the horses back to whoever he bought them from and always at a loss.'

'I admit, they were a touch wild,' Anna conceded, 'but for the most part, he seemed able to keep them under control.'

'Nevertheless, I would ask you not to drive out with him again. He is not a man I would encourage you or any other young woman to spend time with.'

Anna bristled. Having already made up her mind not to see Lord Andrews again, the warning was unnecessary, but she resented Barrington's belief that he had the right to tell her who she should and should not see. 'I think you are too hard on the gentleman, Sir Barrington. He was very pleasant to me. Attentive to my wishes and interested in what I had to say.'

'What do you know about the viscount, Lady Annabelle?' Barrington asked softly.

'Not a great deal,' she was forced to confess. 'He told me his wife died two years ago and that he has three married sisters he seldom sees.'

'He also has four children ranging in ages from six to thirteen and he is looking for a new wife to take care of them.'

'He cannot be looking very hard,' Anna said. 'I've spoken to several young ladies who told me of their desire to become the next Lady Andrews, but apparently, he offered them no encouragement whatsoever.'

'Yet he seemed interested in you?'

'Actually, no. During the course of our drive, he asked me a great many questions about Miss Dora Preston.'

'Miss Preston?' Barrington said quietly. 'Of course. A painfully shy young woman of nine and twenty, who now finds herself in a precarious financial situation as a result of her parents' death. She is neither pretty nor accomplished and has received no offers of marriage. Furthermore, as an only child, she has no brothers or sisters to whom she can apply for help.'

'Then why, given all that, should you not be pleased to hear that Lord Andrews is interested in her?' Anna asked, thinking it a logical question—until she saw the look on his face. 'Don't tell me you know something about him as well?'

'I'm afraid I do. And it is not the kind of information that recommends him to *any* woman, let alone one who is alone in the world and so terribly naïve.'

'Dare I ask why not?'

'Because Lord Andrews can be...unstable.'

'Unstable.'

'He has been known to suffer from hallucinations and bouts of paranoia.'

'The poor man. Is he not well?'

'Not when under the influence of opium, no.'

'Opium! *Lord Andrews?*'

'For obvious reasons, it is not something the man publicises,' Barrington said. 'It started out as a medical treatment for some unspecified condition several years ago, but over time, he grew addicted to its more...pleasurable aspects. It is the reason he has no communication with his sisters. They are afraid for the welfare of his children when he is under the influence. I know for a fact that the eldest sister has tried to remove the children from his care, but has been unsuccessful in her attempts. Marrying someone like Miss Preston leads me to believe he is looking for the kind of wife who will not ask questions. One who will be grateful just to have been asked and who has no family to worry about her. With such a wife in place, Andrews's sisters won't have a hope of taking the children away from him.'

Dear Lord, it was enough to make her feel ill. Anna couldn't believe that the man with whom she had just parted company would be the type to take opium, but neither could she dismiss it out of hand. Not when it was Barrington who had made her aware of it.

'If what you say is true, I must warn Miss Preston not to entertain his suit,' Anna said quickly. 'Though for the life of me, I cannot imagine what reason I am going to give her. She knows what her chances of marrying are. She'll never have another opportunity like this.'

'I have every confidence you will find a convincing explanation. If not, you can always tell her the truth. For her sake, she must not consider his offer. Nor must any other young lady for that matter.'

'I cannot protect them all!'

'I know. Fortunately, Andrews will likely retire to the country before the end of the Season, especially if he meets with no success in London. He will probably marry a woman from the local village. He does not look to marry well, only quickly.'

Anna nodded, aware that once again she was in his debt. 'Thank you for the information, Sir Barrington. Though I do not feel better for having learned of it, I know it will help Miss Preston in the long run.'

'There are, unfortunately, many men like Andrews in

society. Hallucinatory drugs will always hold an appeal for that sort of man.'

Aware that they were still standing on her front step, Anna said, 'Forgive me, I have rudely kept you out here talking. Would you like to come in?'

'Only if your father is at home.'

'I don't believe he is,' Anna said, wondering at the nature of his call. Surely the Marquess of Yew hadn't some further issue with Peregrine. 'He informed me when I left with Lord Andrews that he would be out until later this evening.'

'Then perhaps I will try again later.' He touched the brim of his beaver, then turned to go.

'Sir Barrington?' When he stopped and turned back, Anna said, 'Have you had any luck finding Julia's necklace?'

His expression didn't change, but something in his eyes hardened. 'No, though I have recently been made aware of information pertaining to the theft. But it is nothing I am at liberty to share at this time. Good afternoon, Lady Annabelle.'

With that he walked back down the path and climbed into his waiting carriage. The driver flicked the whip and the horses set off.

Anna walked into the house, unable to shake a feeling of gloom. Finding out the truth about Lord Andrews had not been pleasant and she made a promise to herself to send a note to Miss Preston that very afternoon. But it wasn't only that. Barrington had called to see her father and in finding him absent had made it perfectly clear that he had no desire to spend time in *her* company. Contrary to what she'd believed, it was obvious that the breach between them wasn't healed at all.

The rest of the day passed uneventfully, though Anna was aware of feeling strangely on edge. Even in the carriage en route to an evening engagement, the conversation she'd had with Barrington lingered in her mind. Was there anything the man *didn't* know? He seemed to be in possession of the most disturbing information about almost everyone she knew. Even unassuming Lord Andrews, whom she found herself observing during the course of the evening, harboured secrets that were both dark and disturbing. Watching him speak quietly to an elderly lady, Anna found it difficult to equate the seemingly upright gentleman with a man who indulged in a substance whose prolonged use was known to affect the mind and body in terrible ways.

'Are you sure you did not misunderstand Sir Barrington?' Lydia asked after Anna had acquainted her with Lord Andrew's unsavoury pastime.

'I can assure you I did not,' Anna said, keeping her voice down. 'Sir Barrington was very convincing in his description of the man's activities; given that I've no reason to doubt him, I took the liberty of writing to Miss Preston and advising her not to encourage Lord Andrews's suit. I told her Mr. Atlander would be a far better choice.'

'Until you speak to Sir Barrington about *him*,' Lydia murmured. 'And find out that *he* is not all he seems to be either. Faith, it must be disturbing to know so much about so many people. Only think of the kind of secrets Sir Barrington is forced to keep. He could utterly destroy people if he was of a mind to.'

'Only if they did something foolish. If one is innocent of all crimes, people have nothing to fear from him.'

'And what about you, Anna?' Lydia asked quietly. 'Have you anything to fear from Sir Barrington Parker?'

Anna took a sip of champagne. That was the problem with close friends. They saw far too much. 'I have no idea what you mean.'

'I think you do. You speak of him quite often, you know,' Lydia said, 'and in a tone of voice that leads me to believe you are not entirely indifferent to him.'

'Be that as it may, we both know exactly where we stand.'

'You may know where you stand, Anna, but are you happy about it?'

Anna raised her glass to her lips instead of replying. *That* was a different question altogether.

The house was quiet when Anna got home. Milford met her at the door and took her evening cape. 'Thank you, Milford. Is my father still up?'

'He is, my lady, but he went to his room and said he was not to be disturbed.'

Anna paused in the act of removing her gloves. 'Did Sir Barrington Parker call this evening?'

'He most certainly did,' Edward said, coming down the stairs. 'That will be all, Milford.'

Anna wasn't surprised by her brother's curt dismissal of the servant, but she was surprised to find him still at home. 'You're not usually here this time of evening,' she said as the butler withdrew.

'I had planned on going out, but when Parker arrived, I decided to stay. I'm glad I did, though you won't be.'

Anna flinched at his tone of voice. 'I assume he came to speak to Papa about Peregrine?'

'On the contrary, he came to speak to Father about the baroness's necklace. It seems the thief has been found.'

Something in his face set Anna's heart racing. 'Who is it?' she whispered.

'Can you not guess?'

*Dear God, it was someone she knew?* 'Stop playing games, Edward. Just *tell* me and be done with it!'

'Oh, I'll tell you, but you won't so easily be done with it. Because the thief is someone you know. A man you were raised to love and respect.' Her brother donned his hat and started for the door. 'A man who has lied and deceived us all. Our much loved and revered father!'

*Her father had stolen the baroness's necklace?*

Impossible! In fact, it was more than impossible. It was ludicrous! Her father was a wealthy man. He had no reason to steal anything—and he certainly wouldn't have stolen something from Julia. So why on earth had Barrington come here and accused him of having done so?

Woodenly, Anna made her way to the drawing room. There had to be a mistake. Barrington had been given the wrong information. One of his informants had followed the wrong lead. Tracked down the wrong man. Her father was *not* a thief. She was willing to stake her life on that.

She closed the door behind her and walked on unwilling feet towards the fireplace. She was cold, chilled from the inside out, her mind struggling to come to grips with what she had just learned. What kind of man was Barrington that he could do this to her family? He had *spoken* to her father. Socialised with him. Yet he had still come here and accused him of this heinous crime.

'How could you, Barrington?' she whispered. 'How *could* you do this unspeakable thing to my father?' She bit her lip, fighting back tears. 'To *me.*'

Barrington stood in his study, gazing into the fire, his conscience burning as hot as the flames in the grate. How long would it be? How long before she arrived on his doorstep demanding an explanation to the accusations he had laid at her father's feet?

It couldn't be long. She might even come tonight...straight from having spoken to her father. Unless she didn't get a chance to speak to him. The earl might well have gone out, or refused to speak to her. No doubt he needed time to come to grips with the fact that someone had supposedly seen him stealing the baroness's necklace while she lay sleeping in her bed.

Certainly Barrington had needed time. When the shadowy figure had first mentioned the earl's name, Barrington was sure he must have heard wrong. The Earl of Cambermere a thief? It was laughable! The man was a peer of the realm. An aristocrat. Such conduct would be anathema to him.

Yet, the man had repeated the earl's name several times over the course of the next few minutes, though never once had he vouchsafed the name of the person who was the apparent source of the information.

Not that it mattered, Barrington reflected grimly. He had been given the Earl of Cambermere's name as the person who had committed the crime. And, as his first and only suspect, he was obliged to follow it through. For Anna's sake, he prayed God it wasn't the only name he received.

Anna had no idea how she had passed the hours of that terrible night. It certainly wasn't in sleep. She had lain awake through the long midnight hours, getting up several times to pace the length of the room. At one point, she had opened the curtains and stared at the moon, but it gave her no comfort and eventually she had staggered back to bed. But she hadn't been able to sleep and still lay awake when the first fingers of light began to creep into her room. She watched the blackness of the night sky give way to a dark indigo hue, then to lighter blue as the sun climbed higher in the sky. She heard the sounds of the servants moving about in the house below. Laying fires. Dusting furniture. Setting out breakfast. And still she thought about Edward's words.

*A man you were raised to love and respect...a man who has lied and deceived us all...*

No, she *wouldn't* believe it. Nor would she wait any longer to have it shown up as the lie she knew it to be. She got up and dressed even before her maid arrived to help her, then went down to the library where she knew her father spent most of his early morning hours. He would be off to his club for lunch, but Anna had no intention of seeing him leave *before* she'd had a chance to speak with him. Not today.

She knocked on the library door, but waited until she heard his voice before pushing it open. 'May I come in, Papa?'

'Anna.' He rose as she entered, surprise and uncertainty reflected in his eyes. His complexion was grey and he looked as though he hadn't slept. 'What are you doing here?'

'I came to see you.' Swallowing hard, Anna closed the door and took a step towards him. 'I needed to hear it from your lips that this is all an abominable lie.'

He knew what she was talking about. Anna saw it in the way his eyes closed ever so briefly. The way his shoulders sagged. 'Did Parker tell you?'

'No. Edward did.'

'Ah.' Making no move to deny it, the earl sighed and sank back into his chair.

'I don't believe it, Papa,' Anna said. 'Someone has told a hurtful and outrageous lie!'

'Yes, they have,' he agreed. 'But they have also offered damning evidence to back up their claim.'

'What kind of evidence?'

'Someone told Parker that I was seen taking Julia's necklace.'

'*Seen…?*' Anna gasped. 'But…by whom?'

'He wouldn't tell me.'

'Why not?'

'He said it was an anonymous source.'

'Then how do you know he's telling the truth?'

Her father looked up. 'Because we're talking about Sir Barrington Parker and he doesn't lie.'

'I wasn't referring to Sir Barrington telling a lie,' Anna said tersely. 'I was talking about his anonymous source. How do we know *he* is telling the truth?'

'We don't. Right now, it's my word against his, whoever he is.'

'Then there can be no contest. You are the Earl of Cambermere!' she exclaimed.

'Which means nothing since the person who saw me was apparently *in* the house the night it happened,' her father said wearily.

'But that doesn't make sense. You've never been alone with Julia in her house,' Anna said. 'And how could you steal the necklace if she was there with you?'

She was surprised to see her father's cheeks darken as he turned away. 'Suffice it to say, that *is* what I stand accused of.'

'Well, it's ridiculous and I don't care what the gossip mill is saying. You are innocent and we are going to make sure everyone knows it!'

'Ah, Anna, have you forgotten how society works? It doesn't matter what people believe. It is enough that someone put it about that I stole the necklace for society to cry scandal.'

'But they have no proof!' Anna cried. 'So far, it is one

man's word against another's—and we don't even know who the other man is! Surely people are intelligent enough to know that, without proof, it is only lies and speculation.'

'One would hope so.'

Anna began to pace. 'Why would Sir Barrington not tell you the name of the person who claims to have seen you take it?'

'He told me he couldn't until further investigation was carried out.'

'Then for all we know, it could be someone deliberately making mischief,' Anna said, grasping at straws. Grasping at anything that might banish the wretchedness from her father's eyes. 'Someone who wishes to hurt you for some unknown reason.'

'I did think of that,' her father said. 'But who have I slighted to such an extent that they would wish to destroy my reputation like this?'

Anna bit her lip. 'You don't think Peregrine…?'

'Peregrine?' Anna was relieved to see a look of genuine shock appear on her father's face. 'Why on earth would he turn on me in such a manner?'

'Perhaps because of the situation with Lady Yew. He was angry and hurt that you didn't believe him when Sir Barrington accused him of having an affair.'

'Rightly so, given that it turned out Parker was correct.'

Reminded of the man who had brought this terrible news into the house, Anna felt a red-hot wave of anger. How dare he disrupt her family's life like this? She had been willing to believe him up until now, but not this time. He and he alone was the cause of her father's humiliation and unhappiness.

'Then I shall go to Sir Barrington myself. I will *demand* that he tell me who his source is and have him explain why he would believe such a ridiculous lie.'

'You're bringing emotion into it,' her father warned. 'Parker doesn't deal in emotion. He deals in facts.'

'Not any more,' Anna said tersely. 'This time, he is dealing with emotions. Yours and mine and Julia's. And by the time I'm through with him, he is going to know *exactly* how challenging dealing with an emotional woman can be!'

Barrington was in the long gallery sparring with his brother-in-law when his secretary arrived to tell him that Lady Annabelle Durst had called and was waiting below.

'Shall I inform her that you are engaged, Sir Barrington?' Sam asked.

'No.' Barrington slowly lowered his foil. 'Ask her to wait in the salon. I shall be there directly.'

'Lady Annabelle Durst,' Tom repeated after the secretary left. 'The Earl of Cambermere's daughter?'

'Yes.'

'Interesting. Is she calling on a business matter or may I have the pleasure of telling your sister that a lady has finally caught her brother's eye?'

'You may definitely *not* tell her that because this is not a social call,' Barrington muttered. 'Lady Annabelle is here with regards to an investigation.'

'Pity. A liaison with Cambermere's daughter would do much to lessen Jenny's disappointment over what happened with Lady Alice,' Tom remarked.

'Duly noted,' Barrington said, ushering his brother-in-law towards the door. He wasn't about to tell Tom that appeasing his sister was the least of his worries right now. 'I trust you can see yourself out.'

Without waiting for an answer, Barrington hurried to his bedroom to change into more appropriate attire. The coming confrontation was not going to be easy and he needed to be prepared. A fact proven true when he opened the door to the salon five minutes later and Anna flew at him like a tigress on the attack. 'How could you do this?' she demanded.

'Do what?'

'Accuse my father of stealing the baroness's necklace. You know he would never do such a thing!'

Barrington slowly closed the door behind him. 'I did what I had to after receiving information from a credible source—'

'Damn your credible sources!' Anna cried. 'We're talking about *my father*. And you know as well as I do that he would never steal anything from anyone! *Especially* Julia!'

'Calm yourself, Anna. I didn't say that I *believed* what I had been told, nor did I charge your father with any crime. But I was given a piece of information and it was my duty to follow it up. So I asked him a few questions.'

'What kind of questions?'

'That is between your father and myself,' he replied evasively.

'But I don't understand. If you don't believe him guilty, why are you putting him through all this?'

'Because there are procedures that must be followed.' Barrington linked his hands behind his back and slowly walked towards the window. 'When did he tell you of my visit?'

'He didn't,' Anna said tightly. 'Edward did.'

'Edward?' Barrington's head came up. 'When?'

'Last night. He waited until I arrived home to tell me that you had called to see Father. I assumed it had something to do with Peregrine, but Edward said you had come to see Papa about the theft of Julia's necklace.'

Barrington didn't trouble to hide his surprise. 'I wonder

how he knew? Your brother wasn't in the room when I spoke to your father.'

'He must have been standing outside in the corridor listening to your conversation,' Anna said. 'Edward is not above doing such things, especially if he thought you'd come to see my father about Peregrine.'

'I see,' Barrington said quietly. He was beginning to have his own suspicions about Viscount Hayle, but knew it was best he keep them to himself for the time being. 'What did your father say when you spoke to him?'

'He told me what *you* had accused him of, but said that you would not name the person who had made this foul accusation against him,' Anna said in a low voice. 'How could you not tell him, Barrington? Surely my father has a right to know who is bringing these charges against him.'

'He will. But for now, I thought it best not to reveal too much. To say something out of turn won't do anyone any good,' he advised.

'But you must know what this will do to his reputation,' she said, 'whether it turns out to be true or not. Why can't you just *say* that the other person is lying and proclaim my father innocent?'

'Because until I am convinced of the part that *everyone* has played in this, I'm not willing to say who is guilty and who is not.'

'But you just said my father didn't do it—and why would he? He likes Julia,' Anna said. 'Why on earth would he jeopardise a possible future with her by stealing something so precious to her?'

'Trust me when I tell you that thought has already occurred to me.' Barrington hesitated a moment before saying, 'You said Edward spoke to you about your father?'

'Yes.'

'It hasn't escaped my notice that there is a certain amount of tension between your father and your brother at the moment,' he said.

'It's hardly surprising,' Anna said in a voice of resignation. 'Papa is pressuring Edward to marry Lady Harriet Green and Edward wants nothing to do with it.'

'Why? Is he opposed to the idea of marriage or just the lady your father wishes him to wed?'

'A bit of both, I think,' Anna admitted. 'Papa thinks very highly of Lady Harriet and he's told Edward so any number of times. He says she possesses all the qualities necessary to be the next Countess of Cambermere.'

'And your brother doesn't share his opinion.'

'Edward says that who he marries is no one's business but his own. I suppose he's right, but Papa is concerned about the future of the family. He says Edward has lived the life of the gentleman about town long enough and that it's time he settled down to his obligations.'

'Which means marrying and producing an heir,' Barrington said.

'Precisely.'

'Are there no other members of the family capable of doing so?' Barrington asked. 'I believe your father has several brothers and sisters?'

'Two brothers, one sister,' Anna said. 'Aunt Hestia is married to a Scottish laird and lives in Edinburgh. I remember meeting her when I was about six and not liking her very much. She has two girls. Father's youngest brother, Cyril, went away to France and was eventually killed in battle, and his next eldest brother sailed off to China and never came back. I suspect he knew he wouldn't have much of a life, given that Papa was heir.'

'So it *is* up to Edward to continue the family name,' Barrington said thoughtfully.

'Yes, and given that he is showing absolutely no inclination to do so, it is only to be expected that relations between him and my father are strained,' Anna sighed.

'Yes, I can see why they would be,' Barrington said. 'Anna, I cannot share with you what I was told, but I promise I will do everything I can to get to the truth of the matter.'

'There is only one truth: that is that my father is innocent of this vile charge,' Anna said, raising her chin in defiance. 'I don't care what manner of evidence has been brought against him. He is a good man. An honourable man. And if you don't believe that, we have absolutely nothing more to say to one another.'

# Chapter Ten

The evidence against her father *was* damning, Barrington reflected in the silence after Anna left. It was part of the reason he hadn't been willing to share it with her. He was loathe to provide her with details of a circumstance that would put the blame for the theft squarely on her father's shoulders *and* give her undeniable proof that the earl and the baroness were engaged in an intimate relationship. But that was what the messenger had told him and what he was obligated to follow up on.

A servant in the baroness's household had seen Lord Cambermere take the necklace after leaving the baroness sleeping peacefully in her bed. Apparently, the maid had gone into her mistress's bedroom, expecting her lady to be alone, and had discovered the earl in the act of taking the necklace from the jewellery case. She claimed that Lord Cambermere hadn't seen her, but that from where she had been standing, she'd had a clear view of the proceedings. After locking the jewellery box, the earl had slipped the necklace into the pocket of his coat, and then returned to the baroness's bed.

The baroness had not woken and, shocked beyond words, the maid had backed quietly out of the room.

Barrington sighed. It might be only the word of a servant against that of an earl, but the messenger had provided details too specific to be dismissed as fabrication or hoax. Details of the room's interior. A description of the jewellery box. Even where the dressing table was located in relation to the bed, what colour the curtains were, and what manner of knick-knacks had adorned the top of the bedside table. Only a maid, with unrestricted access to the baroness's bedroom, would have been able to provide details like that.

Besides, what reason had she to lie? She claimed to have no prior knowledge of the earl. She hadn't worked in his household and had no reason to hold a grudge against him. All she cared about was her mistress and how upset she had been when she'd found out the necklace was missing. It was that grief, combined with a sense of loyalty, that had prompted Miss Smith to tell *someone* what she had seen that night. And, in turn, for that person to tell the man who'd met with Barrington in the darkened garden.

If it *was* true, it meant Cambermere had certainly had the opportunity to commit the crime. But he still lacked a motive and Barrington didn't believe anything was done without motive. Dogs barked because they were frightened. Beggars stole because they were starving. Prostitutes sold their bodies because they needed a roof over their heads.

What reason had Cambermere for stealing?

Barrington idly picked up a piece of Venetian glass, turning it over in his fingers as his mind went back over his various encounters with the earl. Was it possible the man had serious debts? His home was quite grand, but there had been an air of genteel shabbiness about the place. Small signs of neglect a less observant person might have overlooked. Worn patches on the arms of the chairs. The burgundy velvet curtains faded, their bottom edges frayed. Even the mahogany desk had been in need of a good polish.

Barrington had originally put it down to a lack of interest on the earl's part, a sad consequence of Lady Cambermere's death. But now he wondered if it might be an indication of something more. Even the earl's appearance had been wanting, now that Barrington thought about it. Signs of wear at the man's cuffs. The style of the coat slightly out of date. Boots that had seen better days.

Still, if the earl was having financial difficulties, he wouldn't be the first peer to fall on hard times. Cambermere owned a house in town and several smaller estates in the English countryside. The upkeep of such establishments commanded a huge outlay of money. It was the reason many cash-strapped peers resorted to marrying heiresses. It was either that or risk sacrificing their family's land and holdings. But was the earl really in such dire financial straits?

Surprisingly, it was Lady Bessmel who provided some insight into the situation as the two of them stood chatting over lobster pâté the following evening.

'Yes, Cambermere has a lovely estate in Kent,' she told him. 'I used to visit him and Isabel there quite often.'

'What was Lady Cambermere like?' Barrington enquired.

'Quiet. And thoughtful. She enjoyed London, but she was far happier in the country. She loved her garden and her horses. And her books, of course. She would read for hours on end, saying she found precious little time for it in London.' Lady Bessmel sighed. 'I was very sorry when Isabel died. She was…a gentle person. The kind who gave of herself. I believe her death hit Peter quite hard.'

'Were they in love?'

The countess smiled. 'As much as anyone in our circle can be, I suppose. It was an arranged marriage, but it turned out quite well. Peter was a good husband. I never heard stories about him keeping a mistress or visiting the brothels. He seemed content with his life, at least until Isabel died. Then he seemed to lose focus. He couldn't settle to anything. That's why it's so nice to see him finally making an effort again.'

'Making an effort?' Barrington asked.

'With the baroness. It can't have escaped your notice that he is very much taken with her.'

'Yes, I had noticed.' Barrington smiled. 'Can you tell me anything more about the earl? Has he vices?'

'What man doesn't? He gambles at cards, but not a great deal, and he drinks no more or less than anyone else. I suppose his greatest weakness is horses.'

'Horses,' Barrington repeated. 'Is he a frequent visitor to the track?'

'More now than he used to be. I never remember him gambling while Isabel was alive, but a woman's death can change a man. In the beginning, I think it was simply a diversion,' Lady Bessmel said. 'Something to think about other than the fact that his wife wasn't there any more. But over time it gets into a man's blood.'

'Does he win more than he loses?' he asked idly.

'Who knows? Dame Fortune can turn either way. One day she smiles on you, the next she spits in your face. I'm sure Peter's had his share of both, but he's a private man so I doubt anyone knows the true extent of his winnings. Or of his losses.'

It was a conversation that stayed with Barrington the rest of the night—because if the earl *was* in serious debt, Barrington had his motive. The baroness's necklace was worth a small fortune, enough to cover most any man's debts. And given Cambermere's position in society, it was unlikely he would have to take the necklace apart. Connections here and abroad would allow him to dispose of the piece without the sale being traced back to him.

But if the earl was hopeful of marrying the baroness, why bother to steal her jewellery? Julia von Brohm was an exceedingly wealthy young woman with more than enough money for the two of them to live on. Of course, being a widow, her money was her own, and, if she chose, she could have a lawyer draw up papers to ensure it stayed that way. If Cambermere needed funds to pay off his gambling debts, he could apply to her, but given that his debts *were* the result of gambling, she might not wish to put any of her money to them. Barrington remembered a remark she'd once made about gentlemen foolish enough to squander their money on the roll of a dice not being worth the time or the trouble to know. That being the case, he doubted she would willingly give any of her money to a man who had bankrupted himself at the tables or the track.

However, if it was Cambermere's intention to pay off his debts *before* he married her so that he could go into the marriage free and clear, he would then be able to use her money to look after the maintenance of his estates. And surely she wouldn't object to that, given that she would be mistress of them all. So it really came down to two questions.

How deeply in debt had Cambermere landed himself? And how far was he willing to go to dig himself out?

The next morning Anna called for her horse to be saddled and went for a much-needed ride. She feared she might explode if she stayed at home any longer. Trying to read, or doing any one of a hundred and one other things that would normally have distracted her, would be of no use today. She needed to get out of the house and away from her thoughts.

Her father had already done so. Having been offered an invitation to a shooting party, he had left for the weekend gathering at a house about ten miles outside London. It was only to be a small gathering of gentlemen, but Anna knew her father would find comfort in their company. But it did leave her at loose ends. Peregrine was still quiet and withdrawn as he struggled through his own emotional healing and Edward was scarcely at home.

And Barrington didn't call.

Anna told herself she was glad of that. After all, they had nothing to say to one another. She'd made it quite plain that to take a stand against her father was to take a stand against her, and Barrington had made his own position perfectly clear. He intended to pursue the investigation against her father; in the absence of any other, her father was still the main suspect.

Well, loyalty and emotion might mean nothing to him, but they meant everything to Anna. She believed unequivocally that her father was innocent. Barrington was trying to prove him not guilty. There was a subtle but distinct difference.

Unfortunately, as much as Anna had hoped that fresh air and brisk exercise might distract her, neither served to ease her mind. She felt no more relaxed when she arrived home than when she'd left. And when Peregrine emerged from the drawing room, white-faced and shaken, her spirits plummeted even further. 'Goodness, Peregrine, what's wrong? You look positively ill.'

'Thank God you're back! Come in here!' he said urgently. 'And close the door.'

Anna did, wearily hoping his agitation had nothing to do with Lady Yew. She wasn't sure she could cope with one more piece of bad news—or with the mention of that woman's name again. 'What's this all about? If you tell me you've seen the marchioness—'

'This has nothing to do with her,' Peregrine assured her quickly. 'This is worse. Much worse!'

Worse? Anna didn't like the sound of that. And when

Peregrine began to pace up and down the length of the room, looking as though he might burst into tears at any time, she knew there was trouble in earnest. 'What's going on, Per? If it's bad news, just tell me and get it over with.'

He stopped pacing, but didn't look at her. 'I don't know *how* to tell you. I'm hardly able to believe it myself!'

'Believe what?'

He looked ready to say something, then squeezed his eyes shut and took a deep breath. 'No. It's best I show you. You won't believe me otherwise.' With that, he took her hand and led her out of the room and towards the staircase.

'Where are we going?'

'You'll see,' was all he would say. At the top of the stairs, he stopped and cocked his head, listening. Then, with a brief nod, he carried on until they were standing outside the last door in the hall.

'This is Papa's room,' Anna said unnecessarily.

'I know.' Peregrine took another quick glance in either direction, then, to Anna's astonishment, opened the door and dragged her in.

'Peregrine, what on earth are you doing?'

'I have to show you something.' Closing the door, he turned the key in the lock. Then, walking over to the door that connected the earl's room to his valet's, he locked that one as well.

'Peregrine, you're beginning to make me very nervous,' Anna said, unconsciously lowering her voice.

'I'm sorry, but I found something in your father's things that you really must see.'

'You were going through his things?' Anna said, shocked.

'I was looking for his watch.'

'His watch?' The story was getting more bizarre by the minute. 'Why?'

'Because Edward asked me to,' Peregrine admitted.

'I don't understand.'

'Edward was supposed to take your father's watch to Mr Munts for repair,' Peregrine explained, 'but he told me he was late for an appointment and asked me if I would take it instead. I said I would and asked him where the watch was. He told me the earl usually kept it in one of two places. I checked the first place and it wasn't there. But when I looked in the second…'

He stopped, prompting Anna to say, 'You found it?'

Peregrine nodded. 'But I found something else as well.' He led her to the large corner wardrobe and, pulling open the doors, pointed to a small drawer. 'Open it.'

Not sure why, Anna did—and saw a leather bag with a drawstring opening lying on a pile of neatly folded handkerchiefs. 'Is that what you want me to see?'

He nodded. 'Take it out.'

The bag was heavier than expected, and Anna felt the contents shift as she picked it up.

'Open it,' he whispered.

'We really shouldn't be going through Papa's things,' Anna whispered. 'This could be something personal.'

'Open it, Anna.'

There was an edge of fatalism in his voice, and reluctantly, she loosened the drawstring and tipped the contents of the bag into the palm of her hand.

The baroness's diamond-and-sapphire necklace twinkled up at her.

'Oh, dear God!' Anna said—and promptly dropped it. 'What on earth is *that* doing here?'

'I have no idea.' Peregrine reached down and plucked the necklace from the depths of the boot into which it had fallen. 'But we both know it's not supposed to be here.'

The discovery left Anna speechless. How could the necklace be here—in her father's room? In his wardrobe? He had professed his innocence and she had believed him. Then she had gone to Barrington and told him that her father was innocent of the charge and that if he didn't believe her, they had nothing further to say to one another. Yet now she found the baroness's necklace nestled amongst her father's things.

'It's impossible,' she whispered. 'Why would he do this?'

'I've been asking myself that all afternoon,' Peregrine said miserably. 'And coming up with nothing.'

Anna stared at the necklace. It didn't make sense. The necklace shouldn't be here. In fact, this was the last place in the world it should be...

'All right, let's not jump to conclusions,' she said, knowing there had to be a logical explanation. 'Just because we found the necklace here, doesn't mean Papa took it.'

'Then how did it come to be in his things?' Peregrine asked.

'Obviously, someone *put* it here.'

'Who? No one else comes into his room,' he said.

'*You* did!' she reminded him.

'Only because Edward asked me to. And I certainly didn't put *this* here.' He was silent for a moment. 'What about the servants? They come and go all the time.'

'But none of them would have an opportunity to steal a diamond necklace from the baroness,' Anna pointed out.

'And we *did*?' Peregrine demanded.

'Of course not! But at least we move in the same circles. We have access to her house.'

'But none of us would have taken it.'

Yet, the necklace was here. In her father's wardrobe. Peregrine was holding it in his hands.

'It really is fabulous, isn't it?' he said, staring down at it in fascination.

Anna didn't want to look, but it was almost impossible not to. She had never seen such amazing stones. Even in the dim light, the sapphires seemed to glow with brilliant blue fire and the diamonds were as white as any she'd ever seen. Truly, it was a necklace fit for a queen.

'A man would never have to work again if he owned something like that,' Peregrine whispered. 'He could buy anything he wanted. Go wherever he wanted. He'd never have to worry about money—'

'Stop talking like that!' Anna admonished, finally taking the necklace away from him. 'This is going back to the baroness where it belongs.'

'*Back* to the baroness? But…aren't you going to tell anyone you found it?'

She stared at him as though he'd suddenly sprouted a second head. 'Are you *mad*? And have Papa implicated in a crime he didn't commit? Not on your life! Whoever put this necklace here clearly intended to make trouble for Papa and I'm not about to see that happen,' Anna said. 'We have been unbelievably fortunate in finding the necklace before he got home. And I am going to return it to Julia at the first opportunity.'

'I see.' Peregrine crossed his arms in front of his chest. 'And where, pray tell, are you going to tell her you *found* it?'

The question stopped Anna in her tracks. 'Oh.'

'Exactly. If you can't come up with a logical explanation, you're better off not giving it back to her at all. It will just make her suspicious.'

'But the longer the necklace is missing, the more time someone has to spread lies about Papa's having taken it,' Anna said.

Peregrine glanced at the necklace and shook his head. 'I

think you should tell Sir Barrington Parker. Isn't he the one the baroness asked to look into the matter?'

'Yes, and I'll tell you right now, he is the very *last* person I intend to tell about this!' Anna said fiercely. 'Can you imagine what he would say if he were to learn that we found it here? He would think Papa took it.'

'I hate to say this, but...' Peregrine looked distinctly uncomfortable. 'Are you absolutely sure your father *didn't* take it?'

Anna's mouth fell open in disbelief. 'Peregrine, how *could* you?'

'I'm not saying he did! It's just that—'

'I don't want to hear it,' Anna said, cutting him off. 'There isn't a doubt in my mind that my father is innocent. He would never do something like this. *Never!*'

'Then what are you going to do?'

'I'll tell you.' Anna slipped the necklace into the pocket of her riding skirt, a plan already forming in her mind. 'First off, *you* are going to take Papa's watch to Mr Munts and make sure you get a receipt for it.'

'A receipt,' Peregrine repeated in bewilderment.

'Yes. Then, upon returning home, you will give the receipt to Milford and make sure you tell him that Edward instructed you to take Papa's watch in for repair, and that either Milford or James can pick it up when it's ready.'

Peregrine's heavy brows drew together. 'Why am I doing all that?'

'Because I want the reasons for your *being* in Papa's wardrobe to be very clear. It's possible that whoever put the necklace here intended that someone other than Papa should find it. Most likely a servant. And knowing how servants gossip, the culprit hoped news of the necklace's discovery *in* Papa's wardrobe would start making its way through society.

Fortunately, *we* found it and can make sure no such rumours leak out,' Anna said.

Peregrine frowned. 'I don't understand the reason for all the secrecy. We certainly aren't going to say we saw the necklace.'

'Of course not. And before this day is out, the necklace will be safely back in Julia's hands. But if, for some bizarre reason, this does fall back on us, I want it made very clear that you went into the wardrobe looking for Papa's watch because it needed to go to Mr Munts for repair, and that you did *not* see anything untoward while you were there.'

'So if anyone asks, we're going to lie,' Peregrine said simply.

'Precisely. It's the *only* way we can protect Papa. Now if you'll excuse me, I have to get dressed. I have a very important call to make!'

There was only one thought on Anna's mind as she turned her phaeton into Mayfair a short time later. She *had* to get the necklace back into Julia's house—and she had to do it without anyone seeing her!

It should be relatively simple. Once in Julia's parlour, she would pass some pleasant time with tea and conversation before making an excuse to leave the room. A visit to the convenience would probably be the best. That would give her time to slip upstairs and make her way to Julia's bedchamber.

Once inside, she would place the necklace on the floor beneath Julia's bedside table, or better yet, under her dressing table, and then return to the drawing room to resume her visit. In the next few minutes, she would bring the conversation round to the necklace and casually ask if Julia had looked *under* the furniture in her room since jewellery could so easily slip off a night table or a dresser and become lost. If

Julia replied that she or the servants had already looked in such places, Anna would simply advise her to look again and casually change the subject; then, after a suitable amount of time, she would bid Julia a good day and leave.

Really, it was so simple. Julia would find the necklace exactly where Anna said it might be, laugh at herself for not having been more careful—and that would be an end of it. There would be no more stories about the necklace having been stolen. No more rumours about her father's possible involvement. And no need to involve Sir Barrington Parker at all.

Anna almost felt like laughing as she walked up to Julia's front door.

Unfortunately, her neatly laid plans began to fall apart the moment she walked into the house. As the butler opened the drawing room door and announced her, Anna was horrified to see Sir Barrington Parker sitting comfortably at Julia's side.

'Sir Barrington!' she gasped, completely ignoring her hostess.

'Lady Annabelle.' He rose to greet her, his voice decidedly amused. 'You look as though you've seen a ghost.'

'Do I?' *Calm.* Above all, she had to remain calm. No one must know this was anything but a routine visit in the course of her social day. Easier said than done given the weight in the bottom of her reticule. 'Perhaps just my…surprise at finding you here. I didn't see your carriage in the street.'

'It being such a lovely day, I decided to walk,' Barrington told her. 'A brisk walk is always good for clearing the mind.'

'So I've heard,' Anna murmured, wishing desperately for something that might clear hers. 'Julia, how rude you must think me. I greeted Sir Barrington without even acknowledging you.'

'No apologies are necessary, my dear,' Julia assured her with a smile. 'You probably came, hoping to have a cosy chat, and were surprised at encountering our mutual friend. I would have been similarly nonplussed.'

'You are too kind in your forgiveness. But how well you look today.' Anna flicked a cautious glance in Barrington's direction. 'Am I to hope you've had news concerning your necklace?'

'In fact, Sir Barrington and I were just talking about it.'

'Really?' Anna felt her heart skip a beat. 'What did he say?'

'I was about to inform the baroness,' Barrington said smoothly, 'that I am following up on several leads and hope to have an answer for her very soon.'

Anna pasted a smile on her lips. 'How encouraging.'

'Yes, isn't it?' Julia said happily. 'At this point, the only thing that matters is recovering the necklace. I really don't care who took it—'

'You don't? I mean…it's important that we know who *did* take it, of course,' Anna said as two pairs of eyes turned to stare at her. 'But surely its safe return is the more important issue.'

'It is to me,' Julia said. 'I was going to tell Sir Barrington that I won't press charges if he feels that might encourage the thief to return the necklace to me intact.'

'Oh, but that is exceedingly generous of you,' Anna said, aware that matters were improving by the minute.

Or were until Barrington said, 'It *is* generous of you, Baroness, but I doubt the authorities will agree. A law has been broken. Someone must be made to pay.'

'But surely if Julia does not wish to press charges, there is no need for the authorities to be involved,' Anna said, annoyed at his interference.

'As I said, a crime has been committed and retribution must

be made. I suspect the baroness's wishes will be taken into account, but I cannot guarantee they will be honoured.'

Anna abruptly stood up, her stomach twisting. 'Julia, will you excuse me for a moment?'

'Of course, Anna, but are you feeling all right? You've gone dreadfully pale.'

'Have I?' Anna clutched at her reticule. 'Perhaps it's the heat. I am feeling a bit faint.'

'Then you must lie down.' Julia immediately got to her feet. 'I would suggest my room—'

'Oh, yes, that would be perfect!'

'Except that I have workmen repapering all the bedrooms,' Julia finished. 'I fear you would have no solitude at all.'

'No, really, that would be fine,' Anna assured her. 'I just need to lie down for a moment—'

'Then you must lie here on the sofa,' Barrington interrupted, getting to his feet. 'And I shall leave the two of you to some quiet conversation.'

'No, please, that isn't necessary,' Anna said, seeing her carefully thought-out plan disintegrating. With workmen in the bedrooms and people coming and going, she wouldn't have a hope of secreting the necklace in Julia's bedroom without being seen. 'I hate to see you leave on my account.'

'Rest assured, I was preparing to depart when you arrived,' Barrington said with a smile. 'I only dropped by to apprise the baroness of my progress. But I do hope the next time we meet you are feeling more like your old self.'

Wondering if she would ever feel like her old self again, Anna murmured, 'Yes, I'm quite sure I shall be fully recovered by then.'

'If you will wait for me at the front door, Sir Barrington,' Julia said, 'I'll fetch that list of names you asked for. Anna, will you be all right on your own for a few minutes?'

'Yes, of course,' Anna said, fighting back disappointment

as she sank down on the sofa. 'I shall just...lie here and wait for you.'

She was aware of Barrington lingering in the doorway, but didn't have the courage to look back at him. The man was too observant by half. Anna was terrified of what he might read in her eyes. As it was, she felt the necklace glowing like a beacon in her hands. But what was she to do with it now? She couldn't take it away again. Not with the clock ticking on her father's exposure. She had to make sure Julia found the necklace today. And if she couldn't safely get upstairs, she would just have to leave the necklace somewhere in here. But where?

The moment the door closed, Anna sprang to her feet and started searching for a likely place. It couldn't be somewhere immediately visible or Julia would wonder why she hadn't seen it before. But if it was too well hidden, she wouldn't find the necklace at all and the point of the exercise was to put it somewhere that it *would* be found.

Then, Anna spotted it—a large palm standing by the half-open French door. If the necklace was found in the branches, it could be suggested that during his escape, the thief had clumsily dropped it and it had landed in the tree. It was feeble, Anna admitted, but at the moment she had nothing better. And she was fast running out of time. She *had* to make sure the necklace was found in Julia's house *today*.

With that in mind she moved towards the palm, scanning for a likely branch. The necklace was too heavy to be supported by the uppermost branches, but it would be obscured if it was dropped directly into the base. She could, of course, put the bulk of it in the base and leave part of it trailing out...

Risking another glance at the door, Anna unfastened her reticule and reached in for the necklace. She would try it in several places and leave it in the one that looked best. Unfortunately, one of the claws holding the centre diamond was tangled in the fabric, causing her to waste precious seconds extricating it. Finally, it came free and, with infinite care, Anna leaned forwards to place it amongst the thicker branches lower down on the trunk. She tried to arrange it in a manner that made it look as though it had fallen, but the dashed thing kept bending the branches and falling into the base.

And then, the unthinkable happened. Hearing a movement behind her, Anna turned—and blanched.

Sir Barrington Parker was standing by the door, watching her.

# Chapter Eleven

Damnation! Caught red-handed—and by the last person on earth she could afford to be caught by!

Seconds dragged by like treacle in winter. Barrington didn't say a word, but she could tell from the look on his face that this wasn't going to be good.

Then Julia's voice, saying, 'Sir Barrington, where are you?'

Anna gasped—and in that split second, Barrington moved. Launching himself across the room, he pushed her aside and scooped the necklace out of the palm, dropping it into an inside pocket of his coat. Barely had it disappeared than the drawing-room door opened and Julia walked in. 'Ah, there you are, Sir Barrington,' she said in surprise. 'I thought you were going to wait for me by the front door.'

'I was until I suddenly remembered there was something I wished to ask Lady Annabelle,' Barrington said, as calmly as though he had been sitting in one of the chairs reading a magazine. 'So I came back and found her up and moving around.'

Julia glanced at her friend. 'Are you feeling better, Anna? Your colour certainly seems to have returned.'

In point of fact, Anna's face felt like it was on fire. 'I am, thank you, Julia. It must have been…the tea.'

'I'm so glad. I've always sworn by it as a restorative. Here is the information you wanted, Sir Barrington,' Julia said, handing him a folded piece of parchment. 'I hope it helps.'

'I have a feeling it will go a long way towards solving the case,' Barrington said, remarkably composed in light of what had just happened. He turned and gave Anna a bow, nothing on his face to indicate that he had just found her depositing a stolen necklace into the heart of an ornamental palm. 'I'm quite sure I will be seeing you again very soon, Lady Annabelle.'

Far too soon, Anna reflected after he left. She had botched the job as badly as it was possible to botch it. She could only imagine what was going through Sir Barrington's head at that moment.

In point of fact, Barrington had so many thoughts running through his head he hardly knew where to begin. Lady Annabelle Durst had come into the baroness's house in possession of the missing sapphire-and-diamond necklace. She had been attempting to hide it in the base of the palm tree when he had unexpectedly walked back into the room and caught her.

Who was she trying to protect? An unusual question given what he had just seen, but in truth, the possibility of *her* having stolen the necklace had never crossed his mind. She had absolutely no motive and likewise no opportunity. It was also highly unlikely that she had simply stumbled upon the necklace and gone to the baroness's house intending to return it to its rightful owner. If that had been the case, she would have given it to the baroness the moment she'd walked into the room.

But she hadn't. She had held on to the necklace; upon finding herself alone, she had taken it out of her reticule and tried to conceal it in the base of the palm. A place the baroness *would* eventually have found it, though not, perhaps, today.

Obviously Anna hadn't wanted the baroness to discover that *she* was the one returning it. That would have necessitated a series of explanations that would have been awkward to say the least. But having been caught red-handed, what kind of explanation would she offer *him*?

Barrington found himself looking forward to that discussion.

The next question was where to conduct the interrogation? He couldn't do it at her home. Her brother or Peregrine Rand might be present, and possibly her father as well. Nor could he do it at his own house. If he invited her to call on a matter of business, it might raise questions in other people's minds. But if she wasn't calling on business, it was morally inappropriate for her to be there at all.

For that reason, as soon as Barrington got home, he wrote Anna a note, asking if he might take her for a drive in the park that afternoon. Being a lovely day, he suggested using the open carriage and assured her that, if she wished, his secretary could come along as chaperon. He doubted she would elect to speak in front of her maid, given the delicate nature of what they would be discussing.

Her response came back with equal promptness. Yes, she was available for a drive, and, no, she would not bring her maid. If chaperonage was required, she was happy to have it provided by his secretary, who had been very pleasant to her on the occasion of their last meeting.

Barrington smiled. Obviously the lady had already considered her options. If she was going to speak in front of anyone, she clearly preferred that it be his servant rather than hers.

He called for her at half past four and was not at all surprised to find her waiting for him. She had changed into a carriage gown of rose-coloured silk, the lace bodice threaded with deeper pink ribbons. Her hair was tucked up under another of her wide-brimmed bonnets and she carried a white parasol trimmed with deep pink ribbons. She looked absolutely enchanting—and completely innocent.

Surprising for a woman who had stepped so easily into the role of accomplice to a thief.

'Good afternoon, Sir Barrington,' she said as she walked down the steps to meet him.

'Lady Annabelle.' He smiled as he handed her into the barouche, 'Thank you for agreeing to meet with me.'

'I assumed there was no point in putting it off.'

'None whatsoever.' Barrington climbed in and sat down in the seat opposite. She waited until Sam flicked the whip and set the horses moving, the clatter of their hooves making it difficult for the conversation to be overheard, before she began to speak.

'I suspect you wish to ask me about what happened at Julia's this morning without my family being present for the interrogation. Just as well, since I suspect you intend to ask some rather problematic questions,' she said.

Problematic. An understatement to say the least. 'Shall we start with how you came to be in possession of the baroness's necklace?' he suggested.

'Ah, but I was not in possession of it,' she told him. 'I was walking by the French doors and chanced to look down and there it was! Lodged in the base of the palm.'

'Really. And how do you suppose it came to be there?'

The look she gave him was comprised of equal parts

surprise and disappointment. 'Really, Sir Barrington, is the answer to that not obvious?'

'Not to me.'

'Clearly, the thief dropped it as he was attempting to make his getaway.'

'His…getaway,' he repeated blankly.

'Yes. After he took the necklace from Julia's bedroom,' she said helpfully.

'So he did not make his escape through her bedroom window, but came downstairs to the drawing room and slipped out through the French doors.'

'Precisely.'

'An interesting theory,' Barrington said slowly. 'And plausible, I suppose, had my timing not been such that I opened the door in time to see *you* removing the necklace from your reticule and carefully inserting it *into* the palm.'

'Ah,' Anna said, sitting back. 'How unfortunate. Then it would probably be safe to say that you would find any attempt on my part to make you believe that I found the necklace quite by chance equally unbelievable.'

'No. I believe you *did* find the necklace and probably by chance, but the question of import now is *where* did you find it?' He sat forwards. 'In your brother's room—or your father's?'

He watched her cheeks turn bright red as her mouth dropped open in an exclamation of surprise. 'I cannot imagine why you would say such a thing—'

'For what it's worth,' he interrupted, '*I* think you found it in your father's room.'

She went rigid. 'Why would you say that?'

'Because Rand is still getting over his affair with Lady Yew and hasn't the clarity of mind to plan something like this. Likewise, if your brother had taken the necklace, I suspect he would either have held on to it until things cooled down, or he would have arranged to have it cut into smaller pieces that he could sell more easily. That leaves your father. Who, as it turns out, had both the motive and the opportunity to take it.'

'Motive?' Anna snorted. 'What possible motive could my father have had for stealing Julia's necklace?'

'The same as claimed by so many gentlemen of the *ton*,' Barrington said softly. 'Debt. In your father's case, through losses incurred at the racetrack.'

'How dare you! My father does not bet on horses!'

'Ah, but he does, dear lady. And though he wins more than he loses, he did suffer an unfortunate streak of bad luck last year from which he has been struggling to recover. A necklace like the baroness's would go a long way towards taking him—indeed, your entire family—out of dun territory.'

He knew immediately that what he'd told her had come as a complete shock. She'd obviously had no idea that her father had amassed such staggering debts, so the thought of him stealing a priceless necklace in an effort to clear himself had never occurred to her.

'If what you say is true—and I am not saying for a moment that I believe it is,' Anna said, 'my father would surely have had other ways of raising the money necessary to cover his obligations.'

'If he has, he has not availed himself of them. But let us not deviate from what we are here to discuss,' Barrington said firmly. 'The fact is, *you* came into the baroness's house with her necklace in your reticule, therefore, I have no choice but to ask you *where* you found it and *how* it came to be there. Unless you also wish to be viewed as a suspect.'

He saw the indecision on her face and knew she was debating as to how much to reveal. To say too much was to condemn someone else. To say too little was to condemn herself.

'Sir Barrington, if I tell you where I found the necklace, would you be willing to let it go?'

'In all honesty, I don't see how I can.'

'But you heard what Julia said. She is willing to drop all charges as long as the necklace is returned.'

'I understand that. But without a logical explanation as to *why* it was taken, we cannot know what the thief had in mind. At the very least, someone is getting away with a crime.' Barrington leaned forwards so that his face was close to hers. 'Someone took that necklace out of the baroness's house, Anna. I need to know who it was and why they did it. Because if their intent was to incriminate the person in whose room it was found, it's possible they may try again when they realise their first attempt has failed.'

'Incriminate!' Barrington saw the brief but unmistakable flash of hope in her eyes. 'Then you're open to the possibility that the person who *took* the necklace may not be the same person in whose room the necklace ended up.'

'I am open to the possibility, yes,' he admitted.

'And to the idea that…foul play may have been involved.'

'Oh, foul play has most definitely been involved, but who was the target? The baroness—or your father?'

His words fell into a strained silence. Barrington didn't have to be a mind reader to know that Anna was waging a silent battle with herself, struggling with how much she should say. Once she told him where the necklace had been found, there was no going back. The guilty party would be exposed and she would have been the one to expose them.

But did she trust him enough to know that he was only interested in finding out the truth? Or would her natural inclination to protect the people she loved stop her from giving him the answers he needed?

'Anna, I'm not out to condemn anyone,' he said softly.

'And what you tell me today will stay between you and me. No one else need know.'

'But you told Julia you would have to contact the authorities—'

'I said that because I couldn't allow her to believe that the perpetrator of the crime would be allowed to go free. Not until I have more information. But if you know something that can put me on the right path, I beg you to make it known.'

He held his breath while she made her decision. It was within her power to compromise the entire investigation. If she refused to tell him where she'd found the necklace, he would have no choice but to make accusations that would ultimately force her hand. And in doing so, he risked sacrificing any chance of ever gaining her good opinion.

Fortunately, something in what he'd said must have got through to her. With a heavy sigh, she said, 'The necklace was in Papa's room. Peregrine found it when he went to retrieve one of my father's watches. The necklace was lying next to it.'

Barrington wasn't sure whether to feel relief or remorse. 'Was it hidden away?'

'No. It was inside a small leather bag, but the bag was in plain sight.'

'So the thief intended that it be found easily,' Barrington said, his mind working. 'Does your father know you found it?'

Anna shook her head. 'Papa went to the country three days ago. He knows nothing about any of this.'

'Then we have no choice but to wait for his return to ask him about it. Either way, you must prepare yourself for the fact that word may leak out about the necklace having been found in his possession.'

'But it can't!' Anna said urgently. 'Papa would be disgraced!'

'I will do whatever I can to keep this quiet, Anna, but other people are involved and we have no control over what they might say. If the necklace was planted in your father's things, someone obviously wished to make trouble for him. The only way they can do that is by spreading rumours about where it was found. All *we* can do is work at uncovering the truth as quickly as possible,' Barrington said.

'But if you *believe* him innocent—'

'What *I* believe has nothing to do with it. Opinions are just that. To unerringly affix blame, I must have proof.'

'Then *find* the proof, Barrington,' Anna urged. 'Do whatever you have to, but find it. There is no question that my father is innocent.'

'May I point out that you were equally convinced of Mr Rand's innocence when it came to the charges levelled against him?' he said gently.

Anna sucked in her breath. 'That was unfair! Peregrine lied to me because he believed himself in love with that wretched woman. The situation with my father is entirely different. He has no reason to lie.'

'From my perspective, no one ever does,' Barrington said softly. 'However, I shall call upon your father when he returns and ask him what he knows about the necklace. His answers will go a long way towards determining where we go from here.'

She was silent for a moment, considering, perhaps, what he had said. 'I want to be there,' she said unexpectedly.

'I beg your pardon?'

'I want to be there when you interview my father. I want to hear what he has to say.'

Foreseeing difficulties she couldn't imagine, he said, 'I strongly advise against it.'

'Why?'

'Because questions will be asked that will be...uncomfortable.'

'For whom?'

'For both of you.'

Anna's face twisted. 'But if they help to uncover the truth, they must be asked. And I wish to be there to bear witness to my father's innocence.'

'Anna—'

'It's settled,' she said. 'I shall send you a note upon his return. And when you reply to it, I want you to make it known that I am to be included. Will you do that for me, Barrington?'

He knew from the stubborn set of her mouth that she wasn't going to back down. She intended to be there to witness her father's absolution. Well, he'd warned her. He could do no more than that. 'I will do this, as long as you know that I do it under duress.'

She smiled, confident of having won the argument. 'I don't need your approval, Barrington. Only your agreement. Besides, I doubt there's anything you can say to my father in my presence that will embarrass me any more than you finding me secreting a stolen necklace in the base of Julia's palm.'

Barrington sat back and sighed. 'I wouldn't be so sure about that.'

Anna was as good as her word. The day after her father's return, she sent Barrington a note advising him that her father was home, and of his agreement to the interview regarding the baroness's necklace. As such, when Barrington called at the house the following evening, Anna met him at the door, saying she had already advised her father of her intention to be present at the interview, given that she was as much involved in the matter as anyone else.

Thankfully, both Hayle and Peregrine were out, though Barrington thought he saw Hayle's carriage pull away just as he arrived. What he might make of it, Barrington didn't know or care. He was far more concerned with what he was about to find out from the earl.

In the drawing room, Anna sat down in the chair by the fireplace and clasped her hands together in her lap. Her expression was composed, but her eyes betrayed the nervousness she was feeling over what was to come.

By comparison, her father's face was untroubled, the result of his being completely unaware of what had transpired in his absence. 'Evening, Parker,' he said as Barrington walked into the room. 'May I offer you something in the way of refreshment?'

'Thank you. I'll have a brandy.'

'I'll join you. Sherry, Anna?'

'Thank you, Papa.'

As Cambermere crossed to the credenza to pour the drinks, Barrington moved closer to where Anna sat. 'This is your last chance,' he said, leaning down to speak quietly in her ear. 'Things are going to be said that *will* be difficult for you to hear. Are you quite sure you wish to stay?'

'Quite sure,' she said, though the slight quiver of her bottom lip told a different story.

Unaccountably annoyed, Barrington turned away. He hated seeing her like this. Hated knowing that the next few minutes were going to be even more difficult than what she had already endured. But there was no easy way of asking the earl what he must; while he wished there was some way of comforting Anna, he realised it was neither his place nor his right to do so. A fiancé or a husband could offer comfort. Not a man charged with finding out the truth about a crime in which her father might or might not be implicated.

'So, Anna tells me you've news about the baroness's

necklace,' the earl said, handing Barrington his brandy. 'Is it good news or bad?'

'A bit of both, I'm afraid. Your good health, my Lord,' Barrington said, raising his glass. 'Lady Annabelle.'

He saw the delicate colour in her cheeks as she tipped back her glass and wondered if it was the potency of the sherry or the unwitting caress in his voice when he'd spoken her name. He'd have to be more careful about that in the future.

Thankfully, the earl seemed oblivious. 'Well, what have you to tell us?'

'The good news,' Barrington began, 'is that the necklace has been found.'

'Has it, by Jove! Excellent!' There was no mistaking the relief in the earl's voice. 'Jul—that is, the baroness will be very pleased. Where did you find it?'

'That, I'm afraid, is the bad news.' Barrington felt Anna's eyes on him, but purposely kept his gaze on her father. 'The necklace was found in your bedroom.'

'My *bedroom*?' There was a moment of stunned silence as Cambermere's smile gave way to a look of utter confusion. 'You found Julia's necklace in this house...in *my* room?'

'Actually, Peregrine found it,' Anna said unhappily.

Her father turned to stare at her in bewilderment. 'And would you care to tell me what Peregrine was doing in my room?'

'He was looking for your watch.'

'My watch.'

'Yes. Edward said you had asked him to take it in for repair.'

'Yes, I did. But I asked Edward, not Peregrine.'

'But Edward had to go out, so he asked Peregrine to take it instead,' Anna said quickly. 'Edward told him where the watch was and when Peregrine went to get it, he found...the necklace.'

'The necklace was in my *wardrobe*?'

Unhappily, Anna nodded. 'In a leather bag next to your watch.'

'But that's impossible!' Cambermere said. 'The last time I saw that necklace, it was around Julia's throat. You were both there, at the dinner party.'

'Then you have no idea how the necklace came to be in your room?' Barrington asked slowly.

'I no more know how it came to be in *my* house than how it came to be taken from the baroness's.' The earl's expression hardened. 'I understood that was *your* job, Parker.'

The note of accusation was unmistakable, but Barrington merely inclined his head. Now came the hard part. 'It was reported to me that someone saw you take the necklace from the baroness's bedroom while she lay sleeping.'

Anna's complexion paled. *'Wh-what?'*

The earl was furious. 'How dare you, sir!'

'Sorry, Cambermere. I'm only repeating what I was told,' Barrington said calmly.

'I don't care what you were told! It's a damned lie!'

'Do you deny being alone with the baroness in her bedroom?' Barrington pressed.

Upon hearing Anna's muffled exclamation, the earl hissed, 'Damn it, man! *Must* we talk about this in front of my daughter?'

Barrington glanced at Anna, aware that her face had gone as red as the glass globes over the lamps. He'd known it would, but it was too late to do anything about it now. 'She asked to be present for the interview and since this is a critical point in the investigation, discussion of it cannot be avoided. If you wish to leave, Lady Annabelle, you are welcome to do so. I will call you back at a more appropriate time.'

'Can't imagine there *being* a more appropriate time

for something like this,' Cambermere muttered under his breath.

But Anna shook her head, struggling to overcome her embarrassment. 'No, I'll stay. And I am sorry, Papa. It isn't Sir Barrington's fault that I'm here. I insisted on being present during his questioning and I am truly sorry if my being here causes you embarrassment. But it is necessary that we get to the truth of the matter.'

'Lady Annabelle isn't mistaken, my Lord,' Barrington said. 'And I regret that the nature of the question had to be so indelicate. But while what you and Baroness von Brohm do behind closed doors is your own business, you would do well to remember that servants talk.'

'Servants!' Cambermere barked. 'Are you telling me it was a servant who claimed to have seen me take the necklace?' At Barrington's brief nod, the earl's face darkened ominously. 'Give me his name, Parker. Give me his name and I'll get to the bottom of this myself. I'm damned if I'll have my name dragged through the mud like some three-legged dog dragging a stick. Whoever told you they saw me take Julia's necklace was telling a lie. An out-and-out lie!'

'Be that as it may, it isn't a lie that you've spent time alone with the baroness.'

The earl coloured. 'No.'

'Then it's possible a servant may have seen you in her bedroom—'

'Perhaps it *is* best I leave.' Anna abruptly stood up, glancing apologetically at Barrington. 'I'm sure it would be easier for my father to talk about this if I weren't here—'

'No, wait,' the earl said. 'Wait.' He cleared his throat, then reached for his glass. After downing the contents, he set the empty glass on the table. 'This isn't the kind of thing one normally discusses in front of...one's children. Especially one's unmarried daughter. But it would be naïve of me to think that…word of this might not leak out and that you wouldn't eventually come to hear of it.' He glanced at his daughter and sighed. 'Yes, I've spent time alone with Julia. We've come to care for one another. I haven't tried to hide that from you, Anna. And given that we are both widowed, we felt there was no harm in…moving forward with our relationship. Can you understand that, my dear?'

Anna nodded, and though Barrington could see that she was still having a hard time meeting her father's eyes, her voice was steady when she said, 'I understand. And I don't blame you, Papa. But it doesn't make things any easier.'

'No, it doesn't,' Barrington agreed. 'Because the question remains, why would a servant make up a story about having seen you take the necklace if there was no truth to it? What would they stand to gain by such a lie? And how do you explain the necklace turning up in your room?'

'I can't explain it.' The earl shook his head, his anger spent. 'I have no answer for any of your questions, Parker. I sincerely wish I did.'

'I think it's someone trying to stir up mischief,' Anna said. 'Someone who holds a grudge against you. The maid, perhaps?'

'I questioned the young lady at length,' Barrington said. 'But she said she doesn't know you and I believe that she's telling the truth, so I doubt a grudge enters into it. Might it be someone to whom you owe money wanting to make things… unpleasant for you?'

The earl's head snapped up. 'What do you know about that?'

'Only that you had a run of bad luck at the track last year,' Barrington said quietly, 'and that you have vowels outstanding to Lords Greening, Featherstone and Blakeley. Your son has also amassed rather staggering debts thanks to losses incurred at the faro table. Debts you have also been endeavouring to pay off.'

He heard Anna's sharp intake of breath. 'Is this true, Papa? Do you and Edward truly owe so much?' When he reluctantly nodded, Anna said, 'Why didn't you tell me?'

'Because it doesn't concern you,' Cambermere growled, though not unkindly. He glanced at Barrington and sighed. 'I can't deny that there are those to whom I owe money, but the debts are not so large that someone need go to these lengths. I assured Greening and Featherstone they would have their money by the end of the month, and Blakely a month or two after.'

'And your son's debts?'

'With luck, they'll be paid off by the end of the year.'

'But what have debts to do with the baroness's necklace being found in Papa's room?' Anna asked.

'They provide a reasonable motive for theft,' Barrington explained. 'A gentleman's debts are seldom a well-kept secret. One has only to read the morning papers. I found out without any difficulty that your father's and brother's combined debts tally to well over sixty thousand pounds.'

Anna blanched. 'Dear God, so *much*!'

'You needn't sound so horrified, it isn't as large as that,' her father muttered. 'I've managed to pay off thirty thousand of it already.'

'Unfortunately, your son accumulated another twenty this past week,' Barrington said quietly.

The earl was aghast. 'Twenty thousand pounds—in *five days*?'

'I'm sorry to be the one to break the bad news to you, Cambermere, but you would have found out soon enough. And I suspect that whoever took the necklace knew of those debts and planned on using them as the justification behind your stealing the necklace.'

The earl seemed to age ten years as he stood there. 'I can't believe that someone would go to these lengths to incriminate me. But I stand by what I said. I did *not* steal Julia's necklace. I wouldn't dream of doing such a cowardly, selfish thing. To think how it would hurt her...' He transferred his gaze to Barrington. 'I don't suppose you have any idea who *is* behind this?'

'Not yet,' Barrington said, 'but I will find out.'

'And until you do, I'm the guilty party,' the earl said heavily.

'You are *not*, Papa!' Anna cried. 'We all know you didn't take the necklace.'

'You and I know that, my dear, but I'll wager Parker has his doubts. And so he should. Right now, the finger of blame is pointing squarely at me.'

'Only as a result of circumstantial evidence.'

'No. As a result of the fact that I was supposedly seen taking the necklace by a member of Julia's staff, and that the said necklace was found in my room by a member of my own family,' her father said bluntly. 'The proof could hardly be less circumstantial.' He clasped his hands behind his back and glanced at the man standing opposite. 'Well, what do you intend to do?'

'For now, I shall tell the baroness that I know where the necklace is, but that I am not at liberty to say where, or to reveal the identity of the person who took it.'

'She's bound to ask,' Anna said.

'Yes, but I am not required to give her an answer. I'll tell her it may compromise the integrity of the investigation.'

'Decent of you, Parker,' the earl said gruffly. 'I'd hate having Julia think she couldn't trust me.'

It was that more than anything else that convinced Barrington of Cambermere's innocence. If a man was that worried about what a woman thought of him, he wouldn't knowingly do something that would destroy his chances of having a relationship with her.

And yet, as he walked home after the interview, Barrington thought about his feelings for Anna and realised he was guilty of doing just that. He was conducting an investigation into the theft of an extremely valuable necklace and, given the lack of any other viable culprit, was still holding her father up as the leading suspect—and earning Anna's resentment as a result.

But *was* Cambermere guilty? Barrington's gut told him no, but he'd met skilful liars before. Men who swore on their children's heads that they were good family men who never lied, cheated, or stole so much as a crust of bread. All the while they were beating their wives half-senseless and mugging old men for brass buttons.

Oh, yes, he knew all about the complexities of deceit. Lies rolled off the tongues of the rich as easily as they did off the tongues of the poor. He'd even come across men he'd *wanted* to believe. Upright, likeable men whom he had respected until he'd found out what they were beneath the polished manners and charming smiles.

Good men turned bad, Barrington called them. Whether by chance or inclination, somewhere along the line they'd made the wrong choices. Some were driven by greed, others by desperation. And once a man faltered, it was only a matter of time until he did so again; the crime becoming a little darker, the stakes a little higher.

Had the earl faltered? Or was it all a carefully constructed plot to make it look as though he had? That was the ultimate question. And until Barrington ascertained who stood to gain by the earl's downfall, the final answer would remain just beyond his grasp. Tantalisingly close, yet agonisingly far.

## Chapter Twelve

Anna had no particular desire to pay a call on Julia the following day. Given what she knew about the necklace—*and* about her father's relationship with Julia—she feared it would be both embarrassing and awkward. But when she received Julia's beautifully written note asking her to visit, Anna knew it would be churlish to refuse. The woman's spirits were desperately low as it was. How could she possibly be so cruel as to avoid her now, simply because she had no idea how to act?

And so she went, determined to appear as positive as possible. After all, there was really no reason for Julia to talk about the necklace. She knew the investigation was ongoing and that Barrington would inform her of any new leads the moment they became available. And she certainly wouldn't bring up her relationship with Anna's father. Married or widowed ladies did not talk to single ladies about matters pertaining to the bedroom, so there was no reason to think she would bring that up.

No, Anna was quite sure she was making a mountain out of a molehill. She and Julia would pass their time talking about the new books they were reading, or the poetry recital at Mrs McInley's, or what they planned to wear to Lady Schuster's masquerade a week from Friday. Safe, comfortable topics all.

Unfortunately, all thoughts of comfort fled when Anna walked into the drawing room and found, not just Julia seated on the blue velvet settee, but her brother, Edward, as well.

'Edward! What are you doing here?' Anna exclaimed.

'Am I not allowed to pay morning calls the same as everyone else?'

'I thought you did not care for the custom,' she said bluntly.

Her brother's handsome face curved into an angelic smile. 'A man's likes and dislikes can change given the right motivation.'

'Pray do not take him to task him, Anna,' Julia said quickly. 'He has been most diverting company. He bade me speak about Vienna and I was amazed at how homesick I became. Then, we started talking about you—'

'Me?' Anna levelled a sardonic glance at her brother. 'I can't imagine what the two of you would have to say about me.'

'Can you not?' Edward said innocently. 'I would have thought the possibilities endless. However, in this instance, we were talking about Sir Barrington Parker and the fact that he seems rather taken with you. He calls frequently at the house and I understand you have driven with him in the park. Although,' Edward added with a smile, 'I think he calls as much to see Father and Peregrine as he does Anna, so I suppose I could be mistaken as to which member of the family he is the most interested in.'

'Perhaps it would be safe to say that Sir Barrington has become a good friend of the family,' Julia said, obviously sensing an edge of conflict in the air.

'You could say that.' Edward turned to smile at his sister. 'As you already know, Parker is something of an expert when it comes to investigating the dark doings of others. And unfortunately, my family is no stranger to infamy. Peregrine, for example, was foolish enough to involve himself in a sordid affair with the Marchioness of Yew—'

'I'm sure the baroness has no desire to hear about that, Edward,' Anna said coldly.

'Why not? I found it extremely amusing,' her brother replied unrepentantly. 'Can you imagine, Baroness, an unsophisticated country boy coming to London for the first time and believing himself of interest to the beautiful Lady Yew? In fact, he even went so far as to claim that she was in love with him and that she had every intention of leaving her husband to be with him.'

'Really?' Julia flicked an uncertain glance in Anna's direction. 'I had not heard.'

'It happened before you arrived in London,' Anna said tightly. 'And my brother has no business speaking of it. Apologies have been offered and given that the marquess is agreeable to putting the matter behind him, I see no reason why my brother should not do the same.'

It was an awkward moment and Anna could practically feel the tension vibrating in the air. But she was damned if she was going to let Edward embarrass her in front of Julia with sly remarks about Barrington or inflammatory ones about Peregrine.

Unfortunately, her brother was a master at turning the other cheek. 'How unfortunate it is that social calls must be of such limited duration, Baroness. I fear my time is up. But I did enjoy talking to you about Vienna. As you say, it is a beautiful city and I look forward to seeing it again, now that travel around Europe is so much easier.'

'You must be sure to visit Schonbrunn Palace,' Julia said,

happy for the change of subject. 'It is one of the loveliest places on earth.'

'If you recommend it, I will be sure to include it in my travels. Perhaps we might even visit it together one day.' Edward rose and bowed over her hand. 'Until tomorrow.' Then, straightening, he nodded at his sister. 'Anna.'

Anna inclined her head, not quite in dismissal, but not far off—and Edward knew it. His eyes cooled as he smiled down at her. 'You may be interested in knowing that just before you arrived, I was telling the baroness that I had stumbled upon some information with regards to her necklace. I expect to have more news very soon.'

He left the room with an elegant bow, but in the silence that followed, Anna felt as though a hand was closing around her throat. *He knew about the necklace. And he was going to tell Julia her father was the one who'd taken it.* There could be no other explanation for what he'd just said. And in exposing their father as the thief, Anna knew it would destroy any chance he might have had for a future with Julia. Worse, it would go a long way towards establishing Edward in a more favourable position with her—which meant she had to convince Barrington not only to tell Julia about the necklace, but to return it to her as soon as possible. Before any more harm could be done...

'Anna, are you all right?' Julia enquired softly.

Anna looked up, aware that her worries must have been reflected on her face. 'Fine. It's just that Edward and I are not on the best of terms these days.'

'No, I thought not. Never mind, I'm told it often happens between siblings,' Julia said, making an attempt at light-heartedness. 'But I am surprised Lord Hayle and Mr Rand are not on better terms. I would have thought they'd be good company for one another, being so close in age.'

'I believe that was my father's hope as well, but it is not to be,' Anna admitted with a sigh. 'They are two very different men and they do not see eye to eye on anything.'

'How unfortunate,' Julia murmured. 'Your brother has been so kind to me. He's called several times this week to see how I was faring and to ask if there was anything I needed. When I enquired as to how your father went on, he said it was unlikely he would call, given the nature of the investigation surrounding my necklace. I didn't know what he meant by that.' Julia chewed thoughtfully on her lower lip. 'Or what he meant when he said he was following up on some leads of his own.'

'I don't know either,' Anna said, hoping she sounded convincing. So, Edward was paying regular calls on Julia and dropping hints as to his father's involvement in the theft. What a dutiful son, she thought cynically.

She *had* to talk to Barrington. If Julia was to hear from Edward that their father had taken the necklace—

'Ah, Jones, there you are,' Julia said as a maid came in with the tea tray. 'I was just about to ring.'

'Beg pardon for the delay, ma'am,' the girl said. 'Cook wasn't able to find the right jam.' She put the tray down hard and one of the sandwiches fell to the floor. 'Oh, I'm ever so sorry.'

'That's all right,' Julia said as the girl bent to retrieve it. 'That will be all.'

The girl's cheeks went as bright as cherries, and hastily stuffing the fallen sandwich into her apron pocket, she bobbed a curtsy and left.

'My apologies, Anna,' Julia said. 'The girl is new and sadly in need of training.'

'What happened to your other maid?'

'Unfortunately, Miss Smith left to attend to her sick mother. At least, that's what she told me, though I wonder if there might not be a man involved,' Julia confided. 'I noticed a definite change in her over the last little while, both in manner and in appearance. She lost weight and didn't seem as competent at her job. When I asked her if she was all right, she assured me she was, but given that I wasn't about to pry into her personal life, I left it at that. But I was sorry to lose her. It's not easy finding good staff.'

No, it wasn't, Anna reflected, but neither was finding a good position. Were Miss Smith's reasons for leaving as simple as Julia made them out to be? Anna hadn't forgotten the sight of her brother and the maid locked in a passionate embrace. Had Miss Smith been caught in the arms of another guest and the discovery forced Julia's hand? If the maid had allowed Edward to kiss her, who was to say that she hadn't allowed other men to do the same—or worse?

Still, Anna knew it was none of her concern. Servants no more appreciated their affairs being discussed by their betters, than those above stairs liked thinking their problems were being discussed by those below. As such, she wasn't at all sorry when the conversation veered back to the upcoming masquerade and to the elaborate costume Julia was planning to wear. They spent the next half-hour happily discussing hairstyles, with neither Edward nor the missing necklace being mentioned again.

It wasn't often that Barrington found himself in a quandary. His nature was such that when he was given a task, he set about resolving it as efficiently as possible. That was the manner in which he had approached the Marquess of Yew's request that he find his wife's latest lover, and the manner in which he had expected to solve the case of the baroness's missing necklace.

But when faced with the daughter of the prime suspect *insisting* that he return the necklace *before* the identity of the thief could be confirmed, Barrington realised that resolution was going to be neither quick nor easy.

*That* was his dilemma as he stood beside her at the Billinghams' soirée two nights later and the reason for his preoccupation. Because by doing what Anna asked, he risked compromising the entire investigation. There were always a series of steps that needed to be followed. Questions that had to be asked. Leads that had to be investigated. Following the steps in order helped ensure that he didn't miss a vital piece of information.

Doing what Anna suggested threatened to throw everything off. It was like closing the barn door after the horse had bolted. Granted, he was relieved to have the necklace back in one piece, but it wasn't just a simple matter of handing it back to the baroness now and calling the case closed. He had to find out what had prompted the theft in the first place. He'd meant what he'd said when he'd told Anna that if the thief found out his first attempt to discredit the earl had failed, he might well try again.

But how could he not try to accommodate her when doing so would make her so happy—

'Barrington?'

Her voice, gently insistent, recalled him to the moment. Guiltily, he looked down to find her watching him. 'Forgive me, Anna, I was following a train of thought.' They had slipped into the comfortable habit of calling each other by their first names when they were alone and Barrington was glad of it. Somehow, it lessened the distance between them. Now, as he gazed down at her, he tried not to notice how glorious she looked in the beautiful cream-coloured gown, the soft swell of her breasts rising provocatively above the edging of fine lace. 'You were saying something about your brother?'

'I was saying that I'm afraid he's going to expose my father in front of Julia,' Anna whispered. 'Why else would he have said what he did?'

'I don't know.' Barrington tried focusing his attention on her face, but that didn't work either. Her smile captivated him, her mouth entranced him. And her lips...her lips were an invitation to seduction—

'Barrington, are you even listening to me?' she accused.

'Yes, of course.' He dragged his mind back with considerable effort. 'What makes you think your brother would turn on your father in such a way?'

'I'm not saying he would. But you said yourself, there's been tension between them of late and that's why I need you to return the necklace to Julia as soon as possible. If she has it in her hands, she won't believe that my father had anything to do with its theft, no matter what kind of rumours she hears.'

'Why would she believe your father guilty of having taken the necklace if she *didn't* have it in her hands?' Barrington asked logically. 'Has she any reason to doubt your father's integrity?'

'No, but Edward can be very persuasive when he wants to be. If he wished to put my father in a bad light with Julia, he is entirely capable of doing so. And I didn't like the way he was looking at her. It was far too...familiar. And Julia admitted that he had been to see her several times since the theft of the necklace.'

Barrington let his gaze travel around the room, his thoughts occupied with what she had just said. So, the son was paying court to the woman his father was in love with and making no attempt to hide it. It wasn't a pleasant situation for anyone and it had the potential to cause considerable harm. 'Anna, I understand your concern—'

'No, I don't think you do. You don't know my brother the way I do. You don't how vindictive he can be.'

Having born witness to Hayle's temper during the fencing match, Barrington was strongly tempted to disagree, but, equally aware that voicing an opinion would only stir up another hornet's nest, he said, 'Very well. If it means that much to you, I will return the necklace to the baroness tomorrow.'

'You will?'

'Yes, but you are to tell no one that I've done so, and I shall counsel the baroness to do the same. The integrity of the investigation *must* be maintained—as much as it is now possible to do so.'

Anna glanced down at the floor, but when she raised her head and smiled at him, Barrington caught his breath. He had been the recipient of a thousand smiles, but none had ever affected him to the degree hers did. 'Thank you, Barrington. I am now and for ever in your debt.'

*And you are now and for ever in my heart.*

The sentiment came unbidden, and Barrington stood motionless, the realisation having caught him totally unawares. *He was in love with her.* He had no idea when it had happened. All he knew was that he wanted to pull her into his arms and whisper a thousand secret longings in her ear. To take her to his bed and make love to her until they were both weak and trembling. To obliterate every thought from her mind that didn't involve him.

But he couldn't do any of those things because nothing had really changed. Anna was still who she was and he was still who he was. Their situations hadn't altered. Only the way he thought of her…

'Parker! A word in private, if you don't mind.'

The crisp, imperious voice had Barrington turning around in surprise. 'Good evening, Colonel.' Curious. Tanner never spoke to him when other people were around. He wondered what could have prompted the change. 'I was just finishing speaking to Lady Annabelle.' He turned back and bowed over her hand. 'Would you excuse me?'

'Of course. But we will speak again soon?'

He saw the glimmer of hope in her eyes and felt it echoed within his heart, though for entirely different reasons. 'You may be sure of it.'

She departed in a whisper of silk, the sweet scent of gardenias lingering in the air. Barrington didn't follow her progress across the room because he knew better than to display an interest in her here, where all the world could see. But he felt her absence keenly. 'You wished to speak to me, Colonel?'

'Damn right I wished to speak to you. I want to know if you've found Elizabeth!'

'I have, but I fear you will not be happy with what I am about to tell you.'

'Why not?'

'Because it turns out that Miss Paisley has come under someone else's protection.'

'The devil you say!' The Colonel's bushy white eyebrows drew together. 'You mean...she's left me?'

'I'm afraid so,' Barrington replied gently.

'But why? I gave her everything she asked for: gowns, trinkets, pretty ribbons for her hair.'

'Can you think of any other reason she might have left?'

The Colonel's cheeks coloured. 'I never asked her to do anything disrespectful, if that's what you're suggesting. Wouldn't consider such a thing.'

Barrington studied the face of the man before him and felt a genuine stab of pity. Tanner obviously had feelings of affection for Miss Paisley, but if *she* didn't care about him in return...

'I have no answers as to why she left, Colonel,' he said quietly. 'I can only tell you that she did.'

'Who is he?'

'I'd rather not say.'

'Why not? That's why I engaged you, isn't it?' Tanner said gruffly.

'No, you engaged me to find out where Miss Paisley was and if she was safe. That's what I've done. There's really no value in my telling you anything more than that.' Besides, he would no doubt find out soon enough on his own, Barrington reflected. The movement of mistresses between society gentlemen was not a closely guarded secret.

The Colonel knew it, too. He gazed across the room, disappointment evident on his face. 'So you don't think she will come back?'

'I have no reason to believe she will, no.'

The older man nodded. 'Right. Well then, I suppose that's an end to it. At least I know she's all right.' He cleared his throat, rocked back and forth on the balls of his feet. 'Appreciate you taking it on, Parker.'

'I'm sorry the news wasn't better, Colonel.'

Tanner nodded, but walked away before Barrington had a chance to say anything more. It was clear that Miss Paisley's defection had hurt him and Barrington was again moved to wonder what had prompted her to leave. The Colonel had taken her off the streets and given her a place to live, paid for the clothes on her back and made sure there was food on her table—yet she had still walked away.

Why? What prompted a woman like that to leave a man who had been so good to her? The arrival of a wealthier lover? One with a loftier title? Surely that could be of no consequence to a woman like Elizabeth Paisley. She was a lady's maid turned prostitute, not a blushing débutante looking for a husband. And while Hayle was certainly the younger man, Barrington doubted he would have given her more in the way of jewels or clothes than the Colonel. It was quite possible he'd given her less, believing that mistresses were twenty to the dozen. Tanner, being older and wiser, knew more about life and love...

*Love.* Oh, dear God, surely that wasn't what had lured Elizabeth Paisley away? The misplaced belief that Hayle might offer her more than just a bed? That he had genuine feelings for her?

As unlikely as it seemed, Barrington knew it wasn't an impossibility. If Miss Paisley had any degree of education, she would know more of the world than the hardened doxies who made their livings on the streets and might well believe that such things happened. According to Tanner, she *had* come from a decent family, only to fall on hard times when her parents had died. She had tried making a living as a lady's maid, but had fallen victim, as so many women did, to the wandering hands of the master and, without the references necessary to obtain another post, had ended up on the streets.

Yes, it was entirely possible that Eliza's move had been prompted by unattainable dreams, Barrington reflected sadly. He'd rather think it was that than something more disturbing. Something that bordered on the devious. Something that was in all ways far less admirable...

Anna stood by the edge of the dance floor and listened to the lilting strains of a waltz. The dance was far less scandalous than when it had first made its appearance in the ballrooms of society, but it was still one of the few that could raise eyebrows. Gentlemen sometimes moved a little too close and, if a mother's watchful eye was turned, a hand might draw a slender waist nearer or hold a lady's hand tighter than was acceptable.

Anna had spent a good deal of time watching the actions of couples on the floor. While it was not advisable for single girls to dance the waltz, there were always those who did and who had required Anna's services not long after. Tonight, however, her thoughts were not on the dancers, but on the situation with her father and her brother, and even more so with the uncomfortable predicament in which she found herself with Barrington.

She knew that by asking him to give the necklace back to Julia, she was asking him to do something that went against his principles, but she was so afraid for her father's reputation that it was more than she could do to withdraw the request. But what damage had it done to her relationship with Barrington? It felt as though they had not been easy with one another for an age. And though she knew they would not have a future together, why, oh, why couldn't she just put him from her mind altogether? This constant thinking about him was wearing her down. Why couldn't she just accept that he was beyond her reach and move on?

*Because you want to be the one,* whispered the voice inside her head. *The woman he turns to in the darkness of the night. The one who smoothes the lines of worry from his brow, and who makes him forget everything but the sweetness of the moment...*

'Anna, where have you been?' Lydia said, coming up to her. 'I've been looking for you all evening!'

'Why?' Anna said, lingering in dreams. 'Is something wrong?'

'I've just heard the most dreadful thing.' Lydia glanced around, lowered her voice. 'About your father.'

The dreams vanished, destroyed in the rush of returning reality. 'Tell me!'

'Not here.' Taking her arm, Lydia led Anna to a far corner of the room. When she was sure they were beyond anyone's hearing, she said, 'There's a rumour going around that—' she broke off, blushing furiously. 'Oh dear, this isn't at all easy.'

'Please, Lydia. I must know!'

'Yes, of course you must. It's just that…I can't believe he would do something like this.'

'He?'

'Mr Rand.'

'Peregrine?' Anna frowned in confusion. 'I thought you said you'd heard something about my father?'

'I have.' Lydia took a deep breath and said, 'Apparently, someone overheard Mr Rand say that…he'd found the baroness's necklace amongst your father's things.'

*'What?'* Anna didn't realise how loud she'd spoken until she saw heads begin to turn in their direction. Quickly forcing a smile, she waited for them to look away again before leaning in closer to Lydia. 'There must be some mistake. Peregrine thinks the world of my father. He would *never* do something like this.'

'That's what I thought, too, but I'm just repeating what I heard. And there's more,' Lydia said unhappily. 'Rumour has it that your brother's debts have been paid off and people are wondering where the money came from.'

Anna's first thought was that they had not acted quickly enough. Her second was to wonder how to stem the damage before matters got any worse. 'Who started the rumour?'

'No one seems to know. But it isn't a secret that your father and brother were having trouble meeting their debts. So when word leaked out that the baroness's necklace had been stolen and that she and your father were…well, involved, it was suggested that your father might have seen an easy way out of his financial difficulties. Then when Mr Rand said he'd found the necklace in your father's things, followed by word of your brother's debts being cleared, it only added fuel to the fire.' She broke off, sick at heart. 'I'm so sorry, Anna, but I thought you should know.'

Anna muttered something unrepeatable, apologised to

Lydia, then quickly left the room. She was seldom moved to profanity, but what else could she say when matters kept going so terribly wrong? Peregrine had been discovered in an illicit affair with Lady Yew. Everyone seemed to know that her father and brother were mired in debt. And now rumours were flying that her father was a thief and that a member of his own family had given him up.

It was enough to make a saint turn to the devil!

But even as anger and disbelief swelled at the thought of Peregrine having betrayed her father's secret, common sense told her it couldn't be true. Peregrine would *never* reveal what he had seen. She had been there with him the day he'd found the necklace. She had seen the anguish on his face and known that he'd suffered over that discovery as much as she had.

No, Peregrine wasn't the one who'd started the rumour. Barrington was right; the person who wished her father harm was definitely the one behind all this. The lie was just one more piece in a carefully devised plot to incriminate her father, and whoever had laid the groundwork for this unspeakable crime had done their job well. Her father's reputation couldn't *hope* to survive a constant barrage of rumours and innuendos. He would be destroyed, given the cut direct by those who mattered in society. Even those who might have the courage to defend him risked being cut, and those who believed him guilty would never speak to him again. But there had to be a way of finding out who it was and of exposing him for what he'd done.

Anna thought back over everything Barrington had said. *...a maid in the baroness's house...gone in to check on her mistress...saw him take the necklace...*

So, a maid had seen her father take the necklace. Which maid? The same one Anna had seen kissing her brother in the darkness of the deserted study? A very pretty maid who'd left the baroness's employ shortly after the necklace disappeared—

Anna gasped. Was it possible? She'd seen Edward and the maid together *before* the necklace had disappeared. Then the maid had left and a few days later Anna had discovered that Edward had acquired a new mistress. She'd overheard him talking to one of his friends about a girl named Eliza.

Coincidence—or something more calculated?

Unlike many of his friends, Edward didn't keep his mistresses close at hand. He preferred to put them up in a house on a quiet street south of Regent's Park. Fortunately, Anna had stumbled upon the address one day whilst cleaning out a desk drawer and committed it to memory.

Now, as she stepped out of the carriage onto what was a clearly less than affluent street, she was glad she'd thought to do so. She scanned the row of plates and found Number Nineteen second to last in the row—an unprepossessing brick townhouse with dark shutters and blackened chimney pots.

Paying the driver a guinea to wait, Anna took a deep breath and started towards the door. Her heart was pounding and though part of her wanted to turn around and get back in the cab, curiosity and a need to discover the truth drove her forwards. She raised her hand to the knocker and brought it down sharply, three times.

An older woman wearing a white apron over a stiff black gown opened the door. Her face was hard and unforgiving as she stared down at her caller. 'Yes?'

'Is Miss Smith in?' Anna enquired.

Watching the woman run a critical eye over her appearance, Anna was glad she'd thought to wear the clothes she had. Dressed in a plain gown and pelisse in a nondescript shade of brown, a straw bonnet the style of which was a few years out of date, and leather gloves that were far from new, she resembled nothing so much as a governess or a servant, an assessment clearly shared by the housekeeper. 'What would you be wanting with Eliza?'

'I'd like to talk to her, if I may. We used to work together at Baroness von Brohm's and I was wondering—'

'Justine, is that you?' a voice floated down from the landing. 'How did you get—oh!'

Eliza Smith was halfway down the stairs before she realised that her visitor wasn't who she thought. Her pretty face fell and her smile disappeared. But when she looked at Anna again and recognition dawned, her expression of disappointment changed to one of fear. With a muffled cry, she bolted back up the stairs.

'Miss Smith, wait!' Anna cried. 'I need to talk to you!' She went to move past the housekeeper, but found her way blocked. 'Kindly step aside.'

'I don't think the girl wants to see you,' the woman said.

'Well, I'd like to see her,' Anna said. 'If you'll just let me through…'

It was like trying to move a mountain. The woman wouldn't budge and, given that the doorway wasn't wide enough for Anna to go around her, she was stuck. 'Why won't you let me see her?'

'Because the master said I wasn't to let anyone in and I know better than to disobey,' the woman said. 'He'd have my job, and I've six mouths at home to feed.'

Recognising desperation, Anna stepped back, her eyes narrowing even as her stance straightened. 'How much does your master pay you?'

The woman's cheeks flushed, both as a result of the autocratic tone and by Anna's sudden change in stature. 'That's none of your business.'

'It could be.' Anna opened her reticule and taking out a

coin, held it in front of the woman's face. 'This would feed your family for a month.'

'That's a guinea!'

'It is. And if you let me pass, it's yours.'

'Who are you?' the housekeeper asked, staring at the coin like a hungry dog eyeing a bone. 'Maids and governesses don't carry that kind of blunt.'

'I am neither a lady's maid nor a governess. And I have plenty more of these.'

It was shameless blackmail, but Anna suspected it was the only way she was going to get what she wanted. She needed the woman's co-operation and, if necessary, she was prepared to buy her way into the house. Fortunately, she didn't have long to wait. The housekeeper grabbed the coin and jerked her head in the direction of the stairs.

'Go on then, but be quick about it. Gold won't keep me safe if he comes round and finds I've let you in. Five minutes is all you get!'

Deciding it would have to be enough, Anna ran up the darkened stairway, her soft-soled boots making no sound on the threadbare carpet. Turning right at the landing, she found herself standing in front of a closed door. 'Miss Smith?' she called, trying the handle and finding it locked.

'Go away!'

'Eliza, please! I need to talk to you!'

'I've got nothing to say!'

'That's not true. You can help a lot of people by talking to me,' Anna insisted.

'I don't care about other people,' came the girl's muffled reply. 'Nobody cares about *me*.'

'*I* care,' Anna said. 'And if you'll let me, I'll get you out of here.'

Silence followed her rashly offered promise, leaving Anna to wonder if she'd said the right thing. If this was the girl's only home, she might not be all that anxious to leave. But looking at the water stains in the ceiling, the faded and peeling wallpaper, and the warped floorboards beneath her feet, Anna couldn't help thinking how lowering it must be to come home to this every night.

'Eliza, please!' Seconds were ticking by. Any minute, the housekeeper would appear at the bottom of the stairs, demanding that she leave, and Anna wasn't so naïve as to think she would get a second chance at getting back inside. 'I promise you won't come to any harm. Just open the door.'

Out on the street, Anna heard a vendor raucously hawking his wares. She heard the sounds of children laughing and the clatter of carriage wheels as they rattled past the front door. Normal, everyday sounds—and still the door remained closed. Which meant Anna had no choice. She only had time for one last desperate attempt.

'You won't get away with it, Eliza,' she said quietly against the door. 'I know you took the necklace. And I *will* go to the authorities if you refuse to talk to me.'

# Chapter Thirteen

That was all she said. Fear or anger would compel the girl to open the door now because it didn't matter whether the accusations were true or not. A servant accused of stealing from her employer couldn't hope to win her case.

Eliza Smith was obviously smart enough to know that. Moments later, the door opened and she stood silently in the doorway.

Anna caught her breath. The girl facing her now wasn't the same pretty maid who had served her tea at Julia's house. Her once-shining hair hung lank around her small face, her complexion was ashen and there were faint purple shadows on her cheeks and around her beautiful green eyes. Dear God, what had Edward done to her? 'Are you all right?'

'Fine.' The girl lifted her chin, but Anna saw the way her lips trembled. 'What do you want?'

'To ask you a few questions.' Anna made no attempt to move forwards. 'I think you know about what.'

The girl didn't say a word. She simply turned and walked back into the room, every step a reflection of her state of mind. Anna followed, mutely taking in the details of her surroundings. The walls were papered in the same faded maroon silk as in the hallway, the curtains were pale grey and frayed at the edges, and the bed and dressing table... well, she'd seen better furnishings in a boarding school. Her brother obviously hadn't expended any time or money on the upkeep of this house.

'How did you get past Betty?' Eliza asked in a flat voice. 'She was told not to let anyone in.'

'I bribed her,' Anna said, closing the door. 'I wasn't going to leave without seeing you.' She took a few steps into the room, and then stopped. 'What happened to you, Eliza? Those bruises on your face—'

'I fell,' the girl said, abruptly turning away. 'And hit my head on the door.'

'Eliza—'

'It was foolish you coming here,' Eliza said, an element of fear in her voice. 'My gentleman could be back at any time.'

'I know who owns this house, Eliza,' Anna said gently. 'And judging from those bruises, you would do well to get away from him as soon as possible.'

'I can't,' Eliza said, shaking her head. 'He'll kill me.'

'No, he won't,' Anna said. Her brother might be many things, but a murderer wasn't one of them. 'But I need you to tell me the truth about your relationship with Edward and about the baroness's necklace.'

The girl collapsed on to the bed, her dark hair falling forwards. 'I can't!'

'Yes, you can,' Anna sat down beside her. 'If you did nothing wrong, you have nothing to be afraid of.'

'But I *did* do something wrong.' The girl looked up and Anna saw tears forming in the huge green eyes. 'I didn't want to, but he told me it would be all right. That I wouldn't get caught.'

'He being my brother,' Anna clarified.

The girl nodded. 'He told me the baroness had so many other lovely bits of jewellery that she'd never miss that one piece. And he told me he'd protect me if anyone came along asking questions.'

'But if you knew that what you were doing was wrong, why did you do it?'

Eliza stared at the dirty bedcover. 'Because he asked me to. He said that...if he had the necklace, he could sell it and then we'd have the money we needed to run away together.'

The cruelty of the lie stabbed at Anna's heart. 'And you believed him.'

'I loved him,' Eliza said, dragging the back of her hand across her eyes. 'I did from the very first time I saw him. I would have done anything to make him happy. *Anything.*'

'But you must have known it couldn't work between you. What about the difference in your situations?'

'Edward assured me that it didn't matter.' Eliza looked at her and Anna saw the naked hope shining in her eyes even now. 'He said that because I spoke properly and carried myself well, no one would know I wasn't a lady. Especially when I was all dressed up. And I did have nice clothes when I met him.'

Suspecting that the clothes were cast-offs from a previous employer, Anna said, 'You were lucky that your former mistress was so generous.'

Eliza bit her lip, guilt adding to the misery on her face. 'They weren't from an employer, my lady. They were from a gentleman. I did work as a lady's maid, but when the mistress found her son trying to break into my room, she said I'd have to leave and that she wouldn't provide me with references. So I left, and when I couldn't find decent work, I ended up in a brothel.'

Anna sighed. It wasn't an unusual story. Girls in Eliza's

position had very few avenues open to them, even those who, like her, were fortunate enough to have some degree of education or training. 'That must have been very difficult for you.'

'It was horrible,' Eliza said bluntly. 'But, it could have been worse. Mrs Brown, the woman who kept the place, made sure we had good food and there was always medical care if any of the girls needed it. She told me her clients were very particular about that kind of thing and that she couldn't afford to have any of her girls getting sick.'

Anna nodded, knowing how miserable the lives of girls forced into prostitution could be. Even for those who had the good luck to find an establishment where the abbess cared about their welfare, a girl's worth diminished with every year that passed. As her looks faded, so did her value. 'Were you there long?'

'No. I met the Colonel…the gentleman I mentioned…on my first night. He was a kind man. I think he knew how frightened I was and he was…very gentle with me,' Eliza said, avoiding Anna's eyes, though two bright spots of colour stood out on her cheeks. 'Afterwards, he asked me about myself, where I'd come from and if I had any family. I told him I'd been born in Leeds, but that I'd moved to London after my parents died. I explained that I'd been a lady's maid and told him why I'd had to leave. He was quiet for a bit, then he asked me if I might consider working for his wife. Apparently she needed a maid; when I reminded him that I didn't have any references, he said it wouldn't be necessary and that I was to present myself at his house at ten o'clock the following morning.'

'And you were given the position?' At Eliza's nod, Anna said, 'You were exceedingly fortunate.'

'Yes, I was. Of course, there was one small…additional requirement,' Eliza added, again avoiding Anna's eyes.

'That you become his mistress?'

Eliza nodded. 'He said he and his wife hadn't shared a bed in years due to her being so poorly. He asked if he could see me, and when I said I didn't like the idea of him coming to me in the attic, he told me he'd be careful. It was all right for a while, but I think his wife saw the way he looked at me and knew what was going on, so she asked me to leave. She wasn't mean about it. She said she knew her husband kept mistresses, but that she wasn't willing to live with one in her own home.'

That was fair enough, Anna thought. She couldn't imagine *any* woman being happy about seeing the face of her husband's mistress in the mirror every morning as she brushed out her hair or fastened her gown. 'What happened after that?'

'The Colonel felt so bad about my having to leave that he said if I was willing to…continue with the arrangement, he'd put me up in a nice little house and buy me clothes and make sure I had everything I needed. Since I liked him well enough and thought it would be an easy life, I agreed.'

'Yet you left him.'

Eliza began fidgeting with the edge of the bedsheet. 'It was never my intention to be somebody's mistress, my lady. Even though the Colonel wasn't demanding, I didn't feel right about…what I was doing. So one day, I looked through a newspaper he'd left on the dining room table and happened to see an advertisement for a lady's maid. I thought I didn't have much of a chance, but I desperately wanted the position, so I put on the nicest of the gowns he'd given me and wore new gloves and a bonnet so I would look respectable.'

'And you went to see the baroness?' Anna said.

Eliza nodded. 'She was ever so nice. She didn't seem to care that I had no references. She said she liked the way I looked and that I had a nice way about me. She told me what the wages were and said I could start right away. And I did, as Miss Eliza Smith. I thought it would be best to start with a clean slate. I left the Colonel's house that very day.'

'Did you tell him about the position?'

Eliza shook her head. 'I didn't have the heart to. But I only took one of the dresses he bought me, apart from the one I wore to the interview.'

'So you didn't leave the Colonel because of my brother?'

'Oh, no, my lady!' Eliza said quickly. 'The first time I saw Edward was just before the baroness's dinner party. I was on Bond Street, picking up some things for her ladyship when I saw him walking towards me. I remember thinking I'd never seen a more handsome man in my life. I saw him twice more after that, and each time I did, my knees would go weak and I'd feel all quivery inside, as if I was filled with feathers. I'd never felt that way about a man before. Then when he turned up at the baroness's dinner party and I saw him with that other gentleman, I thought I was going to faint dead away.'

'But you didn't,' Anna said drily.

'No. Mr Hansen told me to be off and I had to go. But I was that upset, I couldn't settle to anything, so I went into the study to tidy up. Edward must have seen me and followed me. Then when you came in—' Eliza broke off, her face turning bright red. 'Well, you know what happened.'

Anna did, aware that the sight of her brother and Miss Smith locked in a passionate embrace would stay with her for the rest of her life. 'So you became Edward's mistress,' she prompted.

The girl nodded 'I lived for those moments, my lady. They were the only thing that kept me going. Please don't misunderstand, it wasn't just about *being* with him. Or about the fact he was a gentleman. It was just that…no one had ever made me feel the way he did. No one had ever said…they loved me before.'

Anna felt her heart go out to the girl. Poor Eliza. She was no different than Mercy Banks or Cynthia Wicks…or herself when faced with a man who made her bones melt. Reason and logic flew out the window when rational thought was banished by irrational desire.

Because love wasn't logical. The mistake was in trying to make it so.

'When did things begin to change?' Anna asked, her gaze touching on the bruises.

'After I took the necklace,' Eliza said in a dull, flat voice. 'That's when he stopped talking about us being together. He stopped treating me like a lover—and started treating me like a whore.' She looked up and Anna saw the hopelessness in her expression. 'That's when I saw him for what he really was.'

Anna nodded and resolutely got to her feet. 'You can't stay here any longer, Eliza. It will be safest if you come away with me now.'

'I can't!'

'Yes, you can. Obviously the relationship isn't going to continue if this is how he treats you. Besides, I need you to tell someone the truth about the necklace.'

Eliza's lips were pressed tightly together, her head going from side to side.

'Listen to me,' Anna said firmly. 'There's a rumour going around that my father stole the baroness's necklace. A rumour I have every reason to believe my brother started. And if nothing is done to correct it, my father's reputation *will* be destroyed.'

'I know,' Eliza said miserably. 'I felt terrible when I heard that. I asked Edward about it, but that's when he turned on me. He said it was none of my business and that I wasn't to talk to anyone about what really happened. He said if I did, he'd hurt Justine.'

Anna frowned. 'Justine?'

'My sister,' Eliza said, her eyes filling with fresh tears. 'Edward said he'd…make it worse for her if I stepped out of line. That's why he told Betty I wasn't to have any visitors— or to be let out.'

Anna stared. 'You're not allowed to go out at all?'

'Not unless he's with me,' Eliza said. 'I have to do as he says or he'll hurt her. And I couldn't bear that, my lady. Justine's younger than me and she's never been as strong. I've spent the last two years looking after her. That's why I was willing to do whatever I had to in order to get money. I promised our mother I'd take care of her.'

Anna sat back, struggling to come to terms with this disquieting piece of news. Her brother was keeping one girl a prisoner and threatening another with physical harm? What kind of monster was he? He obviously had no conscience at all…

'…and Justine's been so happy working for the baroness.'

'I beg your pardon?' Jerked from her thoughts, Anna said, 'Your *sister* works for the baroness, too? But you were the one I saw—'

And then the penny dropped. Of *course*. Eliza was the girl Anna had *first* seen at Julia's house, but she wasn't the *same* girl who had served her tea on several occasions after that. *That* had been Justine. And if you didn't look closely, it would be all too easy to mistake one for the other. Both girls had the same dark hair and the same elfin face, but where Eliza's eyes were a deep, clear green, Justine's were a pale misty blue.

'Eliza, did Sir Barrington question *you* about the theft of the baroness's necklace, or your sister?' Anna asked shrewdly.

'That was Justine,' Eliza said sheepishly. 'She didn't

know anything about the necklace, so when the butler told us someone was coming to ask questions about its theft, I asked Justine to work in my place. And because she knew nothing, she was able to be convincing when the gentleman questioned her.'

'So you and your sister have been sharing the job without the baroness knowing?'

A guilty flush suffused Eliza's cheeks. 'I didn't think she'd mind, my lady. I was nervous the first time Justine stood in for me, but she said everything went well and the baroness didn't question me about it when I went in next, so we carried on.'

'And none of the baroness's other servants questioned the arrangement?'

'None of them knew. There was only myself and the tweenie on that floor and she wouldn't say boo to a goose. Cook had quarters downstairs and Mr Hansen's room was on a separate floor. And Justine and I were very careful about our comings and goings.'

'But why did you do it?'

'To give Justine the training she needs to become a maid,' Eliza explained. 'I realised I wouldn't be able to look after her all the time, or make enough money to support the two of us, so we decided she would learn the skills necessary to go into service. I gave her as much time as I could when we lived with the Colonel—'

'Justine *lived* with you in the Colonel's house?' Anna interrupted. 'Did he *know* that?

'I made sure he didn't,' Eliza said. 'I had no choice, my lady. Justine had been working as a nanny to a man who worked at a bank. When he started trying to get her alone, I knew I had to get her out of there before it was too late. So I told her to leave and had her come live with me. The Colonel never knew,' Eliza assured her. 'I was the only one who went to him. Justine stayed in the kitchen whenever he came round. She knew what I was doing and she wasn't happy about it, but neither of us was in a position to complain.'

'Where is Justine living now?' Anna asked.

Eliza blushed deeply. 'At Mrs Brown's.'

Anna gasped. 'Your sister's staying at a *brothel*?'

'Only until I can make other arrangements,' Eliza said quickly. 'I couldn't leave her at the Colonel's, but I didn't want to bring her here either, so I let her use my room at the baroness's house until I gave notice. Then both of us had to leave. I couldn't afford to have Edward know where she was.'

'But to arrange for her to stay at a brothel—'

'It's the only place I could afford, my lady, and she's not working,' Eliza said. 'Mrs Brown promised me that. She's letting Justine have a small room in the basement, well away from the other girls. But I have to get her out as soon as I can.'

'Then we shall do so this very afternoon.' Anna abruptly got to her feet. 'You and your sister need to disappear until this situation can be satisfactorily resolved.'

'But Edward will come after me,' Eliza whispered. 'And Justine, too, if he finds out where she is!'

'He won't get the chance,' Anna said resolutely. 'I'm going to take you to the home of a good friend, then go back for Justine. Together we'll work out how to keep both of you safe until someone I know can get to the bottom of this.'

Anna saw how desperately the girl wanted to believe what she was saying, but she also saw the depth of her fear. 'I'd like to believe you, my lady, but—'

'Believe me, Eliza. I won't let Edward hurt you or your sister. Now, pack your things and let's be off.'

'You'll have to get past Betty first!' Eliza whispered. 'And that won't be easy. She knows Edward will make it the worse for her if she lets me go!'

'Then I'll find a place for Betty as well,' Anna said, aware that matters were getting more complicated by the minute—but she had no choice. She refused to see these women's lives made worse as a result of their association with her brother. She opened the wardrobe and took out the girl's tiny valise. 'What will you take?'

Eliza glanced at the array of dresses hanging in the closet and shook her head. 'Nothing. I don't want anything he bought me, because he never really wanted me, did he, my lady? Only what I could steal for him.'

Anna wasn't sure how to answer that. What could she say that wouldn't destroy the poor girl more than she already had been? 'You must forget what my brother has done, Eliza,' Anna said gently. 'When you leave here, you'll have no reason to see him again.'

'I'd like to believe that,' Eliza said again, 'but he won't take the blame for the theft of the necklace. He'll tell people I took it, and once that gets around, I'll be arrested.'

'That's why you're not going to stay in London,' Anna said firmly. 'I know people in the country. Good people who will be only too happy to give you and your sister positions. My brother will never find either of you.'

'But the necklace—'

'The necklace has been found and will be returned to the baroness without her ever knowing how it came to be stolen. Now, come along. We have much to do before this day is over.'

Removing Eliza Smith from her brother's house was one of the easier tasks Anna had to do that day. She hustled her down the narrow staircase and after checking to make sure that Betty was nowhere in sight, opened the front door and pointed her in the direction of the waiting carriage. Then, telling the driver to wait, Anna went back in search of the housekeeper, knowing the poor woman had to be made aware of the situation.

Betty didn't have to be told twice. Aware that her employment would be terminated as soon as Edward learned of Eliza's escape, she threw off her apron, grabbed what few personal belongings she had, and left the house at the same time as Anna and Eliza, with two more of Anna's guineas jingling in her pocket.

'Can we stop and pick up Justine?' Eliza asked when Anna gave the driver the direction of the Park Lane home of the Marquess of Bailley.

'There isn't room,' Anna said. 'I'll go back for her once you're safely out of sight.'

Arriving at the Marquess of Bailley's house, Anna walked up to the front door with Eliza at her side and knocked on the door. It was answered in moments by Hilton, the family's long-standing butler. 'Good afternoon, Lady Annabelle.'

'Good afternoon, Hilton. Is Lady Lydia in?'

'She is, my lady. In the rose salon.'

'Thank you. Would you be so kind as to take Miss Smith down to the kitchen? She would be most grateful for a cup of tea.'

The unflappable Hilton didn't bat an eye. 'Of course, my lady.' Signalling a maid, he told her to take the young lady downstairs. Once that was taken care of, Anna made her way to the rose salon and within minutes, she was giving her friend a terse though somewhat abbreviated version of all that had happened.

'You wish me to keep Miss Smith and her sister *here*?' Lydia asked at the conclusion.

'Only for a little while,' Anna said. 'For obvious reasons, I can't risk having either of them stay with me. And I promise it will only be for a few days. I'm going to see Sir Barrington right now and tell him everything that's happened.'

'He's not going to be happy when he hears that you've involved yourself in this,' Lydia warned.

'Why not? He should be delighted that I've solved his case for him,' Anna protested.

'Not when he learns that you put yourself in harm's way to do so!'

'I was hardly in harm's way,' Anna said drily.

'You think going to Edward's house and kidnapping his battered mistress isn't going to spark a reaction?' Lydia demanded incredulously. 'I shudder to think what he would have done had he arrived and caught you in the act.'

'He would have been angry and told me to mind my own business, but it's silly to suggest that I was in any kind of danger,' Anna said. 'He is my brother, after all.'

'That doesn't absolve him. Edward is a wicked man and wicked men are capable of anything. Have you forgotten what happened to Sarah Wentworth?'

Anna's jaw tightened. How could anyone forget what had happened to that poor woman? Her husband had mistakenly believed her guilty of having an affair and had had her committed to an institution, even though it was clear to anyone who saw her that there was absolutely nothing wrong with her mind. Nevertheless, she disappeared one night and it was months before someone happened to see her in the asylum and made a complaint to the lady's father. Even then, it had taken considerable effort on her family's part to have her released and the resulting scandal had been horrendous.

'Please help me, Lydia. Will you keep Eliza and her sister here? It won't be for long,' Anna said. 'I shall write to a very good friend of mine this very night and see about sending both of the girls to her. Edward would never even think of going there. She runs a small school near York and her sister married well and has a very large house. I'm sure one of them will be able to give the girls some sort of employment.'

'You don't have to convince me, of course they can stay,' Lydia said. 'I shall put them in the room next to mine. In fact, their arrival has solved something of a problem in that my own maid asked for time off to visit her ailing father. If anyone asks, I shall simply say I hired them on a friend's recommendation. And I shall be sure not to send them out of the house on any errands.'

Anna pressed a kiss to her friend's cheek. 'Thank you, dear friend. I'll just go back and fetch Justine—'

'Oh, no, you won't.' Quickly getting up, Lydia went to the writing desk and took out parchment and quill. 'I refuse to see you venture alone into that part of town. It's dangerous; besides, someone might see you and start asking awkward questions.' She wrote a few words on the paper, sanded and folded it, then rang for a servant. 'I'll have John take the carriage and retrieve Miss Smith. A male servant going into that kind of place won't arouse any suspicions. And he can drop you at Sir Barrington's on the way.'

Touched by her friend's willingness to help, Anna gave her a hug. 'You are too good, Lydia. I promise I shall make it up to you.'

'Just get this mess straightened out,' Lydia said grimly. 'That will be thanks enough!'

Barrington had forgotten what a restful sleep was. For five nights in a row, he'd ended up pacing the drawing room because, for five nights in a row, he'd been unable to think about anything but Anna. She'd kept him awake—and aroused—into the wee hours of the morning. He couldn't explain why. He had trained himself to ignore what he couldn't have, to resist temptation in all its wide and varied forms. He couldn't be bought, bribed, or browbeaten. God knew, enough men had tried and failed. Yet when it came to her, it was as though he had no will at all. He became as docile as a kitten. And like a kitten, he craved her touch. He wanted to wrap himself around her, to immerse himself in her warmth and to lose himself in her body.

Knowing he couldn't do any of those things was driving him mad. Even now, as he sat at his desk, staring out the window instead of reviewing papers concerning a complicated case, all he could think about was Anna. Remembering the expression on her face during their last meeting—

'Sir Barrington...'

Recalling how angry she'd been at his refusal to abandon his pursuit of her father, her misplaced belief that he assumed the earl guilty—

'Sir Barrington?'

Her—

'*Sir Barrington!*'

'Yes, what *is* it, Sam?' Exasperated, Barrington turned to see his secretary standing in the open doorway, and right behind him—'Anna!' He leaped to his feet, sending a flurry of papers to the floor. 'That is...Lady Annabelle!'

She stepped in front of the younger man, hesitation and uncertainty written on her face. 'I hope I haven't come at a bad time?'

'Of course not. Come in. Sit down.' He stared at her greedily, devouring the sight of her, wondering how it was possible for a woman to grow more beautiful by the day. 'Thank you, Sam, that will be all.'

The door closed with a quiet click. Anna came towards him. 'Are you sure this isn't a bad time. You seem...preoccupied.'

'I am.' *With you.* 'I was going over the details of a case.' He glanced briefly at the papers on the floor and then walked around to the front of his desk. Leaning back against the edge, he crossed his arms over his chest and tried not to notice how the sunlight danced on her hair, turning it a warm, honeyed gold. Her complexion was as smooth as alabaster, her mouth a bright red berry, ripe for the taking—

Desire exploded, hardening him where he stood. And with a degree of resolve he didn't know he had, he forced it down and away. 'You look like a woman on a mission.'

'I am. I came here to tell you that I know who took Julia's necklace. *And* how it came to be in my father's wardrobe.'

His eyebrows lifted. 'Indeed.'

'My brother's mistress took it.'

'Elizabeth Paisley?'

He said the name without thinking, and watched as a delicate line formed between her brows. 'No. Eliza Smith.'

'Your brother's mistress is a girl by the name of Elizabeth Paisley,' Barrington said. 'I know because I was asked to find her by a gentleman who was…concerned about her welfare.'

'A gentleman by the name of Colonel Tanner?'

Barrington raised an eyebrow. 'How did you know?'

'Eliza told me about him. And I remember you speaking to a gentleman you referred to as Colonel that night at the Billinghams' soirée. I suspected they might be one and the same.'

Hiding his surprise, Barrington inclined his head. 'Elizabeth Paisley was originally Colonel Tanner's mistress. When she disappeared from his house, he began to worry so he asked me to see if I could find her. Initially I was afraid that foul play might have been involved, but when I learned through my visit to Madame Delors that someone else was paying for her clothes, I realised she had simply transferred her affections.'

'Madame Delors?' Anna said, wide eyed. 'Is *that* why you went to see her?'

'Of course. A good modiste dresses a wide range of women and sends the bills to their husbands or protectors. It seemed the logical place to start. Why? Did you think I had some other reason for going?'

Anna coloured, but firmly shook her head. 'No, of course not. Go on.'

'Because I knew the Colonel had ordered clothes for Miss Paisley from Madame Delors, I hoped she might be able to tell me what had become of her. After some careful prompting, she kindly provided me with your brother's name.'

'So you *knew* about Eliza's involvement with Edward.' Anna abruptly sat down. 'Why didn't you tell me?'

'Two reasons. One, because I was investigating her in confidence for another client, and, two, because I was afraid you might ask Edward what his involvement with her was.'

'And so I should! Eliza was the one who took the necklace!'

'Not possible,' Barrington said. 'The baroness's maid said she saw your father take the necklace.'

'That's right. Eliza *was* Julia's maid.'

'Wrong,' Barrington said. 'I interviewed all of the household help. No one matching Miss Paisley's description worked there at the time of the robbery.'

'That's because Eliza wasn't there the day you questioned the staff. Her sister, Justine, was.'

'But I didn't interview a Justine Paisley,' Barrington said. 'The baroness's maid was a girl by the name of Eliza Smith.'

'Exactly. Eliza Smith *is* Elizabeth Paisley,' Anna said patiently. 'She changed her name when she went to work for Julia. And she asked her sister, Justine, to stand in for her on the day you went to interview the staff because she was afraid that if *she* spoke to you, her nerves would give her away. Justine knew nothing of what Eliza had done so Eliza knew she would be entirely convincing.'

'Are you telling me the baroness didn't know she had two different girls working for her?'

'Not when the only difference between them was the colour of their eyes,' Anna said triumphantly. 'Justine and Eliza are twins.'

There it was. The missing piece of the puzzle. Barrington hadn't been able to trace Elizabeth Paisley because she had changed her name to Smith and because she and her twin sister were pretending to be the same person.

He picked up the crystal paperweight and turned it over in his hand, the sunlight sending shards of silver dancing around the room. Elizabeth *and* Justine Paisley. Damn.

'So it all started,' he said slowly, 'when Edward saw Elizabeth Paisley…or Smith as she was then, at the baroness's dinner party.'

'Actually, it started a little before that, but I suspect they first became lovers that night. Eliza told me she spotted Edward the moment she walked into the dining room and he must have noticed her because I saw them together later that night.'

'Where?'

'In the study. After you and I…parted company on the balcony, I went back into the house through another door and came upon Edward and Miss Smith.'

He watched the colour spring to her cheeks and his eyebrows rose a fraction of an inch. *'In flagrante delicto?'* When her colour deepened, he couldn't help smiling. 'That must have been awkward.'

'Apparently more so for me than for Edward,' Anna said ruefully. 'A few days later, I overheard him telling two of his friends that he had installed a new mistress at his house. I put two and two together.'

'So she went to him willingly,' Barrington said.

'Oh yes. Eliza said that while Colonel Tanner had been good to her, she wasn't in love with him.'

*In love with him.* So, his hunch had proven true. 'Is that how Edward convinced her to steal the necklace?' Barrington asked. 'By telling her he loved her?'

'Of course. He told her she would be doing it for them, so they could be together.'

'And she was gullible enough to believe it,' he said wryly.

'A woman in love is all too ready to believe anything she's told,' Anna pointed out. 'Edward made her believe that selling part of the necklace would provide the money they needed to start a new life together. And Eliza was too much in love with him to see how impossible a reality that was.'

'Of course. We always think the best of those we love,' Barrington murmured. 'Only to discover that love blinds us to the truth. Eliza was no different.'

'Until she found out it was all lies. When she threatened to leave, Edward realised she had the power to expose him and his method of persuasion took on a more…physical form.' Anna looked at him and Barrington saw the anger in her eyes. 'That's why I had to take her away.'

He froze, hardly able to believe what she'd said. '*You* took her out of his house? Dear God, Anna, do you realise how dangerous that could have been?'

'The only danger would have been to Eliza if I'd left her there!'

'And what if Edward had arrived whilst you were helping her to escape?' he said.

'He likely would have been angry and put a stop to it.'

'He might have done a damn sight more than that.'

'Why does everyone insist on believing that Edward would hurt me?' Anna asked in exasperation. 'He's my brother, for heaven's sake!'

'He's also a man with a grudge and guilty of having plotted a serious crime,' Barrington retaliated. 'He attempted to destroy your father's reputation and apparently had no qualms about using violence against Miss Paisley or her sister. Speaking of which, we have to find the other sister as quickly as possible. Once your brother discovers what's happened, she won't be safe.'

'I know. That's why a carriage is on its way to pick Justine up now and take her to the Marquess of Bailley's house,' Anna said. 'I asked Lydia if the girls could stay with her until I've had a chance to contact some friends of mine in the country who might be able to provide positions for them.'

'Good girl,' Barrington said approvingly. 'While I don't like involving anyone else in this, Lady Lydia's house is probably the safest place in the short term. Your brother would never think to look for Miss Paisley or her sister there.' He turned away from her, dragging a hand through his dark hair. There was still much to be done, but when he thought of what Anna had already endured, and what could have happened... 'I'm sorry you had to get involved in this, Anna. I would have spared you, if I could.'

'I know,' Anna said softly. 'But none of this is your fault, Barrington. Edward's turned out to be the villain. I would never have believed him capable of such treachery, but it seems I didn't know him *or* Peregrine as well as I thought.'

'You can't know what people don't want you to. That's what makes this such a dangerous business,' Barrington said, walking towards her. 'Please don't do it again.'

His voice was soft, barely above a whisper, yet it reverberated through her with the force of a hurricane. 'You don't have the right to tell me what to do,' she whispered back.

'No, but I'm going to regardless. And do you know why?'
He came to a halt in front of her, so close that he could see
the pulse beating beneath her skin. 'Because if something
were to happen to you, I would never know peace again.' He
raised his hands and placed them on either side of her face.
'If I never had the chance to kiss you again, I would slowly
go insane. Much as I'm doing now...'

He waited for her to pull away, but when she leaned into
him and closed her eyes, Barrington knew there was no turning back. He took her face between his hands and angled
her mouth to his, desperate to feel the softness of her mouth
under his.

It was more than he expected. Her lips, sweet, soft, and
maddeningly erotic, wiped every thought from his mind but
how much he wanted her. He touched his tongue to her upper
lip, heard her breath catch and felt his world shift when she
opened her mouth to him.

The taste of her nearly drove reason from his brain. The
warmth of her in his arms, the hunger he tasted in her kiss,
were all that mattered. And when her arms came around him
and her fingers pressed into his back, urging him closer, he
knew he couldn't let her go. With a groan, he slipped one
hand around to cup the nape of her neck, tilting her head
back, exposing her throat. She smelled like heaven and, like
a starving man, he feasted on her, savouring the scent and the
taste of her skin. Her breasts were warm and heavy against
his chest, rising and falling as the tempo of her breathing
increased.

He reclaimed her mouth, his kiss no longer gentle, his
tongue exploring the shadowy recesses of her mouth. He
kissed the pulse beating at the base of her throat, and when
she groaned and arched against him, he cupped one breast,
feeling the nipple harden through the slight material of
her gown.

Anna moaned, a whisper into his hair, and he went as hard as iron. God, he needed her. Needed to peel away the layers of clothing until they lay skin to skin, to caress her until they were both aching with desire, to hear her cry out his name as he claimed her for his own…

'Anna,' he whispered against her throat. 'Oh, my love…'

He spoke without thinking, the endearment slipping naturally from his lips. He no longer cared if she knew how he felt. All he wanted was to be close to her, as though, in this intimate embrace, all the reservations he'd felt had suddenly evaporated.

But something was different. Anna was pulling back. Her arms fell away, leaving him cold where he had been hot. Empty where he had been full. And when he looked at her, it was to see tears rolling down her cheeks. 'What's wrong, my love?'

'Don't *call* me that,' she protested, her voice tremulous. 'Don't talk to me of love when, by your own admission, you have none to give me.'

Her words stabbed at him like the point of a rapier. 'You know why I said that. I told you of the risks—'

'But you kissed me as though you cared—but you don't.'

'I do! Just—'

'Just not enough to marry me, yes, I know,' she threw at him. 'Then why torment me like this, Barrington? I won't be your mistress.'

'I would never ask that of you,' he said, aware that his own heart was thundering in his chest. 'But neither will I be the cause of you putting yourself in danger. You've already seen what I bring to your life: Rand's life in shambles; your father held up for ridicule; and you, forced to speak out against your brother and forcibly remove a woman from the prison he was holding her in. Do you not see the dangers of being involved with me?'

'What I see,' she said huskily, 'is a man trying to put right what others have put wrong. A man who chooses to expose the weaknesses that turn good people bad and which destroy families along the way. You did not *ruin* Peregrine's life, Barrington. He did that by involving himself with Lady Yew. And you certainly didn't hold my father up for ridicule. That was all Edward's doing.'

'And what of the dangers from Edward now? You've seen what he's capable of,' Barrington said. 'And while you might not want to believe it, *all* men are capable of violence. All it takes is one spark to ignite the fire.'

'Does that include you?' she asked.

He swallowed hard as an image of Hayle raising his hand to her appeared in his mind. 'If it came to the possibility of your being hurt by another, yes, I would most definitely be capable of violence.'

He had no idea if it was the answer she expected, or even the one she wanted. But it was the only one he could give and he knew that she was shaken by the intensity of his declaration.

'I have no wish to inspire such behaviour,' she said in a low voice. 'It has always been my desire to bring out the best in people, not the worst. And violence of any kind can only be the worst.'

'That's why I need you to be careful,' Barrington warned. 'Your brother is guilty of having tried to implicate your father in the theft of the necklace. If he suspects you of going public with that information, how do you think he's going to react? His standing in society means a great deal to him. He won't look kindly upon anyone who exposes him for what he really is.'

'Maybe not, but how *can* I expose him, Barrington? He's

a member of my family. Think of what it would do to my father. How disloyal it would be—'

'Did Edward consider loyalty when he asked the Marquess of Yew to persecute Rand over the affair?' Barrington said brutally. 'Knowing it would cause Rand public humiliation and disgrace?'

She blanched. 'Edward *asked* Lord Yew to bring charges against Peregrine?'

'Yes. The marquess is actually quite proud of his wife's ability to seduce younger men. He doesn't care that she slept with Rand, and neither did Edward. All your brother wanted to do was humiliate Rand in the eyes of society.'

'But why?'

'Because he's jealous.'

'Jealous! Why on earth would Edward be jealous of Peregrine? He's heir to an earldom, for heaven's sake! Peregrine is merely my father's godson—'

'No, Anna. Edward hates Peregrine Rand because he *is* your father's other son—'

*'What?'*

He'd gone too far. The moment he saw the look of disbelief on her face, Barrington knew he'd said too much, because contrary to what he'd believed, she hadn't worked it out. As astute as she was when it came to analysing and fixing relationships between other people's families, she was blind to the truth when it came to her own. 'You didn't know,' was all he said.

'Didn't *know*?' she demanded in a tortured whisper. 'How could I possibly have known? Papa introduced Peregrine as his *godson*. I had no reason to believe he was anything else.'

'What about the physical resemblance between them?'

'I thought it barely noticeable. Even Edward doesn't resemble my father all that much. Or are you going to tell me he's not really my brother either?'

Barrington heard the tension in Anna's voice and, though his first instinct was to apologise, he knew silence was the better choice. It was too late for apologies now. The damage was done. Anna hadn't moved an inch from where she stood, but she was as distant from him as the moon was from the earth. 'It was never my intention to hurt you, Anna.'

'Then why would you say such a thing to me?'

'Because I know it to be the truth. I did some digging into your family history,' Barrington said, not bothering to mention that it was Lord Richard Crew who had discovered the truth about Peregrine's background. 'It was all there, in the parish registers.'

Anna didn't move, but her eyes grew suspiciously bright. 'So that's why Edward hates Peregrine so much,' she whispered. 'He worked it out as soon as Peregrine arrived.'

'I suspect so, yes.'

She was silent for a long time, her expression one of mute despair. Barrington didn't say anything either, knowing it was better that she work matters out for herself. Anything else he said now might only make the situation worse.

Finally, she spoke. 'Why didn't Papa tell us? Surely we had a right to know.'

'Perhaps he thought to spare you the hurt you're suffering now. And while it pains me to say it, he wouldn't be the first nobleman to father a child outside marriage.'

'How *dare* you!' she cried. 'My father *loved* my mother. He was faithful to her until the day she died! How do I know *you're* not the one telling lies? You could be making this all up!'

'Why would I do that?'

'I don't know.' Anna wrapped her arms around her chest, as though to stop herself from shattering into a million pieces.

'You once told me that people lie to protect themselves or someone they care about, but we both know those aren't the only reasons. People lie to influence others, or to make them feel better about themselves. They lie to inflict hurt.'

'So you believe I'm deliberately trying to hurt you by lying to you about your father's relationship to Peregrine Rand?'

Anna shook her head. 'I don't know what you're trying to do. All I know is that my father is an honourable man. He would never have done something like that. It would have destroyed our mother. And he would *never* bring a child he'd had with another woman to live under the same roof as Edward and me. It would be too painful for all of us.' Her chin came up. 'If Peregrine *is* my father's child, he would have told us. I *know* he would.'

Barrington said nothing. What could he say? She was a daughter defending the father she loved. She trusted him, as she'd trusted her brother, believing that she knew the ways of the world. The ways of love.

Yet she didn't know how love could twist and warp until it was unrecognisable to anyone who saw it. She didn't know how it could wound with a single word, or destroy with a single glance. For what was jealousy but love without trust? What was obsession but love without reason?

Hayle was jealous of Rand because he was the product of his father's love with another woman. Elizabeth Paisley had stolen for the man she loved because she believed it would strengthen their bond and allow them to start a life together. And the earl had lied to his family in an effort to protect them from a devastating truth. He probably *had* been faithful to his wife while he was married to her, but Peregrine was his child by a woman he'd met *before* he married Isabel. Likely before their marriage had even been arranged or the two of them had met.

Sadly, none of that mattered now. Anna was looking at

him as though *he* was the serpent in the Garden of Eden. As though he was the source of all the rumours and lies. There was nothing he could do now but finish his investigation and walk away. Out of the case, out of her life.

'I will call upon your brother this evening, Lady Annabelle,' Barrington said quietly.

'Not at home!' she gasped.

He shook his head. 'Lord Hayle spends Thursday nights at his club. I shall speak to him there.'

'What will you say?' she asked, not looking at him.

'That is between your brother and myself. But when the interview is over, I shall send word to your father of the outcome.'

'And what about me, Barrington?' Anna said, finally raising her eyes to his face. 'What would you say to me?'

He stared down at the blotter, knowing there was only one thing he could say. 'I will say goodbye. Because after what's happened between us today, I can't imagine there possibly being anything else appropriate.'

# Chapter Fourteen

Contrary to what he'd told her, Barrington did not find Hayle at his club that evening. He called in at White's on his way to another society event, only to be informed by the manager that the earl's son had not yet put in an appearance.

Thanking him, Barrington left and climbed back into his carriage. Where did he go next? There were any number of hells to which Hayle might have gone, but it would take the entire night to investigate them all. Had he gone to see his mistress? Possible, Barrington reflected. And if so, he would have found the house in darkness and Eliza gone. How would he react to such a development? With anger? Or with fear? Would he suspect Eliza of having revealed the part he'd played in the theft of the necklace and realise that information now existed that could connect him to the crime, thereby exonerating his father?

The likelihood of that was even more possible; afraid of what that might mean for Anna, Barrington gave his coachman the direction of Regent's Park. He intended to keep a close eye on Hayle for the next few days. Anna might like to think her brother was guided by family loyalty, but having seen what loyalty meant to him, Barrington decided it was best to play it safe. Any man that twisted by jealousy and anger was a danger to anyone he came into contact with—and that *included* his only sister.

The carriage pulled into the darkened street a short while later. Barrington knew the number of the house, but even from this distance he could see that there were no lights on inside and that neither a private carriage nor a hackney stood outside. If Hayle had paid the house a call, he hadn't bothered to wait around.

So where was he now—and in what state of mind?

Abruptly, Barrington remembered something Crew had told him during his last visit. As well as providing him with the surprising but very useful information regarding Cambermere and his relationship to Peregrine Rand, Crew had informed him that Hayle had taken to spending time with Lord Andrews. Apparently they were often seen heading in the direction of Andrews's favourite hangout, a disreputable tavern close to the Thames, down a dark alley most decent men knew better than to travel. A place known to opium users needing a place to hide.

Barrington thumped the roof of his carriage and gave the driver the address. Whatever he was going to say to Hayle had to be said tonight. And if that meant following him into the mouth of hell, that's what he'd do. But he'd go in prepared. He reached under his seat and pulled out the ebony cane. If he was to take Hayle on in an unfriendly atmosphere, the cane might well save his life. In places like the Cock's Crown, he was only going to get one chance.

Anna walked listlessly into the drawing room as the clock on the mantel struck nine. She and Peregrine were expected at Lady Bessmel's for cards, but the thought of having to spend an entire evening making light-hearted conversation and acting as though nothing was wrong was far from welcome. She perched on the arm of a high-back chair, only to get restlessly to her feet a few minutes later. She felt cold though the room was warm and even an extra shawl couldn't banish the chill, nor was it likely to given the source of her distraction.

*Was Peregrine truly her half-brother?* Barrington certainly thought so. He would never have made the comment to her otherwise. But the only person who could give her a definitive answer to that question was her father and he had gone out earlier in the day. And even if she knew when he was coming home, would she have the courage to ask him such a question?

How did one go about enquiring if the young man now living with them, a man who had been introduced to them by their father as his godson, was, in fact, their half-brother?

Her father's bastard.

No. Definitely not the kind of question a daughter asked. Because if Barrington was wrong, her father would be devastated by her questioning of his honesty. Indeed, of his very honour. And if he wasn't wrong?

Anna closed her eyes, retreating from the thought.

Unfortunately, Barrington didn't make mistakes. Everything he'd said to her from the moment they'd met had been proven true. What reason had she to doubt him now? His approach to everything he undertook was logical, unemotional and based purely on fact. Sentiment didn't enter into it, whereas with her, *everything* revolved around emotion. People didn't make mistakes because they were logical. They made them because they allowed their emotions to get the upper hand. Emotions like anger and jealousy and hate.

Having to listen to such accusations made against the members of her own family was horrible—but having to

agree with them was even more so. It called into question
the degree of loyalty she owed her family. A responsibility
she'd never questioned until now—and Barrington was the
one who was making her question it. Was it any wonder she
had no desire to see him again?

Yet she *did* want to see him. Desperately, because he had
become the only constant in her life, the one person she
could count on. He consumed her every waking thought. Not
an hour went by that she didn't think of him. Not a minute
passed that she didn't remember every exquisite detail of
the moments they'd spent together: the heady sensation of
his hand caressing her breast; the warmth of his mouth on
hers; the incredible eroticism of his body pressed intimately
against hers.

But what was all that worth if love and tenderness weren't
present as well? Intimacy without love was the reason men
went to prostitutes. Barrington might not be able to deny
the strength of the attraction between them, but he was still
reluctant to encourage anything more. He used the charges
he had laid against the men in her family as proof of the
destructive force he brought into her life.

How was she to tell him that she didn't care about that
any more? That all she cared about was loving him and of
finding some way of getting him to love her in return?

How on earth did she tell a logical man something so
thoroughly illogical?

'Anna? Are you ready to go?'

She looked up to see Peregrine standing in the doorway—
and the sight of him caused her heart to turn over all over
again. Peregrine Rand. Country gentleman—or unknown
half-brother? It was impossible not to wonder in light of
Barrington's stunning revelations.

And yet though she stared hard at Peregrine, she still
couldn't find the confirmation she was seeking. The

knowledge that he truly was her father's son by another woman...

'Anna? Are you all right?'

'Hmm? Oh, yes, of course.' *Don't think about it. It won't help you get through the evening.* 'Are you sure you want to go to Lady Bessmel's tonight?'

Peregrine's mouth twisted and, suddenly, there was no mistaking the hesitation in his eye. 'I'm quite sure I *don't* wish to go, but I can't hide in the house for ever. I'll have to show my face in public at some time.' He walked into the room, hands thrust into his pockets. 'If it was only the affair, I could bear it. But knowing that people are whispering about what I reputedly did to your father is a thousand times worse.'

Anna looked at him and saw how deeply he was suffering. The colour had gone from his face and his eyes were shadowed with despair. Even his attire was subdued: his cravat simply tied, his waistcoat plain, his collar points of moderate height.

'I know you didn't start the rumour about having found the necklace in Papa's possession, Per,' Anna said softly. 'You wouldn't have done that to him.'

His laughter had a hard, bitter edge to it. 'Then you're one of the few who believes it.'

'How did you find out what people were saying?'

'Lord Richard Crew was good enough to inform me.'

Hearing the name of the well-known lady's man, Anna raised an eyebrow. 'I'm surprised *he* would be the one to tell you, given his own less-than-sterling reputation. Did he happen to mention whether or not he believed it?'

'He didn't say and I didn't ask,' Peregrine replied, his expression bleak. 'Frankly, I didn't want to know.'

'Oh, Peregrine,' Anna said, coming to stand beside him. 'This really hasn't been a very good visit for you.'

'No, it hasn't, but much of it's been my own fault,' Peregrine said ruefully. 'Making a fool of myself over Lady Yew wasn't the best way to start and this has certainly made matters worse. But I can't believe people would think I would betray your father like that. Yes, I saw the necklace in his wardrobe. We both did. But I would never say so in public. Your father's been good to me, Anna. He brought me to London and let me live here. He made it easy for me to enter society when my background lends nothing to my being there, and he even forgave me for the débâcle with Lady Yew.'

'He did?'

'He said it was the right of every young man to sow his wild oats.' Peregrine gave her a lopsided grin. 'I just picked the wrong field in which to sow them.'

In spite of the situation, Anna was actually able to laugh. 'Yes, well, I suppose everyone must be forgiven one mistake.'

'Would that it was only one.' Peregrine said. 'I wish I was more like you, Anna. I doubt you've ever done anything stupid or irresponsible in your life. You would never let yourself be compromised by your feelings.'

'Oh, Peregrine,' Anna breathed. 'I am no more sensible than you when it comes to matters of the heart.'

'Nonsense. You're never out of humour. You don't allow familiarity from gentlemen and you act with moderation at all times.'

*Except when in the arms of the man I love,* Anna wanted to tell him. *Waiting for him to say the things I so desperately want to hear...and probably never will.* But all she said was, 'The young ladies I counsel would think me a poor example if I didn't follow my own advice. Besides, we both know how destructive unbridled passion can be. Surely it is better to love moderately than to lose oneself completely.'

'Perhaps, but I would never wish that for you. Or for myself. When I fall in love, I want it to be without reason or logic. I want to feel light-headed over it,' Peregrine said. 'Giddy with the excitement of it all. I want the woman I love to be all I think about—my reason for getting up in the morning and the motivation for everything I do during the day. I want her to be my queen. My Guinevere.'

Anna smiled. 'You're a poet and a dreamer, Peregrine, but I have no doubt that you *will* find your Guinevere one day.'

'And what about you, Anna? Do you think you'll ever find your Lancelot?'

Anna stood up. She already had…and his name was Barrington Parker. But he was lost to her, the bitter words they'd thrown at one another severing the tenuous connection that existed between them. 'I doubt it. There just aren't that many knights in shining armour left.'

As expected, walking into the Cock's Crown was like descending into the dungeons of hell. The dimly lit room was thick with smoke, the cloying scent of opium burning the eyes and addling the brain. Pictures both dark and disturbing hung from the walls and there was a sense of desperation and despair about the place.

It took only a moment to locate the figure of Viscount Hayle. Sitting at a table in the corner, he appeared to be well into his cups, though in truth, he was in better shape than many of his companions. Lord Andrews was sprawled out on the table next to him and a younger man Barrington recognised as the heir to a dukedom lay face down on the floor. The humid air was rank with the smell of booze and fear.

Hayle looked up as Barrington approached. His eyes were bloodshot and, in the dim light, his skin had a decidedly greyish tinge. 'Well, well, if it isn't the admirable Parker,' he drawled. 'A little out of your area, aren't you?'

'It's not one of my favourite haunts,' Barrington said,

resting his hands on the knob of his ebony cane. 'But something told me I might find you here.'

'And why should you wish to *find* me?' Hayle said, enunciating each word.

'You and I have business to discuss.'

'Really? I can't imagine what manner of business would be so important that you would need seek me out here. As you can see, I am with friends, and friends would resent me speaking to you on matters that do not concern them.'

It was hard to tell if Hayle was foxed or drugged, but either way, Barrington knew it was going to be a difficult conversation. 'Your friends can listen if they wish, but we *will* have a conversation.'

'I think not.' Hayle closed his eyes and rocked back on the legs of his chair. 'You take yourself far too seriously, Parker. You should learn to relax and enjoy life, as I do.'

'What, by viewing it through a veil of opium? Thank you, but I prefer reality to hallucinations.'

'Obviously, you've never tried it.'

'No, but it would no more be my idea of fun than forcing a helpless young woman to do my dirty work, then hold her prisoner for fear of her exposing me,' Barrington said contemptuously.

Hayle's eyes opened, the chair slowly righting. 'What the hell are you talking about?'

'I think you know. I'm sure the name Elizabeth Paisley rings a bell.'

'Eliza?' To Barrington's surprise, Hayle actually laughed. 'I'm not holding her prisoner. She came to me willingly. She loves me, don't you know.'

'She may believe herself in love with you, but you and I both know it was fear that kept her from running away from you.'

Hayle's smile slowly disappeared. 'And I suppose I have

you to thank for her unexpected departure. And for that of my housekeeper?'

Not even the most unholy of tortures would have prompted Barrington to tell Hayle it was his sister who had orchestrated Eliza's escape. 'The young lady was too afraid to leave on her own, so it was necessary that I assist her in that regard,' he said quietly. 'Once I realised she was the one who'd stolen the baroness's necklace and given it to you, I had no choice but to speak with her.'

'Gave the necklace to me? What a bizarre notion. And entirely wrong, of course.' Hayle unsteadily picked up his glass. 'My *father* is the thief, Parker. Surely you've figured that out by now. The much revered Earl of Cambermere stole the baroness's necklace and it was none other than his *godson*, Mr Peregrine Rand, who made it known to society. Were you aware that it was Rand who found the necklace amongst my father's things?'

'I did hear something to that effect,' Barrington remarked, 'though it seems a bit strange that you would ask him to fetch something from your father's room…a watch, I believe… when you were the one who was supposed to take care of it.'

The man gave a non-committal shrug. 'My father asked me to attend to it, but I was busy, so I asked Rand to do it for me. I thought him competent enough to undertake a trifling matter like that.'

'So you had no idea he would find the necklace lying right next to the watch when he went in search of it,' Barrington said blandly.

Again, the shrug. 'Had I known, I would have gone myself. I have no desire to see my father humiliated in the eyes of society, Parker. Or to see our family name tarnished by such a dishonourable act.'

'No, I'm sure you do not,' Barrington murmured, impressed

by the man's ability to lie so convincingly when under the influence of the drug. 'And, of course, it makes no sense that your father would steal anything from the woman he has asked to marry him.'

It wasn't the truth, but it got the response Barrington was hoping for.

'He hasn't asked her to marry him,' Hayle snapped. 'Julia would have told me!'

'You wouldn't have heard it from your father first?' Barrington probed.

'My father doesn't confide his plans to me any more. He hasn't for some time.'

Barrington heard the note of resentment in Hayle's voice and knew the loss of his father's confidence, and perhaps his respect, rankled. 'Still, it can't come as a great surprise that he wishes to marry her,' Barrington went on. 'He's made no secret of his affection for the lady. Your father is, in all ways, an honourable man. If he was in love with the baroness, he would naturally offer her marriage.'

'Oh yes, just like he offered Rand's mother marriage,' Hayle said contemptuously. 'But he didn't, did he? He married my mother and ignored his bastard for the first twenty-seven years of his life. Hardly the behaviour of an *honourable man.*'

'It's possible your father didn't know of Rand's existence,' Barrington said. 'It may have been brought to his attention only a few months ago.'

'He knew he'd bedded Rand's mother,' Hayle said with contempt. 'And the consequences of *that* are all too easy to predict.'

'As I said, the relationship may have ended without his knowledge of there being a child,' Barrington said reasonably. 'Rand is older than you, so the association between your father and his mother was an early one.'

'I don't give a damn when he had the relationship or what they were to one another!' Hayle burst out hotly. 'What bothers me is that the moment my father learned of Rand's existence, he brought him to London without so much as a by your leave.'

'What did you expect him to do?'

'He could have asked me how *I* felt about it. I *am* his legitimate son and heir, after all!'

'Perhaps he didn't think it concerned you. Rand is his son by a woman you don't even know. It's hardly surprising that he would be suffering feelings of guilt—'

'If my father was stupid enough to rut with a woman of low birth and then have feelings of guilt, he should have gone to the country, made his apologies to the family and left it at that,' Hayle bit off. 'He should *never* have brought his bastard to London and tried to pass him off as his *godson* so I might be made a laughingstock in society!'

'And that's what really bothers you, isn't it, Hayle? That you have a brother you never knew anything about and whose existence is an embarrassment. A brother who shares your bloodline—'

'He is nothing to me! Less than nothing!'

'He is your half-brother. And because you sensed that the moment he set foot in your house, you set out to humiliate Rand *and* your father by showing them both in the worst possible light,' Barrington said mercilessly. 'You had your mistress steal a necklace from the woman your father loved and then you tried to pin the blame for the crime on him, knowing that by exposing him, you would be humiliating your father as deeply as you felt he had humiliated you.'

If Barrington was hoping for a confession, he was destined for disappointment. 'I don't know what you're talking about, Parker. All I know is that the baroness's necklace was found in my father's possession and that he must bear the consequences for his actions.'

'And Miss Paisley? Would you see her hang for a crime she didn't commit?' Barrington pressed.

'Why should I care? She's a whore. She made her interest in me plain enough the first time I saw her and I wasn't about to pass up the invitation. Unlike you, I have hot blood running through my veins,' Hayle sneered.

Ignoring the slight, Barrington said, 'So you expect me to believe that you didn't take her as your mistress simply because she worked for the baroness and you knew that, through her, you could get your hands on the necklace.'

'That's right.'

'You'd also like me to believe that you didn't feed Miss Paisley a parcel of lies about how much you loved her, telling her that if she could steal the baroness's necklace, the two of you would be able to start a new life together.'

'Most certainly not.'

'Nor did you tell her that you actually wanted the necklace so you could set up your father to look like a thief.'

'You really have got the wrong end of the stick, Parker.'

'Have I?' Barrington shook his head. 'I think you planned the entire affair as a way of getting back at your father. You seduced Miss Paisley and then persuaded her to steal the necklace for you. You planted the necklace in your father's things and made sure Rand would be the one to find it, then *you* started the rumour that he was the one who named your father as the thief. Everyone knew that relations between Rand and your father were strained as a result of the affair with Lady Yew, so you reasoned it wouldn't come as any great surprise if Rand took an opportunity to get back at your father. But the fact is that Rand would never do something like that because, unlike you, he has a conscience.'

'A conscience!' Hayle threw back his head and laughed.

'You have the gall to say that after he slept with another man's wife?'

'Ah, but you laid the groundwork for that affair, didn't you, my Lord?' Barrington said. '*You* told Rand about the state of the Yews' marriage and *you* made a point of introducing him to her, knowing full well that she had a passion for younger men. Then, you made sure her husband found out and you asked him to go after Rand in public, knowing how furious your father would be when he learned what Rand had done. And by doing that, you thought you were giving Rand a reason for revenge against your father. It really was very well thought out. By trying to implicate your father and Rand, you attempted to destroy *both* their reputations at the same time.'

'My God, Parker, you really should be writing lurid Gothic novels for love-struck young females. Either that, or the opium has already got to your brain,' Hayle said derisively.

Barrington smiled. 'Pleading innocence won't wash, Hayle. I *know* what you're guilty of. That's why both Miss Paisley and her sister are safely beyond your reach. And if *you* know what's good for you, you'll confess to the part you played in this whole ugly affair.'

Again, Hayle laughed, but there was a nastiness to it that warned Barrington to be careful. 'Why should I? It's all supposition on your part. You don't have a shred of evidence. And even if I was guilty, it's not something that's going to put me in jail.'

'No, but it would make living in London intolerable and I think to a man like you, that would be almost as bad. When society hears what you've done, they *will* turn against you. No one will receive you and your reputation will be in shreds.'

Hayle's eyes darkened with hate. 'Get out!' he snarled. 'Get out before I forget I'm a gentleman and thrash you to within an inch of your life.' As if to make good on his threat, he rose unsteadily to his feet and took a lurching step forwards.

But Barrington merely stepped back and raised his cane. 'I'd advise you to think again, Hayle. This isn't the typical gentleman's walking stick. It doesn't break when it's brought down with force on a man's head. I know because I've done it before. And my reactions haven't been slowed by the numbing effects of opium or alcohol. I guarantee that if you take me on now, you *will* lose.'

Eyeing the lethal-looking cane, Hayle hesitated, but his voice was rough with emotion when he said, 'You won't get away with this, Parker. By God, I'll make you pay.'

'No, my Lord,' Barrington said. '*You're* the one who's going to pay. Because if I have my way, you won't be getting away with anything.'


It was nearly two o'clock in the morning when Barrington left the Nottinghams' soirée. He'd had enough of glittering society for one night. He was tired of the games he was called upon to play, weary of the desperation he saw in the eyes of so many. When had it all begun to lose its lustre? When had moving in society become a chore rather than a pleasure?

He remembered how it had been when he'd first come home from France. How surprised he'd been at the extent of society's welcome. Within days of his arrival, invitations to select gatherings had begun to roll in, as had sponsorships to the right clubs from gentlemen who had seemed genuinely interested in his welfare. He had been told which families to befriend and which to avoid in the same breath as he'd been told which tailors to patronise and which to ignore.

Then, of course, had come the ladies. All of them beautiful, many of them titled, a fair number of them married. They had shamelessly flirted with him, some in the hopes of eliciting a proposal of marriage, others in the hopes of prompting a very different type of proposal. Had he chosen to partake, he could have had a dozen of them lining up to warm his bed.

But he hadn't accepted their come-hither looks and it wasn't long before the rest of the pleasures had begun to pall as well. A brief affair with the widow of one of his father's friends, though sexually fulfilling, had left him feeling curiously dissatisfied, much like a hungry man who, having sat down to a magnificent buffet, discovered that the wine was bad and the food tasteless.

But the final blow had come during the investigation of the two men his late father had trusted and done business with. Men with whom Barrington had socialised and for whom he'd felt admiration and respect. Men who had turned out to be nothing more than parasites on the flesh of society. Greed had fuelled their quest for power and money and once their masks of civility had been stripped away, Barrington had seen them for the monsters they were.

The discovery had come too late to be of help to his father, but from that night on, Barrington had done what he could to make sure that other decent men were not so foully put upon. He'd begun listening to conversations, and when he heard something he didn't like, he'd started asking questions. Quietly. Unobtrusively. Always careful not to raise suspicions in anyone's mind. But he'd asked the questions he'd needed to get the answers that mattered.

He'd also started cultivating different friends. Friends not as highly placed in society. Friends who put more stock in a man's worth than in his title. People he found himself able to trust. He also stopped putting faith in a person's appearance. A lovely face could hide a heart of stone, just as an ugly one could disguise a generous and giving nature. He'd stopped basing his decisions on emotion and gut feeling and turned to uncovering facts, doing whatever he'd had to in order to get at the truth.

It hadn't always made him popular, but he hadn't done it to win friends.

As the soirée wasn't far from his house, Barrington decided to dismiss the carriage and walk home. He needed time to think through his situation with Anna. They hadn't spoken since their last conversation and Barrington was beginning to think they never would again. Of all the disagreements they'd had, this was by far the worst...because he'd found her vulnerable spot and struck it hard. He had called her father's honour into question. He had accused him of having a child with another woman and of not telling his legitimate son and daughter the truth.

And she, loyal to a fault and believing wholeheartedly in her father's integrity, had retaliated by accusing Barrington of being a liar and completely insensitive to her father's feelings. When he had tried to make her see her brother for what he was, Anna had told him he'd had no right to criticise and had steadfastly refused to believe that she was in any danger from Edward at all.

Unfortunately, Barrington had absolutely *no* doubt that Hayle was capable of violence and it infuriated him that Anna still tried to see the good in him, believing that his role as her brother would prevent him from visiting upon her the cruelty he so freely visited on other people. So it was up to him, Barrington realised, to keep her safe. Until Hayle could be dealt with, his priority had to be in keeping him away from Anna.

But apart from that, there was the other far more emotional situation between them: the one concerning their feelings for one another. Growing slowly but steadily, his had changed from simple liking and admiration to a deep and abiding love. Thoughts of Anna filled his days with longing and his nights with hours of sleepless frustration. He wanted her in his bed. In his heart. In his life.

But the life he offered was not one most well-bred young ladies would wish for—and it certainly wasn't what Anna deserved. For one thing, she would be settling for far less than was her due. As the daughter of an earl, a marquis or a duke wasn't out of the question; given her incredible beauty, Barrington knew she would have no trouble attracting either. And yet she remained single, professing to want *him*. She'd told him as much in the way she'd kissed him, in the way her body had melted into his, in the way her arms had closed around him and drawn him close. She was a passionate woman with a heart that beat for those she loved and she would defend them to the bitter end, Peregrine Rand being a case in point.

So how did he go about resolving this mess? How did he change her opinion of him without hurting her—or convince himself to marry her despite all the reasons he should not?

More importantly, how was he to go on living, if he was unable to do either?

He was passing a small copse of trees when he heard it. The snap of a twig. The sound of laboured breathing. Someone hiding in the bushes, waiting to spring. But even as he jumped to the left and drew the sword from its ebony holder, Barrington knew it was too late. His enemy was upon him, the sudden, sharp pain in his right shoulder proof that the danger was much closer than he'd anticipated.

Clamping his teeth against the pain, Barrington whirled and saw the man standing behind him. Darkness hid the contours of his face, but he had no need of lamplight to know who his enemy was. The hatred emanating from Hayle was a tangible force. And when he lunged again, Barrington knew it was in the hopes of finishing him off.

Fortunately, this time, the lethal blade missed its mark.

'The opium must have muddled your brain,' Barrington said, switching the sword to his left hand, knowing his right was now useless. 'A skilled fencer wouldn't have missed an opportunity like that.'

'I didn't miss with my first strike,' Hayle growled. 'Shall I take pity on you and finish you off quickly, Parker? Or are you as good with your left hand as you are with your right?'

Barrington shifted his weight to compensate for the change in fencing arm. 'I am, by nature, a right-handed fencer, but I learned to use a sword in my left so I might be doubly prepared.'

'Then we shall see how well you were taught,' Hayle cried, lunging again.

The sharp clang of blades echoed in the night, but Barrington knew better than to look for help. No sensible person was abroad this time of night and the watchman was likely asleep in his box. Hayle had chosen the time and place of his attack well.

'I must have caused you considerable alarm,' Barrington said, the edge of his blade gleaming dangerously in the moonlight, 'to provoke you into coming after me.'

'You said enough.' The earl's son aimed a deadly blow at Barrington's right side, obviously hoping to worsen the damage he'd already inflicted. 'I don't intend to let you or anyone else humiliate me again and I certainly don't intend to let you expose me.'

Barrington skilfully deflected the attack, but Hayle was fighting like a man possessed. While his skills were inferior to Barrington's, his anger and fear combined to make him a dangerous adversary. Fortunately, with that much opium in his system he couldn't hope to last long in a sustained fight. 'Killing me won't change the situation with Rand,' Barrington threw out. 'He'll always be your father's son.'

'His bastard, you mean!' Hayle shouted. 'And I'm damned if I'll let him take what's rightfully mine.'

'Don't be stupid, Hayle. Your father won't leave his estate to Rand. You're his legitimate son and heir.'

'But he *likes* Rand,' Hayle spat contemptuously. 'He wishes I was more like him. But I'm not and I'm never going to be. Rand's a spineless interloper who's going back to the country as soon as I can make it happen.'

Barrington felt a sudden wave of light-headedness. He must be losing more blood than he thought. And the pain in his right shoulder was a constant reminder of his carelessness...

'Feeling the strain, Parker?' Hayle taunted. 'It's all well and good to put on a fancy show in front of others, but we both know *this* is what it's all about. The fight to the death.'

Barrington took a deep breath. He *was* getting weaker, which meant he had to change his strategy. If he hoped to survive, he had to convince Hayle that he was failing. Lull him into believing that he could close in for the kill at any time.

Fortunately, Barrington had a feeling his opponent wasn't looking to make this a quick kill. Hayle was the kind of man who enjoyed prolonging the agony. By doing so, he would unwittingly give his opponent the advantage he needed.

Barrington let his arm fall, as though weakening. 'What do you hope to gain by killing me, Hayle? Freedom from persecution?'

'You could say that.' Hayle withdrew a few paces, but kept his fighting arm extended, the point of the blade level with Barrington's chest. 'With you dead, there will be no one to challenge my father's guilt. He won't go to jail, but he will be ostracised. And Rand will go back to the country where he belongs and I'll see to it that Anna is married off to some harmless bumpkin who prefers life in the country. Maybe

I'll push her in Lord Andrews's direction. She'd do nicely for him once he has knocked the spunk out of her.'

Fighting down rage at the thought of Andrews getting anywhere near Anna, Barrington took a step, exaggerated a wince and made sure his opponent saw it. 'You've thought of everything.'

'I always do. It's taken a while, but it's all come together,' Hayle said. 'Rand's humiliation, Father's disgrace and, eventually, my marriage to the lovely baroness. And with it, an end to all my financial worries.'

'So that was the final part of your plan.'

Hayle inclined his head. 'I've already told her it was my father who stole the necklace. She didn't believe me, of course, but she won't have a choice once it all comes out. And I have been very careful in my addresses to her. I am, of course, in utter despair over my poor father's circumstances. But if a man cannot bring himself to act according to the law, he must suffer the consequences. Julia will see that and, in time, she will agree to be my wife. I have expensive habits and they need constant feeding. I intend to make damn sure no lawyer puts her money beyond my reach.'

It was shameless, Barrington reflected, but he couldn't fault Hayle's strategy. Through careful planning, he had removed each of the obstacles that stood in the way of his getting what he wanted. Barrington saw the anticipation of victory on the other man's face and knew he believed success lay within his grasp, confident it was only a matter of minutes before it was his.

But he'd reckoned without his opponent's equally fierce determination to prevent any of that happening. Barrington let his arm fall another inch and saw the smile break out on Hayle's face.

'Well, I think it's time to bring an end to this. Goodbye, Parker. I hope your skills with a foil serve you better in hell than they did here.'

# Chapter Fifteen

Anna stared through the window of the carriage as it made its way home from the card party. Peregrine was dozing quietly beside her, but even though the hour was late, she was far too wide awake to sleep. She had hoped an evening with friends might help her forget her concerns about Barrington and her family, but not even the constant chatter about balls and betrothals had been enough to do so—because she couldn't stop thinking about Barrington. She couldn't stop remembering everything he'd said to her. Everything he had come to mean to her.

And in remembering all that, Anna knew she had no choice but to tell him she loved him and dare him to turn her away! She would suffer the embarrassment of being spurned, take whatever chances she had to, but she was *not* going to let him walk out of her life without having made one last effort to get him to stay. She had no intention of spending the rest of her life alone, knowing she had no one to blame but herself if that's how it ended up.

They were passing the end of the park when she saw a flurry of movement in the trees. Two dark figures—then a shimmer of silver in the moonlit darkness. Swords! She sat forwards and pressed her face to the glass. 'Peregrine! Wake up!' She thumped on the roof of the carriage. 'Stop!'

'What's the matter?' Peregrine said, groggily coming to.

'There's a fight,' she said, throwing open the carriage door. 'In the park.'

'Anna, wait, are you mad?'

She ran across the grass, deaf to his cries. Some sixth sense warned her that this was no ordinary fight. She hadn't seen her brother or Barrington the entire evening, but Lord Richard Crew, appearing late at the home of Lady Bessmel, said he had been at a hell earlier in the evening and that both Barrington and her brother had been there and that neither of them had looked happy. Had Barrington gone to confront Edward about his conduct with Eliza and been met with threats of violence?

Those words echoed in Anna's ears now as she ran towards the two men. One of them was tiring. He was staggering backwards, hunched over, his right arm hanging limp at his side. The other man raised his sword for the killing blow and she felt the scream build in her lungs. *'Barrington!'*

A split second before he heard Anna scream, Barrington straightened. With deadly intent, he lunged, moving at incredible speed and catching Hayle completely off guard. He stabbed him first in the left leg to disable him, then in his right shoulder to render his sword arm ineffectual.

The earl's son screamed in pain as the sword fell uselessly from his hand. As he sank to the ground, Barrington saw the look of disbelief on his face. He hadn't expected that final rally. Hayle had been preparing himself for victory, readying his blade for the killing blow, his wounded opponent all but vanquished.

Instead, he was the one now down on the ground, blood flowing freely from wounds in his leg and his shoulder. He would live, but he would never fight with that arm again. Only then did Barrington turn and see Anna flying across the grass towards him. Anna, her eyes wide, her face white with fear. 'Barrington! Oh, dear God!'

And then she was in his arms, heedless of his blood soaking into her gown. He gasped at the pain her embrace caused, but there was no way in hell he was going to push her away. Not now when he felt the wetness of tears on her face. He closed his eyes and held her close as his knees finally gave way and he sank wearily to the ground.

'Barrington!' she cried, falling with him.

'I'm fine, Anna,' he whispered. 'Fine. I just need to…sit down.'

Seconds later, Peregrine came running. 'What the hell's going on?' He looked in horror at Edward lying on the ground, and then at Barrington bleeding in Anna's arms. 'What in blazes—?'

'Lord Hayle and I had some…unfinished business,' Barrington murmured over Anna's head. He handed his sword to Peregrine with the instruction that he watch Hayle, then he tipped Anna's face up to his. 'It's over, love. Everything's going to be all right now.'

He stared down into her eyes and saw everything that mattered to him. Everything that ever would matter. She was his now and for always. And he was never going to do anything to risk losing her again.

That was his last thought as he slipped into darkness and the pain in his shoulder mercifully disappeared.

It was a tense party that gathered in the Earl of Cambermere's library just over an hour later. Barrington, his shoulder bandaged and wearing a clean shirt lent to him by Peregrine, held a large glass of brandy in his good hand and Anna sat next to him wearing a new gown, her previous one having been liberally stained with his blood. Peregrine sat in the chair in front of the fireplace, looking deeply upset by all that had gone on, and the earl sat behind his desk, looking equally troubled as he nursed an even larger glass of brandy.

Only Edward was absent, his injuries being tended to upstairs by the surgeon his father had called in immediately upon the party arriving home.

A few minutes later, the door opened and the surgeon came in. Instantly, the earl was on his feet. 'Well?'

'Your son will be fine,' Mr Hopkins said with a weary smile. 'I've stitched the wound and given him a sedative for the pain. I doubt he'll wake up for some time.'

'How serious are his injuries?' Anna asked.

'The injury to his thigh was superficial, but he won't have much use of his right arm.' The surgeon glanced at Barrington. 'I suspect the only reason he's still alive is because you knew exactly where to strike.'

'It was never my intention to kill him,' Barrington said quietly. 'Only to prevent one of us from being killed.'

'Then you have my congratulations on a job well done. I've left some laudanum on the table by the door for you, Sir Barrington. It will help ease the pain.'

Barrington nodded. 'Thank you, Mr Hopkins.'

'Yes, thank you, Hopkins,' the earl said gruffly. 'Good of you to come so quickly.'

The surgeon smiled. 'I'll add it to the bill. Goodnight, all.'

Cambermere waited for the surgeon to leave before saying,

'Now would someone please tell me what in God's name happened tonight?'

Barrington glanced at Anna, but realised she was still too shaken to talk about it. Given that Peregrine didn't look much better, Barrington said, 'I think it falls to me to explain, my Lord. And as much as I regret some of what I am about to say, I'm afraid you need to hear it all.'

The earl grimaced. 'Say what you must. I shall bear it as best I can.'

So Barrington told him, beginning with Hayle's taking up with Elizabeth Paisley, followed by the details of his plan to have her steal the baroness's necklace and finally his reasons for placing the necklace in his father's room. He purposely made no mention of the conversation he'd had with Hayle regarding his feelings towards Peregrine, knowing it would reveal more than he—and likely the earl—wished to, but what he did say was damning enough.

At the end of the lengthy telling, the earl abruptly stood up, his face devoid of colour, his brown eyes deeply troubled. 'Why?' was all he said. 'I've never been hard on Edward. Never forced him to do anything he had no wish to do. And I gave him everything he asked for.'

'I'm sure you did all that and more,' Barrington said. 'But when you invited Peregrine to come and stay with you, everything changed. It's time, my Lord,' he said softly. 'You can't keep this a secret any longer.'

He felt Anna stiffen on the sofa beside him, but knew the time for deceit was over. She had to hear the truth and she had to hear it from her father's lips.

Cambermere obviously knew it, too. 'You're right, of course,' he said finally. 'It was naïve of me to think I could keep the secret for ever. A man's past is never truly past.' He looked at Anna and sadly shook his head. 'I'm sorry, my dear. I should have told you the truth straight away. Before Peregrine even got here. But I was afraid you would think badly of me.'

'I could never do that, Papa.'

'You might over something like this.'

'Like what?'

The earl sighed. 'The fact that Peregrine *is* my son.'

Barrington heard Anna's muffled gasp, but it was to Peregrine's starkly white face that his gaze was drawn. 'I'm *what*?'

'It's true,' the earl said. 'I met your mother when I was nineteen. We fell madly in love and it was my dearest wish that we be married. But my father wouldn't allow it. Olivia wasn't well born and I was heir to an earldom. So while my parents didn't object to our friendship in the beginning, they did once they saw it getting serious. When I told my father I was in love with Olivia, he forbade me to see her ever again.'

'Oh, Papa,' Anna said softly.

'We were both heartbroken,' the earl said quietly. 'At that age, love is so keenly felt, as was the pain of our enforced separation. But I had no choice. I had duties and obligations. Responsibilities to my name. So I made the decision to break it off. I never saw Olivia again.'

'But what about Mama?' Anna asked. 'Did you not love her?'

'Yes, but not in the way I loved Olivia. I'm sorry, my dear, but you may as well know the truth. My marriage to your mother was arranged and the love we came to feel for one another developed over time. But what I felt for Olivia was entirely different. Something that only comes along once in a lifetime. Peregrine is the result of that love.'

'But how could you just leave her like that?' Peregrine

asked in a harsh whisper. 'You got her with child and then just...walked away?'

'I never knew she was increasing,' the earl said, the sadness in his voice reflected in the bleakness of his expression. 'I was sent away to Europe. When I got back, it was to find the preparations for my marriage to Isabel already underway.'

'How did Mama feel about the marriage?' Anna asked.

'We liked each other well enough. Your mother was high born and beautiful, everything a man could ask for, and we were married a few months later. The problem was, I was still in love with Olivia.'

'But you never saw her again,' Peregrine said grimly.

Cambermere shook his head. 'I went looking for her when I got back, of course, but she was gone. And I had no idea there was a child until two months ago when the man you believed to be your father wrote to tell me about you.'

'But how did he know?'

'Apparently, Olivia fell ill not long after I was sent away. When she found out she was...dying—' the earl's voice caught, but he forced himself to go on '—she gave you to her sister, Mary, to raise. But she made Mary promise not to tell *anyone* who your father really was. Mary kept that promise until the night before she died. Only then did she tell her husband who you really were and that it was only right I be contacted and made aware of your existence.'

It was a shocking story and Barrington wasn't at all surprised that no one in the room spoke for a few minutes. They all had much to come to terms with. The knowledge that Cambermere had been in love with another woman before he'd met his wife. The fact there had been a child from that ill-fated love, and the fact that only three people had known the truth about Peregrine's existence.

'So, Peregrine really *is* my half-brother,' Anna said, the first to find her voice.

'Yes, my dear, he is,' her father said. 'And I hope you will believe me when I say that I was as deeply shocked when the letter arrived telling me about him as you are now.'

Anna nodded, her eyes heavy with regret as she glanced at Barrington. 'I'm so sorry, Barrington. I should never have doubted you.'

'It doesn't matter.'

'Yes, it does.' Anna turned to glare at her father. 'You should have told us the truth, Papa. As soon as you found out.'

'I know. I thought you might have realised it the first day Peregrine arrived,' Cambermere said. 'Edward saw it straight away.'

Anna shook her head. 'I wasn't looking. You introduced him as your godson. I had no reason to suspect otherwise.'

'But if you knew who I was when you wrote to me,' Peregrine said slowly, 'why didn't you tell *me* when I first arrived in London?'

'Because I wanted the three of you to get to know one another without any kind of prejudice standing in the way,' the earl explained. 'Perhaps that was naïve of me, but I thought it would be easier for you to become friends if you didn't know about the connection. Wrong, I know now, but that was the decision I made.' He glanced at his daughter, his eyes pleading with her to understand. 'I knew it would be difficult to explain my having a child with another woman. You loved your mother deeply and I feared you would see it as a betrayal of her that I had been with another woman, even if happened before your mother and I were introduced. I didn't want you to hold that against Peregrine. It wasn't his fault.'

'But it mattered to Edward,' Anna said sadly. 'He knew who Peregrine was and he wanted nothing to do with him.'

'It was worse than that,' Barrington said. 'Your brother wanted to humiliate Rand, the way he felt he'd been humiliated by your father's bringing Peregrine to London. Edward was convinced that if *he* knew Peregrine was your father's son, so would the rest of society.'

'And did they?' Anna asked.

'I'd be lying if I said there hasn't been speculation about it. Nevertheless, it was Edward's intention right from the start that Peregrine should fail.' Barrington said. 'He introduced him to Lady Yew, knowing her penchant for younger men, and made sure that Peregrine knew the truth about the state of the Yews' marriage. He encouraged him to become Lady Yew's lover, and he used that to try to set your father against Peregrine, and perhaps against you as well.'

'That's why he tried to make it look as though I'd stolen the necklace,' the earl said sadly.

Barrington nodded. 'He knew you wouldn't go to jail, but that your standing in society would be hopelessly compromised. That's what he was counting on. He also planned on courting the baroness in the hopes of eventually marrying her. He felt that by showing you in such a bad light, and himself in such a good one, she would eventually transfer her affections to him.'

'Dear God,' the earl whispered. 'What did I do to deserve such hatred from my own son?'

'He didn't hate you, Papa,' Anna said sadly. 'He was just eaten up by jealousy.'

'And by his fears, irrational as they were,' Barrington said. 'Perhaps he was afraid you might have made Peregrine your heir.'

'No,' the earl said firmly. 'Whatever my feelings for

Peregrine, Edward is my legitimate heir. The title must devolve to him.'

'But what of his future now, Papa?' Anna said. 'He cannot stay here. Not after what he did to you and Peregrine. To say nothing of the fact that he tried to kill Barrington tonight.'

'My lord, if I may…?' Barrington interjected.

The earl nodded. 'Of course.'

'It might be in everyone's best interests if Edward were to…go away for a while.'

The earl frowned. 'Go away?'

'To the Americas, perhaps. Or Australia. A man can do well in such places if he applies himself and your son is far from stupid. He is simply a victim of his own insecurities. This could be a chance for him to make something of himself. More importantly, it would get him away from London and give the rest of you time to work matters through. And, hopefully, to put all of this behind you.'

Anna nodded. 'I think it's an excellent idea. I don't see how any of us would be able to carry on as normal, given what's happened.'

'No, I don't suppose we would. But what about you, Parker?' the earl asked, his voice laced with regret. 'There's no getting around the fact that my son would have killed you. You would be perfectly within your rights to have him brought up on charges.'

'Perhaps, but I have no intention of doing so. I would never wish that kind of grief on your family. Your son acted out of jealousy and fear. He is tortured enough by his demons. There is no need for me to add to his suffering,' Barrington said.

All eyes turned to the earl, who seemed to be considering the suggestion. 'Are you sure you would be amenable to seeing him walk away? You may never wield a sword with that arm again.'

Barrington shrugged. 'Since I am able to fence with either hand, it is of no real consequence. It is enough that Edward experience life elsewhere. Perhaps it will force him to take a closer look at his life and to rethink his priorities.'

'I sincerely hope so,' the earl said heavily. 'A man's son is said to be a reflection of himself. I hate to think that in some way I inspired that kind of belief system in him.' He glanced at Peregrine, who was sitting quietly in the corner, and said, 'And what about you, sir? What have you to say about all this?'

Peregrine looked up, still clearly in shock. 'What *can* one say upon learning that the man he has always believed to be his father is not, and that a man he never knew existed until a few weeks ago is.'

'A shocking revelation indeed,' the earl agreed.

'Also, that I have a half-brother and half-sister I never knew, and that one of them hated me enough to wish his own father grievous harm.' Peregrine shook his head, his eyes troubled. 'It is a great deal to come to terms with.'

'Indeed it is,' the earl said quietly. 'But it is my sincere hope that you will stay here and get to know us better while you are endeavouring to do so. However, if you feel you cannot stay under the present circumstances, you are free to leave. Perhaps you will wish to return to the family you left behind.'

'Actually, I would rather stay in London,' Peregrine said slowly. 'One of the reasons my father…that is, the man I thought was my father wrote asking you to take me, was so that I might have a chance to experience life beyond the farm. I think he knew I wasn't cut out to be a farmer. And while they were good to me, I doubt going back there now would be in anyone's best interests.'

'Then you are welcome to stay,' the earl said. 'If Anna has no objections?'

'None whatsoever,' Anna said immediately. 'I don't like Peregrine any the less for having found out he's my half-brother. In fact,' she added with a smile, 'I like him a great deal more.'

'Good. Then the decision is yours, Peregrine. If you wish to stay in London, we will be happy to have you. And if you do not wish to live in this house, you may choose another,' the earl said. 'I shall see to it that you *are* taken care of and that you are acknowledged as my son.'

Peregrine stared. 'You would do that?'

'Why not? I'm not ashamed of you. Far from it,' the earl said softly. 'You are all I have left of Olivia and I loved her with all my heart. I see so much of her in you and I deeply regret that you did not have a chance to know her. She was… an exceptional woman.'

'Perhaps you could tell me about her,' Peregrine said slowly. 'I would like to know who she was.'

'I would be honoured,' the earl said. Then, roughly clearing his throat, he got to his feet. 'Well, it's late and I think enough's been said for now. Parker, my carriage is at your disposal. Or, you are welcome to stay here if your injuries are such that you would rather not travel.'

'Thank you, my Lord, but I would like to return home.' Barrington stood up, wincing slightly. It was one thing to pretend his injuries weren't serious; it was quite another to believe it. 'You have enough to contend with here, I think.'

'I'll see you out,' Anna said, quickly getting to her feet.

They walked to the front door in silence. Barrington was very aware of Anna beside him, but the situation was too fraught with emotion to speak of important matters now. The embrace they had shared in the park, the passionate words they had exchanged, would all have to be addressed, but not tonight. 'May I call upon you in a few days' time?' he asked as they stood together at the door. 'There are things that need to be said.'

'Of course,' she said, her expression faltering ever so slightly. 'Are you sure you're well enough to drive home, Barrington? You've been through so much tonight.'

He gave her a weak smile. 'We all have. Given that I won't be the one driving, I'll be fine. But I am in need of rest.'

'Yes, of course.' She looked at him then, and to his surprise she stood on her toes and kissed him full on the mouth in a long, intimate kiss that left his head spinning. 'Sleep well, my love,' she whispered against his lips. 'And thank you from the bottom of my heart for everything you did tonight.'

Incredible. As much as his body ached, the touch of her mouth instantly aroused him. 'I did nothing.'

'You let my brother live,' she said. 'But, more importantly, *you* lived. I wouldn't have liked having my brother's death on my hands, but I fear that's what would have happened had you died at his tonight.'

Barrington wanted to believe she was joking, but the look in her eyes told him otherwise. 'You would have destroyed your life.'

'It wouldn't have mattered,' she told him. 'If he had killed you, it would already have been destroyed beyond all hope of repair.'

As expected, over the next few days, Peregrine and the earl spent a great deal of time talking through their unusual situation. There were twenty-seven years to make up for and a lot of ground to cover. And though, at first, the words were slow in coming, it wasn't long before they were flowing freely, bringing the two back on an even keel. Peregrine was anxious to hear about his mother and Cambermere was delighted to talk about her. Given that he'd had to keep the truth about Olivia bottled up for so many years, it was a relief to finally be able to talk to someone about her—especially when that someone happened to be her son. And in learning of his true parentage, Peregrine seemed to mature into the man Anna knew he wanted to be. Lady Yew was never mentioned again.

As for Edward, he had been happy to go away. Aware that his future in London was in jeopardy, both because his family knew what he had tried to do and because it was quite likely society would find out at some point, he elected to go to California, where he'd heard stories that it was possible for a man with a good head on his shoulders to acquire vast tracts of land and make a fortune into the bargain. If there was one thing Edward wasn't lacking, Anna acknowledged wryly, it was confidence in his own ability to succeed.

As for Julia, she was thrilled at having her necklace safely returned to her. So much so that, when she learned the truth about what happened, she decided not to press charges against Miss Paisley and even offered the girl her position back.

'Why ever would she do such a thing?' Lydia asked as she and Anna walked their horses along Rotten Row a few days later. 'Miss Paisley has proven herself anything but trustworthy.'

'I know, but if you could have seen Eliza's face when Barrington told her she wasn't going to be charged and that the baroness was willing to take her back, you would understand. Eliza hasn't had an easy life,' Anna said. 'She told me the happiest she's ever been was during her brief time with the baroness and she apologised to Julia so sincerely that I actually saw tears in Julia's eyes. Eliza said she was willing to do whatever the baroness asked and that she could check her jewellery every night to make sure it was all there. She was just that happy to have a second chance.'

'Well, I'm glad it all worked out for Eliza, but what about Justine?'

Anna laughed. 'I was able to find a position for her and you will never guess with whom.'

Lydia looked blank. 'Who?'

'Miss Mercy Banks. Or, as she will shortly become, Mrs Giles Blokker. I think they will suit admirably.'

'How marvellous! And your father? This must have been a very trying time for him.'

'It has been dreadful,' Anna admitted. 'Learning about the existence of a son he never knew he had and finding out what kind of man Edward was were very hard on him. But some wonderful things have come out of it, too. He has acknowledged Peregrine as his son and Peregrine is delighted that he doesn't have to go back to the country. He's promised us all that he'll forget about sowing wild oats and stick to his papers and archaeological investigations.'

'And what of your father's hopes with regard to Julia?'

Anna slowly began to smile. 'In spite of my brother's best efforts, Julia never believed that my father was guilty of stealing her necklace. She didn't understand Edward's sudden interest in her and says she found it rather sad, since it was obvious he didn't love her the same way Papa did. I believe he will ask her to marry him once a suitable time has passed and the memory of all this has faded.'

'So,' Lydia said with a smile, 'your father and Peregrine are settled and Edward has been banished to the Americas. It would appear that matters have worked out splendidly for everyone…except you.'

'Nonsense, I am perfectly happy.'

'Has Sir Barrington spoken to you?'

Anna felt her cheeks grow warm. 'Not yet, but he did say we had things to talk about.'

'And do you wish to talk to him about these matters?'

'Yes, though there really is no hurry,' Anna said, knowing it for the lie it was.

But Lydia just smiled. 'Perhaps not on your part, but I believe the gentleman is quite anxious in that regard. No doubt that is why he is approaching us now with such a determined look on his face.'

Anna gasped and, lifting her head, saw that Barrington was indeed riding towards them. 'Oh, no, I'm not ready!'

'I don't think we ever are for moments like this,' Lydia said with a wink, 'but they come along regardless. And in case you're wondering, this isn't a chance meeting. Sir Barrington sent a note asking me if we would be riding in the park this morning. I told him we would.'

Anna felt her pulse begin to race. He had planned this? He'd wanted to see her that badly?

'Good morning, Lady Annabelle. Lady Lydia,' he greeted them, resting his hands on the pommel. 'Lovely morning for a ride.'

'It is indeed, Sir Barrington, and I think I shall take advantage of it,' Lydia said, gathering her reins and smiling at Anna. 'I shall return in a little while.'

In the silence that followed, Anna turned to study the face of the man watching her and realised her heart was beating so hard she could barely speak. 'I could say this is a surprise but I understand it was planned.'

Barrington gave her a wry, fleeting smile. 'It has been my experience that important matters are best not left to chance. I wished to speak to you in private, which meant not at your house or at a society gathering. So, I had to arrange for some other meeting place and I thought this the most suitable. I did ask Lady Lydia to stay close by so there could be no question of impropriety.'

Anna looked up and saw that Lydia was still within sight, having stopped under the shade of a large tree just beyond. 'You appear to have thought of everything.'

'I try,' he said quietly. 'Though when it comes to you, I find myself constantly falling short of the mark.'

Anna bit her lip so as not to smile. 'I can't imagine why you would say that. You always seem so completely in control of yourself, no matter what the situation.'

'Because I am used to dealing in logic and reason. Yet all of my dealings with you involve emotions, and rather strong ones at that,' he admitted.

'And emotion clouds judgement so as to totally obscure the truth,' she teased.

'I should have known you would use that against me,' he said wryly.

'It wasn't intended as a slight. I would never knowingly hurt you, Barrington.' Anna's smile faded, her fingers tightening convulsively on the reins. 'You look…much better than you did when last I saw you.'

Clearly intent on setting her mind at rest, Barrington grinned. 'I have fully regained my strength and the surgeon is very pleased with my shoulder, though my valet has been heard to complain that I have, at times, been a rather difficult patient.'

Anna laughed, a welcome relief from the tension she'd been carrying for too many days. 'I was so afraid, Barrington. That night, when I ran across the park and saw you and Edward fighting…when I saw all the blood…I was terrified I was going to lose you.'

'There was really never any danger of that,' he said quietly. 'Your brother was too far under the influence of the opium to be a real threat.'

'But he wounded you all the same.'

'Yes, because I was careless,' Barrington admitted. 'I lowered my guard. Preoccupied with thoughts of you, I wasn't expecting the attack. But he only managed to get in one thrust.'

'One good one,' she whispered, glancing at his arm, still in its sling. 'You may never use that arm again.'

'Not to fight to my previous standard, perhaps, but it is perfectly capable of doing other things. Like holding you close,' he murmured.

Anna closed her eyes, feeling the warmth of his words pierce her heart. 'Is this where you tell me again about the risks involved in loving you?'

She opened her eyes and caught his gaze. A minute passed, and then he slowly began to smile. 'No. It's probably what I *should* say, but I'm not going to. What I feel for you isn't rational, Anna, but I'm not willing to fight it any more.'

'Good, because love isn't rational,' Anna said. 'Elizabeth Paisley did what my brother asked because she loved him and thought he loved her in return. Just as Peregrine lied to me because he thought Lady Yew had deep feelings for him. Love excuses all things and forgives all things.'

'Do you honestly believe that?'

'No. It's a pretty sentiment, but it doesn't justify lies or deceit. Peregrine's belief that Lady Yew wasn't in love with her husband didn't make it right for him to enter into an affair with her. Just as being in love with my brother didn't justify Miss Paisley's stealing Julia's necklace.'

'So you're saying that truth and emotion will always clash,' Barrington said.

'Probably. I suspect men will always do bizarre things in the name of love.'

'Which brings me back to our ongoing conversation.' At her look of confusion, he said, 'The one we started the night we met at Lady Montby's and that we have been having ever since. The one concerning…us.'

Her pulse accelerated. 'I wasn't sure there *was* an us.'

'Oh, there most definitely is an us,' Barrington replied. 'I've spent the last few weeks trying to deny it, but finally realised I'm fighting a losing battle. And you know why.'

Anna stared down at her hands. 'You have taken pains to tell me and on more than one occasion. But you must feel there is hope for us or you wouldn't have sought me out.'

'You're right. Because the idea of *not* having you in my life is one I can no longer contemplate. You *are* all I think about, Anna,' he said quietly. 'And a man cannot be effective if his mind is constantly engaged upon something or someone he believes…unattainable.'

'I have always been attainable…for you,' Anna said, her voice husky. 'It was *you* who chose to believe otherwise. And I don't care if being with you involves risk. I would rather take the risks than live without you.'

'Even if it endangered your life?'

Anna suddenly felt wise beyond her years. 'You said yourself that life is never entirely without risk and you're right. But I like to think I demonstrated that I am not some witless female prone to running away at the first sign of danger.'

'No, you're not.' His mouth lifted at one corner. 'You have proven that most admirably. But would you allow yourself to become intimately involved with a man like me? Knowing that what I do might always put you in danger.'

Anna shook her head. 'The greatest danger to *both* of

us thus far has been from my own family. I couldn't be any closer to the source of the danger if I tried.'

'In that case…' Barrington dismounted and, crossing to her side, held out his hand. Anna placed hers within it and allowed him to help her down from the saddle. His hands lingered on her waist and they were so close she could feel the warmth of his breath on her face. 'I haven't spoken to your father, and if you say you have no desire to *be* my wife, I will not do so. But if you consent to marry me, Anna, I'll make you a promise here and now that there won't be any more risks to either of us, because I won't take on any more assignments.'

Her eyes widened in shock. 'You would do that for me?'

'I would do whatever it took to keep you safe,' Barrington said softly. 'I love you, Anna. There's never been a woman in my life for whom I've felt a deeper or more powerful passion. I love everything about you. Your enthusiasm for life, your unstinting concern for others, the genuine goodness that is so much a part of you. If you refuse to marry me, I will go on, but only because there won't be anything else for me to do. If you accept, you'll never have to worry about your happiness again.'

'Or yours,' Anna said. 'My brother almost killed you, Barrington, and I suspect there are others who would no doubt like to try. A man doesn't make friends by exposing other men's deepest, darkest secrets.'

'That's what I've been trying to tell you.'

'Nevertheless, someone has to try to stop them, and as I've been trying to tell *you*, I don't want you to give up what you do. I love you. There's no doubt in my mind about that. And, yes, I'll be afraid for you, but what you do is part of who you are. I couldn't ask you to give that up for me.'

'You don't have to ask. I've given a great deal of thought

to what I would be giving up and it doesn't compare to what I would be gaining. I want you as my wife, Anna,' he told her fervently. 'I want to hold you in my arms and tell you every day how much I love you. I want to cover your body with kisses and hear you cry out my name when we make love. And I want to see your beautiful eyes in the faces of our children. Marry me, sweetheart, and I'll spend the rest of my life not only telling you how much I love you, but showing you.'

His smile was slow and sensual, filling her with a giddy sense of pleasure. 'Good, because I *am* saying yes, Barrington, so you'd better be prepared to make good on your promise.' Uncaring as to who might be watching, Anna walked into his arms and tilted her head back, her eyes glowing. 'As far as I'm concerned, you can start telling me *and* showing me, just as soon as you like.'

\* \* \* \* \*

# Courting Miss Vallois

## GAIL WHITIKER

To Klas, always.
Thank you for introducing me
to all things Swedish.

To my agent, Sally Harding,
for opening doors and for being there
with a keen eye, a wealth of patience
and an excellent sense of humour.

And to Kimberley Young,
who made me dig deeper,
but in the nicest possible way.
Thank you for guiding me safely through
the perils of the London Underground!

## Chapter One

'We've found them, my lord,' Inspector Rawlings said in a voice of quiet satisfaction. 'And by all accounts, in good health and fine spirits.'

For a moment, no one spoke. Not the portly detective whose long-awaited words brought to an end a search that had begun nearly eighteen months ago. Not the beautiful, dark-haired lady whose briefly closed eyes spoke more eloquently of her feelings than words ever could. And not the tall, slender gentleman whose clandestine missions in France had been the reason for the investigation in the first place. Nothing disturbed the silence of the April afternoon but the steady ticking of the mantel clock and the rattle of carriage wheels on the cobblestones below.

'And there is no doubt in your mind that it is Sophie Vallois and her brother, Antoine?' Nicholas Grey, Viscount Longworth, asked at length.

Rawlings shook his head. 'None whatsoever. I've had my best man on it for months. There can be no mistake.'

'Thank heavens!' Lavinia Grey said with relief. 'To know they have finally been located. I cannot imagine what their life has been like.'

'Neither can I,' the inspector admitted. 'But I suspect they did what was necessary in order to protect themselves from those who would have murdered them in their beds.'

Lavinia's slender fingers tightened on the arm of the loveseat. 'Surely it was not as dire as that.'

'I wish I could say otherwise, but to those loyal to Bonaparte, what Miss Vallois and her brother did would have been viewed as an act of treason. The two would have had no choice but to lose themselves in the back streets of Paris.'

'Which they did most effectively for the best part of three years,' Nicholas murmured. 'Are they aware of having been followed?'

'No, my lord. Budge is my best man. He could follow the Prince Regent into the privy and not arouse suspicion. Begging your pardon, my lady.'

Lavinia inclined her head, though the dimple in her cheek suggested amusement rather than annoyance. 'And my husband's letter. Was it delivered?'

'According to my information, it was put into Miss Vallois's hands at half past four on the afternoon of the tenth,' the inspector said, checking his notepad. 'That being the case, you should be receiving an answer very soon.'

'*If* the young lady has any intention of replying.' Nicholas moved towards the fireplace, seeing in the flames the sweetly innocent face of the child he remembered. 'She might not even remember who I am. And if she does remember, she may wish to have nothing more to do with a man who was so instrumental in ruining her life.'

'You did *not* ruin her life, Nicholas,' Lavinia said with a touch of exasperation. 'Miss Vallois and her brother helped you of their own accord. It isn't fair that you should shoulder all the blame for what happened as a result.'

Nicholas smiled, touched as always by his wife's unconditional support of his actions. She was a remarkable woman, able to comprehend the rationale behind what he did without convoluted explanations or lengthy justifications. Her quick, intuitive mind would have made her an excellent intelligence agent had she chosen to turn her hand to it. And as he walked across the room towards the brocade loveseat where she sat, he thanked God—and his commanding officer—that she had not. 'You are, as always, the voice of reason and logic. Even if the logic is somewhat prejudiced in my favour.'

'Of course it's prejudiced, darling. I am your wife. How could it be otherwise?'

'Not all wives agree with their husbands.'

'Not all husbands are worth agreeing with.' She smiled up at him. 'You have always been a most delightful exception.'

Nicholas bent to press a kiss against her dark, shining hair. 'And you the reason for it.'

Across the room, Inspector Rawlings cleared his throat. 'Excuse me, my lord, but shall I inform my man that his continued surveillance is no longer required?'

Nicholas glanced at his wife. 'Well?'

Lavinia raised her shoulders in a gesture as eloquent as it was elegant. 'I suppose there is nothing to be gained by leaving the poor man in France now. Miss

Vallois and her brother have been found and your letter delivered. There is nothing we can do but sit back and wait for her reply.'

Nicholas glanced at the inspector to see if he had anything to add, but assumed from the expression on his face that he agreed with Lavinia. They had all waited a long time for news that Sophie and Antoine Vallois had been found. Now that they had, and an initial contact had been made, there was nothing any of them could do but sit back and wait for her answer. It was frustrating, to be sure, but it seemed that once again, fate had placed his well-being squarely into someone else's hands. All he could do now was hope it would smile as favourably upon him today as it had all those years ago, when, but for a chance meeting with a young French girl and her brother in the darkened countryside of war-torn France, he wouldn't have been here at all.

The lumbering coach drew to a halt in the bustling yard of the Black Swan Inn; within minutes, a stable boy ran forwards to grab the reins of the lead horse. Carriage doors were thrown open, stairs were let down and a stream of weary passengers began to make their way into the inn.

Sophie Vallois was amongst the first to disembark and as she waited for her brother to join her, she smoothed her hands over the rumpled skirts of her well-worn travelling outfit. Thank goodness she had not worn one of her new ensembles. Quarters on board ship had been cramped, and cleanliness was not an issue with which the captain had concerned himself. Added to that, the rough crossing had been enough to test the mettle of even the hardiest sailor. Fortunately, the wind-swept sea had not sent them to their beds as it had so many others and, come morning, Sophie had been on deck to see the spectacular sight of the sun glinting off the white cliffs of the southern coast of England. Now, countless hours and even more miles later, they had arrived at the coaching inn where they were to spend the night before continuing on to London in the morning.

'So, we are to break our journey here.' Antoine Vallois stepped down from the carriage and cast a dubious glance at the exterior of the inn. 'I hope the accommodation is better than the inn's appearance would suggest.'

'It will be fine,' Sophie replied with confidence. 'Lord Longworth would not have recommended it to us otherwise.'

'Unless it has been some time since the gentleman had occasion to stay here himself,' Antoine murmured as he stepped around a steaming pile of fresh horse droppings. Thankfully, the interior of the inn turned out to be far more pleasant than the weathered timbers and muddy yard might suggest, and the fragrant smells wafting up from the kitchen did much to restore their spirits, as did the roaring fire burning in the grate. Instinctively Sophie moved towards it, anxious to banish the chill of the unseasonably cool April evening.

'Wait here while I see to our rooms and enquire about dinner,' Antoine said, placing their two small bags on the floor beside her. 'If Lord Longworth was unable to secure accommodations, we may find ourselves bedding down with the horses. And while sleeping in a barn is nothing new, I would rather not be plucking bits of straw from my clothes when we arrive in London tomorrow.'

Sophie's mouth twitched as she held her gloved hands out to the flames. 'I'm sure Lord Longworth would not care if you arrived looking like *l'épouvantail*. As long as we arrive safely.'

'The scarecrow, eh?' Antoine chuckled. '*Tiens*, you have no respect for your brother and far too much for this English lord. You seem to forget that our acquaintance with the man was brief and the repercussions far reaching. I would have expected you to be more suspicious of his reasons for asking us to come to England after all this time.'

'I admit, the circumstances are curious,' Sophie agreed, 'but I do not believe he would have asked us to come all this way if his motives were anything but honourable.'

'I hope you're right,' Antoine said, though his eyes remained guarded. 'Wait here and speak to no one. I do not trust these English around my beautiful sister.'

Sophie resisted the urge to smile. 'Do you not believe your sister capable of defending herself?'

'Having seen the way you handle a pistol, I think my sister is *more* than capable of defending herself. It is the well-being of the English I worry about now.'

The remark was typical of the close relationship they shared, and as her brother headed towards the bar, Sophie realised how glad she was that he had agreed to make the trip with her. The last few years hadn't been easy for either of them. The strain of constantly having to move had been exhausting, and when at the beginning of last year they had finally settled into affordable rooms near the centre of Paris, she had nearly wept with relief. It was the first time since leaving home they had enjoyed anything close to a normal existence, so it was only natural that when the letter from Viscount Long-worth had arrived, inviting them to come to England, Antoine would be suspicious. After all, what did they really know about the man whose life they had saved all those years ago? The fact of his having stayed in their barn for two weeks meant nothing given that he had been either delirious or unconscious for much of the time.

It certainly hadn't been the time to ask him what had brought him to France—or why he had been lying in a ditch with a bullet lodged in his side.

Because of her preoccupation with what lay ahead, it was a few minutes before Sophie realised that something was happening in the yard outside. An argument by the sounds of things, though the words were muffled by the thickness of the stone walls. Several of the inn's patrons glanced towards the door, but none seemed inclined to move, reluctant perhaps to involve themselves in something that might have untimely consequences. But when the sharp retort of a pistol split the night air, followed by a woman's high-pitched scream, Sophie knew the argument had turned deadly.

She turned to look for Antoine—and felt her heart stop when she saw him running towards the door. 'Antoine!'

'Stay where you are, Sophie. I have to see if I can help.'

'Then I'll come too—'

'No! If you would do anything, see to our rooms, then wait for me upstairs.'

For the space of a heartbeat, Sophie hesitated. If someone was seriously injured, Antoine would need her by his side. It would be almost impossible for him to do what was necessary without an assistant or the proper equipment. 'Wait, I'm coming with you!'

She was halfway to the door when a hand closed gently but firmly over her arm.

'The gentleman asked that you stay where you are,' a voice said close to her ear. 'I advise you to heed his request. You will only serve as a distraction if you venture outside now.'

The man's voice was as inflexible as his grip, but his high-handed assumption that Sophie would just be in the way rankled. 'You don't understand! Someone may have been injured.'

'I'm sure someone has, but your going out there now isn't going to help. If you promise to stay here, I shall endeavour to find out what has taken place.'

The man did not let go of her arm, and when Sophie finally raised her eyes to look at him, she realised he probably wasn't going to. He stood with legs firmly planted, radiating power and authority in a manner that suggested he was used to being in control. Clearly a man of means, he wore a well-tailored jacket and light-coloured breeches beneath his greatcoat, and though his leather boots were scuffed and in need of a polish, the quality of the workmanship was unmistakable. Dark brown hair fell across a broad forehead, over eyes bright with intelligence, and while his features were too rugged to be called handsome, he was still a very good-looking man. All of which meant nothing given that he was still holding her captive against her will. 'Kindly release my arm, sir.'

'Have I your word you won't do anything foolish?'

'You think a desire to go to the aid of an injured person foolish?'

'I think the intention noble, but the deed reckless.' Nevertheless, his hand dropped away. 'Your husband asked that you see to your accommodation. If you will wait for me at the bar, I shall offer what assistance I can and then return with any details I am able to uncover.'

'Oh, but Antoine is not—'

But the man was already gone, his greatcoat billowing around him as he stepped into the night. Other men followed him to the door, but none ventured out, and, inexplicably annoyed, both with their cowardice and by the high-handed treatment of the stranger, Sophie walked briskly towards the bar. She wasn't used to being cast aside like some helpless female who swooned at the sight of blood. She had often assisted Antoine with his work. Why would he not look to her for help now?

Her mood did not improve when she had to raise her voice to gain the innkeeper's attention.

'All right, all right, you needn't shout,' the old fellow grumbled, shuffling back from the window where he'd been trying to see what was going on outside. 'What do you want?'

'I'd like to see about our rooms. The name is Vallois.'

The innkeeper, whose grizzled eyebrows looked more like slivers of metal than natural hair, opened a well-worn book and ran his finger down the list. 'Nothing like that here.'

Surprised, Sophie said, 'Perhaps they were reserved under the gentleman's name. Viscount Longworth?'

If she had hoped to impress him with the use of a title, her gambit failed. 'No. Nothing like that either.'

'But I was told the arrangements would be made.

His lordship sent me a letter, and said a copy would be sent here. Did you not receive it?'

The old man grunted. 'Mr Rastley might have.'

'Mr Rastley?'

'Him what owns the place. But he had to go off to see to his dying sister and there's no reservation in your name or the toff's.' The man closed the book. 'I can give you a blanket and you can sleep in the stable if you like—'

'Sleep in the stable? Good God, man, what kind of establishment are you running here?'

The remark was uttered by a tall, well-dressed man who came to stand beside her. He was obviously a gentleman. A shiny black beaver sat atop golden curls and a diamond pin was tucked securely into the folds of an elaborately tied cravat. Unlike the first gentleman who'd come to her aid, there wasn't a speck of dust on his boots, and the heavy gold rings on his fingers indicated a degree of wealth most often associated with the aristocracy. But while it was clear he intended to intervene on her behalf, Sophie knew better than to encourage the acquaintance. For all his fine appearance, his expression was cold, his mouth possessed of a cynical twist, his eyes hooded like those of a cat eyeing the helpless bird it intended having for dinner.

'Thank you, sir, but I have no doubt the situation can be resolved to the satisfaction of all concerned,' she told him. 'There has obviously been some confusion over the reservations.'

'Indeed. Confusion that has left you without a comfortable bed in which to spend the night.' The man flicked a contemptuous glance at the innkeeper. 'And to cause so beautiful a lady such a degree of inconvenience is an unconscionable crime.'

The old man blanched. 'Begging your pardon, Mr Oberon, but we don't have any rooms—'

'So you said,' the gentleman drawled. 'However, you cannot expect this young woman to spend the night alone and unprotected.' He turned to her and, as he leaned his elbow on the bar, Sophie saw the expression in his eyes change. 'Who knows what manner of harm might befall her? Better you spend the night with me, my dear, than take your chances elsewhere.'

The ploy was so obvious that Sophie almost laughed. 'Fortunately, I am neither alone nor unprotected. As soon as my brother returns, we will settle this matter to the satisfaction of all involved.'

'Your *brother?*'

'Yes. He ran outside after the first shot was fired...' Sophie faltered, painfully reminded of what had taken place only moments ago. She had no way of knowing if Antoine was all right because she had no way of knowing what manner of contretemps he had stumbled into. Innocent bystanders often came to harm when force was used to settle differences between men. But barely had the thought crossed her mind than it was laid to rest—and by the very man who had prevented her from going to Antoine's side in the first place.

'You will be glad to know that all is well, *madame,*' the gentleman said. 'The matter is settled and the injured man will recover, thanks to the timely intervention of your husband.'

*'Her husband?'* Mr Oberon turned to regard Sophie with an expression of reproach. 'I thought you said you were travelling with your brother?'

'I am. This gentleman mistakenly *assumed* he was my husband.'

'Perhaps because you made no attempt to correct me,' the first man said.

'How could I?' Sophie fired back. 'You ran outside before I had a chance to say anything.'

'By the by, Silverton,' Mr Oberon cut in carelessly, 'what *was* going on outside?'

'An argument, over a lady,' said the man so addressed, his slight hesitation enough to cast doubt as to the lady's respectability. 'An insult was tendered, an apology demanded, and when the offending gentleman refused to give it, the lady's companion took out a whip and struck the man across the face. The first gentleman responded by shooting the second in the leg. A nasty wound, but not life threatening, thanks to the prompt attention of this young lady's brother, whom I assume to be a doctor?'

'He is studying to become one,' Sophie was stung into replying. 'And I would *not* have been in the way. I often help my brother in such situations.'

'But I wasn't to know that, was I?' Mr Silverton said. 'I only heard him ask you to stay where you were. And detecting the note of concern in his voice, I deigned to intervene. Perhaps I should have left well enough alone and let you rush headlong into the fray.'

The reprimand was faint but unmistakable—enough to inspire guilt, but not harsh enough to wound. Sophie was still considering her reply when the door opened and Antoine walked in, his face grim, the front of his jacket spattered with blood. 'Antoine! Are you all right?'

'Yes, which is more than I can say for the fellow

outside.' He glanced at the two men standing beside her and, to Sophie's surprise, offered his hand to her adversary. 'I am in your debt, *monsieur*. Without your help in holding the man down, I doubt I would have been able to staunch the flow of blood. *Merci beaucoup.*'

Mr Silverton's hesitation was so brief as to be almost imperceptible, but Sophie noticed. She watched him take Antoine's hand, shake it briefly, then release it almost immediately. 'I'm sure you would have managed.'

'Yes, I'm sure he would.' Mr Oberon's mouth pulled into a thin line. 'The French are nothing if not resourceful when it comes to dealing with matters of life and death.'

His words fell into a strained silence and Sophie wondered at the look that passed between the two Englishmen. But, more concerned with her own plight, she turned to her brother and said, 'It seems we must look for alternate accommodations, Antoine. Rooms have not been reserved for us and the inn is full.'

His surprise was as great as her own. 'Did you not show the man the letter?'

'There wasn't any point. He said there were no rooms available.'

'Then you will take mine,' Mr Silverton said at once. 'It is not large, but it has two beds and is relatively quiet. I shall make myself comfortable in the bar.'

'Oh, no,' Sophie said quickly. 'We couldn't possibly—'

'Thank you, Mr Silverton,' Antoine cut in. 'My sister has had a long day and is anxious to look her best on the morrow. We are most grateful for your offer.'

Sophie's mouth dropped open. They were *grateful*

for his offer? Since when had they resorted to accepting help from strangers? Especially from a man who hadn't even wanted to shake her brother's hand!

'*Ce n'est pas une bonne idée, Antoine,*' she whispered urgently. '*Nous serons mieux lotis dans la grange avec les chevaux!*'

It was an indication of how distraught Sophie was that she allowed herself to fall back into French. Before leaving Paris, she and Antoine had agreed to speak English whenever they found themselves in the company of others. And while sleeping in the barn with the horses was not what she *wished* to do, it was far preferable to putting herself in a position of debt to this man. She had learned that offers of kindness always came with terms—and that payment was never negotiable.

Unfortunately, Mr Silverton obviously thought it a *fait accompli*. 'The room is at the top of the stairs, second on the left. If you will give me a moment, I shall remove my things and then return to give you the key. Oberon, may I store my valise in your room?'

'If you must, but don't think to spend the night. *I* have only the one bed and I certainly don't intend sharing it with you.'

Mr Silverton's voice was heavy with sarcasm. 'Rest assured, the thought never entered my mind. I'll see you at dinner.'

'Fine. All this high drama has left me with an appetite. In fact...' Mr Oberon glanced at Sophie, his gaze skimming over her with a thoroughness she found insulting. 'Perhaps you would care to join us, *mademoiselle*? The innkeeper has assured us of a decent meal in his private dining room and I can assure you, it will be far preferable to sitting cheek to jowl with the riff-raff out here.'

Resisting the urge to tell him the riff-raff would be *in* the private dining room, Sophie said, 'Thank you, but, no. My brother and I will be fine out here.'

'Very well. Then I bid you a good evening. And may I say that it has been...a pleasure.'

His eyes said everything his words did not and as he turned and walked away Sophie felt her face burn with humiliation. If such was a display of upper-crust English manners—

'You must forgive Oberon's lack of tact,' Mr Silverton said drily. 'He tends to speak before he thinks.'

'You owe us no apology, sir,' Antoine replied stiffly. 'Your conduct more than made up for his.'

Mr Silverton bowed. 'I would not wish you to think English chivalry dead.' His glance rested on Sophie for the briefest of moments before he touched the brim of his beaver and walked towards the narrow staircase.

Sophie followed him with her eyes, not at all pleased with the events of the past half-hour. 'You should not have accepted his offer, Antoine. We know nothing about him.'

'Nevertheless, I wasn't about to see you spend your first night in England sleeping in a barn.'

'Better that than finding ourselves beholden to a man who clearly doesn't like us.'

'I don't care if he likes us,' Antoine said. 'All that matters is that you have a proper bed in which to sleep and hot water in which to bathe. Lord Longworth wasn't able to provide that for you so I wasn't about to turn Mr Silverton down when he did. Besides, I doubt the loss of one night's sleep is going to trouble him unduly.'

Of course it wasn't. Mr Silverton was clearly a man of means, Sophie told herself. If he slept poorly in the bar tonight, he would simply go home and sleep it off tomorrow, no doubt in the comfort of a very fine house with his wife and servants to attend him. He certainly wouldn't be thinking about her. She was just one more person he'd met along the way.

*And that's all he was to her.* One more anonymous face in the crowd. She knew nothing about his life, so what did it matter if he thought her ill mannered for having refused his offer of help? Thanks to him, she would be clean and well rested when she arrived in London for her reunion with Nicholas tomorrow. Surely that was more important than worrying about what kind of impression she'd made on a man she was never going to see again.

# Chapter Two

'So, who do you think she was?' Montague Oberon enquired between bites of underdone potato and over-cooked beef.

Robert Silverton didn't look up from his plate of steak-and-kidney pie, hoping his apparent preoccupation with his meal would discourage Oberon from continuing to talk about her. 'Why would you not think she was his sister?'

'Because you heard what he said about it being important she look her best tomorrow.'

'Perhaps she is meeting with a prospective employer. Or a long-lost relation.'

'Or her new protector. You know what they say about French women.'

'I know what *you* say about French women," Robert said, reaching for the salt cellar. "But I fear they are not all whores, strumpets or ballet dancers.'

'Pity.' Oberon took a piece of bread, his brow furrowing. 'I suppose she could have been his mistress.

There seemed to be a deal of affection between them, and God knows, I've never looked at *my* sister that way.'

'Why would you? You've told me countless times that you despise Elaine.'

'Of course. You would too if she were *your* sister. But I've never seen you look at Jane that way and the two of you are very close.'

'You're imagining things.' Finishing his meal, Robert picked up his glass. 'There were marked similarities in their appearance. The slenderness of the nose, the firm line of the jaw, the shape of the eyes...' *The seductive curve of the lady's mouth. Oh, yes, he'd noticed that. And he'd stared at it far too many times during their brief conversation...* 'I have no doubt they were related. But I could ask the gentleman on your behalf and leave you to the consequences.'

The viscount's son nearly choked. 'And find myself on the other end of a Frenchie's blade? No, thank you. I haven't your skill with the foil.'

'You could if you showed more inclination to learn.'

'I've little inclination to do anything that involves hard work or strenuous exercise,' Oberon said, pausing to flick a remnant of charred crust from the bread. 'Still, I'd give a year's allowance to have her in my bed for one night.'

'It seems to me your money would be better spent on the pursuit of a respectable bride,' Robert said, sitting back in his chair. 'Was that not a requirement of your continuing to receive the exceedingly generous allowance your father doles out to you twice a year?'

'Damned if it wasn't," Oberon muttered. 'The old codger knows me too well. I cannot afford to live without the allowance, so I am forced to legshackle myself to some simpering heiress or some horse-faced widow long past her prime in order to assure its continuation.'

Robert smiled, aware that even under the most dire of circumstances, Oberon would never settle for anything less than a diamond of the first water. 'I'm sure such desperate measures will not be called for. No doubt you'll find at least one young lady amongst this year's crop of blushing débutantes to tempt you.'

'Tempt *us,* don't you mean?'

'No. I've had my brush with marriage, thank you,' Robert said. 'My only goal is to settle my sister in marriage and I intend to devote all of my energies to that.'

Oberon frowned. 'You may have a difficult task there, Silver. Jane's a delightful girl, but there is her affliction to consider.'

'I wouldn't call a misshapen foot an affliction, and I certainly don't consider it an impediment to her making a good marriage.'

'Of course not. You're her brother and honour bound to defend her. But what man would not wish his wife to be the most beautiful woman of his acquaintance?'

Robert raised his glass and studied his companion over the rim. The remark came as no surprise. It was exactly what he expected from a man who valued physical perfection above all and saw anything less as flawed. 'Jane *is* an acknowledged beauty.'

'But she *limps*, Silver. She cannot walk without the use of a cane and is hard pressed even to ride as well as other young ladies her age.'

'But she rides nevertheless.'

'Only when in the country where no one can see her. Be reasonable, old man. Jane's chances of making a good match in London are about as remote as ours of finding a man of wit and intelligence amongst the rabble out there,' Oberon said bluntly. 'Perhaps if you left her in the country, introduced her to the local clergyman—'

'Jane's chances of making a good match in London are no better or worse than any one else's,' Robert said mildly. 'Love enables one to overlook what others see as faults.'

'Blinds one to them, you mean. It sets up ridiculous expectations and does nothing more than pave the way for marital strife. I don't expect the woman I marry to love me, any more than I expect to love her.'

'Then what do you expect?'

'Loyalty, obedience and good breeding skills. I expect her to sit at my table and entertain my guests, manage my households to make sure the servants don't rob us blind and provide me with an heir at the earliest opportunity so I can go off and indulge my other interests.'

'Those being?'

'To find myself in bed with a different woman every night.'

Robert snorted. 'If that's all you require, you may as well marry your housekeeper and spend your nights at a brothel.'

'And pay for the pleasure of bedding a woman? I'd rather eat bad oysters for breakfast,' Oberon said. 'I could give you the names of a *dozen* young ladies happy to warm my bed for nothing more than the pleasure they receive in return.'

'Then why not marry one of them?'

'Because I want a flower of rare perfection. A woman as virginal as Hestia, as amusing as Thalia, as—'

'As exquisite as Aphrodite?'

'That would be my first choice, though if she is not, I shall simply snuff the candles and do the deed as quickly as possible.' Oberon shrugged. 'London is full of tempting young chits only too happy to do what a man likes. Take that stunning young woman we just met. I'd wager even *you* wouldn't mind a tumble with her, despite your stated aversion to all things French.'

'That has nothing to do with it,' Robert said, aware that it wasn't entirely true, but wishing he'd never told Oberon of his antipathy. 'As a result of what happened between Lady Mary Kelsey and myself, I have no intention of involving myself with *any* woman, whether she be well born or otherwise.'

'Ah, yes, the broken engagement. Pity about that,' Oberon reflected. 'Unlike you, Lady Mary is not keeping quiet about her feelings. Last week she called you a heartless bastard for breaking things off without a word of explanation.'

'Trust me, it is better I do not vouchsafe the reasons,' Robert murmured.

'Be that as it may, she is threatening to sue you for breach of promise and society has taken her side. You have been cast out, my friend. Abandoned. Thrown to the murderous hordes. Which means you may as well find yourself a nice little mistress to keep you warm at night—in fact, what say you to a little wager? Whoever establishes the most beautiful woman in London as his mistress before the end of the Season shall be declared the winner.'

'I'd say that apart from it being a totally iniquitous undertaking, it makes absolutely no sense. Have you any idea how many beautiful women there are in London?'

'Ah, but I said the *most* beautiful.'

'By whose standards? Jane is considered a beauty, yet you are offended by her handicap and label her unattractive as a result.'

The viscount's son had the decency to blush. 'I did not say she offended me—'

'Not in so many words, but we both know that is what you meant.'

'Then we shall let a panel of our peers make the decision. And the stakes of the wager will show that he who loses must give the other that which he desires most. I'm willing to put up my stallion,' Oberon said, stabbing the last piece of beef with his fork. 'I recall you once saying that were I to offer you a chance to buy him, you'd take it without second thought. Now you can have him for free.'

Robert sighed. 'Let it go, Oberon. You know this is a complete waste of time.'

'On the contrary, it could be very interesting. We just have to come up with something of equal value for you to put forward.' Oberon tapped his finger against his chin. 'I have it! Your sapphire ring. I've always been partial to it and that is what I claim as my prize.'

Robert stared. 'You think I would risk a priceless family heirloom on something as feeble as this?'

'Why not? A wager must always have a prize *and* a consequence or it is not worth the trouble. So what do you say? Are you in?'

There were times, Robert reflected, when it was impossible to find the words that would adequately describe how he felt about some of the things Oberon did. Just as it was equally hard to imagine that one day, the man sitting opposite him would wear a viscount's coronet and own a veritable fortune in property and wealth. Robert picked up his glass and shook his head. 'No.'

'But why not? It is a harmless enough wager.'

'Not if the terms of the wager become known to the ladies involved.'

'Faith, Silver, when did you acquire such pretty manners? I remember a time when you would have wagered a month's allowance on something as inconsequential as in which direction a flock of pigeons took off.'

'That was before my father shot himself over gambling debts he couldn't afford to repay,' Robert said quietly. 'I swore then I wouldn't follow in his footsteps. And I won't have Jane ending up the same way as our poor mother.'

'But she wouldn't, old man. Unlike your father, *you* never lose!'

'A man's luck can change. Fortune is a fickle mistress.'

'For others, perhaps, but not you. Your prowess at the tables is legendary.'

'Count me out,' Robert said. 'I want nothing to do with it.'

Oberon sat back, rapping his fingers on the table and looking thoroughly peeved. 'Really, Silver, if I didn't like you so well, I'd pass you over for Welton. Unfortunately even he's begun to bore me of late. Twice now he's stood me up for lunch, and the last time I called round, he wouldn't even see me.'

Robert frowned. That didn't sound like Lawrence. When they had all been at Oxford together, it was most often Lawrence Welton to whom Oberon had gravitated. Likely because the affable Lawrence was the only one who had not been openly critical of Oberon's debauched lifestyle. 'Are you sure he's well?'

'Well enough to attend a social engagement the same afternoon he stood me up,' Oberon said. 'No, I've washed my hands of him. He used to be such good fun. Now he's become as staid and as boring…as you.'

Robert was unmoved by the criticism. So what if Oberon thought him boring? *He* knew what was important and it certainly wasn't deceiving innocent young women for the sake of someone else's pleasure or gain. 'Play the game if you must, but I'll have nothing to do with it. However, I will offer a toast. To your future wife,' Robert said, raising his glass. 'May she be as beautiful as Aphrodite, as gentle as Hestia—'

'And as lusty as an Irish farmer's daughter,' Oberon said. 'A toast to the dear lady's health…wherever she may be!'

It was late the following afternoon when Sophie finally stepped down from the carriage into the quiet of the respectable English street, and as far as she was concerned it wasn't a moment too soon. Her serviceable brown jacket and skirt were hopelessly creased, her half-boots were covered in dust, and there was a stain on the palm of her left glove from having touched something black and oily. Added to that, the unsettling events of the previous evening had made it impossible to sleep, leaving her feeling overly tired and decidedly on edge. If it weren't for Antoine, she would have climbed back into the carriage and turned the horses in the direction of home.

A long row of tall, white houses stretched before her, each with four stone steps leading to a shiny black

door. From the centre of each door, a brass lion roared
a warning to those who came near, and to either side
and above, rows of windows glinted in the last rays of
sunlight. A square ran the length of the street, bordered
by trees newly covered in green, and in front of each
house, black wrought-iron posts stood waiting to receive
horses and carriages.

It was a far cry from the crowded *Rue de Piêtre* and
the three small rooms she and Antoine called home.

'Buy some sweet violets, miss?' asked a young girl
passing by with a tray. She was petite and dark haired,
and the sweet smell rising from the flowers brought
back bittersweet memories of home. Mama had always
loved violets....

*'Non, merci,'* Sophie murmured, forgetting the
girl wouldn't be able to speak French. Forgetting they
weren't in France. They were in England, and suddenly
it all seemed like a huge mistake. What in the world
had made her think this was the right thing to do? Too
much time had passed. They should never have come—

'Upon my word, Sophie, is it really you?'

And then it was too late. The past caught up with
the present and the moment of reckoning was at hand.
Sophie looked up to see the door standing open and
a swarm of black-coated servants emerge, like bees
flying out of a hive. A couple stood on the top step, and
while the beautiful woman in the exquisite silk gown
was not known to her, the man...oh, yes, she knew
the man. There might be lines around his mouth that
hadn't been there before, and traces of grey peppering
the dark, wavy hair, but his eyes were still the clear
bright blue of a summer sky and his smile was still as
warm as an August day in Provence. She would have

recognised him anywhere. 'Lord Longworth,' Sophie said, breathing an audible sigh of relief. 'It has been…a long time.'

'A *very* long time.' Nicholas Grey started down the stairs. 'So long I scarcely recognise the beautiful young woman you've become. And I'm not sure exactly what to say except…welcome to England, dear Sophie. And may I say how very, very happy I am to see you again.'

It was almost like coming home. Sophie stepped into his embrace, feeling as though a weight had been lifted from her shoulders. 'No happier than I, for you look much better than when last we parted.'

'I dare say it would have been difficult to look worse. But even the deepest of cuts and bruises heal and I am pleased to say I had exceptionally good care.' Nicholas glanced at the young man standing quietly on the street behind her, and slowly extended his hand. 'Antoine. I was afraid you would not remember who I was. Or choose not to come if you did.'

'Under the circumstances, you would be a hard man to forget,' Antoine said, his greeting more reserved than his sister's, but his tone cordial as he shook the viscount's hand. 'I take it your memory is fully restored?'

'It is, though it was several months after the accident before I could claim a complete recovery.'

'I have learned that injuries like yours often induce temporary memory loss.'

'So it would seem.' Nicholas smiled. 'I understand you are apprenticed to a surgeon in Paris.'

Sophie glanced at him in surprise. 'To Monsieur Larocque, yes, but…how could you know that?'

'I suspect there is very little Lord Longworth doesn't

know about us,' Antoine said. 'No doubt he has had us thoroughly investigated.'

'Antoine!'

'No, it's all right, Sophie,' Nicholas said quietly. 'I regret that such duplicity was necessary, but it would serve no purpose to lie and I will not insult your intelligence by doing so. Yes, I hired someone to find you and they did what was necessary in order to uncover your whereabouts. But the investigation was discreet and nothing of its undertaking made public. So unless *you* told anyone of your reasons for coming to England, I can assure you that no one here knows.'

It was a moment before Antoine said, 'I told the gentleman to whom I am apprenticed that I was coming to visit an old friend, and that time was of the essence given the precarious state of his health. However...' he looked at Nicholas and began to smile '...you appear uncommon well for a man on his deathbed, my lord.'

In full understanding of the situation, Nicholas chuckled. 'I'm glad I was able to hang on until your arrival.' He reached up to scratch his ear. 'Am I in imminent danger of expiring?'

'Not imminent, but the prognosis isn't good.'

'In that case, I suggest we go inside before I take a turn for the worst.'

'Thank heavens,' Lady Longworth said. 'I thought the entire visit was to be conducted on our doorstep.'

Making a sound of disgust, Nicholas said, 'Forgive my abominable manners. Sophie, Antoine, my beautiful wife, Lavinia, who, I can assure you, has been as anxious about your arrival as I.'

'Of course I've been anxious. But you must both be weary after your long journey,' Lavinia said. 'Why don't we retire to the drawing room? I've asked Banyon to set out refreshments.' She extended a slender white hand to Antoine. *'Vous ne viendrez pas avec moi, monsieur?'*

The young man's eyebrows rose. 'Your accent is perfect, *madame. Avez-vous été née en France?'*

'No, I was born in England, but my first husband was French and we lived in Paris for several years after we married. It will be delightful to have someone to speak the language with again.'

'I am surprised you do not speak it with Lord Longworth,' Sophie said. 'I remember his French being very good.'

'Alas, that was over three years ago,' Nicholas said. 'And given that I seldom use the language any more, I am beginning to forget many words and phrases.'

'Understandable. Even my own French is not as good as it once was.' Lavinia turned to Antoine, a hint of mischief lurking in the depths of those lovely eyes. 'I look to you for help in that regard, *monsieur.'*

*'Ce serait mon plaisir,'* Antoine replied, and though he did not smile, Sophie thought she detected a slight thawing of his reserve. Good. If the beautiful Lady Longworth had the ability to make her brother less suspicious of the situation, so much the better. She watched them walk into the house, quietly chatting in French, and found herself alone on the steps with Nicholas.

*'Tu es...très belle, mademoiselle,'* he complimented her. 'And I am sorry my accent is so poor compared to my wife's.'

'Your accent is fine,' Sophie said, wondering why Nicholas still seemed so ill at ease with her. He was a great man—a viscount in the British aristocracy. He had a beautiful wife, a lovely home and was clearly a man of means.

And yet, perhaps it was only to be expected. The last time they had seen each other, she had been a naïve girl of sixteen living on a farm in the French countryside and he an Englishman fighting for his life. She had struggled to make him understand what was happening to him and had done her best to keep him alive by feeding him soup smuggled from the kitchen, and by wrapping his wounds in bandages made from her own petticoats. For that, he had called her his angel of mercy and had gripped her hand when the fever had raged and the terror of his own anonymity had settled in his eyes.

Perhaps that was the problem, Sophie reflected. He was no longer a man on the brink of death and she was no longer the child he remembered. Maybe now that she was here and so little like the person he'd left behind, he was regretting his invitation, wishing he'd left things as they were. So much had changed in both their lives.

'Lord Longworth—'

'No,' he interrupted gently. 'Let there be no formality between us, Sophie. You are the young lady who saved my life and to whom I will always be indebted. I would ask that now, and in the future, you call me Nicholas.'

She looked up at him and tilted her head to one side. 'Is such familiarity permitted in England?'

'I see no reason why not. You are a good friend, and good friends always address one another by their Christian names.'

'*D'accord,* then Nicholas it shall be. As long as I am Sophie to you.'

'You will always be that, even though I now know your full name to be Sophia Chantal Vallois.'

Sophie raised one eyebrow. 'You *have* done your homework.'

To her amusement, he actually looked embarrassed. 'I fear so.' Then, his expression changed, becoming serious. 'Our first meeting seems…a very long time ago now, Sophie. Almost as though it were another lifetime. And there are still parts of those three weeks I don't remember. But I sincerely hope I did nothing to hurt you, or say anything to which you might have taken offence. A man in pain often lashes out at those around him, and I would hate to think I had scarred the child I left behind with a callous remark or a thoughtless word.'

So, that was the reason for his reserve, Sophie reflected. It had nothing to do with the people they were now, but rather with the impression he had made all those years ago. 'You did nothing wrong, Nicholas,' she said. 'Even in the depths of pain, you could not have been more *vaillant*. And if some of your memories of that time are dim, it is probably not a bad thing. It allows you more room for the good memories. For the ones that are worth remembering.'

'I'd like to think so.' He looked at her and a smile trembled over his lips. 'What about you, Sophie? Have you happy memories of the last three years?'

Sophie knew that he wanted her to say yes. She could see in his eyes, the hope that her life had not been an ongoing series of struggles and hardships, and perhaps one day she would tell him the truth. But not today. 'I have many happy memories, but I'm quite sure this is going to be one of the happiest.'

## Chapter Three

'Are you sure I cannot offer you more tea, Sophie?' Lavinia asked. 'Or another scone? Cook was most insistent that you try both the orange marmalade and the raspberry jam.'

'*Merci, non,* I have already eaten too much,' Sophie demurred, sitting back on the loveseat. Nearly an hour had passed since she and her brother had sat down with their hosts in the elegant rose drawing room, and in keeping with the spirit of the day, the formalities had long been dispensed with. 'If I continue like this, I will not fit into my clothes.'

'Nonsense, you could do with a little extra weight,' Lavinia said. 'Don't you think so, Nicholas?'

'I cannot imagine Sophie looking any better than she does.'

Lavinia's lips twitched. 'Spoken like a true diplomat. No wonder you do so well in the House.'

'It does but pass the time.' Nicholas set his cup and saucer on the table. 'But now that we've all had a chance to become better acquainted, I think our guests would like to know why they are here. It isn't every day a stranger from one's past invites you to come to London.'

'Especially when that stranger happens to be a member of the English aristocracy *and* an intelligence agent for the British government,' Antoine added.

'*Former* intelligence agent,' Nicholas said. 'I am happy to say those days are behind me. But it does bring me to the reason for my invitation, the first and foremost being to thank you properly for having saved my life. Without your discretion and most excellent care, I would certainly have died. A man doesn't forget something like that and because I am in a position to repay you, it is my sincere hope that you will allow me to do so.'

'But there is nothing *to* repay,' Sophie said. 'We did what anyone would have done under the circumstances.'

'On the contrary, given the political instability of the time, finding an Englishman shot and left for dead should have raised any number of questions. You asked none.'

Antoine shrugged. 'By your own admission, you had no answers to give.'

'But you must have wondered.'

'*Bien sûr.* But at the time I was more concerned with keeping you alive than with trying to find out why you had been shot.'

'And therein lies the difference, Antoine.' Nicholas got to his feet. 'Where others would have waited *until* they knew why I had been shot, you went ahead and removed the bullet regardless. That is the mark of an honourable man.'

Sophie had no need to look at her brother to know that he would be uncomfortable with the praises being heaped upon him. Whatever services he had rendered had stemmed from a genuine desire to save a man's life: the natural inclination of a man who one day hoped to become a doctor. For that, he expected neither praise nor reward. But equally aware that he was a guest in the gentleman's home, Antoine said simply, 'What is it you wish to do?'

'For you,' Nicholas said, 'a letter of recommendation that will open the doors to whatever university you wish to attend, as well as a financial endowment to help offset the costs of your studies towards becoming a doctor.'

Antoine went very still. 'You are offering me... money?'

'I prefer to think of it as a means to an end.'

'*C'est la même chose.* But we are not in need of your charity, my lord. Sophie and I have managed well enough on our own.'

'Have you?' Nicholas linked his hands behind his back. 'I may not be familiar with all the ins and outs of becoming a doctor in France, but in England, there are considerable fees involved in the study of medicine. Not to mention the costs of establishing your own practice.'

'None of which, if you'll forgive me, are your responsibility.'

'But all of which *became* my responsibility the day you saved my life and so drastically altered the course of your own. Let us not mince words, Antoine. Because of me, you and Sophie had to hide out in the French countryside with the fear of discovery hanging over your heads like the sword of Damocles; upon reaching Paris, you took whatever manner of work you could find. First as a labourer, then as a clerk, then briefly as a—'

'Thank you, my lord. I am well aware of the means by which I earned enough money to cover our expenses,' Antoine said. 'It is enough you had us investigated. Pray do not compound the injury by prying into matters that are clearly none of your concern.'

'But it *is* our concern,' Lavinia said gently. 'We care what happens to you and Sophie.'

'Of course we do,' Nicholas said. 'Why else would we have gone to all this trouble?'

'I really don't know,' Antoine said coldly. 'But we did not ask for your help and our situation is not so desperate that we are forced to come to you with our hands out. It was Sophie's wish to see you again and I agreed to make the trip with her. A decision I am now beginning to regret!' He abruptly got to his feet. 'Now, if that is all you wish to say—'

'It is *not* all I wish to say—!'

'Nicholas, please!' Lavinia said. 'Antoine. *N'ira pas faire vous s'asseoir et nous écouter jusqu'au bout.*'

Her low, quiet voice seemed to inject a note of calm into the escalating tension and Sophie was relieved to see her brother sit back down. She knew this was difficult for him. Antoine was proud. Too proud to accept what he would only see as a handout, even from a man whose life he had saved. 'Listen to what Nicholas has to say, Antoine,' Sophie urged softly. 'Then let common sense, rather than pride, dictate your answer.'

'And please understand it was never our intention to offend you,' Lavinia said.

'Indeed it was not,' Nicholas said gruffly. 'My *only* desire was to try to make things better for you. I apologise if you see that as an intrusion into your lives, but the fact is I was worried about the two of you. Those were dangerous times and hardly a day went by I didn't wonder what had become of you. I owe you my *life*, Antoine. Perhaps to a doctor that doesn't mean very much, but to me—to us,' Nicholas said, glancing at his wife, 'it meant…everything.'

There was a poignant silence as Nicholas sat down and took Lavinia's hand in his. Watching them together, Sophie knew he had spoken from the heart. Whether or not his plans for their future came to pass, his reasons for bringing them to England could not be faulted. They stemmed from a genuine desire to thank them for the most noble gesture one man could make towards another.

Sophie glanced at her brother and was relieved to see that he, too, was regretting his hastily spoken words. 'You have nothing to apologise for, my lord. Sophie's right. Sometimes a man's pride gets in the way and prevents him from seeing what is truly before him.'

'I fear we've all been guilty of that.' Nicholas offered him an apologetic smile. *'Pride goeth before destruction, and a haughty spirit before a fall.'*

'But pride can be a good thing too,' Sophie said. 'It gives us the courage to fight for what we believe in.' She leaned over and touched her brother's arm. 'It enabled you to pursue your dream of becoming a doctor.'

'Yes, it did,' Nicholas agreed. 'But a surgeon is *not* a doctor. And if your wish is still to become a doctor, I can help you. For all the *right* reasons.'

For a moment, Antoine was silent. There was a great deal at stake and Sophie knew her brother would not make a hasty decision. He would take time to think the matter through, weighing his options before giving them his answer. 'And Sophie? What would you do for her?'

This time, it was Lavinia who answered. 'It is our wish that Sophie stay here in London with us for a while. Not only so we can get to know her better, but so that we might introduce her to English society. It is our hope she will form lasting friendships with the young men and women to whom she is introduced.'

'Naturally, we will provide her with all things necessary to a young lady entering society,' Nicholas said. 'A suitable wardrobe. A maid to attend to her needs. A carriage. Or if she prefers, a decent mare to trot around Hyde Park—'

'Why?'

Antoine's one-word question stopped Nicholas in his tracks. 'Why?' He looked at the younger man and frowned. 'Is it not obvious?'

'Not to me.'

But to Sophie, who had been listening with growing concern, the answer was suddenly all *too* clear. 'I think, Antoine, that Nicholas and Lavinia wish me to find…a husband.'

'A husband?' Then, her brother's eyes opened wide. 'An *English* husband? *C'est de la folie!* Sophie has no intention of marrying an *Englishman*! She is perfectly capable of finding a husband in France!'

'But what kind of man would he be?' Lavinia asked. 'The son of a *boulanger*? A shop assistant barely making enough to feed himself, let alone a wife and eventually a family.'

A flush darkened Antoine's cheeks. 'You assume too much, my lady.'

'Do I? You forget that I've lived in France. I am well aware of the practicalities of life as they apply to a young woman in Sophie's position and they are not without their limitations.'

'Let us speak plainly, Antoine,' Nicholas said. 'Sophie's chances of making a good marriage where she is are extremely limited. For all your noble aspirations, a surgeon is little better than a tradesman and your sister will not benefit by the association. Here, we can offer her so much more. She will move in elevated circles; accompany us to soirées and balls held at some of the best houses in London. And when a gentleman does offer for her, as I have no doubt several will, he will have to meet *my* standards as far as wealth and station go, and seek *your* approval as the man who will be your brother-in-law.'

'May I be permitted to say something?' Sophie asked, torn between annoyance and amusement at the conversation going on around her.

'But, of course, dear,' Lavinia said quickly. 'It is, after all, your future we're talking about.'

'Yes, it is. And while I appreciate what you'd like to do, I really have no wish to be married.'

She might as well have said she wanted to strap on paper wings and fly to the moon.

'No wish to be married?' Lavinia said. 'But...*every* young lady wishes to be married, Sophie. It is the only respectable option open to a woman.'

'Perhaps, but since Antoine and I left home I have seen much of relationships between men and women, and I am not convinced marriage is to my benefit. A man stands to gains much whereas a woman loses everything.'

'Not if she marries the right man,' Lavinia said.

'But she will not know if he is the right man until *after* she's married him,' Sophie said. 'And then it is too late. Besides, what gentleman of good family is going to want someone like me? A farmer's daughter, from Bayencourt?'

'Rubbish! You no more resemble a farmer's daughter than I do a tinker!' Nicholas said. 'You are an astonishingly beautiful young woman who carries herself like a duchess, and who speaks the King's English with a slight, albeit charming accent. I cannot think of *any* man who would not be proud to have you by his side.'

'There, Sophie, did I not tell you?' Antoine said. 'If you gained nothing else from your employment with Mrs Grant-Ogilvy—'

'Good Lord. *Constance* Grant-Ogilvy?' Lavinia interrupted in surprise.

Sophie sucked in her breath. *Mère de Dieu,* she had *begged* Antoine not to mention that woman's name. 'Yes. Do you…know her?'

'Not personally, but I understand she is a woman of high moral character and an absolute stickler for propriety. You could not have had a better teacher in the arts of being a lady.'

The moment passed—and Sophie breathed again. 'Nevertheless, I am *not* a lady and I did not come to London looking for a husband.' She turned to Nicholas. 'I came to see *you.* And to meet Lavinia.'

'Yes, well, why don't we talk about all this in the morning?' Nicholas said. 'After you've had a chance to settle in.' He glanced at his wife, seeking support. 'What do you think, my dear?'

'I think that's a good idea,' Lavinia said slowly, 'but we probably owe Sophie an apology as well.'

Sophie blinked. 'An apology?'

'It was never our intention to make you uncomfortable, my dear. We simply thought that if you wished to be married, we might be able to provide you with a better opportunity to do so. However, if that is not the case, will you not at least stay and give us a chance to get to know you? We have both waited a long time to say thank you.'

Sophie began to smile. 'And I have waited a long time to see Nicholas well again. But the final say must be Antoine's. He has been as much guardian as brother to me these past three years and I could not stay if he was not easy with the decision.'

'Well, Antoine,' Lavinia said, 'what do you say?'

Antoine drew a deep breath. '*En vérité, je ne sais pas.* It seems…so much to ask. A great imposition on you both—'

'Then let me tell you one more thing,' Nicholas said quietly. 'My memory of Sophie was of a child. A golden-haired angel who appeared to me through a nightmarish haze of darkness and pain. I really had no idea how old she was and in bringing her here now, I thought to give her whatever a child her age might like. But the young lady who stepped down from the carriage is not a little girl who hankers after sandcastles by the sea. She is beautiful young woman with a mind of her own, and more than anything, we would like to get to know her better. All *you* have to do is say yes.'

Antoine was quiet for a long time, longer than Sophie expected. To her, the question was straightforward, the answer, simple. 'You have concerns about leaving me here, Antoine?' she asked at length.

'No, not really,' Antoine said finally. 'I admit, it wasn't what I had in mind, but as Nicholas pointed out, I have neither the financial wherewithal nor the social connections to make life better for you. And given that I would like to see you married—'

'Antoine—!'

'*Soyez patient,* Sophie. You and I have had this conversation before. I too believe that marriage is the only respectable occupation for a woman, and your chances of making a good marriage here are far better than they would be in France. As to marrying an Englishman… well, that decision must be yours. But if you would like to stay with Nicholas and Lavinia, I won't stand in your way.'

'Please stay with us, Sophie,' Lavinia said. 'It would make us both so very happy.'

Sophie looked at the three people in the room and realised that for the second time in three years, her life was about to change—but this time it would be a change for the better. In the company of Nicholas and Lavinia, she would be able to explore London and all it had to offer. She would have access to good books and fine music, perhaps have conversations about subjects that had always been of interest to her. And if her time in London culminated with a proposal of marriage, she could always say no. But the chance to get to know these two dear people might never come again.

'Yes, I would like to stay,' Sophie said firmly. 'And, if possible, I would like Antoine to stay as well.'

'Sophie! *C'est trop demandez!*'

'No, it's not too much to ask at all,' Lavinia said

quickly. 'We simply thought you would be anxious to return to France.'

'Which, of course, I must or Monsieur Larocque will look for someone to take my place.'

'But surely a few more days won't make that much of a difference,' Nicholas said. 'There are people here who would like to meet you. Friends, who know what you did and who would be proud to make your acquaintance.'

'Why not stay with us for a week?' Lavinia suggested. 'Nicholas and I will be attending a ball tomorrow evening and we would be delighted to have you come with us. It will be the perfect opportunity to introduce you and Sophie to society.'

Antoine frowned. 'If I stay, it will not be with a view to entering English society.'

'Then come for the sport,' Nicholas said. 'Lord Bruxton plays an excellent game of billiards. I can promise you some stiff competition if you're up for it.'

'Antoine is actually quite good,' Sophie said, knowing her brother would always downplay his abilities. 'Monsieur Larocque often invites him to play.' She got up and crossed to his side. 'Please say you will stay, Antoine. It will give you a chance to practise your game before you play Monsieur Larocque again. And I would enjoy seeing *les dames anglaises* swooning over you.'

Antoine snorted. 'They will surely have more sense than that. But, if it will make you happy, I will stay—but only for a week. Then I must go back.'

It was good enough for Sophie. She didn't care if it was Nicholas's persuasiveness or her own pleas that had finally convinced her brother to change his mind. All that mattered was that he was to stay in London for a week—and that she was to stay for at least a month. After such an auspicious start, how could she look upon this as anything but the possible start of a new and memorable chapter in both their lives?

Robert Silverton was not in a good mood as the carriage made its way from Portman Square to Mayfair. Not only because he had no desire to spend an evening being given the cold shoulder by a large number of the three hundred guests Lady Bruxton would have surely invited to her *petite soirée,* but because of what he had heard at his club just that afternoon.

It seemed that despite having told Montague Oberon he had no intention of participating in his ridiculous wager, the man had gone ahead and set it up regardless. Now he and several of Oberon's more disreputable friends were engaged in a race to establish the most beautiful woman in London as their mistress.

'I shouldn't worry about it,' said his sister, Jane, from the seat opposite. 'You need only strike your name from the book and in a few days it will all be forgotten. It seems a silly thing upon which to wager.'

'It is, but Oberon lives to gamble and when the topic of—' Robert shot her a wry glance '—that is, when talk veered in that direction, he couldn't resist putting forward this preposterous wager.'

He watched her lips compress, knew she wanted to laugh. 'You needn't pussyfoot around the subject with me, Robert, I am well aware that most men keep mistresses. What do you think those old tabbies talk about while they are watching their young charges pirouette about the ballrooms of society?'

'How prettily they dance?'

'Not for a moment. They gossip about which gentlemen are having affairs, and about which married ladies
are in love with other women's husbands. How do you
think I found out about Lady Andrews and Jeremy
West?'

'Yes, I did wonder about that,' Robert murmured.
'But it is hardly the kind of information an unmarried
lady should be privy to.'

'Oh, my dear Robert, you have no *idea* how much
scandalous information I am privy to. It is one of the
highlights of my sad little life. But seriously, you must
stop worrying about me all the time. You've done little
else since Mama died and it really isn't fair. You should
be out there looking for a wife.'

'Need I remind you that I *was* briefly engaged to
Lady Mary Kelsey?' Robert said. 'And that as a result,
my name has now been struck from the list of eligible
bachelors.'

'Then why are we going to Lady Bruxton's tonight?'

'Because *you* still need to be exposed to good society
and Lady Bruxton was kind enough to invite us both,
despite my shoddy reputation.'

Jane wrinkled her nose. 'I don't care what anyone
says, you were right to break off your engagement. Life
would have been very unpleasant for both of us had
you gone ahead and married Lady Mary. I *know* she
didn't like me.' She was silent for a moment, but when
she spoke again, there was a delightful wickedness in
her voice. 'I'll wager Mr Oberon would never consider
*me* in the running for the most beautiful ladybird in
London.'

'I should damn well hope not! Apart from your being

a respectable young woman, I cannot imagine you married to a man like Oberon.'

'Why not? When his father dies, Monty becomes a very rich young man. The list of ladies wishing to be his wife *or* his mistress will stretch long, of that you can be sure.'

'And I pity every one of them,' Robert said, suddenly reminded of the French girl he'd seen at the Black Swan Inn. A girl whose beautiful face lingered in the shadows of his mind. He hadn't seen her or her brother again after taking his leave of them that night, but he hadn't forgotten her—and neither had Oberon. He'd talked about nothing else the entire way back to London.

'Well, let's hope there will be a few new faces at Lady Bruxton's tonight,' Jane said. 'Otherwise, I shall be forced to marry a blind man who falls in love with the sound of my voice and does not mind that I hobble on the way to the drawing room.'

'You will marry a man who loves you *despite* the fact you hobble,' Robert informed her with amusement. 'And I have every confidence *this* will be the year you find him.'

'Goodness, such unwavering belief in my ability.'

'Do you not share it?'

'I would like to, but I fear Tykhe has chosen to bestow her favours elsewhere.'

'Then we shall seek our own good fortune,' Robert said boldly. 'Thumb our noses at the Fates.'

'Oh, no, we must never do that,' Jane said, laughing. 'Unless we wish to bring their wrath down upon our heads.'

'Nothing of the sort,' Robert said. 'But we have

endured more than our fair share of bad luck, Jane. It is time the gods smiled favourably upon us for a change.'

Sophie recognised him the moment he walked into the room. Though he was far more elegantly attired than on the occasion of their first meeting, there was no mistaking the confidence in his stride or his ruggedly handsome features. He stood tall and proud, his dark hair gleaming in the candlelight, and though several women turned to look at him as he passed, his warmest smile was reserved for the young woman at his side. A slender lady wearing green and who walked with a cane in her hand. 'I know that gentleman,' Sophie said.

Lavinia's dark brows rose in surprise. 'Which one?'

'The tall one who just came in. Silverton, I believe his name is.'

'Yes. Robert Silverton. And that is his sister, Jane. Where do you know him from?'

'The Black Swan Inn. He and another gentleman were there the evening we landed.'

Sophie had purposely made no mention of the events that had taken place at the inn. Nicholas would have been furious that his arrangements had fallen through, and Lavinia would have been horrified at the thought of a lovers' quarrel erupting into gunfire in the courtyard. But with Mr Silverton in the room and the prospect of an encounter likely, Sophie thought it best to mention that the two of them had spoken. 'I would not have thought them brother and sister. The resemblance is not strong.'

'No. Robert tends to follow his father's side while Jane gets her fair hair and delicate colouring from her mother's. But they come from a very good family. Their father was knighted for services to the Crown, and their mother was the youngest daughter of a baronet,' Lavinia said. 'Sadly, their deaths kept Robert and Jane out of society for many years.'

'Neither of them is married?'

'No. Jane was injured in a carriage accident as a child and does not go about much. You see how she limps. As for Mr Silverton, I regret to say he is out of favour with society at the moment.'

Sophie frowned. 'Out of favour?'

Lavinia glanced around, and then lowered her voice. 'About six weeks ago, Mr Silverton asked a young lady to marry him. She accepted and wedding plans got underway. Then, a few weeks later, he broke it off without a word of explanation to anyone. Naturally the lady was terribly upset and said some very harsh things about him in public. After all, it's one thing for a lady to change her mind, but quite another for a gentleman. As a result, no self-respecting mother will allow her daughter anywhere near Mr Silverton, and many doors have been closed in his face. I'm surprised he's here tonight.'

Sophie watched the good-looking brother and sister move through the crowd and noticed that while some of the guests offered them a reserved smile, others ignored them completely. 'It seems a very harsh treatment,' she said. 'He must have had a good reason for breaking the engagement off.'

'I'm sure he did,' Lavinia agreed. 'But a gentleman simply doesn't do things like that. And the fact he won't say *why* he did it has hurt him irreparably. Lady Mary is telling her own version of the story and it is not kind. Even Jane has suffered for it.'

Sophie switched her attention to the sister. A truly lovely young woman, Jane Silverton stood a good head shorter than her brother and looked to be fairly delicate. And though the smile on her lips was cheery, the paleness of her cheeks told another story. 'I should like to meet her. I think it's cruel that she be shunned for something her brother did.'

'That's very kind of you, dear.'

'I just try to put myself in her place,' Sophie said, for in truth, she *had* been in Jane Silverton's place once, though not for the same reasons. 'And you should know that while Mr Silverton and I did have a conversation that night, we were not formally introduced. He may not even remember who I am.'

'Well, he'll remember you after tonight,' Lavinia said, discreetly raising her hand to attract the couple's attention. 'Madame Delors surpassed even *my* expectations with that gown. You are easily one of the most beautiful women in the room.'

While Sophie took leave to disagree with the latter part of Lavinia's statement, she couldn't deny that the gown of cream-coloured lace over a gold satin slip was the most glorious thing she had ever seen. Cut outrageously low in the front, it displayed a rather alarming amount of skin—which had prompted her to stitch a wide band of lace inset with pearls and tiny satin roses into the neckline—and from a raised waist, the skirt fell in elegant folds to the floor. Delicate slippers of soft kid leather, cream-coloured elbow-length gloves, and a spray of cream-and-pink roses in her hair put the finishing touches on what Sophie could only think to call a truly magnificent ensemble.

Even so, she doubted it would be enough to thaw Mr Silverton's chilly reserve.

'Mr Silverton, Jane, how lovely to see you again,' Lavinia said when the pair finally managed to reach them. 'Allow me to introduce a very dear friend of mine, Miss Sophie Vallois. Sophie, this is Miss Jane Silverton and her brother, Mr Robert Silverton.'

'How lovely to meet you, Miss Vallois,' Jane said. 'Or should I say, *enchantée*?'

The girl's voice was as delightful as her sparkling green eyes and Sophie found it hard to believe that any gentleman would find her lacking. 'How do you do, Miss Silverton,' she replied, before adding more diffidently to her brother, 'Mr Silverton.'

'Miss Vallois.' He briefly inclined his head. 'We meet again.'

So, he wasn't about to pretend ignorance of their first encounter. She awarded him a point for honesty. 'I didn't think you would remember.'

His deep brown eyes were steady on hers. 'On the contrary, I am unlikely to forget.'

'Sophie informs me the two of you met at the Black Swan Inn,' Lavinia said.

'Saying we *met* would not be entirely correct,' Mr Silverton said. 'We were brought together by circumstances less than conducive to pleasant socialising and parted soon after.'

'Then how fortunate you should both end up here tonight in order that the formalities might be observed.'

The gentleman inclined his head. 'As you say.'

'Is your husband not with you this evening, Lady Longworth?' Miss Silverton asked.

'Yes, but he and Sophie's brother just left to play billiards with Lord Bruxton. Apparently they are all quite mad for the game.'

'Your brother plays billiards?' Mr Silverton asked Sophie in surprise.

'When he has a chance, yes.'

'I thought the study of medicine was an all-consuming passion.'

Sophie raised her eyes to his, daring him to disagree. 'A man must take some time away from his studies, lest he become too weary to absorb anything new. Even God rested on the seventh day.'

Was that a hint of a smile? 'A lofty comparison.'

'But fitting under the circumstances. I admire *anyone* who has the determination to strive for something they truly believe in.'

'And I have always been impressed by people who choose to help others in such a way,' Jane spoke up. 'But tell me, how did the four of you meet?'

'Through my husband,' Lavinia said easily. 'Nicholas and Antoine met in France several years ago, and we finally persuaded him to come to London and to bring Sophie with him. Unfortunately, Antoine must shortly return home, but Sophie is to stay with us until the end of the Season.'

'Oh, how wonderful!' Jane said happily. 'Then you must pay us a visit while you are here, Miss Vallois. We will have petit fours, and speak French, and you can tell me all about the latest fashions from Paris. *J'adore la mode française.* Have you seen much of London?'

'Not yet.'

'Then why not join us tomorrow afternoon? Robert

has promised to take me for a drive around Hyde Park. It would be lovely if you and your brother could come too.'

It was an unexpectedly kind offer and one Sophie would have been happy to accept—had she not caught sight of the expression on Mr Silverton's face. Obviously he did not share his sister's enthusiasm for the outing and saw no reason to pretend he did. 'Perhaps another time,' she said. 'I have no wish to intrude.'

'Oh, but you wouldn't be intruding,' Jane said. 'My brother is always delighted to have friends come along. Aren't you, Robert?'

'Of course. I merely thought it too soon after Miss Vallois's arrival for such an outing. She might wish to rest.'

'Fudge! If she has been here since yesterday, she is well over the worst and decidedly in need of a diversion,' Jane said. 'Tell her you were only thinking of her welfare and that you would love to have her come with us.'

Sophie had a difficult time holding her tongue. Had Lavinia not been present, she would have politely but firmly declined the invitation. She had no wish to force her company on *any one* who had no desire to share it, even if it meant disappointing Jane, who obviously did. To her surprise, however, it was Mr Silverton who resolved the problem. 'You are more than welcome to join us, Miss Vallois. Jane is anxious for your company, and I am happy to oblige her. As for your own enjoyment, while it might not be as diverting as a night spent in a barn with the horses, I'm sure you will find it an amusing way to pass an hour or two.'

Jane frowned. 'A night spent in a barn with *horses*? What on earth are you talking about, Robert?'

But Sophie knew *exactly* what he was talking about. And the knowledge that he not only *understood* French, but that he *remembered* every word she'd said to Antoine that night at the inn, brought hot colour sweeping into her cheeks. No wonder he'd been so distant with her.

'Come, Jane,' Mr Silverton said. 'Miss Vallois can send a note if she wishes to join us. For now, we mustn't keep her and Lady Longworth from their evening.'

'No, of course not. Forgive me,' Jane said. 'It's just that I so seldom meet anyone I really like, I tend to get carried away. But now that we've met, I know we are all going to be great friends. Until tomorrow, then, Miss Vallois. Good evening, Lady Longworth.'

'Jane,' Lavinia said. 'Mr Silverton.'

'Lady Longworth.' He bowed, and then turned to Sophie. 'Miss Vallois.'

Sophie inclined her head, but refused to meet his eyes. Why should she when it was so obvious that he didn't like her? His words had been clipped and the warmth he had shown his sister and Lavinia had definitely not been extended to her.

'A charming pair, are they not?' Lavinia asked.

'The sister more than the brother, I think,' Sophie said. 'Imagine extending an invitation to someone she barely knows.'

'Jane has always had a good heart,' Lavinia said. 'Which is why it annoys me so that she is not yet married. At times, I feel like shaking the young men for their fickleness. But I expect she will benefit greatly from spending time with you and Antoine tomorrow.'

'And I look forward to introducing Antoine to her. In fact—' Sophie broke off and slowly began to smile. 'I have a feeling my brother might enjoy Miss Silverton's company very much.'

# Chapter Four

So she wasn't a whore, a strumpet or a ballet dancer, Robert reflected as he and Jane walked away. She was an exceptionally beautiful young woman who, thanks to the kindness of Lord and Lady Longworth, was about to be launched into English society. The prospect did not please him. His own reasons aside, it meant she was fair game for the likes of Montague Oberon, and he did not relish the thought of watching the man salivate over her every time he saw her out in public.

'Behold the prodigal son,' Jane whispered in her brother's ear a few minutes later. 'And more splendidly attired than half the ladies in the room.'

Her assessment wasn't far off. Not many gentlemen could have carried off the colourful waistcoat and elaborately folded cravat with such panache, but Oberon's height and bearing allowed him to do so magnificently. His golden curls were swept back in a manner few men could have worn to advantage and his clothes were immaculate. Pompous prig he might be, Robert reflected, but looks, breeding and a fortune allowed him to carry it off with aplomb.

'Evening, Silver,' Oberon said when he came within speaking distance. 'Jane. Lovely to see you again.'

'Mr Oberon. What a splendid waistcoat. It is surely a modern version of Joseph's coat of many colours.'

Oberon's expression was blank. 'Joseph?'

'You remember. From the bible.'

'Oh, yes, of course. The old fellow whose wife turned to stone.'

'That was Lot,' Robert said. 'And it was salt.'

'Salt?' Oberon frowned. 'What has salt to do with it? We were talking about my waistcoat.' He paused for a moment to glance around the room. 'Jupiter, what an appalling crowd. I vow there weren't this many people at the—' He broke off, his eyes frozen to one spot. 'Good God, it's *her*!'

Jane turned to look. 'Who?'

'The girl from the inn. Aphrodite reincarnated,' Oberon murmured. 'It is her, isn't it, Silver?'

Breathing a sigh of exasperation, Robert said, 'Yes.'

'Splendid. Then I must be introduced.'

'I'd like a word with you first.'

'Later.' Oberon's eyes never strayed from the object of his affection. '*After* I speak to the Goddess!'

'Now. Will you excuse us, Jane?'

'Of course. I see Lady Jennings sitting on her own and looking rather disgruntled,' Jane said. 'I shall go and keep her company. No doubt she will have a few choice things to say about some of the guests here this evening.'

'Not about me, I hope,' Oberon said.

'On the contrary, you are always one of her favourite

topics, Mr Oberon.' And with a smile for him and a wink for her brother, Jane left the two of them alone.

'Impertinent minx,' Oberon said without rancour. 'Is it my imagination or is her limp less noticeable than it used to be?'

'I am hardly the one to ask given that I never thought it *was* all that noticeable,' Robert said, drawing the other man aside. 'Now, would you mind telling me what the hell you think you're doing?'

Oberon's gaze shortened and refocused. 'Doing?'

'The wager. I told you I wanted no part of it, yet you went ahead and put my name to it regardless.'

'Ah, yes, that. Yes, I did set it up because several of the lads thought it would be a great lark. All of them are in the market for a new mistress and when Mortimer wagered a month at his father's hunting lodge in Yorkshire that he would be the first to succeed, Cramby staked a thousand pounds against him, saying Mortimer had more money than sense.'

'There's a lot of that going around,' Robert muttered. 'But I won't have it, Oberon. Take my name off the bet and out of the book. My reputation doesn't need any further blackening by you.'

'Can't do it, old boy. We all put our hand to it, you see. I personally signed for you,' Oberon confided. 'And when you consider what the winner stands to gain, it really makes no sense to call it off. Now, about the French girl. Who is she and how does she come to be here tonight?'

Biting back a scathing retort, Robert said, 'I know nothing more about her than I did at the inn. Except that her name is Miss Vallois and she is here with Lord and Lady Longworth.'

'You mean she's staying with them?'

'Possibly.'

'Interesting.' Oberon's eyes assumed a speculative gleam. 'She must be well born to be moving in their circle. I wonder if the fair Lavinia has taken it upon herself to launch the girl into society.'

'I have no idea.'

'Then I'll find out for myself. Introduce us.'

'No.'

The blunt answer brought Oberon's head around. 'I *beg* your pardon?'

'I said no. If the young lady is being presented to society, she is not some light-skirt for you to trifle with.'

'My dear Robert, did it not occur to you I might have *other* things in mind for the delectable Miss Vallois?'

'It did not.' Robert smiled without warmth. 'I know your reputation, Oberon, and a leopard doesn't change his spots.'

The other man's expression cooled. 'Tread lightly, my friend. 'Tis a fine line between familiarity and contempt, and many a friendship has been lost over a careless misstep. I ask only to be introduced to the young lady. What possible harm can come of that?'

*They were coming.* The man who didn't like her—and the one who did in ways of which no mother would ever approve. Sophie took a deep breath and slowly opened her fan. What a pity Lavinia had chosen that very moment to go off and speak with friends.

'Miss Vallois,' Mr Silverton said, stopping in front of her. 'Pray forgive the intrusion, but my friend has asked to be made known to you.'

Sophie glanced up into his handsome face, aware of

the strength in those chiselled features, and saw again the cool disinterest she had come to associate with Robert Silverton. But she also saw something else. A reserve that seemed to echo her own uncertainty. 'As you wish, Mr Silverton.'

'Miss Sophie Vallois, may I present Mr Montague Oberon.'

'Miss Vallois, what a pleasure this is,' Mr Oberon said. 'I did not think I would be fortunate enough to see you again.'

'It *is* something of a surprise,' Sophie acknowledged, not liking the way his eyes lingered on the low décolleté of her gown. She purposely raised her fan to block his view. 'So you and Mr Silverton are friends as well as travelling companions.'

'Oh, yes. Very good friends.' Mr Oberon raised guileless blue eyes to hers. 'As you saw that night at the inn, Silverton is everything a gentleman should be. Thoughtful, unselfish, steady as a rock. Sadly, all the things I am not.'

Startled by his candour, Sophie said, 'Then what qualities do you possess?'

'Wealth, humour and impeccable taste when it comes to female beauty…which is why you caught my eye the other evening. The gods themselves could not have sent a more divine creature to move amongst us. But I am well aware I owe you an apology. My behaviour was, to say the least, reprehensible. Due, no doubt, to the tedium of travel and the insufferable manners of that wretched innkeeper. Please say you will forgive me or I shall never rest easy again.'

The effusive apology surprised Sophie as much as amused her, and though she believed his words to be little more than pretty flattery, the fact he *had* offered an apology allowed her to look upon him with a touch more charity. 'I accept your apology.'

'I am relieved beyond words.'

'Ah, good evening, Mr Oberon,' Lavinia said, finally returning. 'How nice to see you again.'

'The pleasure must always be mine, Lady Longworth.' Mr Oberon's smile moved smoothly into place. 'I vow you grow more lovely with every passing day.'

'And I vow you grow more fulsome with your compliments. Have you met Miss Vallois?'

'Indeed. Silverton was kind enough to introduce us. Am I to understand the lady will be spending the Season here in London with you?'

'You are.'

'Then perhaps I might call upon you in the near future to exchange pleasantries in a less crowded venue.'

Lavinia inclined her head. 'You are, of course, welcome to call. But now I must steal Sophie away. Lord and Lady Beale are anxious to meet her. Sophie?'

Grateful for the opportunity to escape, Sophie dropped a quick curtsy. 'Mr Oberon.' Then, raising her chin, and goaded by some mischievous impulse she would no doubt regret later, she looked at the gentleman standing quietly beside him and said, 'Please tell your sister that my brother and I look forward to joining you tomorrow afternoon, Mr Silverton. If the invitation is still open.'

His expression didn't change, but Sophie heard the quiet edge of mockery in his voice. 'It is, and I shall be pleased to tell her of your acceptance.'

Sophie smiled as she tucked her arm in Lavinia's. 'Good evening, gentlemen.'

'Ladies.' Oberon barely waited until they were out of hearing before exclaiming, 'Until tomorrow? What was that all about?'

'Jane has invited Miss Vallois and her brother to come driving with us,' Robert said distantly.

'And she *agreed*?'

'Why would she not? By your own words, I am thoughtful, considerate and steady as a rock.'

'I was only trying to flatter you.'

'By making me sound like the trusted family dog?'

'Nothing of the sort. I simply wanted her to know that you and I are very different.'

'I believe she worked that one out on her own,' Robert drawled, but Oberon wasn't listening. He was following Sophie's progress across the room like a hungry lion following a sprightly gazelle.

'By God, she's exquisite,' he murmured. 'Those eyes. That hair. And that complexion! As pink as rose petals and as smooth as alabaster. Imagine her lying naked in your bed, Silver. Imagine the softness of her skin as you run your hand slowly over her throat, and then lower.' He briefly closed his eyes and made a sound deep in his throat. Seconds later, his eyes snapped open. 'I must know who she is. Where does she come from, and why is she here?'

'I have no idea,' Robert said. 'Is it not enough that she is a good friend of Lord and Lady Longworth's?'

'No. The French are as stuffy as the English when it comes to matters of class. And a well-brought-up French girl would have no need of a London Season.'

The same thought had occurred to Robert, but he had no intention of giving Oberon the satisfaction of agreeing with him. 'If you don't think she's well born, why trouble yourself to make enquiries?'

'Because I would hate to miss the opportunity of getting to know her *if* her birth is all it should be,' Oberon said. 'Look at her, man! When did you last see beauty like that? Observe the elegance of her carriage, the unconscious grace with which she carries herself. Who knows? She may well be the daughter of a French count.'

'You could ask Lady Longworth.'

'I could, but if the Longworths are using her extraordinary beauty as a means of capturing a wealthy husband, the truth may be revealed only *after* the vows are spoken. She may be an heiress—or an actress, which means I'm better off making my own enquiries.'

'Which means what? You strap Miss Vallois to the rack and turn the screws until she tells you what you want to know?'

Oberon laughed. 'Really, Silver, my methods are far more civilised. You see, in every person's life, there are secrets. And there are always people who *know* those secrets. It is simply a matter of finding the right people and asking them the right questions.'

'And if they suffer from the antiquated notion of loyalty or friendship?'

'Then they must be *encouraged* to share what they know.' Oberon smiled, but to Robert's way of thinking, it was a singularly unpleasant thing. 'Next to torture, I've always found money to be the most effective way of eliciting the truth.'

Oberon walked away and Robert made no attempt to stop him. The man was like a dog with a bone. Once he sank his teeth into something, he wouldn't let go until there was nothing left to hold on to. Such was the case with Miss Vallois. Oberon had decided she was of interest to him and he would leave no stone unturned until he knew everything there was to know about her.

A daunting prospect for anyone, let alone a young woman newly arrived in London and looking to make a successful marriage. For *her* sake, Robert hoped there was nothing in her past that would preclude that from happening.

By the time the evening came to an end, Sophie was convinced the English were indefatigable. Though it was well past two in the morning, Lavinia and Nicholas were still chatting enthusiastically about the people to whom they had spoken, and about the delight those people had expressed at having been introduced to the charming brother and sister from France.

Sophie was pleased the evening had gone so well, but her feelings of excitement had long since given way to exhaustion. The noise of so many people, the sights and sounds of a grand ball, the necessity of constantly having to be on one's guard to say the right thing, were tiring in the extreme, to say nothing of the difficulties involved in keeping everyone's titles and positions straight. What a confusing jumble of lords and ladies the English aristocracy was!

Then there was the always-disturbing behaviour of one Mr Robert Silverton…

'I think you'll sleep well tonight,' Lavinia said as they climbed the stairs to their rooms. 'I'll have Jeanette bring you a cup of chocolate in the morning.'

'Thank you, Lavinia.' Sophie was so weary she had

to concentrate on putting one foot in front of the other. 'If left alone, I fear I may sleep until noon.'

'In that case, I shall have a breakfast tray sent up as well.'

Thankfully, Jeanette was waiting to help her undress and after the magnificent gown was removed and carefully hung in the closet, Sophie sat down at the dressing table and gazed longingly at the bed. 'I don't suppose I could go to bed without having my hair brushed?'

Jeanette pursed her lips. 'Her ladyship wouldn't like it, miss. She's very particular about that sort of thing.'

'Yes, I'm sure she is.' Sophie sighed as she turned to face the glass. As the maid took the pins from her hair and it came tumbling down around her shoulders, Sophie closed her eyes and let her mind drift back over the events of the evening. Ironically, she found herself thinking about Robert Silverton. Why, she couldn't imagine. The man had made no secret of the fact he didn't like her, yet she was finding it exceedingly difficult to put him from her thoughts. She had followed his progress around the room, watching as he had stopped to speak with people he knew. The young ladies had been careful to keep their distance, but several of the older ones had smiled in a way that led Sophie to believe he was still *very* attractive to women open to *une dalliance*.

'Sophie, are you awake?' Lavinia called from the other side of the door.

'Yes.' Sophie opened her eyes, glad to have something to think about other than Robert Silverton. 'Come in, Lavinia.'

Lavinia did, looking wonderfully exotic and far too wide awake in a dressing robe of deep crimson silk trimmed with layers of snowy white lace. Her long dark hair was caught in a loose knot at the nape of her neck and there was a definite twinkle in her eyes. 'Thank you, Jeanette. That will be all.'

The maid put down the silver-handled brush, bobbed a curtsy and left. Lavinia waited for the door to close before settling herself on the edge of the bed and gazing at Sophie's reflection in the glass. 'I hope you don't mind, but I couldn't wait until breakfast to hear what you thought of your first ball. And to tell you how proud Nicholas and I were of you this evening. I'm sure we will see your name in the society pages tomorrow.'

Sophie turned on the upholstered seat and her mouth lifted in a smile. 'I hope they neglect to mention that I addressed the Countess of Doncaster's eldest daughter as Lady Doncaster.'

Lavinia dismissed it with a wave. 'You apologised so sweetly even Lady Doncaster couldn't take offence. But we could spend some time with *Debrett's* tomorrow, if you like.'

'Or we could just avoid attending any more grand balls. But I did enjoy myself this evening, Lavinia, and I think Antoine did too.'

'Good, because I noticed several young ladies watching him,' Lavinia commented. 'Miss Margaret Quilling couldn't take her eyes from him.'

'Which one was she?'

'The tall girl in white. Quite pretty, with blond hair dressed with feathers and pearls.'

Sophie nodded, remembering the ensemble rather than the lady. It had been of white tulle over satin with a rather unusual band of satin crescents forming a wide border around the bottom. The sleeves had been short and edged with a smaller band of crescents. 'Yes, I remember. She complimented me on my gown and asked if I'd had it made in Paris.'

'Really? I must pass that on to Madame Delors. She will be delighted to know that her gowns are being praised by such illustrious members of society.' Lavinia got up and wandered across to the window. 'Does the room please you, Sophie? I thought you might prefer one facing the square.'

'The room is perfect,' Sophie said, glancing around the spacious chamber. A huge four-poster bed was draped in lavender velvet, with the bedspread and pillows being of a lighter hue. A wardrobe stood against the opposite wall and a writing table was nestled under a window framed by delicate white curtains. 'My mother would have loved it. Lavender was always her favourite colour.'

'It must have been hard for you to leave her.'

'I didn't get the chance.' Sophie's eyes misted as they always did when she thought of the gentle woman who had raised her as best she could, despite the frequent bouts of debilitating illness. 'She died four years ago.'

'Oh, my dear, I'm so sorry. I didn't know.'

'That's all right. She passed peacefully in her sleep.'

Lavinia's face softened. 'And your father? Do you miss him?'

Sophie felt a return of the old disappointment, followed by the inevitable feelings of guilt. 'I wish I could say I did, but after Mama died, Papa became a very difficult man. He grew bitter and argumentative. Always looking for fault. When he found out what Antoine and I had done, he made it very clear we were not welcome in his house.'

'Gracious! How *did* he find out?'

'There was talk of it in the village,' Sophie said, unwilling to say more. 'When Papa heard, he accused Antoine of being sympathetic to the English cause and of disgracing the Vallois name. He said he was never to show his face in Bayencourt again!'

'How cruel!'

'It was, but Antoine and Papa never really got on. By the next morning, we were gone.'

'But why did you go with him, Sophie? You were so young. Surely Antoine would have preferred that you stay behind.'

'Of course, but how could I stay when it was *my* fault he had to leave?'

'Your fault?'

'I was the one who asked him to help Nicholas.'

'Oh, my dear, you must *never* reproach yourself for that,' Lavinia said. 'You should be proud that you cared enough about the life of a stranger that you would try to help him.'

'He would have died if I hadn't,' Sophie said, remembering the extent of Nicholas's injuries when she had found him lying at the side of the road. 'But I was actually more worried about him after he left. With no memory of what had happened to him, I was afraid the man who'd shot him might still be out there waiting for him.'

'He was,' Lavinia said quietly. 'Thankfully, Nicholas was able to track him down and bring him to justice before he was able to harm anyone else. But you were very brave to do what you did. And to leave home like that.'

'It was hard in the beginning,' Sophie admitted. 'We

were afraid one of our neighbours might have alerted the authorities, so after we left Bayencourt, we kept to the back roads and were careful not to draw attention to ourselves. We slept in barns, ate when and where we could. Once we reached Paris, it was easy to lose ourselves in the crowds. Eventually, Antoine managed to find accommodation for us over a small shop, and after working at a number of jobs, he was offered an apprenticeship with Monsieur Larocque.'

'How did you come to be employed by Mrs Grant-Ogilvy?' Lavinia asked.

Sophie's stomach clenched, the way it always did when that name was mentioned. 'I made a gown for the daughter of one of her friends. I remember sitting for hours at a time, handstitching hundreds of tiny beads to the bodice. When Mrs Grant-Ogilvy saw it, she asked to meet the girl who had done the work. As it happens, she was also looking for someone to teach her daughters how to speak French, so I was hired to do both.'

'How long were you with her?'

'Just over a year. I left just before her eldest daughter married.' Sophie decided to keep her other reason for leaving to herself. She had no desire to talk about Eldon. Eldon, with his grasping hands and hot liquored breath...

'Well, it was certainly a valuable association for you,' Lavinia said. 'It explains how you came to speak English so well and to carry yourself with such grace. I'm quite sure you will be married before the end of the Season.'

*Mon Dieu,* that word again. 'Lavinia, I meant what I said about not wishing to find a husband,' Sophie said slowly. 'I know this may sound strange, but I would like to open a shop.'

'A shop? You mean...you wish to be in *trade*?'

The look of abject horror on Lavinia's face made Sophie laugh. 'Oh, Lavinia, it's not that bad. I'm a very good seamstress and I have a definite talent for design. I want to make clothes for ladies who can't afford the expensive *ateliers* of Paris.'

'But if you were married, you wouldn't *need* to work,' Lavinia pointed out. 'You would be able to lead the life of a lady and you would have the respect of society—'

'But not the independence,' Sophie said. 'I would be subject to my husband's whims. Forever at his beck and call, with nothing to call my own. That is not how I wish to live my life.'

'But you are so very beautiful, Sophie,' Lavinia said, trying to make her understand. 'You saw how popular you were tonight.'

'What I saw were ladies far more accomplished than myself dancing with gentlemen of wealth and breeding in a world familiar to them both. That isn't *my* world, Lavinia. And no gentleman of good family is going to bother with an unsophisticated French girl like me.'

'Let me tell you something, Sophia Chantal Vallois,' Lavinia said quietly. 'The young lady I've come to know is not in the least unsophisticated. She is a beautiful young woman who is going to make a lot of men fall in love with her, and when *she* finds the right man, she is going to find out that being loved by him is the sweetest pleasure of all.'

Sophie's mouth twisted. 'I will tell you if it happens.'

'You won't have to.' Lavinia stood up, her face breaking into a smile. 'Your face will say it all.'

## Chapter Five

'So, did you meet anyone at Lady Bruxton's ball with whom you would like to further an acquaintance?' Robert asked his sister as he turned the landau towards Eaton Place the following afternoon.

Jane, who was looking exceedingly stylish in a deep maroon gown with a new cream-and-maroon bonnet, pulled a face. 'Not a one—and please do not suggest I encourage Mr Hemmings. He is surely the most tiresome man on earth.'

'What about Sir Bartholomew Grout?'

'For pity's sake, Robert. Even wearing spectacles, the man is constantly tripping over his own feet. I need someone sturdier than that lest we both find ourselves on the ground half the time. And though I spoke to him for almost ten minutes, he did not smile at me once!'

'A most grievous offence, I'm sure,' Robert said as he drew up before the Longworths' town house.

'It was to me,' Jane said. 'And I suspect it would be to you as well.'

'Thankfully, I'm not keeping a list of anyone's good or bad points at the moment.'

'Well, you should. That way when the right lady comes along, you will be prepared.'

Robert secured the reins. 'Fine. When she appears, I shall be sure to make a note of how many times she makes me smile.'

'Odious man!' Jane said, though she was quick to laugh. 'Perhaps you are better off with a mistress. I don't suppose it matters how many times *she* makes you smile, since smiling is not the purpose of the association.'

It was an outrageous remark for an unmarried girl to make even to her older brother, but to be made within hearing of a gentleman with whom she had no acquaintance at all was as grievous a social error as a young lady could commit. Robert glanced at the darkly handsome gentleman standing at the bottom of the steps and realised his sister had just committed an unforgivable *faux-pas* in front of Antoine Vallois.

'Oh, dear,' Jane said, clearly not sure whether to laugh or to beg an apology. 'That was extremely bad timing. I hope, sir, that you will forgive my unfortunate choice of words. My poor brother is used to such outbursts, but I fear the general public is not.'

The gentleman walked slowly towards the carriage. 'Perhaps I should claim not to have heard the remark, *mademoiselle*. That would, I expect, be the more gentlemanly thing to do.' He looked at Robert and nodded. 'We meet again, Mr Silverton.'

'Mr Vallois,' Robert said, his voice clipped. 'Allow me to introduce my sister, Jane. And while I should offer an apology for what she just said, I doubt she would thank me for doing so.'

'I most certainly would not,' Jane said tartly. 'Pray do not fear that I am always so outspoken, Mr Vallois, but Robert and I were discussing the importance of a smile in the early stages of courtship. I took leave to disagree with him in the way brothers and sisters so often do.'

The gentleman inclined his head. 'I understand perfectly. I'm sure Sophie has often despaired of me in such a way.'

'I have never despaired of you, Antoine. If anything, it is the other way around.'

Drawn by the sound of her voice, Robert glanced up to see Miss Vallois standing in the doorway. She looked radiant in a pale blue gown, her silvery blond hair tucked up under a fetching straw bonnet, her blue eyes bright with anticipation. She looked as fresh and as appealing as spring itself, but with a sensuality that seemed strangely at odds with her innocence. Robert found it a very disturbing combination. 'Good afternoon, Miss Vallois.'

'Mr Silverton.'

'*Bonjour*, dear Miss Vallois!' Jane cried. 'Haven't we a splendid afternoon for our drive?'

'We have indeed,' Miss Vallois said as she approached the carriage. 'And what a fine pair of horses you drive, Mr Silverton. So perfectly matched, even to the flash of white on their faces.'

'Robert is most particular about his cattle,' Jane said. 'Aren't you, Robert?'

'No more so than any other gentleman.' Robert

jumped down from the seat. 'A well-matched pair is always to be preferred.'

'In horses and in marriage, I dare say,' Jane said. 'Which means I must marry a lame man. Isn't that so, Mr Vallois?'

His reaction was one of mild confusion. 'I cannot imagine why you would think so, Miss Silverton. You must marry as your heart dictates.'

'Ah, but my heart is not free to choose. Were I to fall in love with a prince, I should expect to be disappointed, for he would not turn a kindly eye towards me,' Jane said, her unaffected smile stealing the gravity from her words. 'Like Mr Oberon, he would wish his lady to be perfect in all ways.'

'Then I could only think the prince, like Mr Oberon, a fool,' Mr Vallois replied quietly.

Robert was astonished to see his unflappable sister momentarily at a loss for words, but the lapse was brief and, quickly recovering, she patted the vacant seat beside her. 'How droll you are, *monsieur*. I insist you come and sit next to me. It will give me an opportunity to show you that I am not as gauche as you must surely believe me to be.'

The gentleman inclined his head. 'It would be my pleasure to sit beside you, *mademoiselle*, but I will not be joining you this afternoon.'

'Why ever not? Surely your sister told you that you were included in the invitation.'

'I did,' Miss Vallois said, 'but unbeknownst to me, Antoine and Lord Longworth had already made other plans.'

*'Quel dommage.'* Jane studied Mr Vallois thought-fully for a moment. 'I understand you are not staying

long in London. I would regret not having an opportunity to show you that there is a more refined side to my nature.'

'I have no doubt you possess as refined a nature as any other young lady, Miss Silverton.'

'But she does smile a great deal more,' Robert said drily. 'Though whether that is to recommend her, I cannot say.'

'I would consider it a recommendation,' Mr Vallois said. Then, speaking quietly in rapid French, he added, *'Qu'est-ce qui est plus doux que le sourire d'une belle dame?'*

Robert watched his sister's cheeks go bright pink and turned to glare at Antoine. 'Forgive me, sir, but if you wish to converse with my sister, I would ask that you do so in English.'

'But he said nothing impertinent, Robert.' Jane's smile was as bright as a new penny. 'In fact, I do believe it is one of the nicest things anyone has ever said to me. *Merci beaucoup, Monsieur Vallois.'*

*'De rien.'* Mr Vallois held her gaze a moment longer before addressing Robert. 'Please accept my apology, Mr Silverton. It was not my intention to offend. Only to express an opinion that a beautiful lady's smile is truly a lovely thing to behold.' He touched the brim of his hat. 'Enjoy your afternoon.'

Robert stiffly inclined his head. He knew his feelings of resentment towards the French were not shared by his sister, but the strength of his conviction was such that he could not be happy about seeing her offered a compliment by one, especially one as handsome as Antoine Vallois. A man she barely knew, but who had the ability to make her blush. Damn his charming ways.

'Mr Silverton?'

And now the sister sought to distract him. He turned to see her watching him with those perceptive blue eyes, the question on her face a direct result of the confrontation that had just taken place. Had she guessed at the nature of his thoughts? Figured out that his hostility towards her brother stemmed from a natural antipathy towards her countrymen? Judging from the way her smile dimmed as he handed her into the carriage, she knew something was amiss. But he wasn't about to let it trouble him. For Jane's sake, he would be pleasant, but that was all. He wasn't looking for a wife and he certainly had no intention of making the exquisite Miss Vallois his mistress.

She had made it perfectly clear at the Black Swan Inn that she'd prefer the company of the *horses* rather than have anything to do with him.

Sophie knew they weren't off to a promising start. After settling her in the seat beside his sister, Mr Silverton had climbed back into the driver's seat, picked up the reins and set the team off without a word. It wasn't that he was rude, simply that he was distant. And whether *that* was a result of the stilted conversation he'd just had with Antoine, or of *her* unwelcome presence in the carriage, Sophie had no idea. All she knew was that the tension was as sharp as a finely honed blade—and that it cut with equal facility.

Fortunately, Miss Silverton, with her delightful sense of humour, tried to lighten the mood by alternately paying her brother no mind, or teasing him to distraction. 'I keep telling Robert that he needs to get on with his life before he becomes a doddering old fool no woman is interested in,' she confided as they drove through the gates into the Park, 'but he refuses to listen. He simply tells me I must find a husband and settle down. But really, Miss Vallois, at eight-and-twenty, what gentleman is going to look at me with marriage in mind? I do not have sufficient wealth to make up for the loss of my youth or agility—'

'Jane—'

'And now he is going to scold me for having suggested that my handicap stands in the way of my making a good marriage. He believes it does not, but you and I know better.'

'On the contrary,' Sophie said, 'I watched you at the ball last evening and though you did not dance, you got around very well in all other respects.'

'There, you see, Jane,' Mr Silverton said over his shoulder. 'Miss Vallois has not known you above a day, yet she is already of the opinion that your leg is not the handicap you claim it to be.'

'I wonder.' Miss Silverton sent a sidelong glance at Sophie. 'What would your brother say about my handicap, Miss Vallois? He is studying to be a doctor, after all, and is likely to be less emotional about such things.'

'I would venture to say it is the *last* thing Antoine would concern himself with,' Sophie said without hesitation. 'He is far more interested in how people think than with their physical appearance.'

'In which case, he and Oberon have absolutely nothing in common,' Mr Silverton muttered.

'Apart from their looks, for Mr Vallois is certainly as handsome as Mr Oberon,' Miss Silverton said, though she was careful to maintain the correct degree of indifference. 'He must be very popular with the ladies in Paris.'

'Perhaps, though none seem to have made a lasting impression.' Then, refusing to be ignored by Mr Silverton any longer, Sophie said in a voice loud enough for him to hear, 'Like your brother, Antoine is far more concerned with my well-being than he is with his own.'

She saw his back stiffen, but he did not turn around. 'I am adequately concerned with my own well-being, Miss Vallois. It simply takes less looking after than Jane's.'

'No doubt because you are a man and men are so much more self-sufficient than women.'

There was a brief but significant pause. 'Are you trying to provoke me?'

'Yes, I suppose I am,' Sophie said calmly. 'But not unkindly, I hope.'

'That depends. You should be aware that I give as good as I get.'

'Then I shall consider myself warned,' Sophie said, settling back against the cushions with a smile of satisfaction. Well, it was a start. His posture seemed slightly less rigid than it had been when they'd started out, and his tone was a fraction less chilly. If it was an unguarded moment, she hoped there could be more. Miss Silverton, who was blissfully unaware of the milestone, said, 'It must be the way of older brothers to think of everyone else before themselves. It certainly makes sisters seem a great deal of bother.'

Mr Silverton glanced back at her, and Sophie was surprised to see that he could actually smile. 'You are not a bother, as well you know.'

'Yes, but I do enjoy teasing you. Do you tease your brother in such a way, Miss Vallois?'

'Whenever I get the chance.' Sophie turned her head, her eyes narrowing slightly as she gazed across the field. 'Is that Mr Oberon I see riding towards us?'

'It would appear so.' Mr Silverton sounded less than pleased. 'I wondered if he might turn up this afternoon.'

'He rides a magnificent horse.'

'Magnificent he may be, but you would do well to keep your distance. That beast is hellfire on four legs.'

Sure enough, a few minutes later, the peer's son brought the showy black stallion to a prancing, snorting halt in front of them. 'Afternoon, all,' he called in greeting. 'What a glorious day.'

'Oberon,' Mr Silverton said, reluctantly bringing the carriage to a halt.

'Silver. Miss Silverton. And Miss Vallois. What a delightful surprise.'

'Surely not that much of a surprise, sir,' Sophie said sweetly. 'You were there when I informed Mr Silverton of my intention to join him and Miss Silverton this afternoon.'

'True, but in a city as large as London, there are so many other places you could have gone.'

The stallion suddenly shied and Mr Oberon made a great show of restraining him.

'Oh, Robert, isn't he splendid,' Miss Silverton said softly.

Sophie knew Jane was referring to the horse, but Mr Oberon chose to take the remark as a compliment to himself. 'Thank you, Miss Silverton. Years of experience allow a man a certain ease in the saddle.' He smiled broadly, white teeth flashing. 'What about it, Silver—care to take a turn?'

Mr Silverton's smile was coolly dismissive. 'Thank you, no.'

'Rather wait for the pleasure of ownership, eh?' Mr Oberon winked. 'I understand. But we've yet to see how that game plays out. Miss Vallois, I hope we will have the pleasure of your company at Lady White's this evening.'

It was the first Sophie had heard of it. 'I don't know. Lady Longworth has made no mention of it.'

'Oh, but you must come,' Miss Silverton implored. 'An evening spent with Lady White is a treat unto itself. Robert and I are going. You and your brother really should join us.'

'Lady Longworth may already have made other plans.'

'Cancel them,' Mr Oberon said. 'I guarantee you'll have a better time with us.'

Sophie glanced up into the man's impossibly beautiful face and found herself resenting both his high-handed assumption that she would naturally fall in with his plans and his belief that an outing of *his* choosing would be more enjoyable than one of Lavinia's. She almost hoped Lavinia *had* made other arrangements. 'I shall enquire upon returning home, Mr Oberon. If we are free, I may mention it to Lady Longworth.'

'I can ask no more than that. And now, I must be off. Like the god, Thunder grows impatient if forced to stand in one place too long.' As if to prove it, the stallion reared up, its powerful front legs slicing the air, his high, shrill whinny echoing through the park.

'Easy, boy,' Mr Oberon said, bringing him back

under control. 'Wouldn't want to alarm the ladies.' He touched the brim of his hat to Mr Silverton and his sister, then smiled affectionately at Sophie, his eyes lingering on her longer than was necessary or appropriate.

Sophie turned away. Odious man. What a shame that one so blessed in appearance should be so lacking in humility. For all his chilly reserve, she much preferred Robert Silverton's quiet manners to Mr Oberon's smug arrogance...

'What are you thinking, Miss Vallois?' Mr Silverton enquired as the other man trotted away. 'You suddenly look far too serious for such a lovely afternoon.'

'Only that certain gentlemen have been given so much, yet appear to do so little good with it.'

'Oh, but that's splendid!' Miss Silverton said, clapping her hands. 'I do believe you have just given Monty a set-down and he would be devastated to hear it, knowing how taken he is with you.'

'Nonsense, we are barely acquainted,' Sophie said, uncomfortably aware of Mr Silverton's gaze on her. 'Besides, he is far too flamboyant for my liking.'

'But he is rich,' Miss Silverton said. 'And his country estate is said to rival Chatsworth for opulence. You could do much worse.'

'Leave the poor girl alone, Jane,' her brother said. 'Or she will regret having agreed to come out with us.'

'She will not resent me for telling her the facts. The more she knows before having to make the decision, the better off she will be.'

'The decision?' Sophie asked.

'As to whom you will marry, of course. What other

decision of importance is there for a single lady of marriageable age?'

'I can think of several,' Sophie said, less than pleased with the direction the conversation was taking. 'Fortunately, the choice of a husband will not be one of them.'

Miss Silverton gave a soft laugh. 'Do tell! Are you already engaged to a handsome young gentleman in Paris?'

'I am not, nor have I any desire to be. I've already told Lord and Lady Longworth that I have no intention of marrying.'

The remark must have been more outrageous than Sophie thought. Miss Silverton's mouth fell open and her brother actually turned around on the seat to stare at her. 'No intention of marrying?'

'But…what will you do?' his sister asked. 'Marriage is the only viable option to ladies of good birth.'

*To ladies of good birth.* What would they say, Sophie wondered, if they knew the truth of hers? 'I like to think there are many other things a lady might do. Fly over London in a hot-air balloon, for example. Or travel to Egypt on a camel to explore the pyramids. Float down the Amazon in a boat. When you think about it, the possibilities are endless.'

'For a man, perhaps,' Mr Silverton observed. 'Not for a woman.'

'But do you not wish to fall in love, Miss Vallois?' Miss Silverton asked.

'Not particularly.' Sophie thought about the men she had met in the course of her life. All of them had let her down in one way or another. 'Only think how disastrous it would be to fall in love with someone like…Mr Oberon.'

'I'm not sure a woman *can* fall in love with a man like that,' Mr Silverton said. 'He will always be the more demanding of the couple, and if the lady is like the rest of her sex, she will be far more interested in *receiving* love than in giving it.'

Had he intended it as a slight? Sophie wondered. Or was he simply expressing his opinion that, on the whole, women tended to be the more selfish creatures? 'I take leave to disagree with you, Mr Silverton. Women are capable of both giving and receiving love, oftimes at their own expense. A mother will always sacrifice much for her child, whereas a man will often take his pleasures at the expense of the family.'

He directed a glance over his shoulder. 'Your remark leads me to believe that you do not hold men in high esteem.'

'Only in as much as your remark leads me to believe that you hold women in contempt. Not all women are self-serving.'

'Then you have the pleasure of knowing better women than I.'

Wondering if he was thinking of the woman who was to have been his wife, Sophie said, 'Perhaps you expect too much of the ladies with whom you keep company.'

'If honesty is too much to expect, then I must enter a guilty plea,' he said. 'As for being single past my sister's expectations, she neglected to mention that our family circumstances have been such that neither of us has been free to mingle in society these past few years.'

'Indeed we have not,' Miss Silverton said, a cloud settling on her pretty features. 'First Michael was killed in France, then Papa died under the most tragic of circumstances, and not a twelvemonth later, we lost Mama as well. How can anyone think of love when grief is so fresh upon the heart?'

'Perhaps it is in the finding of love that the pain of grief eases,' Sophie said gently. 'One cannot suffer from two such strong emotions at the same time.'

'I wish that were the case, Miss Vallois,' Mr Silverton said. 'But I have learned that a person *can* suffer more than one painful emotion at a time and feel them both with equal strength.'

'Love cannot exist in the presence of hate, Mr Silverton,' she told him.

'But hate can raise its ugly head when love is threatened or destroyed.' He turned to look at her, and for a moment, it was as though there were only the two of them. 'Of that, Miss Vallois,' he said, 'I am entirely certain.'

To Sophie's relief, the rest of the carriage ride proceeded with all felicity and it concluded with the parties being in relatively good spirits. Miss Silverton had begged Sophie to call her Jane, and said how much she was looking forward to seeing Sophie and her brother at Lady White's for cards that evening.

Fortunately, upon arriving home, Sophie discovered that no plans had been made for the evening, and when she put forward the idea of attending a soirée at Lady White's, Lavinia declared that she could not think of a more entertaining way to pass a few hours.

'Lady White is, of course, the very *essence* of eccentricity,' Lavinia said, as the two sat in Sophie's bedroom going through her wardrobe to see what she might wear. 'Her husband died six years ago and left her a very wealthy widow.' She pulled out two gowns and laid them on the bed. 'She must be in her mid-sixties now, but she still rides to hounds every year. Strange. I don't remember ordering this peacock-blue silk from Madame Delors.'

Sophie glanced up. 'You didn't. I made it and brought it with me.'

'You *made* this?' Lavinia took a closer look. 'But... this is exquisite, Sophie. The gathering along here and the beadwork down the front is quite remarkable. And the fabric is exceptional—and very expensive.'

'I know. A lady bought it for her daughter, but when the daughter didn't like it, the mother bought something else and told me I could keep the silk as payment. But if you'd rather me wear the muslin—'

'No, no, the blue will look marvellous against your complexion,' Lavinia said, putting the cream gown aside. 'Perhaps I *should* let you make your own gowns. This is every bit as good as what we get from Madame Delors, and unlike her, you really are French. However, getting back to Lady White, you should know that besides being unconventional, she is the very devil at cards. I have played with her countless times and have yet to win more than a dozen hands.'

'Don't tell me she cheats?' Sophie said in delight.

'Outrageously, but she does it so well it is nearly impossible to catch her at it. Is Antoine going with you?'

'He told me he was.' Sophie's smile widened. He hadn't intended to—until he'd heard that Jane Silverton was also going to be there. Then he had suddenly changed his mind and agreed that a card party given by an eccentric hostess would make for a highly diverting evening. He might have missed the carriage ride, but it seemed the lady had intrigued him enough that he was not about to miss a second opportunity to spend time with her.

For that, Sophie decided she could put up with Robert Silverton's reserve, Mr Oberon's arrogance and the slight-of-hand dealings of their hostess for as long as was necessary.

# Chapter Six

Lady White was, in all respects, an Original. Thin as a rail, she wore unrelieved black against which her snowy white hair appeared wonderfully dramatic. Her lips and cheeks were heavily rouged and she wore a heart-shaped patch next to her mouth. She was also draped in a king's ransom worth of diamonds and gold.

'My husband always said jewellery was meant to be worn,' Lady White explained as she strolled arm in arm with Sophie and Antoine through the elegant rooms of her town house. 'And at my age, I'm not sure how much longer I'll be around to show it off. Best do it now while I still have a skeleton to hang it on!'

Then she laughed. Not the delicate tittering of a society matron, but the full-bodied laugh of a woman who enjoyed life. Sophie liked her immensely.

'Tell me, how is it I haven't seen you before, Miss Vallois?' Lady White asked. 'You're far too beautiful to be missed. The young men can scarcely stop gawking at you.'

Sophie laughed, moved to wonder if she had been singled out for the lady's special brand of attention or if she spoke this bluntly to everyone. 'Thank you, my lady, but my brother and I are only recently arrived in England.'

'Ah, yes, to stay with the Longworths. Excellent family. I knew Nicholas as a boy. Devil of a lad. Always falling into some kind of scrape or another, but he turned out well enough. And dear Lavinia. Such a charming woman. You don't see love like theirs very often. It's all about money and land now. Women marry for social position and men to beget an heir. Oh, get away with you, Walter!' Lady White said when a gentleman ventured too close. 'Miss Vallois isn't interested in you.'

As the crestfallen youth slunk away, Lady White whispered in Sophie's ear, 'A second son with four unmarried sisters. Definitely not the type of suitor you wish to encourage. Unlike this fine strapping young man beside you.' Lady White raised her lorgnette and peered at Antoine through the lens. 'Lud, but you're a fine-looking man. Why ain't you married?'

The question could have been offensive, but Antoine just laughed. 'I have been involved in my studies, my lady.'

'To be a doctor.'

'Yes.'

'Quite an occupation. Constantly surrounded by the sick and dying.' Lady White shuddered. 'Haven't the stomach for it myself, but thank God there are those who do.' She stopped to touch the patch next to her mouth. 'They don't train doctors the same way in France as they do here.'

'I understand there are differences, yes.'

'But the body's the same, is it not? Whether one finds oneself on this side of the Channel or the other.'

'I've always thought so,' Antoine said with a straight face. 'But not having examined any bodies on this side of the Channel, I cannot say for certain.'

Lady White stared at him for a moment, then burst out laughing. 'By God, I like the cut of your jib. If I was forty years younger, I'd give these young fillies a run for their money. In fact, I still might.' She gave him an audacious wink. 'Think about it, lad. I've money enough to keep us both in the style to which a handsome young buck like you should be accustomed.'

Sophie glanced at her brother, half-expecting to see him make a bolt for the door. Instead, he bowed and said, 'You do me a considerable honour, Lady White, but I fear I must decline.'

'Yes, I thought you might. The good ones always do. Still, I hope you'll play cards with me.' She rapped him on the chest with her fan. 'I've a mind to find out if your wits are as sharp as your looks.'

'I would be delighted.' Then, in a courtly gesture that was years out of date, Antoine took the lady's hand and raised it to his lips. *'Je suis très heureux de faire votre connaisance, madame. Vous êtes une Originale.'*

Lady White blinked, and then to Sophie's surprise, her eyes filled with tears. 'Oh, you wretched boy. Now you've gone and made an old lady cry and I may never forgive you for that.' She drew a handkerchief from her reticule and dabbed at her eyes. 'But bless you for having had the kindness to say so.' She blew her nose, tucked her hankie behind her fan and then, with a smile and another loud sniff, moved off to greet her other guests.

'Goodness, Antoine, you may wish to think carefully before rejecting her offer,' Sophie whispered. 'You would never have to work again if you agreed to become her—'

'Thank you, Sophie, I think the less said about it, the better.' But clearly the idea of becoming the *cher ami* of such a woman was more than even Antoine could keep a straight face for, and after a moment, they both burst out laughing.

They were still chucking about it a few minutes later when Robert and Jane Silverton came over to join them. 'What are you two having such a jolly time about?' Jane asked.

'Lady White,' Sophie said. 'You were right in saying she is a treat. She says what she thinks and worries about it later.'

'I'm not so sure she does worry,' Mr Silverton said. 'I don't think she cares a whit what anyone thinks.'

'Well, *I* think she's marvellous,' Sophie said. 'You have to admire a woman who has the courage to speak her mind.'

'Even though society is likely to condemn her for doing so?'

Sophie slowly turned to look at him. As always, Mr Silverton was impeccably turned out. His double-breasted coat, cut square across the front and decorated with a row of gilt buttons, fit him to perfection. Beneath that, a fine cambric shirt clung to a broad chest and around his neck, a perfectly tied, perfectly white linen cravat. A powerful man, in the civilised clothes of a gentleman. Were his thoughts a reflection of the same?

'It takes courage to fly in the face of convention, Mr Silverton,' Sophie said. 'Especially in a society so rigid about what it will and will not allow.'

'Are you saying French society is more lenient than English?'

'No. I'm just saying that in general, women do not benefit from its strictures. The only women who possess any kind of freedom are those who are titled in their own right, independently wealthy or widowed. It seems very unfair.'

'Well said, Miss Vallois,' Jane said with approval.

'And you, Miss Silverton?' Antoine asked. 'Do you mind being criticised?'

'One always minds to a certain degree, but fortunately, I am not as closely scrutinised as others. My affliction absents me from the rest of the pack.'

Antoine glanced at the cane in her hand. 'How did you come by your injury?'

'An unfortunate childhood accident. A badly broken foot even more badly set.'

'But it does not prevent you from getting about.'

'Nothing could do that,' she told him. 'I am most determined when I set my mind to something.'

'I can vouch for that,' Mr Silverton said. 'Shall we play cards?'

Sophie wasn't sure how it happened, but a few minutes later, she found herself at a whist table, partnered with Robert Silverton against Lady White and a young lady by the name of Miss Penelope Green. Antoine and Jane had moved away to play vingt-et-un at another table.

'I hope your brother is skilled at cards, Miss Vallois,'

Mr Silverton said as the hand was dealt. 'My sister is a Captain Sharp of the female variety.'

'Antoine plays well enough,' Sophie said, picking up her cards. 'It is my skills as a partner you may find lacking.'

'Nothing to it, my dear.' Lady White raised her arm, causing a battery of bracelets to jangle. 'You simply try to take as many tricks as you can by remembering which cards have already been played. That's why I like this game. It requires the use of one's brain. I'm not sure you young whelps know how to do that.'

Sophie said nothing, but when she raised her eyes and met Mr Silverton's over the top of her cards, she saw that he was grinning broadly. 'I shall endeavour to do my best, Lady White.'

'You'll have to if you expect to escape this table unscathed.' Lady White turned up a card. 'Hearts are trump. Your lead, Mr Silverton.'

Over the course of the evening, Robert learned quite a few things about Miss Sophie Vallois. He learned that while she was blessed with beauty and refinement, she also had a lively sense of humour and a tendency towards speaking her mind. He learned that when she was silent, it was not because she could think of nothing to say, but because she preferred to weigh her words before offering them up for public discussion. She never forced herself into a conversation, but when asked a question, responded with wit and intelligence. In short, it was hard to find anything to criticise about the lady, yet he still found himself maintaining a distance.

'Are you enjoying your time in London, Miss Vallois?' he asked after Lady White and Miss Green had excused themselves to partake of refreshments.

'I am. It is, of course, very different to the life Antoine and I lead in France.'

Assuming she referred to the customs and language of the two countries, Robert said, 'Have you always lived in Paris?'

'Only for the last two years. Before that I lived near Bayencourt.'

'I'm not familiar with the town.'

'It's a small village in the north of France. My father was born there.'

'And your mother?'

'In Provence.' Miss Vallois smiled. 'Mama always said she would never move to the north, but when she met my father, that was that. I went to Provence with her when I was ten and liked it very much. The lavender fields were beautiful.'

Robert nodded, picturing a young girl running through the lush purple fields. He imagined a slender figure in a white dress, with silver-blond hair flying out behind and laughter ringing across the fields. It made for an engaging scene. 'You speak English exceptionally well for someone who's never been outside France,' he observed.

'I was employed for some time by an English lady who hired me to teach French to her daughters. In turn, I was tutored in English with particular emphasis on pronunciation and diction. I was forbidden to roll my r's, drop my h's, or say *zat* instead of that. The lady was something of a...' She looked to him for help. 'A *termagant*?'

'A termagant.' Robert smiled. 'Yes, it is the same in

both languages.' So, she had been a governess. That, he supposed, explained her polished manners and her refined way of speaking. 'I would venture to say if their French is half as good as your English, you did an exceptional job.'

Miss Vallois wrinkled her nose. 'I fear I did not. The eldest daughter was not interested in learning the language and took pains to tell me so on a regular basis. But the younger one was very sweet and more than made up for her sister's deficiencies.' She looked at him with renewed interest. 'Have you ever been to France, Mr Silverton?'

The question stabbed at his heart. 'Briefly. I held a commission in the cavalry, but sold it when my eldest brother was killed.'

'Yes, I'm so sorry. I cannot imagine what that must have been like,' Miss Vallois said. 'If I were to lose Antoine, it would be like losing a part of myself. I don't know that I would ever feel whole again.'

Robert stared at her, aware that in a few simple sentences, she had summed up exactly how he'd felt at the time of Michael's death. He'd been shattered, his world cast into darkness by the death of the one person he'd been closer to than anyone else. 'There are still times I don't feel whole. Even now, when I walk into a room, I expect to see Michael there. To be able to walk up to him and laugh over some amusing and totally inconsequential event.'

'Were you close growing up?'

'Inseparable. He was only two years older than me so we shared many of the same interests. He taught me how to ride and he was there when I took my first bad spill in the field.' Robert's mouth twisted. 'It was my first time hunting and, caught up in the excitement, I tried to take a gate at full tilt. I don't remember hitting the ground, but I remember Michael picking me up and carrying me back to the house. He called for the surgeon and stayed with me while my arm was set.'

'That must have been painful.'

'It was, but it hurt a great deal less than my father's indifference.' Robert tried to keep the resentment from his voice. '*He* was more concerned about my horse. Said I could have ruined a prime bit of blood. I wanted to lash out, but Michael put his hand on my good arm and said it wasn't worth it. Told me I'd only regret it in the morning. And, as always, he was right.' Robert stopped, swallowing hard. 'I never expected Michael to die in the war. When the letter came informing us that he'd been killed, I thought it must be a mistake. I didn't want to believe it. To me he was…indestructible.'

'I don't think we ever really believe that someone we love will fall. I suppose that's the best part of the human spirit,' Miss Vallois said. 'The unshakeable belief that the worst will never happen to us or to those we care about. I sometimes wonder if we would venture into the unknown at all if we did not hold that belief true.'

'Indeed. We are fragile in body, yet indomitable in spirit,' Robert murmured. 'And how fortunate that is the case.'

He hadn't expected her to reach out. But when he felt the gentle pressure of her hand on his arm and looked up to see compassion in the depths of those remarkable blue eyes, he knew the sympathy she offered wasn't feigned. Whatever she thought about him as a person was secondary to her need to offer reassurance and warmth. He found that strangely comforting.

'Ah, Silver, thought I'd find you here,' Oberon said, blundering in and destroying the mood. 'And Miss Vallois. I'm so pleased you decided to heed my advice and come.'

'Mr Oberon.' The lady slowly withdrew her hand. Robert was surprised at how keenly he felt its loss. 'As it turned out, Lady Longworth had not made other plans and agreed that it would make for a pleasant evening.'

'Excellent. The company is not always the best, but the variety of entertainments more than makes up for it.' Oberon put his hand on the back of her chair and leaned down to whisper, 'I hope you received the small floral tribute I sent to the house.'

A delicate pink blush stained her cheeks. 'Yes, the roses were beautiful, thank you.'

'My pleasure. They will always pale in comparison to you, of course, but I wanted you to have a token of my affection and esteem.'

Robert drummed his fingers on the table. So, Oberon had already begun sending gifts. He should have known. The wolf would waste no time in getting the hunt underway. Damn him.

'And how fares your luck at the tables tonight, Silver?' Oberon asked, straightening. 'You should know, Miss Vallois, that Silver has the luck of the Irish when it comes to cards. In fact, he's something of a legend in the gambling hells of London. There's not many who'll wager against him.'

'It's all in the turn of the card,' Robert said, his voice cool. 'Most games are pure luck.'

'Speaking of luck, Butterworth was wondering how you were faring in that matter we were speaking of the other day.'

Robert purposely kept his eyes down. 'You should know better than to ask.'

'Fair enough. Are you going to ask me how I go on in *my* endeavours?'

'Which endeavours would those be, Mr Oberon?' Lady White demanded, returning to the card table. 'I'm sure we would all like to know.'

Oberon's mouth thinned. 'You'll forgive me, but they are of a private nature and not meant to be shared.'

'Then I wonder at you bringing them up at all. Especially in front of Miss Vallois, with whom you can have only the slightest of acquaintance.'

Robert reached for the deck of cards and slid them across the table. Point to Lady White. She obviously had no qualms about giving Oberon a set-down in front of others. Unfortunately, he was nothing if not adept at turning a floundering situation to his advantage. 'You are right to admonish me, Lady White. Miss Vallois, pray forgive my poor manners. Perhaps I can make it up to you by offering to take you to an entertainment tomorrow evening. I understand *Don Giovanni* is playing to great reviews at the Covent Garden Theatre.'

'The theatre!' Lady White said huffily. 'In my day, such things were not considered suitable entertainment for a young lady of refinement. Have you secured the Longworths' agreement to the outing?'

'Not yet, though I have no reason to believe Lady Longworth would withhold it,' Oberon said. 'I hear tell that as a girl, she saw Mary Robinson play Perdita and was much moved by the performance.'

'Of course she would be moved.' Lady White deftly shuffled the cards. 'Mrs Robinson gave an outstanding performance. Pity she was such a trollop. Made a com-

plete fool of herself over the Prince, and he no better.'
She cut the cards and began to deal. 'The theatre can
offer a most enjoyable experience if the performers are
worth their salt. My sister once entertained thoughts of
a career on the stage. Nearly put my father in the grave.
But she was very good at that sort of thing.'

'Acting, my lady?' Miss Vallois enquired. 'Or of
provoking her father?'

The question was so unexpected that Robert burst
out laughing. Even Lady White chortled. 'So, there is
spirit beneath that pretty exterior. Good. I cannot abide
humourless people. So, shall you go to the theatre with
this rapscallion, do you think?'

Robert raised his head in time to see an impish smile
lift the corners of Miss Vallois's mouth. 'Yes, I think I
shall. If Lady Longworth does not object.'

'I don't suppose she will if you take that handsome
brother with you,' Lady White said. 'No doubt he would
enjoy a good love story. He's the stuff of which they're
made.'

Oberon was quietly fuming. 'I thought it would make
a pleasant evening for Miss Vallois and myself,' he said
stiffly.

'I'm sure you did. But if I were in Lady Longworth's
shoes, I would much rather have Miss Vallois go with
a large contingent of friends.' Lady White levelled a
keen glance in Robert's direction. 'You should go too,
Mr Silverton. Do you good to get out. And take that
delightful sister with you.'

'I might just do that,' Robert said, beginning to enjoy
himself. 'Jane adores the theatre.'

'Excellent. The more the merrier, eh, what?'

Robert risked a quick glance at Oberon, whose hopes

for a romantic evening were now well and truly shattered, and tried not to laugh. 'As you say, Lady White. The more the merrier indeed.'

Not surprisingly, Lady White and Miss Green took four of the next five hands and though Robert knew the woman cheated, he couldn't bring himself to expose her. Not when he was so in charity with her for having totally disrupted Oberon's plans. He thought he would have been ambivalent about the man's intentions to court Miss Vallois, but the more time he spent with her, the more he realised how wasted she would be on such a man. A man without sensitivity or the capacity for love. A man to whom winning meant everything...

He heard a noise—and looked down to see that he had snapped the stem of his wineglass in two.

'Good Lord, Robert, whatever is the matter?' Jane asked, coming up to him. 'If looks could kill, there would be several dead bodies strewn about the floor. Or perhaps...just one,' she said, following the direction of his gaze. 'What has Oberon done now?'

'Nothing. I just don't care for his attentions towards Miss Vallois.'

'Are they inappropriate?'

'He has invited her to the theatre.'

'A trifle bold, but hardly reprehensible. Which play?'

*'Don Giovanni.'*

'Oh, how splendid! I've heard it is a very good performance.'

'Would you care to join us?'

*'Us?'*

'I plan on going as well.'

Jane looked at him in surprise. 'Surely that was not Mr Oberon's idea.'

'No. Lady White suggested we make up a party when Oberon was foolish enough to invite Miss Vallois in front of her.'

'I am amazed he would be so careless—or so obvious in his attentions.'

Intrigued, Robert said, 'Why should he not be obvious?'

'Because as lovely as Sophie is, I doubt she is well enough born for his father's liking,' Jane said. 'I hear tell he is keeping a very close eye on his son, and on the ladies with whom he is keeping company.'

'I didn't think his father cared so long as Oberon married *someone.*'

'That may have been the case in the beginning, but Lady Jennings told me Lord Mannerfield is growing more and more concerned about his son's wayward nature,' Jane confided. 'He is afraid Monty will be trapped into marriage by some penniless fortune hunter who uses her wiles and her beauty to ensnare him. Word is he is hoping his son marries a title, or a lady with a fortune of her own, neither of which Sophie has.'

'That's true, but I'm not sure how much Oberon cares about that any more. He talks about her incessantly, and you and I both know how single minded he can be when it comes to getting something he wants.'

'But are you sure it's marriage he has in mind, Robert? After all, he was the one who initiated the mistress wager, and we both know he won't give up his stallion without a fight.'

'No, but he stands to lose a great deal more if he doesn't marry,' Robert said. 'And his conversations to this point lead me to believe he is considering Miss Vallois.'

'Well, unless she is secretly the daughter of a French count, I doubt his father will look kindly upon the match,' Jane said bluntly. 'You should do everyone a favour by finding out where she comes from. And if her birth is not what it should be, you should tell Mr Oberon she is not suitable to being his wife. Either that, or court the lady yourself.'

'I *beg* your pardon?'

'Well, why not? I've seen the way you look at her, Robert. And while she may not possess wealth or a title she has everything else a man could ask for in a wife.'

'Have you forgotten that she's not *looking* for a husband?' Robert said. 'She'd rather explore the pyramids in Egypt, or float down the Amazon on a raft.'

'Boat,' Jane said, laughing. 'And, no, I haven't forgotten, but you don't really think she's serious about that, do you?'

'Who knows? The French think differently than we do. But, even if I was interested, what have I to offer her? A tarnished reputation? The knowledge that she would be cut by good society if she were to associate with me? Higher-placed gentlemen than myself have left the country after being given the cut direct, and Oberon tells me Lady Mary is now thinking of suing me for breach of promise. That won't win me any allies.'

'Then *tell* people why you jilted her, Robert!' Jane implored. 'They can't forgive you if they don't know why you did it. I know Lady Mary isn't blameless or you would never have broken it off.'

No, he wouldn't, Robert acknowledged. But after overhearing a conversation between his then fiancée and several of her closest friends, the reasons had become painfully clear. Imagine telling people that your future sister-in-law was repulsive and fit only to live in an institution. Imagine coldly laying out your plans for removing her to the country so that you might never be in the same house at the same time. That was the nature of what he'd heard, and once he had, Robert had known he couldn't go through with it. As his wife, Mary would have had total control of the household and all who lived in it. If she'd wanted to make Jane's life miserable, she could have done so without argument from anyone.

And so, he had brought it to an end…and kept silent as to his reasons. He had no wish to denigrate Lady Mary in the eyes of society, but neither was he about to risk Jane being made to suffer for an error in *his* judgement.

'It doesn't matter,' he said. 'Better I be the one to deal with the fallout than her.'

Jane crossed her arms in annoyance. 'You are too good, Robert. You are in disgrace because of her.'

'Exactly. And if I was to show an interest in Miss Vallois now, she would be tarred with the same brush. Ignored by virtue of her association with me. She deserves a better chance at a future than that.'

'With whom? Your good friend, Montague Oberon?' Jane snapped. 'Seducer of woman and gambler par excellence?'

'That's enough, Jane,' Robert said. 'Cynicism doesn't become you.'

'And martyrdom doesn't become you!'

'I'm not trying to be a martyr. But if I am not willing

to involve myself in Miss Vallois's life, I'm better off out of it.'

Robert glanced across the room to where Oberon and Sophie were engaged in a private conversation, and thought about what Jane had said.

*Find out where she comes from; if her birth is not what it should be, tell Oberon she is not suitable to be his wife.*

Even if it was that simple, there were still consequences to making known such information. The first being the irreparable damage it would do to Sophie's reputation. If she was discovered to be low born, doors would be closed in her face. She would not be entertained by good society and her chances for making a good marriage would dry up faster than a puddle in the desert. He wasn't willing to inflict that on anyone.

Not even a French girl who didn't appear to like him all that well regardless.

# Chapter Seven

The vestibule of the theatre was already buzzing by the time Sophie and Antoine arrived for the performance of *Don Giovanni* the following evening, but she had no trouble in picking out the figure of Mr Silverton in the crowd. He seemed to tower over those around him, his broad shoulders emphasised by the excellent cut of his evening jacket, his snowy white cravat arranged in simple but elegant folds. Mr Oberon stood closer to the door, equally well dressed, but with a superiority of manner that would always set him apart from lesser mortals. 'Ah, Miss Vallois,' he said, coming forwards to greet her. 'What a radiant vision you present. A most fitting tribute to this elegant temple.'

Sophie only just refrained from rolling her eyes. 'You are too kind, Mr Oberon. I think you remember my brother, Antoine?'

'Of course.' Oberon gave him a curt nod. 'I am so pleased you could join us.'

Antoine's greeting was equally cool. *'Mon plaisir.'*

'And here is Silverton come to add his sparkling wit,' Mr Oberon said. 'But where is Jane? I understood she was coming too.'

'Yes, here I am,' Jane called. 'I was just waiting for Lady Annabelle.'

It was then that Sophie noticed the exceedingly lovely young woman walking by Jane's side. She was taller and more slender than Jane, with perfect skin and finely formed features. Her hair was a shade of gold that glistened in the candlelight and her gown of pale pink satin was of the first stare. Pearls glowed warmly at her ears and throat, and her movements were blessed with effortless grace, making Sophie feel like an impostor at the ball—or a cuckoo in a nest of swans.

'I hope you don't mind,' Mr Silverton said, 'but I took the liberty of inviting Lady Annabelle Durst to join our party. Apparently she is very fond of Mr Scott's plays.'

'Not at all,' Mr Oberon said. 'How could we mind so beautiful a lady joining our party?'

'You are very kind, Mr Oberon,' Lady Annabelle said in a low, melodic voice. 'But when Mr Silverton and I met at Lady Chesterton's musicale this afternoon, he told me several of you were attending the performance this evening and I was bold enough to ask if I might come along. *Giovanni* is one of my favourite operas.'

'As it is mine,' Mr Oberon said. 'Pray allow me to make known the rest of the party to you, Lady Annabelle. This is Miss Sophie Vallois and her brother, Mr Antoine Vallois.'

Lady Annabelle nodded pleasantly at Sophie and then turned to greet Antoine. 'Monsieur Vallois. I understand you and your sister are visiting from Paris. How long do you intend to stay?'

'My sister is remaining for the Season, but I am only here until next week.'

'What a shame. You will scarcely have time to see any of London's many attractions.'

'I will see as many as I can,' Antoine said, 'and let Sophie tell me about the rest when she returns.'

'I am sure she will do an excellent job, but it is never the same as seeing the sights for oneself. Would you not agree, Mr Silverton?'

'I've found that nothing is ever as good as experiencing life's pleasures first-hand, Lady Annabelle.'

When the two exchanged a smile, Sophie was astonished to feel a tiny pinprick of jealousy—a reaction that both shocked and troubled her. She had no feelings of affection for Mr Silverton. His conduct towards her had been anything but encouraging, and given that *her* plans did not include marriage, it made no sense that she should be jealous of the way he looked at another woman. But jealous she was, and the fact the two spoke to one another with such ease only heightened Sophie's awareness of being an outsider. Mr Silverton might have been cut by polite society, but he was still more a part of it than she would ever be.

A few minutes later, the party made its way up the sweeping staircase, stopping to admire the Ionic columns and the elegant Grecian lamps hanging from the ceiling. Sophie pretended to study the elaborate décor, but her eyes lingered more often on Mr Silverton and Lady Annabelle than they did on the gilt-covered woodwork. Mr Oberon might be the strutting peacock, but

Mr Silverton was definitely the hawk, darkly handsome in black and white, his waistcoat embroidered with silver thread.

At the top of the stairs, prior to entering the antechamber, the party drew to a halt. Sophie noticed Jane cast a covert glance at Antoine, only to look away as her brother stepped forwards to take her arm. 'May I escort you in, Jane?'

'Yes, of course.' She placed her gloved hand lightly upon his arm. 'Thank you.'

Antoine, catching Sophie's eye, started in her direction, but was intercepted by Mr Oberon. 'Miss Vallois, I wonder if I might have the honour—'

And just as smoothly, *he* was intercepted by Lady Annabelle. 'Pray forgive the intrusion, Mr Oberon, but I really must ask Miss Vallois about her gown.' She stepped forwards and slipped her arm companionably through Sophie's. 'It is simply perfection. You must have brought it with you from Paris.'

'In fact, it is one of Madame Delors's designs,' Sophie said, relieved to see Mr Oberon step back.

'Madame Delors? I would never have guessed. I shall have to pay her a visit this very week,' Lady Annabelle said. 'Mama is insisting I have three new gowns made before the Wistermeyers' ball next month and I was at a loss to know where to go.'

And so, they proceeded into the box: Mr Oberon leading the way with Mr Silverton and Jane following, Lady Annabelle and Sophie coming next, and Antoine bringing up the rear. Fortunately, there was more than enough room for the six of them to be seated comfortably and for a few minutes there was jostling as everyone selected their chairs. In the end, Antoine sat beside Jane in the second row with Lady Annabelle on his right, while Sophie sat in the front row between Mr Oberon and Mr Silverton. And it truly was splendid. Slender pillars heavily encrusted with gilt separated the boxes, and from a bracket that extended over the top of each pillar hung a glorious cut-glass chandelier.

Even more decorative than the trim, however, were the ladies and gentlemen who occupied the boxes. Sophie saw the flash of diamonds and rubies, heard the rustle of expensive silks, and wondered how the crowds in the two-shilling gallery must feel at seeing such wealth and opulence all around them. There didn't look to be an empty seat in the place.

'Do you like opera, Miss Vallois?' Mr Silverton asked.

Sophie turned her head to smile at him. 'I really cannot say, never having been to one before.'

'I remember seeing Edmund Kean play Shylock,' he said. 'It was a stunning performance. Lady White is correct when she says that much depends on the skill of the performers.'

'If you don't mind, I would rather *not* hear Lady White's name mentioned this evening,' Mr Oberon muttered. 'As far as I am concerned, the woman has already said a great deal too much.'

Sophie quickly looked down, but not before catching a flicker of a smile on Mr Silverton's face. Had his good spirits to do with Mr Oberon's antipathy, she wondered, or to the unexpected presence of the beautiful Lady Annabelle Durst?

A sudden flurry of activity in the box next to them heralded the arrival of a family well known to Mr Oberon, and when he excused himself to speak with them, Sophie took a moment to glance back at her brother and Jane. They were talking quietly between themselves, Jane looking young and carefree in a becoming gown of pale amethyst silk with clusters of violets tucked in her hair and a delicate strand of pearls around her throat. Her cheeks were unusually flushed, and when she laughed at something Antoine said, Sophie couldn't help but be aware of how happy they seemed to be in each other's company.

'Has your brother made any mention of when he is returning to France?' Mr Silverton asked quietly.

Sophie turned back to find his warm brown eyes fixed on her. 'He has not mentioned a particular day, though I believe he intends to leave next week.'

'He is dedicated to his profession.'

'He is dedicated to *learning* his profession. At the moment, he is apprenticed to a local surgeon and very grateful for the opportunity.'

'It can't be an easy life. Calls at all hours of the night. Injuries of a wide and often heart-wrenching nature. It takes a special kind of dedication to do what he does.'

'That, and a talent for healing,' Sophie admitted, thinking of some of the truly awful things Antoine had encountered. Filthy hospital wards. Soiled linens. Unsanitary food. It was a wonder he hadn't contracted something himself. 'I am not so blessed.'

'Perhaps not in that area, but you have gifts aplenty in others.'

As if afraid of having said too much, Mr Silverton quickly turned away, but Sophie found her gaze lingering on his profile. Was it her imagination or did his voice seem warmer tonight? Several times he had made a point of touching her when they were together. Nothing to which she could object. A hand at her waist to guide her. A light touch on the arm to draw her attention to something she hadn't noticed. And sitting together here, she was very conscious of his thigh close to hers; of the heat of his body warming her through the thin fabric of her gown—

'—to become a doctor?'

Belatedly, Sophie realised he was asking her about Antoine. 'Forgive me, Mr Silverton, my mind was elsewhere.'

'I was just asking if your father approved of your brother's decision to become a doctor. It is not the usual choice of occupation for the eldest son.'

'No, and…Papa wasn't at all pleased.' Why was she so flustered all of a sudden? Heat was rising in waves, and even now, her heart was beating too fast. 'He… wanted Antoine to stay home and help in the fields.'

Mr Silverton smiled. 'The fields?'

'Yes.' Goodness, why hadn't she brought her fan with her? 'The idea was that…Antoine would take over once Papa got too old, but Antoine never had any interest in farming. Even as a boy he wanted to help people.'

Sophie was about to say more, when Lady Annabelle suddenly leaned forwards to whisper in her ear. 'Forgive my boldness, Miss Vallois, but I do believe your brother is rather taken with Miss Silverton. They seem to be caught up in their own little world.'

Sophie moved uneasily in her chair. Had Mr Silverton overheard the remark? She knew he wasn't fond of Antoine, in which case he wouldn't be pleased at the idea of Antoine and Jane striking up a friendship. 'Perhaps I should ask Jane to sit up here,' she said quickly, slanting a quick glance at Mr Silverton. 'The view of the stage is that much better.'

But he wasn't listening. He was staring straight ahead, his mouth grim, his brow furrowed as though deep in thought. Sophie bit her lip. Obviously, he *had* heard, and it was clear he wasn't pleased about it.

Fortunately, Lady Annabelle's laughter bubbled up like sparkling champagne. 'You can ask her, Miss Vallois, but I have a feeling that tonight, the company in the box has far more appeal for Miss Silverton than the play.'

Robert was dimly aware of the sounds swirling around him. Of Lady Annabelle's bell-like laughter. Of a low murmur of conversation from the box next to them. Of a whistling sound from the stage below. But none of it mattered because what Sophie had just told him caused everyone and everything else to fade into insignificance.

'*...Antoine never had any interest in farming...*'

How simple a statement, yet how utterly destructive…because it meant Sophie was not well born. She was the daughter of a farmer, a man who laboured in the fields on someone else's land. Her skills with the language had been learned from an English woman who employed her to teach French to her daughters, and her manners and refinement were likely sprung from the same source. Apart from her stunning natural beauty, Sophie Vallois had absolutely nothing to recommend her. And the ramifications of that were inescapable.

Oberon would never consider taking her as a wife now. When he found out the truth, one of two things would happen. He would either stop paying attention to her and look for a well-bred lady to be his bride. Or, he would realise that the object of his obsession, now never to be his bride, would in fact make an enchanting mistress.

It was the latter possibility that had Robert gritting his teeth. Oberon was a master at seduction. He had dazzled lonely widows, shamelessly sweet-talked virgins, and skilfully compromised married women, all in the pursuit of his own pleasure. He didn't give a damn about reputations and once he knew marriage to Sophie was out of the question, his efforts would be aimed in an entirely different direction. He would pay court to her, much as he was doing now, but his *coup de grâce* would be an assignation rather than a proposal of marriage.

He would compromise her. One night was all it would take. One carriage ride into the darkness. And with her reputation in tatters, she would have no choice but to return to France, either to keep house for her brother or to find work in a rich man's home. Oberon might offer to set her up in the house he kept in Kensington for just such a purpose, but how long would it be before his interest in her waned and the next lovely face stepped forwards to take her place? To a man like that, the chase was always more exciting than the capture.

No, the damage was well and truly done. Sophie's unintentional slip had certainly cost her the coronet of viscountess. Only time would tell if it would jeopardize something more valuable.

Despite the undercurrents swirling around her, Sophie thoroughly enjoyed the performance of *Don Giovanni*. Its central character was the quintessential rake, a man who lived to seduce women, and it was his inability to settle on only one that eventually condemned him to an existence in hell. She alternately laughed and gasped, or held her breath in anticipation of the unrepentant Lothario's eventual descent into the underworld. Certainly the crowd seemed to enjoy it. Only once during a poorly enacted scene did a handful of orange peelings make their way on to the stage. Otherwise, the boisterous crowd heartily approved of the drama.

Only Mr Oberon appeared unmoved, his attention fixed more often on her than it was on the actors on the stage below.

'Are you not enjoying the performance, Mr Oberon?' Sophie asked when at last she could no longer ignore the intensity of his stare.

'I have seen the opera before, Miss Vallois, but it does not compare to the enjoyment I am having in watching you.'

'But surely your lack of attention dishonours the talent of the composer.'

'Nothing could do that. But in watching you, I see the joy of one who is hearing the music for the first time. That, in itself, is a pleasure to behold.'

'I think the *story* of Don Giovanni is equally entertaining,' Lady Annabelle observed. 'The composer obviously wishes us to take a message from it.'

'Indeed. That a man should settle for just *one* lady,' Mr Silverton said darkly, 'instead of casting his nets so wide.'

Oberon seemed impervious to the slight. 'That is what we all aspire to do, but the trick is to find that one woman who surpasses all others. One who captures our heart in a way no other can. Don Giovanni never found his lady whereas I...' he stopped to gaze at Sophie '... am hopeful of finding mine.'

A sudden burst of applause drew Sophie's attention back to the stage, and, grateful beyond words for a chance to look away, she likewise began to applaud. What in the world was the man about? To make an admission to a lady in private was one thing, but to say such a thing in a crowded theatre box was quite another. Especially with Mr Silverton glowering at him the entire time. What if he thought her flattered by the man's unwelcome attentions?

Unfortunately, once the cheers came to an end and the theatre began to empty, Sophie knew she would have to make her way back downstairs. But how was she to do that without Mr Oberon claiming her hand like an overbearing master?

To her surprise, it was Lady Annabelle who again came to her rescue. Timing her exit so that she stepped out of the box at the same time as Mr Oberon, Lady Annabelle casually slipped her arm through Mr Oberon's and proceeded to ask his opinion on some of Mozart's other works, in particular his horn and his violin concertos that were becoming so popular. Sophie was quite sure Mr Oberon had no idea he had been manipulated. Why Lady Annabelle had done it was anyone's guess, but at least it had spared Sophie a potentially awkward descent to the vestibule below.

On a happier note, she was pleased to see Antoine helping Jane navigate her way past the chairs, holding her arm in a manner that was neither condescending nor familiar, and Jane was clearly enjoying the attention. Her pretty face was even more flushed than before and

Sophie felt sure it had nothing to do with the heated confines of the theatre.

'It would seem my sister is not immediately in need of my help, Miss Vallois. Perhaps you are?'

Sophie turned to see Mr Silverton holding out his arm. Surprised but pleased, she placed her fingers lightly on his sleeve. 'Thank you, Mr Silverton. Are you all right now?'

'All right?'

'You went very quiet earlier. I wondered if I had said something to upset you. Or if Lady Annabelle had.'

It was as direct a question as she could ask—and she was relieved to see him smile.

'No. I was simply…lost in thought.' He turned his head and met her gaze. 'But forgive me for not having told you that you are the most beautiful woman in the room, and that you have been on more than one occasion.'

His voice was low and sincere, and as she fell into step beside him, Sophie marvelled that she had ever thought him lacking in any way. His face might not have the classical perfection of Mr Oberon's, but to her, he would always be the more handsome. In his evening clothes, his stature was enhanced rather than diminished, and when he smiled, his entire face lit up, his eyes coming alive with warmth and tenderness.

How would he gaze upon a woman he cared for? Sophie mused. A woman he loved.

The thought was unexpected—as was her resultant confusion when she realised that, just for a moment, she had pictured herself as that woman. Ridiculous, of course, because Mr Silverton didn't see her that way. To him, she was just a stranger—an unknown woman he had encountered at a coaching inn. One his beloved sister had all but bullied him into taking on a carriage ride and one a meddling hostess had insisted he accompany to the theatre. It was laughable to see herself in the role of the woman he might revere, for while passion could flare in the blink of an eye it took time for true affection to grow.

And love…?

Sophie sighed. Love took the greatest time of all. It was impossible to be in love with someone you had only just met. With someone you were quite sure did not like you.

With someone, she admitted, like Robert Silverton.

The party dispersed shortly after, and though Robert would have liked to have spent more time with Sophie, he noticed that Jane's colour was still unusually high and decided to order their carriage straight away. He couldn't risk letting Jane wear herself out, knowing it often took days before she was fully recovered.

He waited with Oberon on the road, as servants hailed carriages for their elegant lords and ladies, and sharp-eyed lads of eight or nine watched for unsuspecting victims.

'I think your sister would have preferred to be escorted home by Vallois,' Oberon commented, oblivious to it all. 'They seem to have struck up a friendship.'

Keeping his eye on the street, Robert said, 'Be that as it may, Jane and I came together and we will leave that way.'

'Pity. That would have left me free to drive Miss Vallois home and I would have enjoyed that very much.

Since you were determined to spoil my evening with her, it was the least you could have done.'

The idea was so preposterous that Robert actually laughed. 'I did not spoil your evening. It was Lady White's suggestion we all come together.'

'You *could* have said you and Jane were otherwise engaged.'

'But we were not. And it wouldn't have mattered regardless. Lady White suggested Miss Vallois invite her brother and you saw as well as I did how pleased she was by the idea. At that point, I judged there was nothing wrong with my joining the party. And with inviting Lady Annabelle.'

'You take a great deal upon yourself, Silver,' Oberon said distantly. 'If I didn't know better, I would swear you didn't trust me to behave properly with Miss Vallois. But we both know that makes no sense. If I hope to earn the lady's affection, what would be the point in compromising her beforehand?'

A muscle twitched in Robert's jaw. 'In my experience, there is often a great deal of room between intention and action.'

Oberon grunted. 'I'm not sure I like your tone. I thought you would have been pleased with the way I've been courting Miss Vallois. I am still considering offering her marriage, you know, and I believe the Longworths would approve. Why would they turn down the chance of their young friend becoming a viscountess?'

*Tell him what you know! Tell him what she is and put an end to this once and for all.*

But Robert couldn't bring himself to say the words. Too many questions needed to be asked and too many people's lives would be affected by the answers. He had to be sure of his facts before he said anything. Especially to a man like Oberon.

'They will wish her to marry the man she loves,' Robert said. 'Although Miss Vallois told me to my face that she has no desire to be wed.'

'No desire be hanged! All young women wish to be married, Silver. She was obviously just being coy. And if it's love she wants, I'll make her love *me*,' Oberon said confidently. 'I can be very persuasive when I set my mind to it.'

'I take it you've found no impediment to marrying her?' Robert forced himself to ask.

'I've made no specific inquiries, but I've seen nothing in her conduct that leads me to believe she is anything but what she seems.'

The remark was disquieting. Oberon *never* took anything at face value. In his search to uncover the truth, he turned over every rock, uprooted every tree, until those secrets were ferreted out and exposed. His all-too-ready acceptance of Sophie led Robert to believe that none of that mattered any more. That Oberon didn't care for the consequences...and he found that even more disturbing. It suggested an attachment that wasn't healthy. An attachment that bordered on...obsession.

'Well, as you said yourself, she could be an heiress or an actress,' Robert said casually. 'But if your father requires that you marry a lady of title or fortune, you will have to look elsewhere. Miss Vallois has neither.'

'It matters not since on the day she becomes my wife, she acquires both. My father, for all his lofty intentions, cannot stop me from marrying whom I please.'

'And if his displeasure takes the form of a threat of disinheritance?'

Oberon's smile turned into a sneer. 'As it happens, I have discovered a few things about my father's past he would rather not be made known. Some…youthful indiscretions, if you will, that would be embarrassing for all concerned.'

Robert stepped back as a young boy ran past. 'I'm surprised he told you of them.'

'Oh, you can be sure he did not. But letters kept for the wrong reasons often become an excellent source of information for those who know how to use them. I doubt my mother or the lady in question would appreciate the errors of their youth being made public after all these years.'

Robert stared at the man standing next to him as though he were a stranger. So, the son would blackmail the father with letters written years ago about an affair that would be damaging to all. Oberon knew his world well. A peer might be above the law, but he was not above being cut by good society. The fact Oberon would *use* that information to wilfully destroy his father's reputation and those of several other people, said a great deal about his character—or lack thereof.

'Tell me, Silver, why are you suddenly so interested in my courtship of Miss Vallois?' Oberon asked. 'Surely it cannot be that you have developed feelings for the lady yourself? You, who've sworn off matrimony and despise all things French.'

'I do not despise all things French, and my reputation is such that I have nothing to *offer* a lady,' Robert said. 'But I do not wish to see Miss Vallois hurt.'

'Then you have nothing to worry about for I have no intention of hurting her. Now, why don't you send your sister home and join me for some serious gambling?

There's money to be made on greenheads who don't know a trump from a tart.'

'Thank you, but I've no interest in fleecing innocent young men who haven't the brains to stay out of the hells.'

''Pon my word, sir, that almost sounded like a lecture, and I am not of a mind to take a lecture from you. Act the hero if you must, but don't forget—I *know* the games you've played. I was a willing participant in many of them.'

'Be that as it may, the past is the past. Leave it where it belongs.'

'Leave it where it belongs? Oh, that's ripe coming from you!' Oberon said as his carriage drew to a halt and the footman hurried to let down the stairs. 'A man who still hates *all* Frenchmen because *one* shot his brother in the back. You're the one living in the past, Silverton. Not me.'

Oberon climbed up into the carriage and the moment the door closed behind him, the coachman whipped up the team. Robert stepped back as the stylish equipage passed, his thoughts as dark as the night that swallowed it up. So what if Oberon thought he'd lingered too long in the past? He was the *first* one to admit that Michael's death had prevented him from moving on. It was the reason he had delayed his return to society. The reason he hadn't looked for a wife until a little over a month ago. Anger had plunged him into an abyss of bitterness and despair from which he'd thought there was no escape.

But there *was* life after death, and eventually, his world had begun to right itself. He had emerged from the darkness to pick up where he'd left off, resuming his place in society. Doing the rounds of the civilised gentleman. And if some of the shadows remained, they were no longer a source of despair. He was able to work around them.

And then Miss Sophie Vallois had arrived. Sophie, with her quicksilver smile and her sparkling blue eyes. She had marched into his world and splashed colour on to a drab grey canvas. She had challenged and provoked him. Stimulated and disobeyed him. And she had made him laugh at the idea of a lady wanting to float down the Amazon in a boat. No wonder Jane was her slave. Even old Lady White couldn't get enough of her. She truly was a breath of fresh air.

And if he continued on his present course, he would lose her. It was as simple as that. Oberon intended to do everything in his power to make her see him as an ideal husband, and the only person who stood in his way... was Robert. Because he alone held the ace. Sophie had handed it to him in the theatre tonight. All he had to do now was to decide if, when and how to play it.

## Chapter Eight

The sky was grey and overcast when Sophie and her maid set out for Oxford Street the next morning. Not the best time to venture out perhaps, but with Lavinia's birthday the following day, Sophie had no time to waste. She had to pick out a gift today.

Fortunately, she knew what she wanted to buy. The last time she and Lavinia had been out together, they had paused to admire a selection of fans displayed in a shop window. Lavinia had pointed out one in particular and Sophie had agreed it was exquisite. Then, when an acquaintance had hailed them, the fans had been forgotten—until this morning, when Sophie had returned to the shop to buy it.

Now, with the gift tucked safely in its case, she set out for her next destination—only to be forced into the doorway of a gentlemen's clothier when the clouds finally burst and the promised rains came pelting down.

'Miss Vallois, what on earth are you doing out in such dreadful weather?'

Startled, Sophie turned to find herself face to face with Robert Silverton, who was just emerging from within. 'Shopping, as it happens.' Goodness, did the man draw on some secret elixir that made him appear more handsome every time she saw him? 'But I think we will have to cut it short. This rain doesn't look like it's going to let up any time soon.'

'Then perhaps I could offer you a ride home?' He glanced apologetically at her maid. 'Unfortunately, my carriage only has room for two.'

'Don't you worry about me, sir,' Jeanette said. 'A bit of rain won't hurt me. But I'd hate to see Miss Sophie get her fine clothes all spattered with mud. You go on. I'll make my own way home.'

'Here, take a hackney.' He pulled out a coin and pressed it into the maid's palm. 'My conscience will not allow me to see you walk home through a downpour like this.'

Jeanette blushed and bobbed a curtsy. 'Thank you, sir. I'll take those parcels, miss, and put them in your room without her ladyship seeing.'

'Thank you, Jeanette.' Sophie gratefully handed them over, then dashed into the street and quickly climbed into the waiting carriage. 'This is very good of you, Mr Silverton,' she said as they got underway. 'We should both have been drenched had you not come along.'

'I'm glad to be of assistance.'

'How is Jane this morning?'

'She was in good spirits when I left, though I was concerned about her last night. She is prone to chills, and when I saw how flushed her cheeks had become, I feared she might be coming down with something.'

Suspecting it had more to do with her reaction to

Antoine than it did to an illness, Sophie nevertheless said, 'I could mention it to Antoine. He is not an apothecary, but perhaps he could suggest a tonic.'

'Thank you, but Jane has no need of a doctor, especially a—'

He clamped down hard on the words, but not soon enough to prevent Sophie from sliding a startled glance his way. What had he been about to say? That he didn't want Antoine involved because he was still learning his profession? That he was not experienced enough to treat his sister? 'If you are concerned about Antoine's skills, I can assure you—'

'This has nothing to do with ability,' Robert assured her. 'I watched your brother in action. I know how talented he is.'

'Then why did you not finish what you were about to say?'

She waited a long time for his answer. Finally, he said, 'Because to do so would be to reveal something about my past I have no wish to talk about. Or to explain.'

He looked at her then, and Sophie caught a glimpse of a shadow that dwelt in his soul. Of an old wound slowly healing. But what had that to do with his reluctance to accept help from Antoine? Her brother was no more a part of Robert's past than she was. Until a week ago, they'd all been strangers to one another. Yet she couldn't shake the feeling that the root of Robert's animosity lay buried in that past.

Had it something to do with the fact that Antoine was not well born? Sophie hadn't meant to divulge that particular piece of information, but she had been so flustered by her sudden awareness of Robert that the words had inadvertently slipped out. And once they had, there was nothing she could do to take them back. But Robert hadn't learned that truth until last night, and his reluctance to shake Antoine's hand had been evident from the first, when all he'd known about him was that he was French and that—

Sophie blanched. *Mère de Dieu,* surely that wasn't the problem? Robert didn't want Antoine to help his sister…because he was French?

*Non, c'était impossible!* The war was over. Napoleon had been banished. There was absolutely no reason for Robert to harbour feelings of resentment simply because he and Antoine had been born on opposites of the Channel!

And yet, how else did she explain the tension she felt every time the two men were together? A tension that *had* been there the first time they'd met. She'd never forgotten Robert's hesitation when it came to shaking Antoine's hand. And while he might be willing to compliment her brother's skills when it concerned patching up a gunshot wound, she couldn't forget that he had been brusque, almost to the point of rudeness, when he'd spoken to Antoine outside Nicholas and Lavinia's house that morning…

'You've gone very quiet, Miss Vallois,' Robert observed. 'Have I said something to offend you?'

How did she answer that? If what she suspected was true, he most definitely *had* offended her. But if she was mistaken…

'Do you *like* my brother, Mr Silverton?' she said, knowing the question had to be asked.

She watched his expression change, saw the shutter come down. 'I really don't know him.'

'But you went to his aid the night a man was shot. And you have been in his company on at least two other occasions. Surely that is time enough to know whether you like a man or not.'

'On the contrary, it is barely enough time to form even a fleeting impression.'

Sophie quickly turned away, struggling for the right words; not sure what the right words were any more. 'That day you came to take me driving...when you spoke to Antoine. He offered Jane a compliment and you all but *demanded* that he speak English to her.'

'Of course, because we are in England,' Robert said quietly. 'If we were in France, I would have expected him to speak French, as I would myself.'

To anyone else it might have seemed like a reasonable excuse, but Sophie wasn't fooled. Robert had refused Antoine's help because he was French.

How did she respond to something like that? What was she supposed to say? To find out that a man, of whom she'd thought so highly, should be prejudiced in such a way came as a huge disappointment. While she could understand one man hating another given sufficient cause, to despise an entire nationality over a matter that was clearly restricted to him alone, demonstrated a narrowness of mind of which she could not approve.

'I am surprised at your willingness to be seen with me,' she said quietly, 'given that your dislike of the French is so all encompassing.'

He shot her a dark look. 'I said nothing about disliking the French.'

'You didn't have to. It is the *only* reason you could have for saying what you did.' She turned to face him. 'Why else would you not allow Antoine to offer even the slightest assistance to your sister, even after admitting that he is very good at what he does?'

Robert's jaw tensed, but he returned his attention to the road. 'I would prefer we speak no more about this.'

'But I *must* speak of it! You resent my brother because he is French, yet you are unwilling to tell me why.'

'And *you* seem unwilling to accept that certain matters *are* private and not open to discussion with those not personally involved.'

'Not personally involved? You are speaking of my *brother*, Mr Silverton! That *makes* it personal!'

Sophie hadn't realised they were home until Robert drew the carriage to a halt in front of Eaton Place. But she refused to wait for him to help her alight. She pushed open the door and started to get out.

'Miss Vallois, let me—'

'I will accept nothing from you, sir!' Sophie said as she climbed down. 'I would not wish to give offence by *forcing* you to take the hand of a Frenchwoman!'

Even through the rain, she saw him flush. 'Don't be ridiculous!'

'I am not the one being ridiculous!' Sophie said, fully aware that she was. For the first time in years, her temper was getting the better of her—and the stupid reasons why made her even more angry. 'I am not the one who has condemned an entire nation for reasons of which you will not speak.'

'I told you. The matter is personal and extremely painful.'

'Very well. Then let our acquaintance be at an end so you will not be forced to think of it every time you look at me! Good day, Mr Silverton.'

She was halfway to the front door when his words stopped her in her tracks. 'My brother was murdered. By a Frenchman. They found him in a deserted barn, ten miles outside Paris.'

The words, torn from his throat, caused Sophie to turn around, the sudden pounding of her heart deafening in her ears. 'How do you know...he was murdered?'

'He'd been bound hand and foot. Someone had put a sack over his head, and his hands were bloodied, as though he'd been fighting. He'd been shot once, in the back of the head. At close range. I don't think I need tell you the kind of damage a bullet fired that close to a person's body can do.'

Sophie pressed her hands to her mouth, trying to shut out the horrific images. *'Mère de Dieu!'*

'He went to France to fight for England, Miss Vallois. If necessary, to die a soldier's death. Not to be butchered by a man who hadn't the courage to face him. Only a coward shoots his enemy in the back,' Robert said bitterly.

From somewhere deep within, she found the courage to whisper, 'How do you know...it was a Frenchman?'

'Because they found a note stuffed in Michael's pocket. A note, covered in his blood, and hailing Napoleon Bonaparte as the future Emperor of England. No Englishman would write something like that, or shoot a compatriot in the back. I cannot forgive that of your countrymen. God knows I've tried. I'm sorry if that offends you, but you asked for the truth.'

Yes, she had. And as she stood looking back at him, mindless of the rain, Sophie was totally at a loss to find the words that would make sense of such a tragedy. What did you say to a man from whom so much had been taken, and in such a brutal fashion? What could she say that would exonerate her countryman? And why had she not been able to accept that, whatever Robert's reasons for despising the French, they were deeply personal and not meant to be shared?

Drawing his own conclusion from her silence, Robert flicked the whip and the horses set off, the carriage disappearing into the dull, grey morning.

Sophie didn't move. She stood where he'd left her, rain streaming down her face, the wind tugging at her cloak. She should have let him keep his secrets. She had no right to demand answers to questions that were none of her business. And she had been wrong to lash out at him simply because he refused to satisfy her curiosity. He was right. She had intruded where she didn't belong. And only time would tell if he would ever forgive her for that.

It came as no surprise that Robert made no attempt to contact her over the next few days. Why *would* he, given the nature of what had passed between them? Bitter words, spoken in anger, were never easily forgotten, and the petty accusations she had flung at him now seemed exactly that.

How ironic that *both* of them should have been so ill served by her countrymen. Robert's brother had been brutally murdered by a Frenchman, and *she* was staying at the house of a man who had likewise been shot and left for dead by one. Perhaps the French as a whole were a hot-blooded mob who preferred to make peace with swords and gunfire than with cool heads and clear thinking. Only look at the bloodiness of the Revolution. How many innocent people had been put to death during that dreadful time?

Even she and Antoine had not escaped their ire. They had been forced to leave their home when the sentiments of their neighbours had turned against them. When the man she was to have married had betrayed her.

It still hurt to think about that painful time. In her youthful naïveté, Sophie had believed herself in love with Gismond D'Orione. Their parents had agreed that when the time came, they would be married, and there had never been anyone else in her life but Gismond. She had grown up with him. Gone for walks with him. Experienced her first kiss with him. And because she'd loved him, she hadn't thought twice about telling him about Nicholas.

But Gismond had been afraid. He'd told his father about Sophie finding a wounded Englishman in the road, and about Antoine saving his life, and then his father had told others until eventually, the entire village knew. And when their father had found out, she and Antoine had had no choice but to leave. And so they had, stealing away in the middle of the night without telling anyone of their plans. Antoine had said it was better that way. Safer. They had packed a few clothes, taken some bread and cheese and disappeared into the darkness.

Sophie had never heard from Gismond D'Orione *or* her father again.

It did not make for pleasant memories and when the butler appeared to say that Mr Oberon had called, she was almost glad of the diversion. Even Lavinia seemed more kindly disposed towards him than usual.

'Mr Oberon, how nice of you to call,' she said, putting aside her magazine.

Mr Oberon strolled in, dashing as ever in gleaming Hessians, skin-tight breeches of fawn-coloured doeskin, and a cutaway coat of dark blue superfine. But his waistcoat was unusually subdued and his neckcloth was tied in a simple but elegant knot. 'Good afternoon, Lady Longworth, Miss Vallois. I came in hopes of taking you both out for a drive. The weather has turned fine and I thought it might be pleasant to take a turn about the Park.'

'You are very kind to ask, Mr Oberon,' Lavinia said. 'But I have Mr Harris coming to see me about new curtains. Sophie may go, if she wishes.'

Had it been a few days earlier, Sophie would have declined, having no wish to offer any kind of encouragement to Mr Oberon. But at the moment, she didn't want to be alone. After what had happened, she felt a desperate need to get out into the sunshine, to dispel the darkness of her thoughts by talking to someone who would naturally try to flatter her and make her laugh. If such was a flagrant abuse of his time, she would do her best to suffer the guilt.

'I would like that, Mr Oberon,' she said. 'If you will wait but a moment, I shall get ready.'

Fifteen minutes later, she allowed Mr Oberon to help her up into his dashing, high-perch phaeton.

'I vow I am carrying a ray of sunshine in my carriage,' he said as he climbed into the seat beside her. 'And never did one look lovelier.'

Sophie smiled as she opened her parasol. The carriage gown of buttery yellow muslin had seemed perfect for the occasion, but she had not worn it with a view towards inviting compliments. Mr Oberon needed no encouragement for that. But as if sensing she was not herself, he set out to be more charming than usual. He kept the carriage to a sedate pace and assumed the role of guide, pointing out houses of interest along the way and regaling her with amusing stories as they clipped along. But when after five minutes had passed and the only sound was the steady thud of the horses' hooves, he turned to her and said, 'You are noticeably quiet this afternoon, Miss Vallois. Dare I ask what is troubling you?'

Sophie sighed, aware that despite her best efforts, she had been a less than obliging guest. 'Forgive me, Mr Oberon, I admit my thoughts have been somewhat distracted.'

'I hope with nothing of a serious nature.'

'Serious enough.'

'Does this concern our mutual friend, Mr Silverton?'

Sophie was too unhappy to hide her surprise. 'How did you know?'

'A lucky guess. You seem to enjoy the gentleman's company and given that you were in such good spirits when we parted the other night, I wondered if it might have something to do with him.' He flicked a perceptive glance in her direction. 'Am I close?'

It was hard to know how much to reveal. Was the murder of Robert's brother something one discussed with a man who was little more than a stranger?

It was, if she had any hopes of understanding Robert better.

'Are you familiar with the nature of the tragedy concerning Mr Silverton's brother?' she asked.

'With Michael? Oh, yes, I know all about that. It was a terrible thing,' Mr Oberon said. 'I've always wondered how Robert and Jane got through it.'

Sophie blinked. Compassion? From Mr Oberon? 'I suppose it was because they had each other.'

'I dare say that's true.' Oberon looked at her again. 'I am surprised he told you.'

'He did not wish to.' Sophie averted her gaze. 'I goaded him into it.'

'*You* goaded Silver? I doubt that very much, Miss Vallois. You are anything but pushy.'

'I was the other morning,' she said miserably. And in as few words as possible, she told him of her conversation with Robert and of its distressing outcome.

'Ah, I see why you are downcast. You wish to have Robert's good opinion and fear now you may have lost it.'

'I am not as concerned with what he thinks of me, Mr Oberon, as I am with knowing how clumsily I brought back the memory of something he obviously wishes to forget.'

'But if we are speaking honestly, just being around you is likely to do that. Your delightful accent, slight as it is, betrays your origins and will always come between you.'

The words cut like a knife, partly because Sophie knew them to be true and partly because they had been uttered by someone who knew Robert much better than she did. 'You do not think he would ever be able to see beyond it?'

'I think it unlikely,' Oberon said. 'Robert has very strong opinions about the French. I'm telling you this because he and I have been good friends for years. We were even closer before his brother was killed. But all that changed after Michael's death. And it didn't help that his father committed suicide not long after.'

Sophie gasped. 'Suicide?'

'Not many people were willing to come right out and say that, of course, but I believe Sir William took his own life,' Oberon said. 'He was never the same after word came back from France that Michael had been killed. He'd been so proud of his eldest son. Michael was a captain and his father thought him the best of all men. He loved Robert, but Michael was the apple of his eye, and he took his death very hard. He shut himself away for weeks on end, refusing to see anyone. The gambling started shortly thereafter. Robert tried to stop him, but his father would have none of it. It was an addiction, you see, and Sir William could no more stop himself from gambling than he could bring his eldest son back from the grave. The family carried on as best they could, but it was impossible to ignore the fact that he was getting worse, as was their financial situation.

'Ironically, it was Robert who saved the family from total ruin,' Oberon went on. 'He had a knack for winning and was able to recoup much of what his father lost. But it was a dreadful situation and everyone feared for the outcome. Then, some months later, Sir William said he was going north to a hunting lodge in Scotland. It seemed a sudden decision, but he told Robert he was meeting friends for some shooting. Many of us hoped it was a sign Sir William was on the mend, but as it turned out, nothing could have been further from the truth. One of the gamekeepers found him in the far woods a few days later. Some say it was an accident, but I don't believe he ever had any intention of coming back.'

'How terrible!' Sophie said in a hushed voice.

'It was. And not long after, Lady Silverton fell into a dreadful decline. The doctors said there was nothing they could do. That she had lost the will to live.'

It was almost too much to bear. Sophie tried to imagine how devastating three deaths in close succession must have been for Robert and his sister, but it was completely beyond her. 'I cannot imagine how they endured it.'

'Neither can I, but I know it was the start of Robert's bitterness towards the French. I suppose, in many ways, he blames them for the loss of his entire family. Naturally, I tried to make him see that despising an entire nation over the thoughtless actions of one lunatic made absolutely no sense, but he couldn't see it. Wouldn't see it, I suppose. And he resented me for having tried to change his mind.'

'I'm sorry to hear that,' Sophie said, gazing at the road ahead. 'It isn't fair that you were made to suffer for trying to make him see reason.'

'Robert was set on a course from which I could not dissuade him,' Oberon said regretfully.

It was everything Sophie hadn't wanted to hear because, with every word, Mr Oberon confirmed that her chances for any kind of reconciliation with Robert were virtually non-existent. 'I wonder that his sister does not share his antipathy towards the French,' she said at length. 'The first time we met, she told me how much she was looking forward to speaking to me of Paris.'

'Jane is not as hard as her brother. She's had her own challenges to deal with and in overcoming those she has learned the meaning of tolerance. Dealing with disappointment at such an early age has enabled her to look more kindly, perhaps with more forgiveness, upon the world.'

Sophie turned her head to look at him. 'You surprise me, Mr Oberon. I would not have expected such compassion from you. Or such understanding.'

He smiled, the brim of his hat shading his eyes. 'I am often judged more harshly than I deserve, Miss Vallois. But I do not trouble myself over it. Trying to correct the opinions of others serves no useful purpose. It is enough that those of whom I think highly know who I am.' He turned to look at her. 'I hope I may consider you one of those people.'

It seemed impossible to believe, but Sophie realised her opinion of the man had changed. How could it not given everything she had heard today? 'You may consider me so, Mr Oberon. And thank you for telling me more of Mr Silverton's sad story.'

'You understand, of course, that he would not wish to know I had told you of it,' Oberon said, returning his attention to the road. 'Robert is a proud man, and proud men do not like their weaknesses being shared with others.'

'I will, of course, make no mention of our conversation,' Sophie assured him. 'I am well aware of how deeply I hurt Mr Silverton. I have no desire to make matters worse.'

'Thank you. I value Robert's friendship too, what little I have left of it. He is, in all ways, an admirable man, as I told you the second time we met.'

'Yes,' Sophie whispered. 'Quiet, honest and steady as a rock.'

She felt his gaze upon her, but did not turn her head. 'You have an excellent memory, Miss Vallois.'

'For some things, Mr Oberon.' An image of Robert's face appeared in her mind: the firm line of his chin, the broad sweep of his forehead, the smile on his lips when he was pleased or amused. A smile she was afraid she might never see again. 'For some things.'

As a result of the carriage ride with Mr Oberon, Sophie's spirits were only marginally restored by the time she and Antoine joined Nicholas and Lavinia for a soirée at the home of Sir David and Lady Hester the following evening. Everything Mr Oberon had said convinced her that the gulf between her and Robert was too wide to bridge. Even the sound of her voice would remind him of that painful time in his life. How could anyone enjoy a friendship under such strained conditions?

Fortunately, Antoine more than made up for her lack of good spirits as a result of having spent the best part of the day at Nicholas's club.

'I must admit you were right in everything you said about Nicholas,' Antoine commented as he and Sophie stood by the edge of the dance floor later that evening. 'He has introduced me to several of his closest friends and they are all excellent fellows. Lord Marwood invited me to come shooting with him, and Mr Kingsley said we would be most welcome to pay a call on him and his wife, either here or at their country house.'

'I'm happy for you, Antoine,' Sophie said, wishing she could find the strength to match his enthusiasm. 'You are moving with a very smart crowd and seem to be enjoying it.'

'It has all been Nicholas's doing,' Antoine said, looking out over the floor. 'If it were not for him—'

He stopped so abruptly that Sophie turned her head to look up at him. 'If *what* weren't for him?' Then, following his gaze, she saw Robert and Jane Silverton standing at the other side of the room.

In an instant, her breath caught. *What shall I say to him?* To ignore him would be craven, but how did she *begin* to apologise for what had happened the other morning?

'I did not think Miss Silverton would be here this evening,' Antoine said softly.

That was all it took. It was there, in his voice. And in a moment of heartbreaking insight, Sophie realised she was not the only one wrestling with demons. Her brother was in love with Jane Silverton—and Sophie knew it was doomed to fail. Robert would never give his approval. 'I suggest you not stare at her so boldly, dearest,' she cautioned, 'lest people begin to wonder at the nature of your feelings.'

Two spots of colour appeared high on her brother's cheeks. 'There is nothing between myself and Miss Silverton,' he said too quickly. 'I simply enjoy talking to her.'

'Then pray do not stare at her as though you wish you could do more. I am not the only one in the room with observant eyes.'

As if to confirm her fears, Sophie saw old Mrs Templeton smile and nod in their direction, and then lean in closer to her eldest daughter. When she whispered something in her ear, the daughter also turned to look and likewise smiled in that knowing kind of way.

'I suggest you ask Miss Templeton to dance,' Sophie

said quickly. 'Inform her that you are oft in the habit of staring at people when your thoughts are actually preoccupied with thoughts of...medical procedures.'

'Medical procedures? What are you talking about, Sophie?'

'Just do as I say unless you wish Miss Silverton to be at the heart of rumours over which you have no control. In fact, you might like to stare at Miss Templeton in just such a way before asking *her* to dance.'

'Now you're talking nonsense.'

'No, I'm not. I may be younger than you, but I understand the rules of the game far better.'

'And what are you going to do while I am playing these games?' he asked drily.

'I am going to speak to Mr Silverton.' Sophie took a long, deep breath. 'I fear I have already said too many things for which an explanation is required and an apology offered.'

Robert had not wanted to come this evening. Not only because the last thing he felt like doing was socialising with people who resented his presence, but because of his last agonising conversation with Sophie. She hadn't deserved the harshness of his reply. When he had begun relating the details of Michael's death, he had seen how deeply she was affected, yet he had still gone on talking, adding detail upon detail until her face had turned white and her eyes had reflected the horror of his words. It had been a heartless thing to do, entirely unnecessary, and if it were within his power, he would have taken back every single word.

But it was not within his power. The damage was done and he had no idea how to undo it. He had started a hundred letters…and thrown them all away. He had stood in the silence of his room and rehearsed the words of his apology. And every one of them had rung hollow and meaningless—

'Mr Silverton.'

And then, she was there, standing before him in yet another new gown—this one sweeping over the curves of her body and revealing just enough of the seductive roundness beneath to stir a man's blood. Her white-blond hair was caught up with a sprig of tiny white roses, and she looked, Robert thought sadly, like spring come to life. A virgin goddess sent to tempt and distract. And she did both…exquisitely. 'Miss Vallois,' he said, fearing the huskiness in his voice would betray him. 'I trust you are well?'

'Tolerably well. You?'

'Tolerably well.'

A moment passed, and, as if realising that was the extent of his conversation, Sophie turned to greet his sister. 'Good evening, Jane. Lavinia and I were sorry not to see you at the musicale this afternoon. The young woman Lady Staynwell engaged to perform was very good. Miss Roundtree, I believe her name was.'

'Yes, I was sorry not to be there,' Jane said, appearing somewhat distracted. 'I understand her mother taught her to play the pianoforte at a very young age. My goodness, it is warm, is it not?' She opened her fan and fluttered it vigorously in front of her face.

Robert, who was actually finding it cooler than usual, said, 'I could fetch a glass of punch—'

'Yes, punch would be excellent,' Jane said. 'But do stay here and talk to Miss Vallois. I am perfectly capable of fetching it myself.' Which she did—walking away

with a degree of alacrity that both surprised and concerned Robert.

'Jane must be very thirsty indeed. I don't think I've
ever seen her move so fast.' He turned to the lady standing beside him. 'Would you also care for some refreshment, Miss Vallois?'

'Thank you, no.'

The silence lengthened…and became awkward.
Robert desperately tried to appear at ease, but as the
memory of what happened returned in full force he
knew he had to say something. 'Miss Vallois, there is
something I must say—'

'No! It is I who must begin.' She paused, catching
her lower lip between dainty white teeth. 'I've not been
able to stop thinking about…what passed between us
earlier in the week. I feel terrible for having caused you
such distress and I owe you an apology.'

'You owe me nothing,' Robert ground out. 'You were
right to speak to me as you did.'

'Not given what happened—'

'You had no knowledge of what happened and I went
at you like a bull at a gate,' he said, feeling the tightness
of guilt at the back of his throat. 'That was wrong, and
unkind. I saw how it made you feel.'

'It shocked me for the terrible things that had happened to you,' Sophie said urgently. 'It made me see
why your feelings towards the French are what they
are. And it helped me to understand that your feelings
towards my brother, and perhaps, myself, are not so
much personal as they are…instinctual.'

'Miss Vallois—'

'No, please let me finish. You owe me no apology
or explanation, Mr Silverton. Because it all makes

sense now. *Any* reminder of the French, no matter how small, will always bring to mind that which you wish most dearly to forget. It was selfishness on my part that caused me to demand a justification for your reaction towards me, and I deeply regret that.'

He couldn't speak. She was apologising to him when it was he who should have been begging *her* forgiveness. Making excuses for herself when there were no excuses to be made, and tearing herself apart into the bargain. 'You were entirely within your rights to challenge me about my feelings towards the French,' Robert said huskily. 'I was allowing my hatred for one man to colour my opinion of everyone else, and in doing so, I demonstrated not only a blatant disregard for the truth, but a shocking narrowness of mind. It would be like you saying that all Englishmen wear green because you happened to meet *one* Englishman who did. But every person must be judged on his or her own merit, and even a condemned man must have his hearing. I can forgive someone for disliking a man if they know he has done wrong, but not before.' He was relieved to see her smile. More than relieved. Hopeful. 'And now that we have cleared the air and offered apologies that are not required, do you think we might start again... as friends?'

Her expression lightened, the darkness leaving her eyes. Did she feel as relieved as he did? Did the stars suddenly seem a little closer than they'd been a moment ago? 'I do hope so, Mr Silverton. In fact, I should like that above all.'

'Then perhaps, if you are not engaged for the next dance, I might claim the honour?'

'You may, though I should warn you, I am not the

best of dancers. My employer taught me how to speak, but she did not think it necessary that I knew how to dance.'

'I don't care.' He looked down at her, wanting to trace the line of her jaw with his fingers, to stroke the sensual curve of her throat. 'I just want to dance with you. And perhaps to talk and to make you laugh. Is that asking too much?'

She shook her head. 'Not at all. I should like to dance, and to talk, and to laugh.'

And when the quadrille came to an end and the minuet began, that was exactly what they did.

Lavinia stood with a group of ladies by a cluster of ferns and tried to pretend an interest in what they were saying. In truth, she was far more interested in what was going on elsewhere in the room. She had watched Sophie cross the floor to talk to Robert and Jane, and then a few minutes later, saw Jane leave and Robert and Sophie take up what looked to be a far more serious conversation. But it wasn't until they laughed, and Lavinia saw the expression on Robert's face, that she realised what was happening.

'Good evening, Lady Longworth,' a smooth voice said beside her.

*Danger.* Lavinia sensed it immediately, recognised it for what it was, and with the composure of a duchess, turned to face her adversary. 'Mr Oberon. Is it not a pleasant evening?'

'It is an exceedingly pleasant evening and the company equally delightful.' Oberon held the stem of his champagne glass between long slender fingers. 'But how careless of Lord Longworth to leave you all alone.'

'Ah, but I am not alone. I am surrounded by friends and now have you to keep me company.'

'Which I am most happy to do.' He raised the flute to his lips, but his eyes were on the floor. 'I had hoped to find Miss Vallois with you, but I see she is engaged with our friend, Silverton.'

'Yes. She thinks very highly of Jane and is often in her company.'

'Yet, Jane is not with them.'

Years of rigidly instilled training allowed Lavinia to open her fan with no visible sign of concern. 'She was a moment ago, but left to secure refreshments.'

'And found Mr Vallois instead.' Oberon's mouth lifted, little more than a grimace. 'It would appear both the Silvertons are very much taken with your guests, Lady Longworth.'

'Why would they not be? Sophie and Antoine are both likeable young people. You must have discovered that during the time you spent with Sophie the other afternoon.'

'I did, and as a result, it is my sincere desire to spend *more* time with her. But frankly, I am surprised to see Silverton looking so engaged. His dislike of the French is well known to both of us, I think.'

Hearing an edge to Oberon's voice, Lavinia sensed the need to tread carefully. 'Mr Silverton is, first and foremost, a gentleman. He would never allow his personal feelings to affect his conduct towards a lady.'

'And yet that is precisely what he did, and in doing so he upset Miss Vallois greatly. She spoke of it to me during our drive.'

'Did she? I am surprised. Sophie usually keeps her own counsel.'

'Do not condemn her for it, Lady Longworth. It was obvious to me she was in distress and when I enquired as to the nature, she told me. So now to see them conversing so amiably, I must confess to some surprise. I had believed Silverton firmly established in his intention to keep her at a distance. And given his current standing in society, I am surprised you would approve of their association.'

Lavinia slowly plied her fan, careful to remain impassive. 'I am aware of society's views with regard to Mr Silverton, but he has chosen to keep his own counsel and I respect him for that. Furthermore, if he spoke out of turn to Sophie, he would naturally be regretful of it and I am sure he is attempting to make amends, even now.'

'And succeeding, by all appearances.' Oberon raised his glass and finished the last of his champagne. 'However, it is of little concern. No doubt you and Lord Longworth are anxious to see Miss Vallois settled in the most advantageous manner possible.'

Lavinia waved at an acquaintance across the floor. 'My husband and I are more concerned that she is happy, Mr Oberon.'

'Of course, but surely you agree that the suitability of a husband *must* be a factor in the final decision. Love is all very well, but it is nothing compared to the benefits that wealth and position can bestow. Benefits someone like myself, for example, would be in a position to confer.'

It took every ounce of acting skill Lavinia possessed to appear calm in light of his admission. 'You, Mr Oberon?'

'Surely you are not surprised by my interest. I have

taken no pains to conceal my admiration of Miss Vallois.'

'But you have spent so little time in her company.'

'Sometimes very little is required. Besides…' his smile grew smug '…after our drive in the park, I believe she now looks upon me with more favour than she did in the past. And only think, Lady Longworth, if Miss Vallois were to become my bride, she would become your equal in society.'

His *bride.* 'I am well aware of what you would be able to give her, Mr Oberon,' Lavinia replied quietly, 'but I think it only fair to tell you that Miss Vallois has no interest in marriage.'

Oberon laughed. 'Yes, so Silverton informed me. But you and I both know that's not true. All young ladies wish to be married. Even poor Jane.' Oberon glanced towards the refreshment table where she and Antoine were still chatting in a most amiable fashion. 'Pity. She is so obviously smitten, yet he, by virtue of being French and what he hopes to become, can offer her nothing. And soon he returns to Paris. No doubt thoughts of marriage are far from his mind.' Oberon smiled. 'Please give my regards to your husband, Lady Longworth. And perhaps you might tell him…' he took a last look towards Robert and Sophie '…tell him there is something I wish to discuss with him at his earliest convenience.'

# Chapter Nine

Robert was reading the newspaper when Jane finally came down the next morning. She wore a morning gown of pale lavender and the soft colour put roses into her cheeks and deepened the green in her eyes. 'Good morning, Robert.'

'Jane.' He put down his paper. 'You look in fine spirits today.'

'I slept better than I have in days and awoke to the sound of a robin singing outside my window.' She helped herself to coddled eggs and toast from the sideboard. 'Did you enjoy yourself last evening?'

'Very much.'

'Sophie looked so very lovely. I would never have thought to dress up a plain white gown with lace in quite that manner. But it was most flattering.'

Robert decided it best to withhold comment. As far as he was concerned, Sophie could have draped herself in burlap and still looked beautiful.

'She dances quite well,' Jane said, spreading a thin

layer of marmalade on her toast. She took a bite and paused in thought. 'Do you think I would have been a good dancer had I not been troubled with this wretched foot?'

'I think you would have been a very good dancer if it was something you enjoyed doing.'

'Does that matter? You do not particularly enjoy dancing, yet you are very good at it.'

'Sometimes we do things whether we like them or not.' Robert remembered the long hours spent with his tutor learning the intricacies of the steps so he would not embarrass himself when the time came. 'Dancing is a necessary part of a gentleman's education.'

'Mr Vallois acquitted himself very well,' Jane commented in an offhand manner. 'I saw him partner Miss Templeton in the minuet and she is not an accomplished dancer at all.'

Robert shrugged as he returned his attention to his paper. 'I suspect dancing is as widely done in France as it is here.'

'But one would not expect a man who intended to become a doctor of having time for such frivolous pastimes. Although Mr Vallois does not strike me as being like other doctors.'

'How many other doctors have you known?'

'You know what I mean. Mr Vallois is passionately interested in a wide variety of subjects, not only in the study of medicine. He can speak intelligently on matters pertaining to science and archaeology, and he is very well read. He can recite Shakespeare as well as any actor on the stage today.'

Aware that Mr Vallois's name was coming up a little

too often for his liking, Robert said tersely, 'A talent that will no doubt prove useful in his chosen career.'

'That was unkind, Robert.'

He looked up. 'Was it? I thought I was simply being honest.'

'Why do you not like Mr Vallois? Apart from that one occasion when he paid me a compliment to which *you* took exception, he has been the perfect gentleman.'

'I never said I didn't like him.'

'You didn't have to. I can tell from the way your voice changes when you speak of him. It's because he's French, isn't it?'

'My voice does not change when I speak of him,' Robert said, putting the newspaper aside. 'But he is due to return to Paris at any moment, so there is no point in *you* losing your heart to him.'

'I have not lost my heart to him!'

'Then why does *your* voice change every time you speak of *him*?'

Jane said nothing, obviously loathe to answer a question to which Robert already knew the answer. 'It wouldn't work, Jane,' he said more gently. 'What Antoine Vallois wants from life and what you want are entirely different. He would not make you happy and I would resent him for not being able to do so.'

'You know nothing about him,' Jane whispered. 'You resent him because he *is* French.'

So, they were back to that, Robert thought wearily. A subject neither of them wished to discuss and for which there were no acceptable answers. 'If my resentment of the French was an issue, I would hardly be spending time in Sophie's company, now would I?'

'It was a *man* who shot our brother, Robert. I suspect that is how you are able to rationalise your interest in her.'

He folded his napkin and stood up. 'I'm going out. Is there anything you would like me to fetch for you?'

'Yes. A book. From Hatchard's.' She scribbled the name on a piece of paper and thrust it at him. 'If it's not too much trouble.'

He took the piece of paper and tucked it in his pocket. 'It never has been before.'

She had the grace to look embarrassed, but she did not relent. She glanced towards the window, her back as rigid as her voice. 'Shall I tell Cook to expect you for lunch?'

'No. I've sent a note round to Lawrence Welton, asking him to meet me at his club.'

'Mr Welton?' Jane frowned. 'Is he not a close friend of Mr Oberon's?'

'He was, but they seem to have fallen out and I haven't seen Lawrence in weeks. I just wanted to make sure everything's all right.' He bent to kiss her cheek. 'I'll see you later this evening.'

'Fine.'

He stood up, hating the brittle tension between them. What was he supposed to say? That he was *happy* about her affection for Antoine Vallois? That he *liked* the idea of her marrying a Frenchman and possibly moving away to France? It would take Edmund Kean himself to make that performance believable. 'Look, why don't you order the trap? It's a lovely day for a drive and it might be pleasant for you to get out of the house for a while.'

For a moment Jane refused to look at him, her expression as stiff as her posture. But Robert knew his sister well. She could no more stay angry with him than he could with her—and as if realising the argument would only serve to prolong an unnatural state of conflict, she gave in with a sigh. 'Yes, it is a lovely morning. Far too nice to waste on pointless arguments.'

'I only want what's best for you, Jane,' Robert said. 'You know that, don't you?'

She looked up at him and eventually nodded. 'Yes, but sometimes I wonder if either of us knows what that really is.'

Lawrence Welton did not arrive at Watier's at the specified hour, nor within the half-hour Robert waited for him. Both struck him as strange, given that Welton was normally a very punctual fellow. But finally giving it up as a bad deal, Robert turned and headed towards St James's. He'd send Lawrence a note later, suggesting they reschedule.

He was just passing White's when he heard someone hail him. 'Mr Silverton!'

Turning, he saw Lord Longworth crossing the street in his direction. 'My lord.'

'I'm just on my way in for some lunch. Care to join me?'

Robert inclined his head. 'That would be most agreeable.'

Being a predominantly Tory club, White's was not an establishment Robert frequented. But Longworth was greeted by several gentlemen whose names were well known in society and then shown with some deference to a table next to the tall window. After ordering a bottle of claret, Longworth said, 'I was supposed to have lunch with Mr Oberon, but he sent word he would be unable to attend.'

'Really.' Robert smoothed the linen napkin across his lap. 'It would appear his loss is my gain. But I am surprised by your invitation, given my current standing in society.'

'Yes, well, I expect that will resolve itself soon enough,' Longworth said. 'Once Lady Mary marries, all will be forgotten and society will find someone else to pick apart—' He broke off as the butler arrived with their wine, and waited until after he'd left to continue. 'Besides, you've had far more serious matters to contend with. Tell me,' he said casually, 'with regard to Michael, did you ever find out how your brother came to be where he was?'

'You mean in a deserted barn miles from anywhere?' Robert shook his head. 'Very little information was made available to us. I know my father tried to get details, but it was almost as though no one wanted to talk about it. Other men were given heroes' burials, but it seemed to me Michael's death was hushed up.' He raised the glass to his lips. 'I thought it damned unfair.'

Longworth rubbed his finger along the stem of his glass. 'There are things you don't know, Robert. Things that couldn't be made public at the time.'

'What are you talking about?'

'I won't go into detail. Suffice it to say we were in a difficult situation in the days leading up to Waterloo. Napoleon intended sweeping into Brussels and had established a presence at both Mons and Charleroi. But from which place would the main thrust be launched?'

'I thought Wellington suspected Mons because it was

on the main Paris to Brussels Highway and ten miles closer to Brussels than Charleroi?' Robert said.

'But did that mean his presence in Charleroi was simply a diversionary tactic? We couldn't know for sure. Though Napoleon was outnumbered two to one by the coalition forces by the time he reached Beaumont, Wellington knew better than to underestimate him, especially after what happened at Leipzig. But with no idea how many men Napoleon had, it made it difficult for Wellington to plan any kind of counter-offensive. So, a handful of men were sent out to collect whatever intelligence they could.'

'Sent out,' Robert said, his eyes narrowing. 'You mean, as spies.'

'Exactly. And eventually, a report came back from Mons indicating that Napoleon intended to launch the offensive from Charleroi. Wellington received it in time to plan a counter-offensive and the coalition forces intercepted Napoleon at Waterloo.'

Robert had no trouble following the series of events. The news of Napoleon's defeat at Waterloo had been front-page news and the cause of much celebration. What he didn't understand was why Longworth was bringing it up now. 'What has this to do with Michael?'

'The men selected for that mission were the very best Britain had,' Longworth said. 'They were men who could be counted on to get the job done. And they did get it done, but not without casualties. The reason I'm telling you this now is because I think you need to know why no one told you the truth at the time. You see, Robert...' Longworth looked around, then dropped his voice even further '...your brother Michael was one of them.'

For a moment, shock stole the breath from Robert's lungs. *Michael, an intelligence agent for the Crown?* Impossible! His brother would never have kept such a secret from his family. He had been the most honest, the most decent man Robert had ever known.

And yet, the more he thought about it, the more he realised it made sense. It explained why Michael would abruptly leave London and not tell anyone where he was going. It explained why he would be absent for weeks on end and then suddenly reappear, but not be able to tell them where he had been. His brother an agent for the British Government. Why the hell hadn't he figured it out for himself? 'Why weren't we told?'

'The Department felt it too dangerous, so the men were sworn to secrecy. Most wives never knew their husbands or sons were employed by the government.'

'We never even suspected,' Robert said ruefully. 'And yet, now that you've told me, it all makes perfect sense. But why am I hearing this now? And why are *you* the one telling me?'

'Because I think it's time you knew the truth. Something went badly wrong on that mission, Robert,' Longworth said bluntly. 'Michael wasn't supposed to be on his own the night he was killed, but the letter that should have gone out advising him the mission had been cancelled was never sent. He was betrayed by one of our own—the same man who killed several of our best agents.' Longworth's blue eyes blazed. 'The same man who tried to kill me.'

Robert stiffened in shock. 'Dear God, *you're* one of them too?'

'Keep your voice down,' Longworth said. 'Yes, I was, and though I didn't work with your brother, I know many of the men who did and they all said he was as brave as any man out there. He did a lot of good before…'

'Before they got to him.'

Longworth nodded, his eyes heavy with regret as he took a deep swallow of wine.

Robert said nothing. It was almost too much to take in. Being told of his brother's true occupation. Of hearing Longworth's admission as to his own involvement in the covert operations. Of hearing how badly the mission had gone wrong… 'Does Lady Longworth know about your involvement?'

'She had to. On my last mission to France, after I was shot by the man who killed your brother, I was found by a young French couple who took me in and saw to my injuries. But when I returned to England, it was with no memory of who I was or what my life had been. Because I was engaged to Lavinia at the time, my commanding officer felt she might be able to help in my recovery, so he told her the truth about what I was doing in France. We still needed to find the man who'd shot me and murdered a dozen other agents. Eventually, we did.'

Robert sat back, digesting what was turning out to be an incredible story. 'How many people are aware of this?'

'Very few and I'd like it to remain that way,' Longworth said, his tone leaving Robert in no doubt as to the seriousness of the matter. 'Napoleon may be banished, but some men carry grudges for years. I only told you this so you would understand how your brother came to lose his life. The Englishman who shot him—'

'The *Englishman*?' Robert gasped. 'But the note found in Michael's pocket—'

'Was put there to throw us off the track,' Longworth admitted. 'Havermere was a double agent. He'll likely spend the rest of his life serving at his Majesty's pleasure, but before he was apprehended, he took a lot of good men down. Your brother was one of them.'

In that split second, Robert's world turned upside down. Everything he'd come to believe about the French since the night his family had received word of Michael's death shattered like glass. His hatred of the French was completely unfounded. His brother's murderer had been one of their own.

It was nearly two o'clock before Robert said his good-byes to Lord Longworth, but still in need of time to review all he had learned, he decided not to go home, but to take a stroll through the bustling streets. It was easier to hide one's confusion in a crowd than to face a sister who was far too perceptive for her own good. He lost track of time as he walked, his mind going over and over what Lord Longworth had told him. *Michael, an agent for the Crown. His only brother, murdered by an Englishman.* What a fool he'd been—

'Silver! What the devil are you doing? Didn't you hear me calling?'

Pulled from the turmoil of his thoughts, Robert lifted his head and saw Oberon striding towards him. 'No.'

'Bit out of your area, aren't you?'

Robert looked up and realised he was almost at Grosvenor Square. 'I wasn't paying attention.'

'Obviously not. But never mind that. I want to talk to you about Miss Vallois.'

'What about her?'

'Only that I saw you with her last night and wondered what you were playing at.'

The proprietary note in Oberon's voice set Robert's teeth on edge. 'Playing at?'

'You assured me you weren't interested in the girl. That your only concern was that she not get hurt. Yet last night, I could have sworn I saw something between you.'

'What you saw was an apology being offered for the way I spoke to her the other morning. I was endeavouring to set things right.'

'Is that *all* you were doing?'

Robert's eyes narrowed. 'I fail to see what business that is of yours.'

'Perhaps you'll have a better understanding when I tell you I intend to speak to Lord Longworth about Miss Vallois. I would have done it today, but I was held up. And I would take it as a personal favour if you were to stay away from her. I can't have my future wife associating with people like you.'

People like *him*? Robert bit back the reply that sprang to his lips, saying instead, 'If the lady chooses to seek out my company, I'm not going to turn her away. But speak to Longworth if you must. The choice will ultimately be hers.'

'The choice? Are you saying you intend to go after her?'

There it was. The question, poised like a sleeping cobra. A line had been drawn and Robert knew that if he stepped over that line, the cobra would strike. But the time for doing nothing had passed. 'That is a matter between Miss Vallois and myself.'

The hiss was audible, the creature awakened. 'You're a fool, Silver. What have you to offer her in comparison to me? Not wealth. Not title. Certainly not a position in society. How will she feel when doors keep closing in her face? When the invitations don't come and your social life dwindles to a handful of people as dull as yourselves. I can give her *everything*,' he said. 'Beautiful clothes. The finest jewels. A silver carriage drawn by four white horses, with her very own tiger to ride behind. And in time, people will make their curtsies to the exquisite Viscountess Oberon. You can give her *nothing*. Face it, Silver, Miss Vallois is as good as mine.'

Robert couldn't argue with a word Oberon said. But the fact the man was stupid enough to believe any of those things mattered to Sophie told him how little he really knew about the lady he hoped to make his wife. 'I've always thought,' Robert said quietly, 'that as good as is a *long* way from being a sure thing.'

Oberon's voice hardened. 'I don't like your tone.'

'And I don't like being warned to stay away. Now if you'll excuse me—'

'Not so fast.' Oberon's hand snaked out, his fingers closing on Robert's wrist. 'I've expended a great deal of effort on Miss Vallois's behalf. I've modified my behaviour, changed my appearance, and I do believe the lady has noticed.'

'In that case...' Robert shook him off '...you have nothing to worry about.'

'Don't do this, Silver,' Oberon said, his expression turning dark and resentful. 'Take my advice. Stop now before it's too late.'

'And if I don't?'

'You *will* come to regret it. I can make things very unpleasant for you and those you care about.'

Robert forced himself to look at the man standing beside him. A man he thought he knew. A man he'd once liked. 'If you hurt anyone I care about, I *will* see you burn.'

'Fine.' Oberon stepped back, the cold mask of the gentleman replaced by the face of the cobra. 'Just don't say I didn't warn you.'

Robert was halfway home when he remembered Jane's book. He'd been in such a foul mood after his confrontation with Oberon that he'd forgotten all about it. And knowing it wouldn't sweeten Jane's disposition to return empty handed, he headed back in the direction of Hatchard's—only to find Sophie inside, perusing a selection of books set out on a small table. For a while, he just stood and watched her. She picked up a slim, leather-bound volume and opened it to the first page. While she read, her lips curved upwards, bringing into view the dimples he was suddenly finding so damned irresistible.

He took off his hat and approached, hoping the truce they had established last night might yet be in place. 'Miss Vallois?'

When she looked up, he was pleased to see a warm glow of welcome in her eyes. 'Mr Silverton.'

'I hope I'm not disturbing you.'

'Not at all.'

'You seem to be enjoying the book.'

'Not really.' She closed the volume and set it down. 'The subject matter was not to my taste.'

'Yet you smiled.'

'More for the unusual style of the author's prose than for its brilliance.'

Robert stared down at the floor. Conversation had never been difficult for him, yet when it came to Sophie, he felt as awkward as a schoolboy. 'You enjoy reading?'

'Very much. I share my brother's belief that it is the best way to expand one's knowledge and understanding of others.'

He relaxed slightly. Good. Books. A common interest. 'Have you a favourite author?'

'I confess to enjoying Miss Austen's works at present, though I probably have a better knowledge of the classics.'

'You obviously share your brother's partiality for them,' Robert said drily.

He felt the curiosity of her gaze. 'How did you know Antoine likes the classics?'

'Jane mentioned it over breakfast this morning. I gather they were speaking of it last night.' He stopped and cleared his throat. 'Miss Vallois, you said in the carriage that you'd like to explore the ancient pyramids. Have you had a chance to visit the British Museum?'

'Not yet.'

'Then perhaps it's time you did. Though not as atmospheric as wandering through the desert, the Egyptian display is most impressive and I would be happy to show it to you.'

Her smile left him breathless. 'Thank you, Mr Silverton, I'd like that very much. Probably better than getting all that sand in our shoes anyway.'

'I dare say.' Unbidden, his mind conjured up an image of Sophie walking barefoot across the sand towards him. Of her sitting on his lap, her arm around his neck as he gently brushed the grains from her feet. He could almost feel the heat of an ancient sun burning through his clothes—and the heat at the thought of holding her in his arms burning him everywhere else—

'Fine.' His voice roughened. 'Shall we say, tomorrow afternoon?'

'Yes.' Her smile was blinding. 'Tomorrow would be perfect.'

They parted at the door and as Robert started for home, he felt a hundred times better than he had after his dismal confrontation with Oberon. But one thing had become painfully clear. He had to keep Sophie away from Oberon. The man didn't want a wife. He wanted a beautiful china doll he could parade around town. One he could dress up and show off and keep under lock and key. He certainly didn't want a woman with opinions or dreams of her own. He would scoff at her wanting to fly above London in a hot-air balloon. Laugh at her dreams of exploring the pyramids. God only knew what he would say about her wanting to float down the Amazon on a raft...

'Boat,' Robert murmured under his breath. No, Oberon was right about one thing. There *could* only be one winner in the battle for Sophie's heart. And while circumstances might prevent it being him, Robert was damned if he'd ever let it be a self-centred snake like Montague Oberon!

Sophie was barely through the door when Banyon informed her that Mr Oberon was waiting to see her. 'I've put him in the parlour, miss, to await your answer.'

'Thank you, Banyon. Is Lady Longworth at home?'

'She is not and I did inform Mr Oberon of that, but

he asked if he might have a brief moment of your time. He said it was on a matter of some importance. Regarding…a mutual friend.'

It was clear from the butler's expression that he was no fonder of passing along cryptic messages than Sophie was of receiving them, but, curious about Oberon's reference to a mutual friend, she said, 'Thank you, Banyon. I'll see him in the drawing room.'

Once there, Sophie paused to take a few deep breaths. Moments later, Oberon arrived. 'Miss Vallois. Thank you for agreeing to see me.'

'Your message was intriguing to say the least. Will you sit down?'

'Thank you, but I don't intend to stay long. I am aware that Lady Longworth is from home, but I came here out of concern for you.'

Sophie arched an eyebrow. 'Am I in some kind of danger?'

'Not of a physical kind, but you could be when it comes to…matters of the heart.'

Tempted to inform him that matters of her heart were none of his business, Sophie said, 'Banyon said you wished to speak to me about a mutual friend.'

'Yes. Robert Silverton. A man for whom I know you hold a special affection.'

Aware of the need to tread carefully, Sophie said, 'Mr Silverton *is* a friend, but nothing more. As you pointed out, there are issues that would always come between us.'

'Nevertheless, given the way I saw the two of you talking at Sir David and Lady Hester's last night, I thought you might have…resolved that issue.'

A warning bell rang. So, he had been spying on her.

Watching her while she was talking to Robert. 'What you saw,' Sophie said slowly, 'was Mr Silverton offering me an apology for what had passed between us with regard to his brother's death. An apology I was happy to accept.'

'Has he asked to see you again?'

The words came at her like the flick of a whip. 'I really don't think that's any of your business, Mr Oberon.'

'Ah, but it is, Miss Vallois. Because I came here today with a view to making you aware of two things. One of which you will find very distressing. About Mr Silverton.'

So, he had come to tell tales on his friend. 'I cannot imagine what you could say about Mr Silverton that would make me think ill of him.'

'Not even that his sudden interest in you may have more to do with his hopes of winning my stallion than with any genuine feelings of love or affection for you?'

The statement was so bizarre that Sophie felt shock rather than outrage upon hearing it. 'Kindly explain yourself, sir.'

'Of course. I happen to know that Robert recently entered into a wager. One of his own devising, with the goal being to make the most beautiful woman in London his mistress. And given that he's told me more than once that he has no intention of marrying, I can only wonder at the reasons behind his sudden interest in you.'

Sophie was glad she was standing by the window. It allowed her to pretend an interest in the goings-on of passers-by in the street below. So, he would have her believe that Robert's interest in her was motivated by a desire to make her his mistress? Truly he did not know his friend well. 'I couldn't help but notice that you said Mr Silverton hoped to win your stallion. Does that mean you were also a party to this wager?'

'I regret to say my name was taken down,' he admitted, 'but I can assure you it was not with my agreement and it certainly wasn't over the acquisition of a mistress. I had already informed Silverton that it was my intention to seek a wife and settle down to married life. At least he had the decency to record my participation as such.'

'So you're telling me that Mr Silverton wagered his ability to find a mistress against yours to find a wife, with the prize being your stallion.'

'I fear so,' Oberon said. 'He's always coveted the beast. He once told me that if an opportunity ever presented itself whereby he might take Thunder from me, he would do so without hesitation. That, I believe, was his primary motivation in suggesting the wager. And to be fair, he did offer up a prize of his own. A rather pretty little ring, but one I know to be a cherished family heirloom.'

Sophie kept her gaze fixed on the view outside the window. 'I am surprised he would risk such a valuable item.'

'I did try to persuade him against it, but he said it meant nothing to him. You must understand, Miss Vallois, Robert is a long-standing knight of the elbow. His passion for gambling runs as hot as the blood in his veins. It became his solace when his world turned upside down, and though he hides his craving beneath a civilised veneer, it is there none the less.'

Sophie let the curtain fall back into place. So, now

Oberon would have her believe that Robert was a heartless gambler to whom winning meant everything. A man whose interest in her was of the most scandalous kind. 'What do you think Mr Silverton would say,' she asked softly, 'if I were to question him about what you've just told me?'

'I suspect he would try to justify his conduct to you by whatever means he could. There would certainly be no point in his trying to deny the wager exists. You could verify what I've said easily enough. I simply wished you to hear the details of the thing from me so that if he told you differently, you would be in a better position to judge who was telling you the truth.'

'And you would have me believe that *you* are the one doing that.'

Oberon smiled, managing to look both guilty and humble at the same time. 'I may have been a trifle bold in my conduct towards you in the past, Miss Vallois, but I like to think I have always been honest. And I'm not saying Robert is a bad man for, indeed, he is not. But he has been through a great deal, and sometimes, when a man is pushed to the very limits of his endurance, the darker emotions rise up to consume him. I would not wish to see you become...an unwitting victim of that weakness.'

Sophie tapped her fingers on the sash. It was hard to believe they were talking abut the same man. Yes, Robert had been pushed to the limits, but it was impossible to reconcile the desperate, unfeeling gambler Oberon made him out to be with the caring, honourable gentleman she had come to know and admire. Her intuition told her she could not be that far wrong. Besides, experience had taught her it was never wise to judge a person's conduct until one was in full possession of the facts. Oberon had told her his side of the story. She had yet to hear Robert's.

'You said there were two things you wished to see me about, Mr Oberon,' Sophie said, meeting his gaze. 'The possibility of my becoming Mr Silverton's mistress would seem to be one. Dare I ask about the other?'

He smiled, though his expression reflected an element of chagrin. 'I should have known you would not be so easily persuaded. Your loyalty does you credit, Miss Vallois, as does your willingness to believe the best of the people you care about. I hope I may be counted amongst those people, because my affection for you *is* the other matter I've come to see you about.'

Sophie caught her breath. Surely he was not about to declare himself. 'Mr Oberon, I would rather not—'

'Please hear me out. The only reason I've kept silent about my feelings was a result of being unsure of my place in yours. But now that I know Silverton has not stolen a march on me, the time has come to tell you that I care deeply for you, and that I have ever since we met. It would please me greatly if you would do me the honour of becoming my wife.'

No, no, no, this was not what she wanted to hear! 'How can you ask me such a question after admitting you were also a party to this wager?' Sophie said. 'By knowing you are as anxious to hold on to your stallion as you say Mr Silverton is to win him, I can only question the motive behind your proposal.'

He affected a look of pain. 'My dear Miss Vallois. Horses are nothing more than commodities to be bought and sold. *You* are one of a kind. And did I not tell you that I became a party to the wager entirely without my knowledge?'

'Yes, but then everything you've told me today is unsubstantiated,' Sophie said. 'I have no proof that the claims you make against Mr Silverton are valid, or that your feelings for me are as honest as you would have me believe.'

'Nevertheless, they are what they are, and only consider what you stand to gain by marrying me. Wealth, status, a title. Everything a woman could ask for.'

But not love, Sophie reflected. He said nothing about being in love with her—because he wasn't. 'Thank you, Mr Oberon. Though I am flattered by your offer, I cannot possibly accept. Apart from the fact I have no wish to marry, I do not love you. And I would *never* consider marrying without love. And now, I bid you good afternoon.'

He didn't look surprised. He didn't even look regretful. As he started towards the door, he actually began to smile. 'I understand. But if you think about it a bit longer, you'll come to realise that in this case, love is not the only consideration. You stand to gain a great deal by accepting my proposal, Miss Vallois, but you stand to lose even more by turning me down. You might like to think about that before giving me your answer. And I *will* call again,' he said as he opened the door. 'Of that you can be sure.'

# Chapter Ten

The memory of Mr Oberon's visit stayed with Sophie long after he'd left, as did his ominous parting words. She had no idea what he'd meant by saying she stood to lose much by turning him down, but she wasn't foolish enough to believe he was speaking in jest. What little she knew of Oberon convinced her he was a man used to getting his own way. As such, it was with a definite feeling of trepidation that she accompanied Nicholas and Lavinia to a soirée at the home of Lord and Lady Chiswick that same evening. She felt quite sure Mr Oberon would be there and that he would be watching her every move. As she settled into the carriage for the short ride to Park Lane, she couldn't shake the feeling that something very bad was about to happen.

'So, this is the young lady we've been hearing so much about,' Lord Chiswick said upon being introduced to her. 'I can see why.' He was a large man, with a large nose, large hands and ears that stuck out from two tufts of unruly grey hair. 'You are an uncommonly beautiful young woman. I'll wager the young bucks are beating a path to your door.' His bushy eyebrows twitched as his hand closed hot and heavy around hers. 'I know I would, had you been part of *my* circle thirty years ago.'

'Put the poor girl down, Wallace, you'll give her nightmares,' Lady Chiswick said with a long-suffering sigh. 'You must forgive my husband, Miss Vallois. He is just returned from safari and killing wild animals always tends to fire his imagination. So, are you and your brother enjoying your visit to London?'

'Yes, very much,' Sophie said, disengaging her hand as tactfully as possible. 'There is so much to see and do.'

'London is the finest city in the world,' Lady Chiswick said proudly. 'I wasn't at all impressed with Paris when I went to visit my brother and sister-in-law there last year. The filth was appalling.'

'When did you go?' Lavinia asked.

'December. Wretched time to travel, but my niece horrified everyone by falling in love with some well-to-do Frenchman and marrying him. Shocking mess. Constance insisted I be there to lend the family moral support.'

Sophie felt a chill run down her spine. *Constance... and a December wedding.* It had to be a coincidence...

'Naturally, my brother wasn't at all happy,' Lady Chiswick was saying. 'The moment Georgina left on her wedding trip, he sold the house, packed up all their belongings and brought the entire household back to England. I think he was afraid his son and youngest daughter might do something equally foolish. He vowed none of them would ever set foot on French soil again.'

Sophie closed her eyes. Constance Grant-Ogilvy had had three children: one son and two daughters.

The wilful, eldest daughter had been called Georgina, and before Sophie had left their employ, Georgina had hinted that she was in love with a man of whom her parents would not approve.

It *had* to be the same family. And if they were related to Lady Chiswick, they might well be here tonight...

'Sophie, are you feeling all right?' Lavinia asked softly. 'You've suddenly gone quite pale.'

'Have I?'

'Probably the heat,' Lady Chiswick said. 'It always affects the newcomers. Have you smelling salts with you, dear?'

'No! That is, thank you, but...that won't be necessary,' Sophie said haltingly. 'I just need some air.'

'Why don't you take a turn around the garden?' Lavinia suggested. 'The night air should put some colour back in your cheeks.'

'Excellent idea, Lady Longworth,' Lady Chiswick said. 'You'll find the entrance through there, Miss Vallois. I'm sure a few minutes will be all you need.'

Sophie inclined her head, grateful for the opportunity to escape. But as she headed towards the French doors that led out into the garden, she knew she needed more than air. She needed to get out of this house. Now... before anything dreadful happened. She hadn't told anyone of her reasons for leaving Mrs Grant-Ogilvy's employ. Accusing the eldest son of inappropriate behaviour was never a recommended course of action for a servant. After all, what an Englishman did on his own property was nobody's business but his own. Sophie had been told that more than once. Fortunately, Eldon hadn't succeeded in ravishing her. She'd been too quick for him. And several well-placed jabs from her elbow had been enough to cool his ardour, as had the veiled threat that she carried a pistol and knew how to use it.

But the fear that *one* day he might catch her off guard had eventually forced Sophie to turn in her notice, and she had left that very day. As expected, Mrs Grant-Ogilvy had been furious. She'd vowed that Sophie would never find work with a decent family again, and had gleefully predicted that she would be on the streets within a week—which, of course, she hadn't. With several good clients bringing her custom on a regular basis, and the small amount of money Antoine brought in, they were able to get by. She didn't need the pittance Mrs Grant-Ogilvy paid her, and she certainly didn't need her snooty disdain—

'Miss Vallois?'

Sophie looked up, startled to see Robert coming towards her. 'Mr Silverton. What are you doing out here?'

'I could ask you the same thing.' He walked along a winding path illuminated by candles set in metal boxes. 'Shouldn't you be inside mingling?'

'Probably, but the room grew unbearably hot.' Sophie frowned. 'I vow English hostesses vie with one another to see who can squeeze the greatest number of people into their houses.'

'It is an ongoing competition,' Robert agreed. Stopping before her, he rested his foot on the stone bench. 'I was taking a walk in the lower garden, wrestling with my thoughts.'

Wrestling with his thoughts? Sophie stared into the dark waters of the ornamental pond, convinced that his thoughts couldn't be half as troubling as hers. For one thing, he wouldn't be worrying about a proposal of marriage from an unwanted suitor, complete with thinly veiled threats of retribution should she refuse. He also wouldn't be troubled by the knowledge that her hostess was related to her former employer, and that the latter might well be in the house tonight. And he certainly wouldn't be worrying about the fact that he had discovered her here, alone in a moonlit garden, with thoughts running through her mind that were both sweet…and forbidden.

'I wasn't aware you were here,' she said, adding feebly, 'I didn't see Jane inside.'

'Jane didn't come with me.' He looked pained for a moment. 'We had words the other morning and she decided to stay home.'

'Words? I find it hard to imagine you and Jane having an argument.'

'Nevertheless, it does happen. I am not the perfect brother Jane would have you believe.'

'We are none of us perfect,' Sophie said distantly. 'I am constantly amazed by the number of mistakes I make. I thought as I got older they would diminish.'

His laughter was as soft as the night air. 'We all like to think we improve with age, but somehow, I suspect it's more wishful thinking than anything else. But I cannot imagine a lady who wishes to float down the Amazon in a boat, or ride in a hot-air balloon, being overly concerned with mistakes.' He straightened, then came to sit down beside her. 'Jane thinks you're marvellous.'

'She does?'

'Oh, yes. You're the closest friend she's ever had. People tend not to want to associate with those who are afflicted in some way,' he said quietly. 'I suppose it's the law of the jungle. Only the strong survive. The weak are weeded out and destroyed.'

'You mustn't speak of her that way!'

'Who better? I know first-hand how cruel people can be, having seen examples of it all my life. Her chances for happiness are few.'

'I think you worry needlessly, Mr Silverton—'

'Robert, please.'

Her heart did a silly little flip. 'Robert. Your sister is a beautiful young woman with a warm and giving nature. She will be loved for those reasons alone.'

'I wish that were the case, but at eight-and-twenty, Jane's chances of marrying well are non-existent and at this stage, her chances of marrying at all are slim. Had she a sizeable portion, I might hold out more hope,' Robert said, 'but much of what we had went to pay off Father's gambling debts. And while we manage well enough, Jane will always be dependent on me for her living. I don't begrudge that for a moment, but I would have liked her to know the sweetness of a husband's love and the joy of holding her own children in her arms.'

Sophie had to turn away lest she reveal too much of her own longings. 'What kind of husband would you wish her to find?'

'One for whom she can feel a deep and abiding love, and who will love her deeply in return. He must respect rather than pity her, for Jane would hate that above all. And he must take her as she is and not look to change her.'

'Do you believe such a man exists?'

'I have to. For her sake, if not for mine.' Robert reached for her hand and slowly raised it to his lips. 'But thank you for being her friend. It means a great deal…to both of us.' Then, turning it over, he pressed a soft, lingering kiss into her palm.

Sophie inhaled sharply. The caress was unexpected…and disturbingly intimate, as was the warmth of his breath on her skin. The air suddenly thickened and grew hot. And when he looked at her…ah, the way he looked at her…

'Miss Vallois?' called a voice from the house. 'Where are you, child? Miss Vallois?'

Sophie gasped, all but wrenching her hand back. 'Lady Chiswick!'

'Does she know you're out here?' Robert asked.

'I'm afraid so.'

His expletive made her blush. 'Then it's best she not find us alone. We don't need *both* of us being shunned by good society. Come, I'll take you back inside.'

Unfortunately, barely had they stood up before Lavinia, Lady Chiswick and Mr Oberon appeared in the doorway. 'Miss Vallois!' Lady Chiswick cried in horror. 'Alone in the garden with a man? What is the meaning of this?'

'Well, well, if it isn't my old friend,' Mr Oberon murmured. 'Enjoying a moonlight rendezvous in the garden. How terribly romantic.'

'It wasn't a rendezvous!' Sophie said, glad for the darkness that hid her blush. 'Mr Silverton and I met quite by—'

'Mr *Silverton*?' Lady Chiswick wheezed. '*Robert* Silverton?'

'Yes, that's right,' Robert said, frowning. 'Is something wrong?'

'There most definitely is.' Lady Chiswick's eyes went

as hard as bits of stone. 'How *dare* you show your face in my house, sir! You were most definitely *not* invited.'

'As a matter of fact, he was,' Mr Oberon said smoothly. 'By your husband. I delivered the invitation myself.'

The lady turned an alarming shade of red. 'My husband does *not* extend invitations to my gatherings, Mr Oberon. And even if he was foolish enough to do so, Mr Silverton should have had the decency to decline.' The lady's voice dropped to a sepulchral tone. 'He is guilty of the *most* unconscionable behaviour towards my goddaughter—'

'Goddaughter?' Lavinia said…and then gasped. 'Oh, dear Lord. Lady Mary Kelsey is your *goddaughter*?'

'Yes, she is, and she has been treated abominably by this man! I want you out of my house, sir. Now!'

'But, surely you are being too harsh, Lady Chiswick,' Lavinia said, quickly drawing the glass doors closed behind them.

'Do not try to placate me, Lady Longworth. If a member of *your* family had been treated in such a manner, you would feel as I do. My poor Mary did nothing to deserve the treatment she received at this man's hands.' She pointed a bony finger at Robert. 'Leave my house at once, sir!'

'*Le bon Dieu*, how can you be so cruel?' Sophie said, shaken by the woman's ferocity. 'Mr Silverton is a gentleman—'

'He is a bounder, Miss Vallois, and you would do well not to waste your time defending him!'

'Miss Vallois is not defending me.' Robert's quiet voice cut through the night like the blade of a scimitar. 'She is speaking from the goodness of her heart and without knowledge of what happened.' He turned to glare at Oberon. 'Unlike some people who know very well.'

'No, he is *not* a bounder,' Sophie said emphatically. 'He would not have ended his engagement to Lady Mary unless he had a very good reason.'

'A good *reason*?' Lady Chiswick was close to apoplectic. 'There is no *good* reason except that he is a selfish and fickle man!'

Sophie's temper flared. 'He is none of those things! He is fine and decent and—'

'Miss *Beaudoin*? What on earth are *you* doing here?'

No one had heard the French doors open, but the commanding voice that rang across the terrace instantly silenced all arguments. Sophie just closed her eyes. She had no need to turn around to see who the newcomer was. She would have recognised that imperious voice anywhere!

'What is the meaning of this, Eudora?' Mrs Constance Grant-Ogilvy demanded of her sister-in-law. 'What is Miss Beaudoin doing here and why is she dressed like that?'

The woman's enunciation would have put an Oxford scholar to shame, and for the first time that evening, Lady Chiswick seemed completely flummoxed. 'I have no idea what you're talking about, Constance. This is Miss Sophie Vallois. She and her brother are here as guests of Lord and Lady Longworth.'

'Sophie Vallois? What are you talking about, the girl's name is Chantal Beaudoin and she is a French seamstress,' Mrs Grant-Ogilvy informed her. 'I employed her to teach the girls French.'

'Well, well, it would seem we have a case of double

identity,' Mr Oberon murmured. 'Perhaps we should give the young lady a chance to explain herself.'

Lady Chiswick drew herself up. 'Well, Miss Vallois. What have you to say for yourself?'

Sophie pressed her hand to her stomach, feeling it pitch and roll a thousand times worse than when she'd been on board ship. 'I—'

'You don't have to answer that, Sophie,' Lavinia said. 'It's nobody's business but your own.'

'No, it's all right, Lavinia.' Sophie knew she had no recourse. She had to be honest. 'Mrs Grant-Ogilvy is not mistaken. I *am* Sophie Vallois, but I was using the name Chantal Beaudoin when she hired me.'

'Then you *did* work for my sister-in-law,' Lady Chiswick hissed. 'And you admit to changing your name. Why?'

'I really don't think that matters,' Robert said, stepping forward. 'It is enough that Miss Vallois told you the truth.'

'On the contrary, I should think the reasons for *pretending* to be someone else always matter,' Mr Oberon said silkily.

'Stay out of this, Oberon,' Robert snapped. 'You've already said quite enough. Miss Vallois, allow me to take you home.'

'Not without answering my question!' Lady Chiswick barked.

Robert dismissed her with a glance. 'With your permission, Lady Longworth?'

'Thank you, Mr Silverton, but I think it's time we all left.' For once, Lavinia's eyes were as cold and as hard as ice. 'I suddenly find the atmosphere oppressive and the company…suffocating.'

Lady Chiswick gasped. 'Well, I *never*!'

Robert walked up to Sophie and held out his arm. 'Miss Vallois?'

His voice was soft, the way it had been when they'd been alone in the garden. In silence, Sophie tucked her hand into the crook of his arm, feeling the much-needed strength of his body beneath her fingers. Warm. Firm. Reassuring. And with Lavinia on her other side, they walked across the terrace and into the house.

'You're doing well,' Robert whispered as they passed through the crowds of milling guests. 'Keep your head up and don't give them the satisfaction of seeing you break.'

Sophie nodded, reminding herself to keep breathing. Thankfully, the further they moved into the house, the fewer people turned to look. Obviously, Mrs Grant-Ogilvy's voice had only carried so far, but by the time they reached the street, Sophie was trembling. Nicholas was already there with the carriage and she let herself be bundled inside, felt a warm rug placed over her knees. As the carriage drew away, Sophie turned to see Robert standing alone on the street and felt her heart break at the expression on his face. It was all out now. Her make-believe castle was in ruins. The dragon had come—and he had come breathing fire.

Antoine and Lavinia were still in the breakfast parlour when Sophie finally came down the next morning. She had passed a restless night and barely touched the breakfast tray Lavinia had sent up. Her stomach was in knots, her mind spinning like a top. So much had happened. Mr Oberon's shocking revelations and equally disturbing proposal. Lady Chiswick's embarrassing discovery of her and Robert on the terrace, followed by the nightmarish appearance of Mrs Grant-Ogilvy.

And Robert, kissing her hand in the garden. Robert, walking strong and confident beside her. How fiercely she clung to that memory. To the remembrance of him putting his hand over hers and squeezing it gently during that long, endless walk. If it hadn't been for him...

'Sophie! Good morning,' Lavinia greeted her. 'Banyon, fresh coffee and toast, if you please.'

'No, just...coffee,' Sophie said. 'Thank you.'

The elderly servant nodded and withdrew. Lavinia turned back and her expression was deeply concerned. 'Did you get any sleep at all?'

'Not much,' Sophie admitted. 'But then I don't suppose any of us did.'

'That wretched Lady Chiswick,' Lavinia said, fuming. 'And that insufferable Mrs Grant-Ogilvy. I wanted to knock their heads together!'

Sophie managed a smile as she sank into a chair. Under normal circumstances, she would have laughed at seeing the usually unflappable Lavinia in a state of such high dudgeon. But given the situation, it was hard to imagine laughing at anything. 'Thank you, Lavinia, but Mrs Grant-Ogilvy was perfectly within her rights to question me. I *was* Chantal Beaudoin when I worked for her, so her confusion is understandable. Imagine if you were to see Banyon dressed in formal attire, pretending to be someone else and hobnobbing with lords and ladies at a society gathering. I dare say you would have had something to say too.'

'But you were there as our *guest*,' Lavinia said. 'You weren't pretending to be someone else.'

'Mrs Grant-Ogilvy thought I was.'

'It's all my fault,' Antoine said unhappily. 'After we left Bayencourt, I thought it would be safer if we changed our names. People were looking for Sophie and Antoine Vallois, not Chantal and Henri Beaudoin. And, when the months passed and nobody came, I saw no reason to change them back. I only did so after Sophie left Mrs Grant-Ogilvy's employ so it would be easier if she wanted to find work.'

Sophie closed her eyes, feeling a return of the headache that had plagued her for the past three hours. She couldn't help wondering how Robert was feeling this morning. He had been humiliated too. What he was thinking now? Was he remembering the events of last night and wishing he'd never met her? Or was he remembering, like her, the sweetness of that kiss…?

'Is Nicholas home?' She pushed the memory away, aware that it hurt too much. 'I should speak with him as soon as possible.'

'He's in the library, but won't you have something to eat first?'

Sophie glanced at the plates of food set out along the sideboard and shook her head. Even if she had any appetite for food, it was more important that she speak to Nicholas. A piece of toast and a helping of eggs wasn't going to make explaining last night's débâcle any the more palatable.

Nicholas stood up as soon as she entered, the lines on his face reflecting the depth of his concern. 'Sophie, dear girl. How are you?'

'I've been better,' Sophie admitted as she closed the door. 'You don't look to have slept much.'

'What little sleep I did get was punctuated by uncharitable thoughts of those two dreadful women!' he growled. 'I'm so sorry about what happened last night. I would have done anything in my power to have prevented it.'

'There was nothing anyone *could* have done, Nicholas. Who was to know that Lady Chiswick was Mrs Grant-Ogilvy's sister-in-law? *And* Lady Mary Kelsey's godmother? Certainly not you or I.'

'No, and I suppose we must be exceedingly grateful that Lady Annabelle Durst and a friend happened to be in the garden when you and Robert were discovered,' Nicholas said, 'or the consequences would have been considerably worse.'

Sophie's brow furrowed. 'Lady Annabelle was *in the garden*?'

'Yes. Didn't you see her?'

'No. And Rob—Mr Silverton made no mention of her being there.'

'Perhaps he didn't know. But apparently, after we left Lady Chiswick's last night, Lady Annabelle made sure everyone knew that she had been in full sight of you and Mr Silverton the entire time, and that nothing inappropriate had taken place.'

It was almost too much to believe. Once again, the lady had come to her rescue. Sophie was beginning to wonder if Lady Annabelle wasn't some kind of...fairy godmother!

'I don't care as much for myself,' she said, 'but I do regret the embarrassment this will surely cause you and Lavinia. Soon all of London will know that I was employed by Mrs Grant-Ogilvy, pretending to be someone else, and that I had the audacity to mingle with guests at the home of her sister-in-law. To say nothing of poor Mr Silverton's disgrace at the hands of that dreadful Lady Chiswick.'

Nicholas sighed. 'Lady Chiswick has never been one of my favourite people, but she was perfectly within her rights to ask him to leave, Sophie. He should never have gone there in the first place.'

'But if he wasn't aware of the relationship between Lady Chiswick and Lady Mary, he cannot be held to blame,' Sophie said, stung by Nicholas's unexpected criticism. 'He is not the type of man who would knowingly offend anyone.'

'Nevertheless, ignorance does not absolve him of guilt. What he did to Lady Mary put him beyond the pale.' Nicholas leaned back against the edge of the desk, propping his hands on either side of his hips. 'Had he gone ahead and honoured his obligation to her—'

'But if she was the cause of the rift—'

'Had he gone ahead and married Lady Mary,' Nicholas repeated gently, 'none of this would have happened. A man's word is his bond and a promise, once given, cannot be retracted.'

'Not even if there is just cause?'

Nicholas sighed. 'Sometimes, not even then. However, the important thing is that *you* did nothing wrong, and that you told the truth in the face of a very difficult situation. That took courage and I'm proud of you, Sophie. Lavinia and I both are.'

'Then you're not sorry you invited me to come to London?'

'Sorry? My dear girl, you've brought us nothing but joy and I know Lavinia is dreading the thought of you going home. Frankly, so am I, but I'm not supposed to show it. Now, why don't you go and have something to eat? I'm sure you had nothing before you came to see me and you didn't have much last night. Then, later on, you and I will sit down and have a little talk about your future.'

'My future?'

'Yes. If it's not to be marriage, we must look at alternatives.' Nicholas put both hands on her shoulders. 'We just want you to be happy, Sophie. And we're willing to do whatever it takes to make that happen.'

It was with decidedly mixed feelings that Sophie accompanied Lavinia to the drapers shortly after lunch. She had already received a note from Robert, saying that, under the circumstances, it was probably best they not go to the museum together, and she had quickly sent one back, saying how sorry she was that the excursion had to be postponed. She'd added a postscript that she deeply regretted *most* of what had taken place the previous evening, and hoped he would be able to read through the lines to see that the time they'd spent alone in the garden…and his kiss…were definitely *not* part of her regrets.

Now, as she wandered up and down the well-stocked aisles, trying to pretend an interest in the brightly coloured bolts of fabric, lethargically looking at lace, she was unable to order her thoughts—

'…of course, it's not as though she ever *had* much of a chance of making a good marriage,' a lady standing with her back to Sophie said. 'Her being crippled and all. But it's shocking behaviour all the same…'

*Crippled.* Sophie's head slowly came up. Two ladies were chatting a few feet away from her. Neither one was known to her, but the fact they were talking about a single, crippled lady made the idea of doing the polite thing and moving away unthinkable.

She edged a little closer, suddenly very interested in a roll of elegant Alençon lace…

'Still, it's only speculation she went to his rooms,' the taller lady said. 'No one's come forward to say they actually saw it happen.'

'But if a gentleman's word can't be taken as truth, whose can? And when I was at Mrs Coldham's yesterday afternoon, three of the ladies were saying there was talk of her meeting that tall dark fellow in the park.'

Sophie's blood ran cold. Surely they weren't talking about *Jane*?

'It will be the ruin of her, of course,' the first lady said. 'She won't be accepted by good society now. Mrs Coldham said as much and no one disagreed with her. I dare say her brother will have no choice but to send her down to the country. And *if* he's fortunate enough to marry, which is doubtful given what he did to poor Lady Mary Kelsey, his wife will have the business of looking after her, and I don't envy her that.'

'Still, it is very sad,' the second lady said. 'I always thought so well of Miss Silverton. She seemed such a genteel young lady, and so well brought up. Certainly her mother was. But judging from the stories, she's not at all what we thought…'

The women carried on talking, but Sophie had heard more than enough. Forgetting her own concerns and dropping all pretence of shopping, she quickly went to find Lavinia, who had been standing too far away to hear any of it. 'Lavinia, I've just overheard the most appalling conversation.'

'Dear girl, whatever is the matter? You've gone as white as a sheet.'

'Come outside. I have no wish to speak of it here.'

Lavinia dropped the bolt of cloth she had been studying and the two quickly made their way into the street. Once Sophie was sure the other ladies were still inside, she told Lavinia all she had learned—and watched Lavinia's face go white. 'And you're sure you heard them say Jane's name?'

'Quite sure. At first, when they spoke of the lady being crippled, I hoped they were talking about someone else. But once they mentioned her name, there certainly wasn't any doubt.'

'This is very serious indeed,' Lavinia said. 'They actually *said* Jane went to a gentleman's rooms?'

'They did, though it was only speculation.' Sophie kept her voice low. 'But apparently several people saw her talking to a gentleman in the park.'

'Quite likely, for I know that Jane often takes the trap and drives out on her own. But she would *never* go to a gentleman's rooms. Even the rumour of such behaviour would be enough to ruin her.'

'Unfortunately, that is the rumour now circulating,' Sophie said. 'The ladies said Mr Silverton would have no choice but to take her down to the country.'

'Oh dear, this is dreadful.'

'Are we to tell her?' Sophie asked.

'Not yet. I am expected at a poetry reading at Lady Henley's later today,' Lavinia said. 'No doubt it will be well attended and I shall make discreet enquiries as to how far the rumours have spread. But if it's true, we will have no choice but to tell Jane and her brother. They must be made aware of what is being said and given a

chance to refute it. Even so, I fear it may be too late.'
Lavinia's expression said it all. 'Jane's reputation may
be lost to all hope of salvation.'

# Chapter Eleven

Sadly, upon Lavinia's returning home later that afternoon, Sophie discovered it was worse than either of them thought.

'Of course, no one seems willing to say who saw Jane enter the gentleman's rooms,' Lavinia said, hardly able to contain her anger. 'Speculation has it that a well-placed gentleman let it slip at one of the clubs, whereupon it soon became common knowledge at all the rest. Then it found its way into the drawing rooms of society.'

'But why will no one say which "well-placed gentleman" made the comment?' Sophie asked.

'Because that's not the way it's done.' Lavinia pulled off her gloves. 'Some misplaced notion of honour amongst thieves, I suppose. Besides, it doesn't matter. Several other people saw Jane speaking to a gentleman in the park, and when you add that to what I truly believe is an out-and-out lie, the damage is done.'

'Did they say who the gentleman in the park was?'

'Several names were mentioned, but no one could say

for certain. And there is no way of knowing if it is the same man whose rooms she is reputed to have visited.'

'I cannot believe this,' Sophie said. 'Who would wish to harm Jane in such a cruel and inhumane way?'

Lavinia sighed. 'I don't know, but I fear we have no choice. We must pay a call on Jane and Robert as soon as possible. They must be made aware of what is being said.' She walked towards the window and drew the curtain aside. She was quiet for a long time. 'I feel terribly guilty for saying this, but it seems one good thing has come out of all this.'

'What's that?'

Lavinia turned and gave her a crooked smile. 'Nobody is talking about what happened at Lady Chiswick's any more.'

Fortunately, both Jane and Robert were at home when Lavinia and Sophie paid their call half an hour later. Jane was reading in the drawing room, and Robert came down shortly thereafter. He was dressed for going out and looked exceedingly handsome in his black-and-white evening attire. Sophie couldn't help wondering where he was going and who he was going to see. Lady Annabelle Durst, perhaps? To thank her for speaking up on their behalf? Or for reasons of his own...

'I'm sorry to be calling so late,' Lavinia said when the four of them were seated in the drawing room, 'but I thought it best not to waste any time.'

'You appear distraught, Lady Longworth,' Robert said. 'Has this something to do with what happened at Lady Chiswick's?'

'I fear this is actually worse. It seems, Mr Silverton, that someone is out to damage your sister's reputation.'

And with as much detail as she could provide, Lavinia told them what she knew of the situation.

The clatter of Jane's cane falling to the floor made everyone jump. But when Sophie saw the girl slump forward in her chair, she quickly ran to her side. 'Jane!'

Lavinia was on her feet. 'Smelling salts?'

Robert nodded. 'I'll fetch them.'

Sophie clutched the girl's limp body in her arms. '*Sapristi!* If I ever find out who did this—'

'Calm yourself, Sophie, we will find out,' Lavinia said. 'For now we must keep our wits about us.'

Sophie nodded. 'Help me sit her back up.'

'Salts,' Robert said, coming in and handing them over.

'Thank you.' Lavinia removed the lid and held them under Jane's nose.

The effect was immediate. The girl's head snapped up and her eyes flew open, only to fill at once with tears.

'No, Jane, you mustn't cry,' Sophie said as Lavinia handed the bottle back to Robert. 'We shall ask the maid for tea—'

'No! I don't want anyone to come in!' Jane cried.

'But you must have something!'

Robert walked to the sideboard and poured a glass of brandy. 'Here, dearest,' he said, handing it to her. 'The fire will put some colour back in your cheeks.'

Jane took the glass and gazed up at her brother through her tears. 'It's not true, Robert. I swear it's not true. I have never visited any gentleman in his rooms. I would never—'

'I know.' His smile was infinitely gentle. 'It never

occurred to me you would. And we *will* get to the bottom of this.'

'Robert, I'm so sorry,' Lavinia said, 'but we thought you needed to know what was being said.'

'I am grateful to you and Miss Vallois for having the courage to come and tell us.' He paused. 'Given what happened at Lady Chiswick's, I would understand you preferring to have nothing more to do with me.'

Sophie and Lavinia exchanged a glance. 'Mr Silverton,' Lavinia said, 'were you aware of the relationship between Lady Mary Kelsey and Lady Chiswick before you went to Lady Chiswick's house?'

'No. I wasn't even acquainted with Lord or Lady Chiswick. I went at Oberon's insistence. He told me Lord Chiswick was most anxious to show me his collection of hunting trophies.'

'Hunting trophies.' Lavinia sniffed. 'God help you if *all* your friends are so caring of your welfare, Mr Silverton. However, having now established that you did not wilfully intend to provoke Lady Chiswick, and with Lady Annabelle's assurances that you and Sophie were not alone in the garden, I think we can dismiss the matter. The fact that people know Sophie was employed by Mrs Grant-Ogilvy is a trifling matter at best. Your sister's defamation is what we must now turn our attention to.'

'At least now I know why I was getting such strange looks at the club this afternoon,' Robert murmured. A shutter dropped down over his eyes. 'I know it is an imposition, but would it be possible for one of you to stay with Jane for a little while? I have to go out.'

'I'll stay,' Sophie said, disappointed that his social

engagement should take precedence over Jane's predicament. 'And it is no imposition.'

His smile rested on her for a moment, the tenderness of his gaze causing her pulse to beat erratically. 'Thank you. I shall return as quickly as possible. Jane, will you be all right without me?'

Wearily, Jane nodded. With a last look at Sophie, he left, closing the door behind him.

'Well, I suppose I had best go and apprise Nicholas of what's happened,' Lavinia said, getting to her feet. 'Perhaps he can find out more details. Send word when you want the carriage, Sophie, but stay as long as you need. Goodnight, Jane. Try to get some rest.'

'Thank you, Lady Longworth, I will.'

With a nod, Sophie closed the door. When she turned back, it was to see a trace of colour seeping back into Jane's pallid cheeks. The brandy, no doubt. 'Don't worry, Jane,' Sophie said, sitting down beside her. 'Your brother will not allow these lies to be perpetuated. This will all be put to rights.'

'Unfortunately, the damage is already done,' Jane said quietly. 'You don't know how society works, Sophie. From what you've told me, it is my word against a gentleman's and society will never take mine over his. I know what they say about me. That I am a cripple and that...I shall never marry. They probably think I had no *choice* but to throw myself at a man in such a way.'

'No one who knows you would ever believe such lies!' Sophie said fiercely. 'I cannot imagine who would wish to hurt you like this.'

'Perhaps Lady Mary has decided to take her revenge,' Jane said. 'If I have no hope of marrying, Robert will be for ever forced to look after me.' She sniffed and reached for her handkerchief. 'I can't imagine what your brother must think.'

'I'm not sure Antoine knows. He and Nicholas were out most of the afternoon.'

'He will hear soon enough,' Jane said, fresh tears welling. 'And he must have nothing to do with me, lest he be the one people believe I visited and his own reputation suffers as a result.'

'But he doesn't even *keep* rooms in London.'

'No one will care about that. They will say he rented a room for the night, or borrowed a friend's home. They will say he compromised me beyond all hope of redemption. Only think what that will do to his reputation.'

'I don't imagine he would care greatly,' Sophie said. 'I've seen the way he looks at you, Jane. And the way you look at him.'

This time when the girl's cheeks reddened, Sophie knew it had nothing to do with the brandy. 'Is it really so obvious?' Jane asked.

'It is to me. I'm not sure it is to anyone else.'

Jane was silent for a time, twisting her handkerchief around and around in her hands. 'I'm so sorry, Sophie. I think I lost my heart to Antoine the first time I saw him. I'm sure you can understand why.'

Yes, Sophie could, though her acceptance of it made it no better for any of them. 'Has he made you any promises?'

'He knows he cannot. Without my brother's consent, it would be impossible for us to marry and Antoine does not wish to incur Robert's anger. Besides, he has to return very soon to France and I cannot go with him.'

'Oh, Jane, I wish I knew what to say.'

'There is nothing to say. The circumstances are all

wrong.' Jane's voice was light, but her eyes were filled with sadness. 'I'm not the first woman to love a man she cannot have and I certainly won't be the last.'

'You make it sound so final.'

'I learned a long time ago that life isn't always fair. But I will have the memory of his love, and I believe he will remember me when he returns to France. I just worry what he will think when he hears these dreadful stories.'

'He will think the same as the rest of us,' Sophie reassured her. 'He will *not* believe these lies. Indeed, he will be as furious as your brother.' She thought about the look on Robert's face as he'd walked out the door. 'And something tells me Mr Silverton in a temper is not a thing *any* man would wish to experience.'

There was only one thought on Robert's mind as he strode into Oberon's favourite hell—and it was not charitable. It became even less so when he found his enemy in one of the upstairs rooms seated at a table with four other men, all of them titled, all of them rip-roaring drunk.

'Silver! What a surprise!' Oberon called around the whore in his lap. 'Hutton, give Silver your chair—'

'I'm not here to gamble,' Robert said. 'I've come for a word with you.'

'Perhaps later. As you can see, I'm very busy—'

'Now!' Robert gently, but firmly, pulled the half-naked woman from Oberon's lap. 'In private or I'll know the reason why.'

In an instant, Oberon's smile disappeared. He glanced at the faces of the men seated around the table, aware of the curiosity burning in their eyes, and said,

'Very well. But you'd better have a damn good explanation for this.'

'Trust me. I do.'

Oberon downed the rest of his brandy. He stood up and led the way out of the room into the darkened corridor. Stopping at a second door, he opened it and they walked into a room that looked to be an office. 'Now, what's this all about—'

'You know damn well what it's about.' Robert slammed the door. 'Someone's been spreading lies about Jane.'

'Really? I can't imagine who would do such a thing,' Oberon said.

'Can't you? A name leaped immediately to *my* mind.'

The cobra reared up, its black eyes as cold as the death it would surely deal. 'Careful, my friend. Damaging stories can be told about a gentleman as well as a lady.'

'So you admit to telling lies about my sister.'

'Who is to say what is truth and what is a lie? Certainly not those who listen with equal fervour to both. But I admit to nothing,' Oberon snapped. 'And if you attempt to put it about that I did, you *will* suffer the consequences. To call the son of a peer a liar is a serious offence.'

'No more serious than destroying the reputation of an innocent young woman.'

'If such is the case, I am sorry for you, Silver. But don't say I didn't warn you.'

It was as good as an admission of guilt—and they both knew it. 'You won't get away with this,' Robert said. 'As God is my witness, I *will* bring you down.'

He left before the man had a chance to respond, fearing that if Oberon said another word, he would call him out on the spot. Duelling might have been outlawed in England, but there were still places where it could be done and circumstances under which it would be forgiven. Robert had a feeling that before this despicable affair was over, he would be intimately acquainted with both.

It was several hours before Robert was of a mood to go home. He wandered through the empty streets, too angry to be of comfort to Jane, too incensed by the nature of injustice done to be pleasant company for Sophie.

*Sophie.* He couldn't even think about her in the same breath as Oberon, that cunning, immoral bastard. How like him to try to turn this back on Robert. As though it was his fault Jane should be made to suffer. The man had no more conscience than a corpse, and thinking of that brought to mind something else he'd once told Robert...

*'I hold people's lives in the palm of my hand and offer them back in exchange for a favour. No one cares if making good on that favour destroys someone else's happiness. All they care about is restoring their own. So it all comes down to choice. The question is...whose happiness will it be? And what price are they willing to pay?'*

Certainly not the happiness of the person who'd gambled it away in the first place, Robert acknowledged bitterly.

He was so lost in thought that he didn't see the person stumbling towards him until they actually collided. 'Watch where you're going, man!' Robert grunted, already reaching for the dagger concealed in his sleeve. London after dark was a dangerous place, rife with pickpockets and thieves. But when he looked up to see the face of his would-be attacker, he realised it wasn't a thief at all. It was Lawrence Welton. 'Lawrence, are you all right?'

The poor fellow looked ghastly. His face was riddled with lines and his eyes were two dark, shadowy pools of despair. 'You're not well. Let me call you a carriage.'

Welton looked up, his eyes finally focusing. 'S-Silverton?'

'Yes. I'm going to take you home—'

'Can't,' the man muttered. 'Not…mine…'

Welton had obviously been drinking heavily. He sagged and would have fallen had Robert not caught him and held him up. 'You need a doctor!'

'Nothing a doctor can f-fix,' the young man said, his words badly slurred. 'Owns it all…'

'Who owns it?'

'Trusted him, you s-see. But it was…all lies. Should have checked…' Welton went on, his eyes glazed, his mouth slack. 'Nothing left.'

Robert's mouth tightened in anger. He'd never seen Welton in such a state. One thing he knew for sure, he couldn't leave the man alone in the middle of the street, at the mercy of pickpockets and thugs. Instead, he hailed a hackney and gave the driver Welton's address. Once inside, he tried to get the information he needed. 'Lawrence, who did this to you?'

'Thought he was…m'friend,' the man mumbled, shaking his head. 'Enemy, more like.' Then he laughed—a rough, grating sound that was filled with despair. 'Stuck a knife in my back.'

'Then you must speak to someone. If you've been cheated—'

'Never prove it…' He unsteadily raised his hand and pointed a finger at Robert. 'Not a friend of yours.'

He passed out soon after—which made getting him out of the carriage even more difficult. Had it not been for the help of Welton's valet, Robert wasn't sure he would have managed. And once inside the house, it took both of them to get the poor man up the stairs and into his bed.

'I'll see to him now, sir,' the valet said. 'Thank you for bringing him home.'

'It's Finch, isn't it?'

'That's right, sir.'

'Is your master in trouble? He mentioned something about…losing it all.'

The valet's face fell. 'So it's happened. I feared it might. But he kept on saying the gentleman wouldn't do it.'

'What gentleman?' Feeling completely in the dark, Robert said, 'Can you tell me what's going on?'

'He wouldn't wish me to, sir,' the servant said, glancing at Lawrence's unconscious figure. 'A proud man is Mr Welton. Far better than those who've used him.'

It was clear that something very bad had happened to Lawrence Welton and that his servant was reluctant to say anything. Robert could appreciate that. He wouldn't wish his own man to divulge anything of a personal nature with regard to his affairs. 'Please give him my best,' Robert said. 'Tell him I'll call round in the morning to see how he is.'

The valet looked grateful. 'Thank you, sir. I'll do that.'

\* \* \*

As it turned out, however, Welton was not in town the next morning. He sent Robert a note thanking him for his help and informing him that he was removing to the country for an indefinite period of time. The letter was brief, the handwriting that of a man unsteady of mind and body...

...no doubt you will hear soon enough that I have been ruined. The details do not matter, the fault is my own. I should have known better than to deal with the devil. But I deeply regret that other truths will never be known and that innocent people will be made to suffer. Beware the company you keep, Robert, for serpents hide behind handsome eyes...

Robert dropped the letter on the table— '...*serpents hide behind handsome eyes.*' He would have had to have been blind not to understand that reference.

Oberon!

'Excuse me, miss, but Mr Oberon is asking to see you,' Banyon said from the doorway of the drawing room.

Sophie stiffened, the magazine in her hands forgotten. She hadn't seen Oberon since the night of the fiasco at Lady Chiswick's and she wondered why he had come now. No doubt, thoughts of marriage were far from his mind. 'Please tell him I am not at home.'

The butler sighed. 'He said that if that was your answer I was to give you this.' He handed her a sealed note. 'He said it had to do with Miss Silverton.'

Sophie quickly broke the wafer and read the note

through. 'Show him in.' She refolded the note and got to her feet. 'But come back in five minutes with the message that Lady Longworth wishes to see me.'

'Very good, miss.' The butler withdrew, concern etched deep into his normally imperturbable features.

Moments later, Oberon appeared in the doorway. 'Miss Vallois. I hope you will forgive the boldness of my letter, but I knew you would wish to hear what I had to say about Miss Silverton.'

Sophie nodded, her mouth as dry as old paper. 'I am interested, of course, though I am surprised you would wish to come here after what happened at Lady Chiswick's.'

'Yes, a most unfortunate incident for all concerned,' Oberon said, not quite meeting her eyes. 'Truths revealed in such a way always leave a bitter aftertaste. But I think we shall put that aside for the moment. I've come to talk to you about Miss Silverton and the tragic situation in which she finds herself.'

Sophie's hand tightened on the parchment. 'It is only tragic because it is all lies.'

'Unfortunately, it is the word of a gentleman against hers,' Oberon said. 'A well to do gentleman, so my sources inform me.'

Sophie stilled. 'Do you know who he is?'

'What would you do if I said I did? Beg that I might tell you so you could go and confront him?'

'Most certainly! I would tell him to his face that he was a coward and demand that he exonerate Miss Silverton at once!'

'My word, such passion,' Oberon mused. 'If I were Miss Silverton, I would consider myself fortunate in having your friendship.'

'It is I who consider myself fortunate in having hers,' Sophie answered. 'Someone has told a hurtful and outrageous lie. Jane would *never* behave in such a manner. Surely you know that. You, who have been acquainted with her *and* her brother for such a long time.'

'Yes, I have known them, and I agree they are both exceptionally good people—which is why I've come to see you. I have a proposition for you.'

Her eyes opened wide. 'A proposition.'

'Yes. A few days ago, I asked you to accept my proposal of marriage.'

'Which, given what you learned at Lady Chiswick's, you now wish to retract.'

'Not exactly.' Oberon strolled around the room, his hands linked loosely behind his back. 'Though I was not…pleased to learn of your former employment, I am willing to overlook it. You would not be the first governess to be raised to the position of a nobleman's wife. As to the confusion over your…identity, I seem to remember Jane once mentioning that your middle name was Chantal, and I suspect Beaudoin to be a maiden name, perhaps on your mother's side?'

Sophie suddenly felt cold, as though an icy draught had blown through the room. 'Yes, that's right.'

'So in essence, you told no lies at all.'

'Perhaps not, but what of my claim that I do not love you?'

'*Love.* That is the *least* of my concerns,' Oberon said dismissively. 'An antiquated notion, best left to poets and the publishers of gothic romances. *I* am in need of a wife and *you* are an incredibly beautiful woman who has bewitched me in every sense of the word. Therefore,

I make you an offer. *If* I could resolve Miss Silverton's unhappy situation, would you agree to marry me?'

Sophie took a quick, sharp breath. 'Resolve it? How?'

'I am not without influence in society. I know the ears in which to whisper. If I said I could prove the gentleman was lying—?'

'You would do that for Jane?'

'No. I would do it for *you*. All you have to do is say yes. And I will give you three days in which to decide.'

'Three days?' A quiver of fear rippled down Sophie's spine. 'You did not set a time limit on my answer before.'

'I think we both know the circumstances have changed. However, I am willing to make it a week. But do not ask me again.' He turned and slowly closed the distance between them. 'I am far too generous with those I care about—'

'Excuse me, Miss Vallois,' Banyon said, appearing in the open doorway, 'but her ladyship has returned and is asking to see you right away.'

*Dieu merci!* It had been the longest five minutes of her life. 'Thank you, I shall come at once.' Sophie turned back to her visitor, her mind in turmoil. 'Good afternoon, Mr Oberon. Banyon will see you out.'

The dismissal was plain. Oberon bowed, but the look in his eyes was far from amiable. 'Thank you, but I know the way. And I will call again in one week from today, Miss Vallois. When I look forward to hearing the words that will make me…a very happy man.'

## Chapter Twelve

Sophie didn't bother telling Nicholas and Lavinia about Mr Oberon's outrageous offer. What would be the point? They would never advise her to accept it, and in fact would probably have told her she was mad for even hearing the man out! But while refusing his offer was certainly in *her* best interests, what would it do to Jane? *She* was the one who stood to lose everything if the rumours weren't laid to rest.

No, there *had* to be a way around the problem, Sophie reflected as the Longworth carriage rattled and bounced its way to Lady White's town house. The gregarious hostess had again invited the four of them to attend one of her impromptu soirées, and while Antoine had declined, Sophie had accepted with alacrity. She knew that Robert would be there, given that he had once told her that Lady White actually *enjoyed* the notoriety of having him present, and with luck, she might be able to talk to him about her predicament. Maybe he could think of a way to persuade Mr Oberon to help Jane without asking the impossible of her.

It might be grasping at straws, but she was running out of time! She had to convince Mr Oberon to save Jane's reputation without making her agreement to marry him a condition of his doing so. She had to make him understand that marriage without love would be anathema for both of them. Difficult given that he'd already told her love was the purview of poets and penny novelists. But make him understand she would. Because now, more than ever, her future happiness depended on it.

'Nicholas, Lavinia, how lovely to see you both again,' Lady White greeted them. 'And Miss Vallois, looking as elegant as ever. How are you, my dear?' She leaned in close and winked. 'I understand you've been having quite the goings on of late.'

A little embarrassed, Sophie nevertheless managed a smile. 'I'm fine, Lady White.'

'Good, because no one really cares what Eudora Chiswick thinks. She's an insufferable mushroom whose husband only married her because her father made a fortune in trade and the Chiswick estate was falling into total disrepair. You're better than the lot of them and that includes her stuck up sister-in-law, Constance. As for poor Miss Silverton—' Lady White broke off, sighing. 'Now there is a truly unfortunate turn of events. I despaired of the poor child marrying before, but there's not a hope she'll find a husband now. Dreadful state of affairs. I wish I could do something to help. But now, here is our dashing Mr Silverton. I dare say you won't mind spending a little time with him.'

With that, Lady White drew Nicholas and Lavinia away, no doubt to quiz them about exactly what *had* happened on the terrace at Lady Chiswick's, and the details of poor Jane's disgrace.

'She is an incorrigible gossip,' Robert said, 'but she means well. And there are times when we all need the company of those who don't give a damn about society.' His jaw clenched. 'I also knew there was absolutely no chance of running into Oberon here.'

At the mention of the man who held both Jane's future and her own in the palm of his hand, Sophie said, 'I was hoping you would be here tonight, Mr Silverton—'

'I was Robert to you in the garden,' he interrupted quietly. 'Am I not Robert to you any more?'

Sophie felt the familiar quickening of her pulse that told her this was more than just nerves. It went deeper… to a longing she couldn't put a name to. That she was afraid to put a name to. 'Forgive me, but I wasn't sure… after what happened between us at Lady Chiswick's, and I received your note cancelling our outing—'

'Surely you understood why I did that?' Robert said. 'I couldn't allow my desire to see you to add to the stories I feared might already be circulating. We were fortunate Lady Annabelle spoke up on our behalf, but if people saw us together, they would suspect there was… something more. I couldn't risk having you share in my humiliation.'

'But when Lavinia and I came to see you the other night, you left so abruptly,' Sophie said.

'Yes, to see Oberon. I had to meet with him, and it was not pleasant.'

'Oberon!' Sophie said, the name torn from her. 'I am

sick to death of Mr Oberon! Robert, there is something I must speak to you about and it is awkward in the extreme. But I don't know who else to turn to.'

'Come,' he said, lightly putting his hand on her waist. 'I know of a place where we can talk.'

And he did. A few minutes later, Sophie found herself seated across from him at a table in a small alcove just off the drawing room. Five card tables had been set up in the main part of the room, and several foursomes were already engaged in play. Conversation was brisk, laughter was frequent, and though Sophie and Robert were separate from the rest, there was no question of their being alone. Robert was right. Neither of them could afford a repeat of what had happened in the garden at Lady Chiswick's. Lady Annabelle Durst would not be waiting around the corner to save them this time.

'Well, Miss Vallois?'

Sophie bit her lip. Where did she start? There was so much to say. 'This is not going to be easy to tell you, but earlier this afternoon, Mr Oberon came to see me.'

She saw his hands tighten on the table. 'And Lady Longworth didn't throw him out on his ear?'

'Lavinia wasn't home. And I did ask Banyon to send him away, but Mr Oberon said he had news that would be of interest to me.'

'And had he such news?'

'He did. He told me he intends to find the man who started this terrible rumour about Jane and to use his position in society to make the man confess to lying.'

'Did he indeed?' The words were carefully non-committal, but Robert's eyes glittered like shards of ice. 'A generous offer. What did he ask in exchange for this boon?'

Sophie swallowed, knowing this was going to be the hard part. 'My acceptance…of his proposal of marriage.'

Robert's face went as still as death. 'Tell me you didn't agree.'

'Of course not! I was too shocked by what he suggested even to think straight. So he told me he would give me time to consider my answer.'

'How long?'

'One week.'

'Do you need that long to decide?'

'Of course not. I do not love Mr Oberon and I certainly don't want to marry him. But he has the power to restore Jane's good name, Robert, which is why I cannot simply dismiss this out of hand. I have been desperately trying to think of a way around it.'

'Jane would be the *last* one to wish you to marry for such a reason,' Robert said harshly. 'And as much as I love my sister, restoring her reputation is no reason for you to throw *your* life away. Oberon is not a kind man.'

'Yet he has offered to set this terrible matter right.'

'Perhaps because he was the one who set it wrong in the first place.'

Sophie gasped. 'Surely he would not do something so reprehensible. He is your friend.'

'He *was* my friend. I have since come to learn that friendship means something entirely different to Oberon.'

Their eyes met across the table, and Sophie saw how deep Robert's enmity went. 'He said something else. About a wager made some time ago, involving his stallion and a ring belonging to your family. Do you know what he was talking about?' She saw his shoulders stiffen and knew she had her answer. 'I see that you do.'

'There would be no point in my trying to deny it. The wager is written down in a place where any gentleman in London could see it. But I am far more concerned with what he told you *about* it than with the fact that it exists.'

'He said you were looking for the most beautiful woman in London to be your mistress,' Sophie said quietly. 'He said the wager was your idea—'

'*My* idea?'

'Yes. He believes gambling is your way of dealing with what life has thrown at you.'

There were times, Sophie realised, when words were not enough to describe the depth of anger in a man's soul. This was one of those times. 'I trust Oberon mentioned that he was also a party to this wager?'

'He did, but he said you put his name to it against his will.'

His anger became a cold, dangerous fury. 'By God, even I had not thought him so devious. For what it's worth, the wager was *not* my idea and I did *not* agree to participate in it. Oberon has told you a monstrous lie, and I suspect a good many others as well. But only one thing matters right now, Sophie. Do you believe him? After all, it is my word against his.'

'Yes, it is, and I do *not* believe him, Robert. How could I, knowing what I do of you?' She looked down, reluctant to meet his eyes. 'Knowing what has…passed between us. But neither did I wish to keep my knowledge of the wager, or anything else he said to me, a secret from you. I would have honesty between us, if nothing else.'

'If nothing else.' Robert stared at the table, as if to see answers magically appear in the surface. But there were no easy answers. They both knew that.

'Sophie,' Robert said finally, 'this is neither the time nor the place, but I must say something because this cannot go on a moment longer.' He looked up, and his burning gaze held her still. 'If I was to secure Lord Longworth's approval, would you allow me to speak to you?'

For a moment, it was as though her brain shut down. As though his words failed to penetrate the fog swirling around her. He wished to *speak* to her? But...a gentleman did *not* ask to speak to a lady unless he intended to speak of marriage. And he had already told her he had no intention of marrying. Besides, there was the issue of her being French—

'Your hesitation leads me to believe you are not as firmly fixed in your affections as I had hoped,' Robert said slowly. 'If that is the case—'

'No, I know exactly where my affections lie.' Sophie pressed her hand to her throat, aware that her heart was beating so loud he must surely hear it. 'But I thought... that is, we have both stated our intentions not to marry. And yet...' She looked at him and her breath cut off. 'Here we are.'

To her surprise, he smiled. 'Yes, here we are—and you still haven't answered my question.'

Laughter erupted from one of the card tables. Sophie heard the clink of a glass and the muted sounds of a string quartet coming from another room. Candles sputtered and perfume wafted and, wonder of wonders,

Robert wished to speak to her. 'Yes, I would allow it,' she said. 'Most happily, I would.'

It was not triumph she saw in his eyes. It was… peace. He reached for her hands and drew them to his lips, oblivious to anyone who might be watching. 'Do not consider Oberon's offer. Ignore him. Stall him. Lie to him, if you must, I really don't care. All I know is that he *is* the man behind these rumours, and that once I have proof, I'm going to expose him for the blackguard he is. He'll never bother you again, Sophie. On that, you have my word!'

It was with that same sense of purpose that Robert set out the following morning. His brief conversation with Lord Longworth before he'd left Lady White's had resulted in the meeting he was about to have, and over the last few hours, he had gone over the details of what he wanted to say. In light of recent developments, matters had reached a point where something had to be done.

Oberon had betrayed him. Heartlessly. Unemotionally. Irreparably. He had lied *to* him and told lies *about* him—and to the only woman who had ever mattered. For that, Robert would make him pay. He was shown into Lord Longworth's library and found the gentleman waiting for him. 'Good morning, my lord.'

'Robert.' Longworth waved him into a chair. 'Can I offer you something in the way of refreshment? I fear it's a bit early for brandy.'

'Thank you, but I won't take up much of your time. I've come to speak to you about Mr Oberon and Miss Vallois.'

'Have you indeed?' Longworth sat down in the chair opposite. 'What is it you wish to say?'

'I am aware that Oberon has spoken to you about his interest in Miss Vallois and that you have given him your permission to speak to her. I would ask you now to revoke that permission at the earliest possible opportunity.'

A brief hesitation. 'I take it you have a good reason for asking?'

'I have two. The first is that I believe Oberon to be a liar and totally without character. The second is that I am in love with Miss Vallois and wish to marry her myself.'

Longworth's brows rose. 'Perhaps not too early for that drink after all.' He got up and crossed to the sideboard. Pouring two glasses of brandy, he handed one to Robert, tossed back his own and sat down again. After a moment, he said, 'You've made some very strong statements. Would you care to back them up with fact? Apart from your feelings of affection for Sophie. I think I understand those well enough.'

'I do not make the claims lightly, my lord, but because of something that happened between Oberon and myself a few weeks ago, I believe he is behind the despicable stories circulating with regard to my sister.' And then briefly, but succinctly, Robert told the man everything. His conversation with Oberon at the Black Swan, the nature of the mistress wager, and the depth of his concern about the other man's growing obsession with Sophie. The only thing he left out was Oberon's most recent proposition. Judging from the expression on Longworth's face, Robert suspected Oberon would have been facing pistols at dawn. As it was, Longworth swore viciously under his breath. 'By God, if what you say is true, the man should be shot!'

'I have every reason to believe it is true, but he will certainly deny it if asked. When I spoke to Miss Vallois yesterday about my concerns regarding Oberon's involvement in Jane's disgrace, I saw how shocked and displeased she was. It was last night at Lady White's that I asked if I could speak to her, if you were to give your approval. I'm well aware that my own position in society does not recommend me in any way.'

'No, I can't say that it does,' Longworth agreed. 'Nor do you have the wealth or position I would have liked for Sophie.'

'Surely I have enough,' Robert said softly, 'for the daughter of a farmer from Bayencourt.'

The look of shock on the viscount's face had Robert bracing for an explosion—but it never came. Longworth's expression of anger slowly gave way to grudging acceptance. 'She told you, yet you said nothing to me. To anyone.'

'I was afraid of how she would be treated by the *ton* if word of her origins leaked out,' Robert said. 'I know better than most how cruel people can be and I did not relish the thought of Miss Vallois being exposed to ridicule and censure. I also thought that since you and Lady Longworth had not made mention of it, you would not be pleased at hearing it spread around by someone else.'

Longworth sighed. 'Perhaps it would have been better if it *had* leaked out. We might not be in this predicament now.'

'Don't be too sure. Oberon's obsession has no basis in logic. As for myself, while I may not be rich, I'm far from being a pauper. More importantly, I would love her with all my heart.'

Longworth studied him in silence for a moment. Finally, he nodded. 'Very well. If Sophie will have you, you have my blessing. I am more concerned that she be happy than anything else.'

'Thank you, my lord.'

'One thing. If you are able to prove Oberon's misdeeds, come to me at once. He must be held accountable for what he has done.'

'I will not come without proof, though I fear it will be difficult to obtain.'

'Devious men seldom leave well-marked trails for others to follow. And the people they hold in their hands, they hold on to tightly.'

Robert nodded, thinking of poor Lawrence Welton. 'Indeed, my lord. Of that, I am most painfully aware.'

For Sophie, the hours ran all too quickly into days. She lived in a constant state of nervous anticipation, waiting for the next blow to fall. As the countdown to her meeting with Mr Oberon approached, she began to fear that even Robert might not have the power to stop him. And then, three days into her allotted time, another rumour began to circulate throughout the drawing rooms of society. A rumour accusing a certain gentleman of having made up the bold-faced lies about Miss Silverton visiting a man in his rooms, when, in fact, nothing of the sort had happened. Furthermore, if Miss Silverton *had* spoken to someone in the park, it was nothing more than the polite exchange of greetings expected between a lady and a gentleman during the course of their social day. Certainly nothing grievous enough over which to defame her character.

The reason for the man's lies was not made clear,

but neither did it seem to matter. Montague Oberon had been heard to speak up strongly in the lady's defence, and with his name behind the rebuttal, no one was going to argue.

'And so, there we have it,' Lavinia said at the conclusion of her recounting. 'It would appear Jane's name is cleared and her reputation fully restored.'

Sophie raised the teacup to her lips. What would Lavinia say, she wondered, if she knew how steep a price Mr Oberon had demanded in exchange? 'Does Jane know?'

'I suspect the news will have reached her by now. It was the only topic of conversation at Lady Orville's this afternoon and given that most of the ladies arrived already in possession of the news, I can assure you it has been widely discussed.'

Again, Sophie could feel nothing but relief for her friend. It was over, the terrible stories finally laid to rest. Jane was once again free to move about in society, knowing that she would be welcome at any house she chose to visit, and that churlish whispers would not follow her wherever she went. That it put society in a dismal light was a fact Sophie could not deny. If people were so willing to believe a pack of lies on the strength of one man's word, what did it say when they were so ready to put it all aside on the strength of another's?

'I fear it is a rhetorical question,' Lavinia said. 'Society is what it is and I doubt it will ever change. People were willing to believe the lies when they were nothing more than rumours, so they could hardly *not* believe Mr Oberon when he came forwards to dispute them and publicly condemn the man who started them.'

Sophie's eyes widened. 'He actually *named* the perpetrator?'

'Oh, yes. And I was deeply saddened to learn of it.' Lavinia looked unhappy. 'I never thought a fine young man like Lawrence Welton would do such a thing.'

Robert was at his club when he heard the news. 'Lawrence Welton?' he repeated in stunned disbelief. 'But that's impossible!'

'Of course it is,' said Captain John McIntosh, the gentleman imparting the information. 'But Oberon was most definite in his naming Welton. He said he had spoken with him a few days earlier and gained the man's confession, after which Welton bolted.'

Robert was too angry for words. So that was what Welton had meant in his letter. Oberon obviously held a packet of Welton's vowels and Welton's agreeing to become the foil for Oberon's monstrous plan was the price he demanded for discharging them.

'Still, it's cleared your sister's name,' McIntosh said.

'And made Oberon look like a hero into the bargain,' Robert muttered. 'And that bothers me no end. Lawrence would never do something like this.'

'Of course not.' McIntosh drained his glass. 'But he has a weakness for cards and, by his own admission, only a fool gambles with the devil. Well, I'd best be on my way. Good to see you again, Robert.'

'And you. I appreciate the information.'

The captain's smile held more than a trace of regret. 'I'm just sorry it couldn't have been better.'

Robert sat quietly after the other man left, thinking over all that he had heard. So, Jane's life had been made better at the expense of Lawrence's. Obviously that was what Oberon had meant when he'd said he held people's lives in the palm of his hand. He had no qualms about using whomever he pleased in the achievement of his own ends, and this time, his old friend Lawrence had been the expendable one.

But where did that leave Sophie? She was now in the unenviable position of believing herself indebted to Oberon for having restored Jane's good name when nothing could have been further from the truth. Robert knew the entire episode had been a carefully devised plot to strike back at *him* for having dared to interfere, and to put Sophie in a position of obligation to Oberon. And Oberon's price for revealing the so-called deception was her hand in marriage.

It was unthinkable! An outcome that must be avoided at all costs. Whatever it took, Sophie must not be allowed to become a prisoner to Oberon's tricks. The man was evil, and if Robert was able to do only one thing, it would be to ensure that his sweet Sophie never became prey for the monster.

Robert called on her the same afternoon. He was told that Lord Longworth and Mr Vallois were not at home, but when he advised Banyon it was Miss Vallois he wished to see, he was taken into the morning room where Sophie and Lavinia were sitting quietly doing their embroidery.

'Mr Silverton, what a pleasure to see you,' Lavinia said.

'Lady Longworth. Miss Vallois. I called to apprise you of the good news regarding my sister.'

'Indeed, sir, we have already heard and we are both overjoyed at the outcome. Speaking of which,' Lavinia said, rising, 'I have written a note to dear Jane and would ask that you take it to her. I shall just go and fetch it.' She left, giving Robert a knowing smile as she passed.

Finally, it was just he and Sophie alone. He walked towards her slowly, suddenly anxious as to how she would receive what he wanted to say. 'Well, Miss Vallois, it would seem at least one problem has been put to bed.'

'It has, and I am so very pleased, for Jane's sake. Thank you for coming to tell us.'

'That wasn't the only reason I came.' He halted in front of her. 'I think you know that.'

Her eyes rose to his and then fell, long lashes casting shadows on her skin. But she smiled, and he heard her take a quick breath as she said, 'And what is this other reason?'

As he looked down at her, he wished for the first time in his life that he had been blessed with a poet's gift for words. 'I believe it safe to say that you and I did not get off to an auspicious start that night at the inn. I won't ever forget you telling your brother that you'd rather sleep in the barn than accept an offer of help from me.'

She laughed, but sent him a reproving glare. 'You are not kind to remind me of that, sir.'

Robert smiled. 'No, perhaps not. But I've since come to learn that I was wrong about so many things. We talked in the garden at Lady Chiswick's about making mistakes. Well, I've made more than my fair share with you. I let ignorance cloud my judgement to the point where it almost blinded me to the truth, and you, dear Sophie, suffered for that ignorance.'

'You were only acting on your beliefs.'

'Misplaced beliefs. I saw a man I thought would do

me no harm destroy the reputation of my sister and cause a fine gentleman to lose his home and his good name. I saw a woman I…cared deeply about forced into an untenable position as the result of her own desire to protect someone who wasn't able to protect herself. And I let my steadfast belief in my own lack of suitability stand in my way of my telling her how I really felt about her. But all that's in the past. From now on, I intend to tell her every single day how much I love her.' He slowly sat down beside her. 'Sophie Vallois, would you do me the very great honour of becoming my wife?'

He waited, heart in his mouth, for her answer. Never had he believed the seconds could move so slowly. That he would feel himself age as he waited for her response. That he might see his world fall apart at the thought of her saying no. But such was not her response. 'Yes, I will,' she whispered. 'Just as soon as matters can be arranged.'

He felt almost lightheaded with relief. He stood up and held out his hand, drawing her to her feet. 'Lord Longworth already knows of my intentions, but I will speak to your brother immediately upon his return. I would like to have his approval, but I'm prepared to marry you without it.'

Her smile was golden, like the sun emerging after the rain. 'Antoine will approve, as long as he knows I love you. He only wants me to be happy.'

'Then I shall do my best to convince him of it. And I shall arrange for a special license, and we shall be married on the day of your choosing. I want you as my wife as soon as possible.' Then, drawing her close, he kissed her, his lips gently tracing the outline of her mouth. There was no experience to her kiss, but the

taste of her nearly drove him mad. And when his tongue
teased her lips apart and he delved into the sweetness
of her mouth, he was lost.

'Enough!' He set her gently away, blood coursing
through every part of his body. 'I have no wish to fright-
en you.'

Her smile reassured him. 'You don't frighten me,
Robert. I want this too. Can you not feel it when you
hold me?'

'I feel that, and more.' He reached for her left hand
and raised it to his lips, gently kissing the finger
that would soon wear his ring. Then, at the sound of
approaching footsteps, he reluctantly released Sophie
and stepped back. But when the door opened and
Lavinia walked in, he knew she saw their happiness.

'Oh, my dears, I am so very pleased for both of you.'

'Thank you, Lady Longworth,' Robert said. 'Perhaps
you would be good enough to send me a note as soon
as your husband returns. I would speak to him, and to
Mr Vallois, at the earliest opportunity.'

'Of course, I shall be happy to do so. As it happens,
we are all engaged for dinner with Lord and Lady Otter-
ham this evening, but would you and Jane care to dine
with us tomorrow? To celebrate this most wonderful
news?'

Robert glanced at the lady who would soon be his
wife, and when she smiled, he thought she had never
looked more beautiful. 'We would be delighted.'

'Excellent.' Lavinia was positively beaming. 'I am
so pleased everything has worked out. I do not think
the story could have had a happier conclusion had dear
Miss Austen written the ending to it herself!'

# Chapter Thirteen

The meeting with Lord Longworth and Sophie's brother went better than Robert could have hoped. Though Antoine was quiet to begin, once Robert convinced him of the depth of his affection for Sophie, he seemed to relax and accept the news, and even to appear happy about it. Longworth had no such reservations. He shook Robert's hand and told him how pleased he and Lavinia were with Sophie's choice, then he assured Robert that they were very much looking forward to having everyone together at dinner the following evening.

Robert thought it an encouraging start.

Given that Sophie was engaged for the evening, he decided to take his sister to Vauxhall, as much to celebrate her good news as his own. It went without saying that Jane's mood had improved immeasurably since learning that her reputation had been restored, though she was deeply troubled at hearing it was Lawrence Welton who had been falsely named as the villain in the piece.

'I would not have believed it of Mr Welton, even if you hadn't told me the truth,' Jane said as they strolled arm in arm down the Grand Walk. 'He always struck me as being such a fine, honourable young man.'

'He is,' Robert said, tipping his hat to an acquaintance. 'Unfortunately, no one is going to challenge Oberon over it. Everyone's afraid of him.'

'With good reason.' Jane was silent for a moment. 'I would not have thought him so evil. Arrogant, perhaps, and vain, but not cruel and hurtful. To destroy a man in such a way…'

'If you could have seen Lawrence that night, you would have understood my desire to call Oberon out.'

'And yet, what crime could you have accused him of, Robert? Nothing was known for certain. You could not have laid the blame for the rumours at his feet, any more than you could have accused him of lying to you when you asked him about them. But it is truly unfortunate that Mr Welton chose to leave London when he did,' Jane said. 'By doing so, he lent credence to Mr Oberon's story.'

'Indeed, but I'm sure that was part of Oberon's strategy.'

'Poor man. I hope he fares well in the country,' Jane said. 'Still, we must not dwell on it when there is so much happier news to celebrate. You are to be married to dear Sophie and I am so very pleased for you.' Then, he felt her stiffen. 'Robert, look!'

Oberon was coming towards them. He had a doxy on his arm and was laughing as though he hadn't a care in the world—until he spotted them. Then a cold, calculating look settled in his eyes. Stopping a few feet in front of them, he touched the brim of his beaver. 'Evening, Silverton. Miss Silverton.'

'Mr Oberon,' Jane said, her voice cooling noticeably. 'I understand I am in your debt for having restored my good name.'

Oberon's acknowledgement was perfunctory. 'It was my pleasure. It would have been a crime to allow a good lady's name to be dragged through the mud while the perpetrator was allowed to go free. What say you, Silver?'

'I'm not so sure the perpetrator of this crime will ever be brought to justice, but I'm very glad to see my sister absolved of all wrongdoing.'

Oberon did not smile. 'Not exactly the thanks I had in mind, but it is of no consequence. The only thanks I seek will be found in another quarter. Good evening.'

'Will you not congratulate my brother on his good news, Mr Oberon?' Jane said. 'He is to be married.'

Robert squeezed his sister's arm, but it was too late. The cobra had turned and stood poised, ready to strike. 'Married? Indeed, I had not heard. Who is the lucky lady?'

'Miss Vallois,' Jane said.

Did Robert imagine the soft hiss? ''Pon my word, Silver, I hardly know what to say. You made no mention of this the last time we spoke.'

'There was no need. I thought we understood each other well enough.'

A shadow of anger rippled across Oberon's face, transforming the handsome features into a stone-like mask. 'A moment in private if you please, Silverton.'

'I would rather not leave Jane—'

'I said a moment, sir!'

Robert felt Jane stir uneasily at his side. 'It's all right, Robert. I shall walk on to the Cascade and wait for you there.'

Oberon didn't bother looking at the female at his side. 'Be gone,' he snapped, and she was.

Robert waited until Jane was safely out of distance before remarking, 'How gallant, Oberon. Do you dispense with all of your harlots with such tact and diplomacy?'

'Do not try my patience, Silverton! I am not in the mood.' Oberon took a threatening step towards him. 'How dare you go behind my back and ask Miss Vallois to marry you. She was already promised to me!'

'No, sir, she was not. And do not think I am unaware of the terms you tried to exact from her.'

Oberon's face went white. 'I would have you explain yourself!'

'You promised to restore Jane's good name in return for Miss Vallois's promise of marriage.'

'Which she gave me!'

'On the contrary, you asked her to marry you and gave her a week to consider your proposal. I asked her to marry me today and she agreed.'

For a moment, Robert thought Oberon would strike him, so vicious was the anger that flashed in those obsidian eyes. 'You'll be sorry you did this, Silverton. I will make you pay.'

'There is nothing more you can do. You cannot defame my sister again and you have already destroyed your good *friend*, Lawrence Welton.'

'Lawrence was a fool,' Oberon spat. 'But there are others who can be made to suffer. I will not allow you to stand in my way again.'

'I don't care for threats,' Robert said. 'And it is *you* who would do well to take care. The aristocracy is not above reproach. Society *will* turn its back on *any* man if the crimes are heinous enough.'

Oberon's face could have been carved from stone. His anger vanished, replaced by a quiet loathing that was far more dangerous. 'I *will* bring you down, Robert. And by God, I'll enjoy watching you fall.'

Robert stood his ground, but he felt a chill run down his spine. The façade of the elegant dandy was gone, devoured by the snake and lost for ever. He had no doubt the creature would strike again…and that when it did, it would strike more viciously than ever before.

Sophie was emerging from Clark and Debenham's the next morning when she saw Mr Oberon leaning against a lamp-post, looking in her direction. She was tempted to go back inside, but it was too late. Oberon pushed away from the pole and came towards her. There was a thin smile on his lips, but his manner was as cold as a blast of Arctic air. 'Miss Vallois, what a pleasant surprise.'

'Mr Oberon.' She was eminently grateful for Jeanette standing quietly behind her. 'I was just on my way home.'

She went to move past him, but was stayed by his words. 'I would have but a moment of your time.'

'Lady Longworth is expecting me—'

'This will not take long.'

'I'm sure it will not. But first, there is something I must tell you—'

'Say nothing. Have your maid stay well behind us and keep your voice down,' Oberon advised. 'I shall walk you the length of this street and then back to your carriage. What I have to say will take no longer than that.'

Aware that there was nothing she could do, Sophie handed her maid the few packages she was carrying and instructed her to follow them at a distance. Then she fell into step beside Oberon and they began to walk.

'It has come to my attention,' he said in a conversational tone, 'that you have agreed to marry Mr Silverton. No, do not answer. Simply smile and nod, as though we were discussing the weather.'

Sophie did, though the knot in her chest tightened until it threatened to choke her.

'It also strikes me that in doing so you have failed to honour your side of the bargain,' he continued.

'I was not aware we had entered into a bargain.'

'Were you not?' He turned to her, his beautiful smile unbearably cruel. 'I thought I'd made it plain. *I* was to restore Miss Silverton's good name and *you* were to accept my proposal of marriage.'

'You said you would *endeavour* to restore her good name, and you gave me a week to consider my answer.'

'Spare me the argument, Miss Vallois. I was to exonerate Miss Silverton and you were to marry me. Simple. Had you told me at the time that you had no intention of agreeing, the outcome for your friend would have been very…different.'

In that moment, Sophie knew she was dealing with a man without conscience, a man who would not hesitate to use any weapon in his arsenal to secure what he wanted. 'You made me believe you cared as much for Miss Silverton's reputation as I did,' Sophie said, keeping her eyes on the road ahead. 'Now I see it was simply a means of buying my affection.'

'Call it what you will, the end result is that you have accepted Mr Silverton's proposal and do not think to hear mine. Well, I am here to inform you that you *will* hear my proposal, and that you *will* agree to it.'

'That, sir, I cannot do. I have given my promise elsewhere.'

'A promise that need mean no more to Silverton than yours did to me.'

'He asked for my hand and I was free to bestow it. I am not in that position now.'

'And if he had not spoken to you and I had come to you as agreed? Would you have accepted *my* proposal?'

Sophie stopped dead, forcing him to halt as well. 'I would not, sir. I told you I did not love you and that has not changed. If I led you to believe my answer would be yes—'

'Say no more, Miss Vallois. It is I who must now speak my piece,' he said, taking her arm and forcing her to walk again. 'Perhaps it will help soften your heart towards me.'

'There is really no point—'

'There is always a point, dearest Sophie.'

'Please do not address me in that way—'

He raised his hand to silence her objections. 'It has not escaped my notice that you and your brother are very close. And, indeed, he is a fine fellow for all his being French. But it has also come to my attention, through the most reliable of sources, that in the past he committed an act which, to certain factions of the government, might be viewed as treasonous. No, keep on walking,' he said when her step faltered. 'See, there is your carriage just ahead. We only have a few more

minutes in each other's company and there is still much
I would have you know.'

'What do you want?' Sophie said, dreading what he
was about to say.

'What I want is your agreement to be my wife. I
thought after what happened at Lady Chiswick's to
make you my mistress, but that would still leave you
free to marry Robert Silverton and I'll see *hell* freeze
over before *that* happens. So, you will agree to be my
wife or I shall make known your brother's doings to
certain people in Paris who, I think, would be very
interested in knowing the whereabouts of a man who
once saved the life of a much sought-after English spy.
For if your brother would do that, who knows what other
conspiracies he might have been a party to?'

'You're bluffing! You don't know anyone who would
wish him harm!'

He smiled, coldly. 'You seem to have forgotten that
your former charge, Miss Georgina Grant-Ogilvy, married a Frenchman who just happens to be in an area of
government very interested in the activities of men like
your brother. And since that illuminating night at Lady
Chiswick's, I have taken it upon myself to develop a
close and most useful relationship with both the lady
and her new husband while they are here in London.'

'You would not dare!' Sophie whispered fiercely.
'Antoine has done nothing to you!'

'Ah, but you, dear Sophie, have. You have bewitched
me and I intend to spend the rest of my life showing
you how much I love you.'

Knowing that love would have nothing to do with it,
Sophie said, 'I will *not* marry you!'

'I think you will. Because you are no longer the only

one whose future hangs in the balance.' Oberon turned to bestow an angelic smile upon her. 'If you do not agree to marry me, I shall see to it that the moment your brother returns to France, he *will* be apprehended and clapped in irons. And from what I understand, life expectancy in a French jail can be...alarmingly short.'

'This will *never* come to pass!' Sophie whispered furiously. 'I will tell him of your monstrous plan. If Antoine knows you conspire to trap him—'

'Ah, but you will not tell him or anyone else of our conversation this afternoon, for if you do, I will make life very difficult for two *other* people I know you hold in high regard. In case you fail to realise it, the lives of an English spy and his wife are never completely without danger either. Not to mention dear Robert. Who knows what manner of...accident may befall him?'

Sophie felt the blood drain from her face. 'I don't believe you! Even *you* would not be so vicious as to threaten them in such a way.'

'My naïve child, I would threaten *anyone* who stood in the way of me getting what I want—and I want you. But I prefer to think of it as having the upper hand. I always do, you know,' Oberon said amiably. 'As I once told Silver, everyone has secrets. All one has to do is find out what they are and then put them to use. I make it my business to find out as many secrets as I can, and you would be amazed at how many people's lives I could destroy. Titled ladies and their lovers. Grand dukes and their paramours. Shady businessmen and dissatisfied bankers.' He smiled, as though the conversation was of the most trivial in nature. 'So you see, Sophie, you really cannot win. Refuse me and I will cause you more pain and heartache than you can imagine. Accept, and everything goes on as normal. Your brother can safely return to France, the Longworths can go on as usual, and Robert and Jane will continue with their boring little lives. And you will become my beautiful viscountess and the envy of all society.'

Sophie could think of nothing to say. The proposal was monstrous, as was the creature who uttered it.

'I can see I have given you a great deal to think about,' he said as they approached the carriage. 'So I will honour my original commitment and formally call upon you tomorrow. That is fair of me, don't you think?'

She turned her head away, unable to look at him, so great was her loathing.

'What, no kind words to offer your future husband?'

'If I had words,' Sophie ground out, 'they would not be kind.'

'Ah. Then I suggest you find some. I expect you to convey all appearance of happiness when I inform Lord and Lady Longworth of our betrothal.'

As the world around her began to spin, Sophie placed her hand on the side of the carriage. 'I am surprised at your determination to marry me, Mr Oberon. I would have thought a viscount's son could do better than to marry the penniless daughter of a farmer from Bayencourt!'

'A farmer's daughter?' The look he gave her was one of amused disbelief. 'Come, come, Sophie, surely you do not expect me to believe such a Banbury tale.'

'You mean you didn't know?' She wanted to laugh, even as fear and indecision tore at her insides. 'Your *reliable sources* failed to inform you as to the details of my birth?'

'There is nothing to tell. Your conduct betrays you for what you are.'

'I was born to Gaston and Aimee Vallois in the kitchen of their farmhouse,' Sophie said. 'I grew up helping my mother keep house and sometimes helping my father in the fields.'

'Rubbish! A farmer's daughter would never be able to speak such impeccable English! She would never appear so elegant in manner and dress!'

'Have you forgotten about my employment with Mrs Grant-Ogilvy? You were there when it all came out. *She* taught me English so that I might speak to her daughters. And because I was often required to accompany the family when they went visiting I was given thorough instruction in deportment, elocution and manners. I may have been taught to behave like a lady, but I can assure you, my origins are quite humble. Only think what society will say when they learn the truth about *that*!' she flung at him.

For a moment, Oberon said nothing, clearly unwilling to believe that she was telling him the truth. His pride and his belief in his ability to control others would naturally prevent him from seeing it as anything but lies. But the longer he looked at her, and the firmer she stood, the more Sophie realised he was coming to accept it. 'So this has all been a sham,' he said, his eyes narrowing to slits. 'An elaborate ruse to trick an unsuspecting public into believing a lie!'

'Not at all. Nicholas and Lavinia never tried to make anyone believe I was anything more than I am. *You* are the one whose motives have been suspect. You've never *loved* me. Your interest in me has always been as a result of my appearance. You said as much the first time we met.'

During the long, tense silence that followed, Sophie felt as though her breath was cut off, her heart thudding noisily within her chest.

'Does he know?' Oberon enquired nastily.

Anxiety shot through her. 'Who?'

'You know damn well who! Silverton! Does he know you're a farmer's brat?'

For the first time, Sophie began to smile. So, the polished veneer was finally being stripped away to reveal the ugliness beneath. 'Yes, he knows. I told him.'

'Yet you did not think to tell me. Pity.'

She knew a fleeting moment of hope. 'Then you withdraw your proposal.'

'I do not!' Oberon's fury nailed her to the spot. 'Nothing has changed, Miss Vallois. I will never let you go so that you can marry him. *Never!*'

With that parting thrust, he left, his steps hard and angry on the cobblestones. Sophie sagged against the side of the carriage. *What had she done?*

'Are you all right, miss?' Jeanette said, hurrying to her side.

'I'm fine.' But Sophie felt the perspiration on her palms; as she climbed into the carriage, her spirits were as heavy as the thunderclouds over her head. What on earth was she going to do? She knew Oberon would make good on his threat. He had done so on every other occasion, and having witnessed what he was capable of, she no longer doubted that he was the one behind Jane's fall from grace. Or that he had done it as a warning—or a punishment—to Robert. The man would stop at nothing to achieve his ends.

And now it was her turn to experience his ire. Just when the happiness she had always longed for seemed within her grasp, it was to be snatched away, like sweets from the mouth of a child.

The monster of her nightmares was real…and his name was Montague Oberon.

'Excuse me, sir, this note was just delivered,' the butler said, holding the tray out to Robert.

Jane looked up from her lunch of bread and butter and cheese. 'Who is it from?'

Not recognising the handwriting, Robert broke the wafer and opened the parchment to see a single line scrawled upon the page.

I must see you. Please come as quickly as you can.
Sophie

Fear lodged like a bullet in his gut. 'Something's wrong.' He got up from the table and kissed his sister on the forehead. 'I have to see Sophie.'

Jane's cheeks paled as she read the discarded letter. 'What does this mean, Robert?'

'I have no idea, but I don't like the sound of it.'

Not long after, he was shown into the Longworths' drawing room. Sophie stood alone by the window, her complexion as pale as her gown, her eyes rimmed with red. She looked ready to shatter into a thousand pieces.

'What's wrong?' he asked as the door closed behind him.

'Thank you for coming so quickly.'

'My darling girl, you have no need to thank me. What has happened?'

'I fear I have had a change of heart, Robert. No, please, stay where you are,' she said as he started towards her. 'Do not make this any harder than it already is.'

'What do you mean you've had a change of heart? Do you no longer love me?'

'My feelings are unchanged,' she said. 'But I can no longer marry you.'

'Why not?'

Her voice shook. 'Mr Oberon—'

'Oberon!' In two strides Robert was across the room. 'What has he said to you?'

'Nothing!'

'Your face betrays you, sweetheart. Come, sit down beside me.'

But she shook her head. 'It's best we not spend time together, Robert. It is too late.'

He put his hands on her arms and realised she was trembling. 'What has he said to make you act this way?' When she didn't answer, he drew her into her arms and held her. 'Tell me, Sophie,' he whispered against her hair. 'I can't help you if you won't tell me.'

'You can't help me regardless. Oberon holds all the cards. There is nothing he will not do, Robert. No one he will not destroy in order to get what he wants. It is simpler…better…if I just marry him.'

'It is neither simpler nor better to marry a man you don't love!'

'But he has the power to destroy everyone I do, and I can't let that happen.' Pulling free of his arms, Sophie moved like an automaton towards the window. 'I won't!'

Robert searched for the words that would make her change her mind. She was slipping away from him and there was nothing he could do to stop it. 'Can you tell me nothing, Sophie? Nothing that can be of use?'

'Only that he knows things,' she whispered. 'I don't know how he found out, but he knows things that can destroy people's lives.'

'Then we will talk to whoever he is threatening,' Robert said. 'Find a way to refute the lies—'

'They are not lies,' she said sadly. 'He knows the truth and that is even more damaging.'

'Then at least tell me *who* has he threatened!'

Sophie put back her head and laughed. 'Who has he *not*? You. My brother. Nicholas and Lavinia. Everyone I hold most dear in my life. And he will make good on his threats, Robert. I know he will.' She looked at him, and the darkness of despair was reflected in her eyes. 'He will never let you have me. He told me as much. If I walk away from you now, everything will be all right. If I do not…'

'You unleash the monster,' Robert said quietly.

'Exactly. Jane is the only one safe from him now. And poor Mr Welton. He cannot touch either of them again.'

It was more than Robert could bear. To see the woman he loved set on a course of action that would ultimately destroy her was beyond all endurance. Because he knew that if she went ahead with this marriage, she *would* be destroyed. If Oberon was willing to use her so abysmally now, what could she expect of their life together? There would be nothing of love or respect. Their marriage would be about possession and revenge. A partnership made in hell.

A marriage to suit the devil himself.

## Chapter Fourteen

Not surprisingly, Sophie's unexpected change of plans was met with expressions of shock and dismay when she told Nicholas, Lavinia and her brother of them shortly after Robert left.

'You are going to marry *Oberon*?' Nicholas said. 'But…you have already accepted Robert Silverton.'

'Yes, and I have just told him I've had a change of heart.'

'But I thought you loved him, Sophie,' Lavinia said in bewilderment. 'You told me as much only yesterday.'

'I know what I said,' she whispered. She had to be strong—and the only way to do that was by studying the welfare of the people standing before her. 'But when I thought about all I would be giving up, I realised how foolish I would be to turn Mr Oberon's proposal down.'

'All you would be giving up?' Antoine said. 'You're telling us you've chosen to become a viscountess and accept all that goes with it? *Pourquoi es-tu de nous mentir, petite?*'

'I am not lying to you!' Sophie said. 'Nicholas, you said you wished me to marry well.'

'Yes, and if I thought it was in your best interests to marry him, I would rejoice in your selection of Oberon as your husband,' Nicholas said. 'But information has come to light about which I cannot be happy, and I would *beg* you to reconsider.'

'I cannot. I've made up my mind,' she forced herself to say in as convincing a tone as possible. 'I *am* going to marry him.'

A heavy silence fell, during which Sophie watched the people she loved struggle to come to terms with the news she had just imparted. It was obvious they didn't know what to say. That all they wanted to do was try to convince her of what a terrible mistake she was making.

Little did they know that she understood better than *any* of them exactly how terrible a mistake it was.

Lavinia slowly got to her feet. 'Well, I had best advise Cook we will only be four for dinner.'

'Three.' Nicholas abruptly stood up. 'I'll be at my club. Antoine?'

Her brother shook his head. 'No, I'll stay.'

'Fine. Then I'll see you both in the morning.' With that, Nicholas left. Lavinia hesitated, looking as though she wanted to say something, then, obviously deciding it wasn't the best time, turned and followed her husband out of the room.

Sophie stayed where she was. She didn't look up. Didn't try to stop them. She knew how disappointed they were, but she couldn't let that matter. She had no choice but to see this through to its painful conclusion.

'So, are you going to tell me what's really going

on, *petite*?' Antoine asked. 'What's really behind this change of heart?'

Sophie shook her head, wrapping her arms around herself and holding on tight. 'It is better you do not know.'

'Why? Has he hurt you?' Antoine's eyes darkened with an unspoken threat. 'Because if he has—'

'Please, Antoine, don't ask me again. I have made up my mind and there is nothing you can say to change it. I *will* marry Mr Oberon. And you must see that this is very good for you. Now you can ask Jane to marry you.'

'Marry Jane?' Antoine stared at her as though she were a simpleton. 'Robert will never agree to my marrying his sister now.'

'Of course he will. If he was willing to marry me, he can have no qualms about allowing you to marry Jane.'

'And condone a marriage between his sister and the brother of the woman who jilted him for a man he despises?'

Sophie winced at the harshness of his reply. 'He only wants Jane to be happy. If he knows she will find that happiness with you—'

'And be forced to think about *you* every time he sees me? To be reminded of what he lost every time Jane talks about her sister-in-law?'

'Please don't, Antoine,' she whispered, turning away.

'I'm sorry, Sophie, but I know you're holding something back. You wouldn't do this unless there was a very good reason.'

When she still said nothing, he came around the table and sat down next to her. 'You have never lied to me.

Never kept anything from me. Why would you do so now when there is so much at stake?'

'It is *because* there is so much at stake that I must keep this to myself. If it were anything less important, I would tell you.'

Antoine's hands fell away and Sophie suddenly felt cold, and terribly alone. 'Then there is nothing more to say,' he said, getting up.

'There *is*! You must speak to Robert. You must marry Jane!' Lord knew, *one* of them had to salvage something out of this pitiful situation!

But Antoine only shook his head. 'If I had one wish, it would be that Jane and I might never be separated again. But that cannot be. I know what Mr Silverton's answer would be, and it is the right one. After all, what kind of life could I offer her?'

'You could offer her the very *best* life!' Sophie said urgently. 'A wonderful life with the man she loves. What more could Jane ask?'

'Respect. Security. Wealth. All of which she deserves, none of which I can give her.'

'But I am to be married to a rich man!' Sophie cried, grasping at straws. 'I will have money. Money that you and Jane can live on.'

Antoine looked at her for a long time. 'Tell me this is not why you consented to be his wife.'

'Of course not! But if I must marry him—'

'*Must?*'

Sophie could have kicked herself. 'If I *want* to marry him, why should my family not benefit?'

Her argument fell on deaf ears. Antoine was not to be swayed. 'I will take nothing from him, Sophie. Even if it comes through you. You do not know what they say about him in the clubs—'

'And I beg you, do not tell me!' she whispered, turning away. 'I do not wish to hear it.'

'Why? Because it confirms what you already suspect?'

'It would not be his money,' Sophie tried again. 'It would be mine to do with as I please.'

'You would have only what he gave you. If he decided to give you nothing, you would have nothing.'

'Then I shall ask Nicholas to negotiate a settlement for me,' Sophie said. 'I have heard that such things are done. And I will be given…pin money. To buy dresses and shoes. You and Jane can live on that.'

'And what will you say when your husband asks why you have no new gown to wear to the ball, or bonnets to wear when you go out in society? How will you explain where the money has gone?'

'I will not explain myself.' She raised her chin. 'If the money is given to me, it is mine to do with as I please. And if I wish to give it to you so that you and Jane can be together, that is what I will do! It would be worth all the gowns and jewels in London to see the two of you happy together!'

'Ah, my sweet Sophie.' Antoine struggled for a moment, and then pulled her into his arms. 'It tears me apart to see you so unhappy.'

'I am not unhappy and everything will be fine,' Sophie lied. She closed her eyes and rested her face against his chest. 'You'll see. It will all work out.'

'And how will you feel when you see Robert Silverton in society? How will you feel when you see him with another woman? Perhaps with the children the two of you might have had.'

The image appeared all too clearly in her mind, and Sophie felt her heart break. 'I will wish him happy in his new life and hope he thinks of me with kindness now and then. That is what I will feel, Antoine. Because that is how it has to be.'

The announcement of the engagement between the Honourable Montague John Phillip Oberon and Miss Sophia Chantal Vallois was published in *The Times* two days later and instantly became a source of speculation and gossip in the drawing rooms of society. Much was made of the fact that the son of a peer was marrying an unknown French woman—a woman who had once been a servant to Mrs Grant-Ogilvy. Oberon's mother initially refused to acknowledge Sophie as her future daughter-in-law until her husband had intervened to settle matters. And while he did not come out and publicly endorse the marriage, neither did he forbid it or threaten to disinherit his son if he went ahead with it. When asked how he felt about Miss Vallois, however, his expression grew stony and no response was offered before he abruptly turned and walked away.

Naturally, the polite world drew its own conclusions as to the family's reactions. Nothing was better loved than a scandal and the haste with which Oberon planned his wedding to the beautiful Miss Vallois was remarked upon in several of London's most elegant drawing rooms. There were also those who commented upon the fact that the newly engaged pair did not seem to spend a great deal of time together at the glittering society events to which they were invited, while others said it was only to be expected. Nothing was as tasteless as an overt display of affection.

Robert did not attend any of the parties. Loving Sophie as he did, he could not celebrate her marriage to his enemy. He could not pretend happiness at seeing her wed to a man who was as bestial as the creatures living in the forest. No, that was unkind to God's creatures, Robert reflected. God's creatures were *better* than Oberon. They did not plot revenge against their fellow beasts, or try to cheat them out of what they owned. Truth be known, he would rather spend the night in the forest with a pack of wolves than he would in a fancy ballroom with the Honourable Montague Oberon.

'I say, you're looking rather glum,' Captain McIntosh said, stopping by the table. 'I thought you would have been out celebrating your friend's engagement to the young French lady. I believe Sir David and Lady Hester are holding a masked ball in their honour this evening.'

Robert set his fourth empty glass on the table. 'Oberon and I are no longer speaking and I have no intention of celebrating his good fortune tonight or at any time in the future.' Then, aware that he sounded as miserable as he felt, he made an effort to be social. 'Care to join me for a drink?'

'If you're sure you want company.'

'I'm not at all sure that I do, but I would rather not drink myself to oblivion alone.'

'In that case...' McIntosh sat down in the chair opposite and signalled for the butler. 'Brandy, if you please, Mr Gibbons.'

'And another for me as well,' Robert said.

The remark drew a sympathetic glance from his companion. 'You're going to regret this in the morning.'

'Most likely, but since the morning and its attendant misery are still ten hours away, my concern is not immediate.'

'So you and Oberon have fallen out,' McIntosh said. 'Can't say I'm surprised. I've never had much time for the fellow myself, and I certainly don't trust him. Welton found that out the hard way.'

'Welton should have known better than to gamble with him,' Robert muttered. 'Oberon's a devil when it comes to cards.'

'I wasn't talking about cards. I was referring to the investment swindle Oberon pulled on him.'

Robert looked up. 'I've heard nothing about a swindle.'

'Hardly surprising,' McIntosh said. 'Why do you think Oberon banished Lawrence to the country?'

'I assumed because Lawrence had debts he couldn't afford to pay back and Oberon's price was his name on my sister's defamation.'

McIntosh sent Robert a pointed look. 'Are you sure the two of you are no longer friends? I'd hate to think any of this might get back to him.'

'Trust me, I'd rather see Oberon in hell than shake his hand.'

'In that case…' McIntosh leaned in closer '…I can tell you that Lawrence got into his cups one night and lost a fortune to Oberon. Naturally Oberon assured him he would be happy to take his vowel with no pressure to repay, but when he suggested that Lawrence might take a look at an investment he was putting together that was guaranteed to pay a high rate of return, Lawrence agreed, no questions asked. But when he went to see Oberon about the investment a few months later, he was told the scheme had gone sour and that he'd lost every penny he put in. So Oberon took his house instead.'

'Poor bastard,' Robert said. 'Was there ever really a scheme?'

'Your guess is as good as mine. If there was, Oberon likely played up the potential for profit far beyond any reasonable expectation of return.'

'Lawrence should have made enquiries,' Robert said.

'Of course he should, but Oberon was his friend. Lawrence signed the letter without asking any questions. And I suspect that when it all fell through, that's when Oberon told Lawrence he would forgive some of his debts if he agreed to play a part in a small subterfuge, namely be the foil for your sister's supposed transgression. Lawrence had no choice but to agree. It was either that or end up in debtor's prison.'

'But if Oberon was stringing Lawrence along, pretending to invest his money in a fraudulent scheme, he's guilty of a criminal offence.'

'Aye, but who's to prove it?' McIntosh asked. 'Oberon would sell his own mother if he thought it to his advantage.'

And blackmail his father into the bargain, Robert reflected bitterly.

'Problem is,' McIntosh went on, 'there's not many who'll risk running afoul of him.'

Robert slowly looked up. 'Except someone who already has and has nothing left to lose.'

The Captain's eyes narrowed. 'Lawrence?'

'Who else? If Oberon *believes* Lawrence destroyed, and Lawrence likewise believes himself ruined, perhaps he would be willing to tell us what happened. We need to show that Oberon's investment scheme was fraudulent from the start. If we could find proof of a criminal act, we could use it against him.'

McIntosh sat back in his chair. 'You'd have to prove it beyond the shadow of a doubt. Leave no stone unturned, as it were.'

Robert thought of his beloved Sophie and of the bleakness in her eyes during their last encounter. 'I would raise the Rock of Gibraltar if I thought a clue lay concealed beneath it.'

'Would you now.' McIntosh smiled. 'I wasn't aware Lawrence was that good a friend.'

'He isn't,' Robert admitted. 'Though I would gladly see him cleared of any wrongdoing, there is someone else far dearer to me who stands to lose a great deal more. I would give my life,' he said quietly, 'not to see that happen.'

Sophie did not expect to see Robert again. Though he was never far from her thoughts, the feelings they had for one another and the nature of what had passed between them would make it impossible for them to be easy in one another's company. The debilitating pain she would feel at seeing him, the knowledge that she might have been his wife, would always be there between them.

Besides, she was betrothed to Mr Oberon now and must endeavour to play the part. And so she shopped with Lavinia for wedding clothes and talked of flowers and churches, and showed her ring of rubies and emeralds, an ugly, ostentatious thing drawn from the bowels of the Oberon family vault, to the young ladies who asked to see it, and professed herself suitably pleased with her good fortune. More than that she could not do. She could not feign an appearance of happiness, or act light-headed and giddy as newly engaged girls were supposed to do. Instead, she grew quiet, locking her pain deep within, keeping the secret of her broken heart from those she loved the most.

And then the final axe fell. Antoine was called back to France. A distraught letter from Monsieur Larocque's wife explained that her husband had fallen on broken glass and badly lacerated his hands. She wrote that he was incapable of performing even the most basic of surgical procedures and begged Antoine to return as quickly as possible, saying there were many patients in desperate need of his care.

It had been a heart-wrenching decision for Antoine. Weighted against his desire to stay and see his sister through what would surely be one of the hardest days of her life was an equally strong desire to go back and help those who were in need of his skills. It pained him to know that without his assistance, some of those people might well lose limbs, or their sight—or even die.

Nicholas tried to make him stay, saying he would do whatever was necessary to enrol Antoine in a university where he could begin his studies towards becoming a doctor in earnest. Even Lavinia had pleaded with him not to go, saying that Sophie would be heartbroken if her only brother was not there to see her get married. But Antoine's life was *about* helping the sick. To turn his back on them now would be to deny his life-long calling—and Sophie had no intention of asking him to do that.

And so she told him to go back to Paris. She convinced him that to ignore Monsieur Larocque's cry for help would be poor repayment for everything the man

had done for him, and said that if he did not immediately return, she would always wonder about his true
desire to be a doctor.

It was of little comfort to her that he agreed. They
had been through so much the last three years, growing closer as brother and sister than many wives and
husbands ever would. But she knew that going back
was the *right* thing for Antoine to do. Not only was he
was finding it increasingly difficult not to see Jane, but
Sophie knew how he felt about her marrying a man she
did not love, a man for whom he could feel no respect
or affection.

'There will be no turning back from this mistake,
*petite*,' Antoine said the night before he left. 'When you
are his wife, you will belong to him. I will not be able
to help you. If he wishes it, you will be lost to me for
ever.'

And Sophie had walked into his arms and held him
tightly because she'd known he was speaking the truth.
A man could beat his wife or have her committed to an
institution without fear of retribution. When a woman
married, she and her husband became one person—and
in the eyes of the law, that person was *the* man.

But, marry him she would, because she had made
a promise to protect the lives of the people she loved.
Surely it was better knowing that Antoine was living
the life he wanted in Paris than to sit here wondering if
the next person who walked into his surgery might be
there to arrest him. Surely it was better knowing that
Nicholas and Lavinia were able to move freely about
London than to live with the fear that someone might
jump out at them from the shadows of a darkened alley.

Surely it was better knowing that Robert was going

on without her than to lie awake at night wondering if
he would meet an unfortunate *accident*, as Oberon had
so casually suggested that morning outside Clark and
Debenham's.

How much happiness could she have known with
that kind of fear dogging her every step?

And so it was that on the day Sophie walked out of
the drapers after the final fitting of her wedding gown,
that she was able to find the strength to look Robert
Silverton in the eye after all but colliding with him.
To speak to him in tones resembling those of a normal
conversation.

'Mr Silverton. Forgive me. I should have paid more
attention to where I was going.'

'The fault was not yours, Miss Vallois.' He bent to
retrieve one of the parcels she had dropped. 'I should
have known better than to walk so quickly along so
crowded a street.' He straightened to look at her and she
saw the pain reflected in his eyes. 'Especially during
the height of the shopping hour.'

Sophie closed her eyes. She had been so close. So
close to convincing herself she had the strength to do
this. To know that she would not crumble the first time
she saw him again. But meeting him like this was her
undoing. An inadvertent collision on a busy street
served as a bittersweet reminder of all they meant to
one another—and all they were destined to lose. And it
took every ounce of courage she possessed to pretend
an indifference she was far from feeling. 'I trust your
sister is well?'

'Well enough.' Robert's voice was quiet, but strained.

'She spends a great deal of time in her room. Writing letters.'

'Yes, writing can be…a pleasant pastime,' Sophie agreed. Poor Jane. The girl's heart was as badly broken as her own. Since Antoine's return to Paris, she had received not a single word from Jane, and the girl had been all but absent from society.

Sophie bit her lip and glanced behind her, hoping to see Lavinia emerge from the shop.

'I was surprised your brother decided to return to France before the wedding,' Robert said, fixing his attention on a nearby curricle. 'I thought he would have wanted to be here to see you…marry.'

'He did, very much,' Sophie said, unhappiness falling like an iron bar across her chest. 'But he received a letter concerning the gentleman to whom he is apprenticed and learned that he himself had been badly injured. His wife begged Antoine to return to take care of his patients. Naturally, Antoine wished to help in any way he could.'

'Of course. Your brother is dedicated to his work.'

'It means everything to him.' Oh, *why* did Lavinia not come out? This unbearably polite discourse was growing more painful by the minute. And then Robert made it even worse.

'I have no right to say this to you, Sophie, but I cannot let you go to Oberon without telling you that I love you with all my heart and that if you ever have need of my help for *any* reason, you have only to come to me and I will—'

'Mr Silverton,' Lavinia said, finally emerging from the shop. 'What a pleasant surprise.'

Robert stepped back. His jaw tightened as he belatedly offered her a bow. 'Lady Longworth.'

'Nicholas and I were talking about you just the other
day. He said he sees very little of you about town these
days.'

'I think it merely that our paths do not cross.'

Lavinia smiled. 'Of course. And how does dear Jane
go on?'

'She engages herself with writing. I think she pens
a novel in secret.'

'A novel! How exciting,' Lavinia said. 'I have always
wanted to write a book, but find myself sadly lacking
in imagination. No doubt it would be a very dry and
boring effort.'

'I'm sure you underestimate your abilities, Lady
Longworth.'

Sophie felt him glance in her direction, but knew
better than to meet his gaze. It was heartbreaking to see
him like this, knowing he would never be more than a
passing acquaintance. How would she ever bear it...?

'Well, I suppose I had best be on my way,' Robert
said at length. 'Good morning, Lady Longworth. Miss
Vallois.'

'Mr Silverton,' Lavinia said quietly, only to breathe
a deep sigh a few minutes later. 'Poor man. He thinks
he conceals his pain, but it is there for all to see. And
dear Jane obviously pines as much for your brother as
you do for Robert.'

Dangerously close to tears, Sophie whispered huskily, 'I do not pine for Mr Silverton.'

'Of course you do. Oh, you can say what you like to
everyone else, but I know what's in your heart, Sophie,'
Lavinia said as they turned and walked in the other

direction. 'I too married one man when I was falling in love with another. And I cared a great deal more for François than you do for Mr Oberon. And though you refuse to explain your reasons for marrying Mr Oberon, I know there *is* an explanation. Oh, no, dear, please don't cry! I didn't mean to make you cry.'

Sophie shook her head, dashing away tears. 'It was just so hard to see him again.'

'Of course it was, and I shouldn't have said anything,' Lavinia said. 'I know how deeply you're suffering. But if you will not change your mind, there is nothing we can do but carry on. The wedding is only a few days away and we still have much to do.'

Sophie nodded, swallowing hard. 'Where are we to go next?'

'We *should* go to Madame Egaltine's for gloves. However...' Lavinia smiled as tucked her arm in Sophie's. 'I think we shall call at Gunter's for ices instead. I believe we are both in need of a little refreshment.'

# Chapter Fifteen

Given the nature of Oberon's crime, Robert suspected there were very few people who would know the full extent of the scheme, or the scope of the financial damage done to Lawrence Welton. Oberon would, but there was no point in looking to him for answers. And while Lawrence might know, it seemed he was unwilling to disclose any details as to what had really happened.

'I signed the papers,' was all he would say. 'I gave them back to Oberon and he assured me he would send me a copy once the lawyer had finalised the details. But he never did. And by the time I realised I had nothing in writing, it was too late.'

The disappointing results forced Robert to focus his attention on two other possible sources of information, the first being the legal firm where the papers had been drawn up, and the second being Mr Stanley Hunt, Welton's man of business. Unfortunately, discreet investigations carried out over the course of the next few days yielded little of use. Having been as effectively deceived by Oberon as his employer, Mr Hunt was deeply embarrassed at being asked about the case and sought to bring the interview to a close as quickly as possible.

As for Sir Thomas Buckley, senior partner with the law firm Buckley, Stevens and Mortimer, the results were equally disappointing. Sir Thomas had worked for both the present Lord Mannerfield and his father for many years; though Robert was not granted an interview with the lofty barrister, he was informed by the clerk who guarded that gentleman's office with the ferocity of a Trojan that much of the work done for the son had been handled by a Mr Adrian Brocknower.

When Robert asked to see Mr Brocknower, the clerk informed him in the most discouraging of tones that the gentleman was no longer in the employ of the firm and that he had no idea where he lived or for whom he might be working—both of which convinced Robert that he had to find Brocknower as soon as possible. A position with a prestigious company was hard to come by. Had Brocknower left of his own volition, or had he been forced out by circumstances beyond his control?

Unfortunately, *finding* Adrian Brocknower turned out to be even more of a challenge. After asking endless questions and checking out three addresses, Robert still had nothing. The rooms were all empty and the landladies had no idea where their tenant had gone. Nor did they care, since, unlike many of the young men who passed through their doors, this one had paid his account in full.

It was enough to drive a sane man to drink and, in a mood to work off some of his excess frustration, Robert made his way to Angelo's. There were always a number of cocky young men anxious to perfect the finer points of the thrust and salute, and while few of them were up to Robert's level of play, they would serve to take the edge off his anger. Unfortunately, by the time he arrived, most of the better fencers had already paired themselves off, and those who were new to the game were happy to practise their lunges in front of a mirror.

Robert made his way to a bench along the back wall and set down his foil. He'd just have to wait it out.

'Are you engaged to meet a partner, sir?'

The voice was quiet. Refined. A mellow baritone perfect for reciting Shakespeare. Robert turned to find a tall gentleman in fencing garb standing opposite him. The man's hair was almost black, and though his face was partially covered by a mask, Robert knew from what little he could see that the man was a stranger to him. 'I am not, sir.'

'Then perhaps you would care to spar with me?'

Robert inclined his head. 'By all means.'

The man led the way on to the floor, walking with the unconscious dignity of a prince. Robert noticed he kept a distance from the other fencers, but was equally aware that no one seemed to be paying them any mind. 'I don't believe I've seen you in here before,' he said casually.

'I usually practise in private, but I thought this afternoon I might benefit from the company of others.' He stopped and turned around. 'Are you ready?'

Robert up took his position. 'When you are.'

The match was surprisingly good. Robert soon determined the man's skill to be equal to his own, if not slightly better. He moved quickly, expending no unnecessary effort, but his swordplay was quick and well aimed. He struck three times before Robert managed his first hit, and when they drew even at six, they agreed to take a break.

'You fence well, sir,' Robert said, breathing harder than his opponent. 'It is evident I have been too long from the game.'

'You present an excellent form and style, Mr Silverton,' the gentleman said. 'I think only your physical stamina is lacking.'

Robert reached for a towel and wiped the sweat from his face. He hadn't missed the fact that the stranger had addressed him by name. 'Perhaps you have more time to practise than I.'

'I agree that technique generally improves with regular practice, but I find extra tutelage also helps. There is a gentleman near Covent Garden who gives private lessons.' The stranger pulled out a card and handed it to Robert. 'You will find him at this address. But I suggest you go tonight. And if he asks, tell him Parker sent you.'

Robert took the card, his eyes widening at the sight of Adrian Brocknower's name and address. 'How did you know—?'

'Let's just say it has come to my attention that you have been asking questions about a common enemy. I happen to be in possession of information that may prove useful to you.'

Robert inclined his head. Whoever this Parker fellow was, he obviously had a grudge against Oberon too. Strange he didn't want to settle it himself. 'I am indebted to you, sir.' He tucked the card securely into his pocket. 'Can I interest you in another match?'

He saw the gentleman's mouth curve behind the

mask. 'Always. But I give you fair warning, Mr Silverton. *This* time, I intend to play.'

There was nothing Sophie could do to alter the path upon which she had set out. But when she thought about Robert's last words and realised what the rest of her life was going to be like, she knew she could not go any further without allowing herself one brief moment of happiness. Insanity it might be, but it was surely no worse than the madness she was already contemplating.

As she stepped out of the hackney late that afternoon, she looked up at the house on Portman Square and was aware of feeling strangely calm. Was this how a condemned man felt as he enjoyed the last few hours of his life? Was this heady feeling of freedom common amongst women who were on the verge of betraying their husbands or lovers?

As she walked towards the front door, she took some comfort from the fact that she had not yet stood before God and his angels and sworn fidelity to a man she despised.

The door opened to her knock and, ignoring the butler's quickly concealed look of surprise, she was shown into the drawing room. It was well past the hour for social calls, but Sophie had sent Jane a note advising her of her intention to call, and asking if she could please make sure her brother was there. She had also asked that Jane not tell him she was coming. It was best he had no opportunity to prepare for her arrival.

Jane was waiting for her in the drawing room. She rose as Sophie entered and Sophie saw how deeply she suffered. She seemed to have lost weight, and her beautiful green eyes were dark and haunted. 'Dearest Sophie, I am so glad to see you again.'

'And I you,' Sophie said, kissing Jane on both cheeks. 'But you do not look at all well.'

'I am not,' Jane said with a sigh of resignation. 'But I shall recover, in time.' She glanced towards the door. 'Robert will be down shortly.'

'You didn't tell him I was coming?'

'You asked me not to.'

Sophie nodded. It was only natural that Jane should be curious, but she had no intention of revealing any of what she planned. That would be for ever between herself and Robert. If she was to burn in hell for what she was about to do, she would go to the devil alone.

Suddenly, the door opened and Robert walked in. 'Jane, I thought I heard someone at the—?' He broke off and his face went pale. 'Sophie!'

'Good evening, Mr Silverton.'

For a moment, they stood there: three actors in a play, each waiting for the other to speak his lines. When no one did, Jane walked over to Sophie, kissed her on the cheek and left. And in the seconds that followed, Sophie knew how a prisoner must feel while waiting for the judge to pronounce sentence. She'd had no idea that silence could be so terrifying.

'What has happened to bring you here?' Robert said softly. 'Dare I hope you've changed your mind?'

Sophie stared at his tall, upright figure and wondered how was it possible to be so vibrantly aware of a man, so desperate for his touch that her body quivered at the very thought of it. 'The only thing that's happened is that I've realised what my life is going to be like once I am married to Mr Oberon.' Sophie slowly untied the ribbons beneath her chin and slipped off her bonnet. 'And I knew I could not go to him without seeing you one more time. Alone.'

She heard his harsh rasp of breath. 'Don't marry him, Sophie. I beg you!'

But she only shook her head. 'I will not change my mind, but if the rest of my life is to be lived in darkness, I would ask for one bright memory to carry into it. Give me that memory, Robert,' she said, stopping before him. 'You're the only one who can.'

They were so close that Sophie could feel the warmth of his breath on her face. At one time, she would have thought it impossible that she would be willing to sacrifice everything for one brief moment of intimacy, but she had lain awake too many hours going over what she wanted to say to back down now. Before she'd met Robert, she'd had no idea what it was to truly be in love. Now, she did. And with the thought of losing him, nothing else seemed to matter.

When he didn't move, Sophie placed her bare hands against his chest, tilted her face up to his and kissed him. Kissed him with the desperate longing of one who knows it will be the last time. And though his lips remained stiff and unmoving beneath hers, she didn't back away. If he rejected her, it would not be because she hadn't done her best to seduce him.

But Robert didn't reject her—and Sophie knew the exact moment his resistance broke. She heard his anguished groan and felt his arms come around her, crushing her against him. His mouth covered hers hungrily and she trembled as his tongue slipped between her lips, coaxing them apart. Sensation flowed through her veins like liquid fire. The taste of him was intoxicating, the scent of him enough to make her senses swim. There was only this man, this time, this moment. She felt his hand at her breast, a light, fleeting caress, but it was as though a whirlwind swept through her body.

*More*. She *needed* him to go on caressing her so that when another man touched her, it would be Robert's caresses she remembered. Robert's face she saw. Robert's love that filled her heart.

'Dear God, Sophie.' His voice was tortured, his breathing harsh. 'If I don't stop soon—'

'I don't want you to stop!' she said urgently. 'Make love to me, Robert. Just once, so I'll know what passion really is.'

She felt his lips against her hair. 'You haven't thought this through, beloved. If you truly intend to proceed with this abysmal marriage, it would be madness for us to be together. You *must* know that!'

Sophie weakly rested her forehead against his chin, her body thrumming with emotion. 'I do. But for once in my life, I don't care. I don't want to be sensible. Please don't ask that of me.'

'I have no choice. I can't do something that will make your life more a living hell than it already is. The body doesn't lie, Sophie,' he whispered. 'Oberon will know you've been with another man.'

'But he doesn't need know it was you!' Sophie gazed up into his eyes. 'He already believes the worst of me. Let him think it happened *before* I came to England.'

'It would not make his rage any the less terrifying, nor would it lessen the punishment he metes out. I cannot do what you ask, Sophie,' Robert said. 'God help me, I would never know a moment's peace again.'

With that, he put his hands on her arms and gently pushed her away.

Sophie closed her eyes, fighting to quell her feelings of disappointment and frustration. He was right, of course. It would be madness to go to Oberon after having made love to Robert. She could tell him what she liked, but she knew he would suspect Robert of being the one, and there was no telling what form his anger and revenge might take. And was the purpose of this marriage not to *ensure* the safety of those she loved?

'Forgive me,' he whispered, standing with his forehead pressed against hers.

Sophie closed her eyes, fighting back tears. 'No. I'm the one who should be asking forgiveness. I was thinking only of what I wanted, without regard for the future. The choice to marry him is my own. I should not have asked you to put yourself at risk by indulging me in such a way.'

'I would indulge you in every way imaginable,' Robert said, his voice heavy with longing. 'There is nothing I want more than to make love to you, Sophie. But not when I *know* what he will do when I'm not there to protect you.'

'Then kiss me goodbye,' she said, gazing up at him. 'And know that whatever he has to take from me, I give you willingly.'

His mouth was not gentle. The kiss was savage. Demanding—and Sophie welcomed it. She buried her fingers in his hair, dragging his head down as she pressed her body even closer to his, seared by the passion that burned between them. This was all she would ever have. One moment in an eternity of loneliness. One moment that would become the memory she would cling to for the rest of her life.

All too soon, it was over. Robert kissed her once more, then gently pushed her away. Numbly, Sophie picked up her bonnet and put it on, tying the silken ribbons beneath her chin. Without looking at him, she turned and started towards the door.

'Sophie.'

She stopped, but didn't turn around. 'Yes?'

'I'm following a lead. I can't tell you more because I don't know what I'll find. But I won't let you go until I've exhausted every possible avenue.'

Sophie nodded, but kept her gaze on the floor. 'Then I will go to bed hoping for good news, my love. Because if you cannot find that avenue within the next twenty-four hours, there will no longer be any need to look.'

# Chapter Sixteen

Adrian Brocknower was leaving. That much became
evident the moment Robert stepped into the dilapi-
dated room at the top of the stairs, on a street where no
self-respecting gentleman would ever admit to keeping
rooms. The narrow bed was bare, the wardrobe doors
flung back, and there was a portmanteau lying open on
the rough wooden floor.

'I'm glad I didn't wait any longer,' Robert said as he
watched the sole occupant of the room throw clothes
haphazardly into the case. 'Or I would have been forced
to add yet another vacated address to my list.'

The young man whirled, his face twisted in fear.
'Who the hell are you?'

'A friend. Parker sent me.'

'Parker?'

'Yes. We met this morning at Angelo's,' Robert
explained. 'He gave me your card and said to mention
his name. I take it you *are* Adrian Brocknower?'

Hearing Parker's name seemed to have a calm-
ing effect on the younger man, but his look was still

guarded as he returned to his packing. 'For now, but I won't be much longer.'

Robert quickly took stock of the other man. In his early twenties, he was of middling height and slim build. His dark hair was unkempt and his long, narrow face bore the unmistakable stamp of fear. 'You're running away.'

'Disappearing, actually.' Adrian reached for the small collection of books on the desk and dropped them into the case. 'I don't intend to be here when he finds out what I've done.'

'He?'

'You know who.' Adrian looked up. 'If Parker sent you, he's the reason you're here.'

'All right,' Robert said, crossing his arms in front of his chest. 'What exactly *have* you done?'

Adrian pulled open a drawer and emptied the contents. 'I've uncovered a fraud, haven't I? And I was foolish enough to tell my employer about it.'

'Your employer being Sir Thomas Buckley.'

'That's right. I told him I'd found inconsistencies in the paperwork. Documents that should have been registered left unsigned. Monies that should have been invested. And when I brought it to Sir Thomas's attention, he told me I'd meddled in areas that were none of my concern and said my services were no longer required.'

'He turned you off?'

'On the spot. When I tried to explain I was simply following procedure, he had me escorted from the premises, without a letter of recommendation or my final pay. He also threatened me with legal action if I breathed a word of this to anyone.'

'And have you?' Robert enquired.

'Parker knows. He advised me to write it all down, so I did. All the names, all the dates, as well as how much money each person invested and where it was supposedly allocated.'

'Supposedly?'

'You can't put money into something that doesn't exist.'

Robert's eyes widened. 'So there *was* a scam. No wonder Sir Thomas's clerk didn't want to talk to me.'

Adrian tensed. 'You didn't go round the firm, did you? Asking questions? Looking for me?'

'I did go round, but not because I was looking for you. I was hoping to speak to Sir Thomas,' Robert said. 'But after being politely but firmly rebuffed, I learned that *you* had handled much of the paperwork for Sir Thomas and that made me think you might be the one I needed to see—especially once I found out you were no longer with the firm.'

'Yes, well, that's probably for the best,' Adrian said. 'I wouldn't want to be in Sir Thomas's shoes when word of this gets out. From what little I've heard, Mr Oberon is not a forgiving man.'

'Would he have reason to suspect you?'

'I'm not willing to take the chance. He didn't know Sir Thomas handed most of the paperwork off to someone else, and Sir Thomas didn't think I was smart enough to find anything wrong.' Adrian shot him a derisive look. 'I was only a clerk, after all.'

Robert smiled. It never paid to underestimate one's subordinates. 'Where is this list of information you've compiled?'

'Before I tell you that, I want your word as a gentleman that you won't tell a soul who gave it to you.'

'You have it,' Robert said without hesitation. 'But when Oberon is charged, he's bound to know someone betrayed him. And there aren't that many people in the game.'

'That's why I'm getting out of London. If this all blows up, Sir Thomas will point the finger of blame at me, and by the time that happens, I'll have changed my name and be living somewhere Oberon will never find me.'

'With luck, he won't get out of prison long enough to try.'

Adrian laughed. 'Oberon won't go to prison. His father's a peer.'

'He will if I have anything to do with it,' Robert said quietly. 'He's ruined too many lives to go free.'

'Well, I wish you well with it, sir, but I've seen money and power triumph over justice and truth too many times to believe it works the other way round.' With that, Adrian walked across to the open wardrobe and leaned in. There was a sound of wood splintering, and moments later, he re-emerged holding a slim, leather-bound journal. 'You can read it if you like,' he said, handing it across. 'I never want to see it again.'

Robert took the journal, but didn't open it. 'Why didn't you show this to the authorities?'

'And risk going up against the likes of Lord Oberon? Not a chance. They'd have charged *me* with fraud rather than put the blame where it belonged. No, if you hadn't come along, this book would likely have ended up in the Thames. Or with Parker.'

Robert looked down at the journal. Parker again. He was growing curious about this man who operated in secret and seemed to know things about people most others didn't. 'I'm very glad to have this, Mr Brock-nower. Perhaps I can use it to help some of the people Oberon has swindled.'

For the first time, Adrian smiled and in doing so, looked less like the fearful young man circumstances had forced him to become. 'I just want to see justice done. Wealth and privilege don't deserve to be in the hands of a man like that.'

'No, they don't.' Robert put the journal on the bed and pulled an envelope from his pocket. 'I don't know where you're going, but this will either help get you there, or establish you once you arrive.'

Adrian stared at the envelope, his face flushing when he realised what it was. 'I'd like to say I don't need this, but I do. Thank you, sir. I'm glad I had the pleasure of meeting you.'

'The pleasure's all mine, Mr Brocknower.' Robert turned to go, and then stopped. 'By the by, who is this Parker chap?'

'Sir Barrington Parker?' Adrian laughed. 'To tell you the truth, I don't know much about him. He came to see Sir Thomas a few times and I once heard him mention Mr Oberon's name. I thought he might be a friend of his, until I chanced to meet him in the street and he told me to watch myself around him.'

'Did he say why?'

'No, but I found out soon enough.'

Robert smiled. 'I'll leave you to your packing. I have a few appointments of my own to keep before this night is over.'

Oberon was at his club when Robert caught up with him. Just as well. He was less inclined to commit murder with that many witnesses around. 'Evening, Oberon.'

'Well, well, if it isn't my old friend, Silver,' Oberon said, leaning back in his chair. 'And looking very serious, I might add.'

'I have been engaged on serious business,' Robert said.

'Why don't you join me for a drink and tell me about it?' Oberon invited. 'I shall enjoy spending my last hours as a bachelor in the company of my good friend. Stokes! A brandy for Mr Silverton!'

Robert studied the man with whom he had gambled away more nights than he cared to remember and wondered that he had ever thought him a friend. Now, he could only see him for what he was: a desperate, conniving man who took no responsibility for his actions. One who felt no qualms about destroying other people's hopes and dreams.

A man who would ruin an innocent young woman's life in a twisted attempt to thwart another's.

'So, Robert, what business have you been engaged upon that has you looking so glum?' Oberon asked. 'Although, perhaps before you tell me, I should demand that you settle the terms of our wager. You owe me for not having told me the truth about my bride.'

Robert didn't so much as blink. 'The truth?'

'About her being a farmer's daughter, of course,' Oberon said, laughing. 'What a turnabout, eh? A viscount's son marrying the daughter of an impoverished French farmer. My, how the *ton* would laugh if they were to hear such a tale. How I would be roasted for having allowed myself to be taken advantage of by a beautiful face. But they won't, of course, because I have already concocted a delightful new background for my beautiful bride. Shall I tell you what it is?'

'Oberon—'

'No, really, I insist you listen. You'll find it quite amusing. The young lady is actually the only daughter of the Comte de Shaltiere, a noble Frenchman who, sadly, was killed in a tragic accident just north of Lyon. His wife, the beautiful Comtesse de Shaltiere, died too, leaving Sophie and her brother to be raised by a kindly aunt whose name I cannot remember and who no one is ever going to find.'

'You're wasting your time, Oberon.'

'No, in fact, I am making extremely good use of it,' Oberon said. 'I've had to because you've not been the good friend I believed you to be. A good friend would have told me about Miss Vallois's origins, as I understand you learned of them some time ago.'

'It came up in conversation.'

'And you did not think it important enough to share with me?'

Robert met the belligerent gaze with equanimity. 'My decision not to say anything had more to do with protecting *her* good name than yours.'

'Yes, no doubt you and the Longworths were in collusion. Making sure no one ever found out that the beautiful Miss Vallois was actually a farmer's daughter.'

'There was no collusion and it was never the Longworths' intent to make anyone believe Miss Vallois was something she was not.'

'Then why dress her up in fine clothes and present her as though she were a lady?' Oberon snapped. 'What was *that* if not a calculated attempt to convince society she was well born?'

'Miss Vallois may not be well born, but she is every inch a lady.'

'Rubbish! She is a farmer's brat. The sad consequence of peasants rutting in the fields.'

Robert had to fight the urge to lean across the table and grab Oberon by the throat. 'If you feel that way, why not call the whole thing off?'

'Call it off? What, so that you can march in and marry the chit yourself? Oh, no, Silver, I won't let you trump me in this. There's far too much at stake. Besides, I have my pride.'

'But I *love* her,' Robert said quietly. 'Can you make the same claim?'

'Good God, no, nor would I want to! But she still stirs my blood and I want her in my bed.' Oberon's eyes darkened with lust. 'French women are passionate creatures. With the right encouragement, she'll quiver like a finely plucked bow. In truth, if it were a simple matter to make her my mistress, that's exactly what I would do. But I'd no doubt find myself facing pistols at dawn with you or Longworth or that bothersome brother of hers. So, I shall marry the wench and make sure the story I've come up with is the *only* one society is allowed to hear. Then I shall bury her in the country with my sister. No doubt she and Elaine will be delightful company for one another.'

A red mist boiled in Robert's head, but when he spoke, his voice was like cold steel. 'And how do you think Lord and Lady Longworth will take to your spreading lies about Miss Vallois?'

'I don't really give a damn. They should have told me the truth when I informed them of my interest in her,' Oberon said in a silken voice. 'But they didn't, did they? They *allowed* me to believe the chit was worthy of my attention, and like a fool, I went to them and asked permission to court her. Imagine! The son of a peer asking permission to address a French peasant. Well, it will do well for them to keep the information to themselves. I can make life very unpleasant for both of them if I choose.'

Robert's voice hardened. 'As you've said, you hold people in the palm of your hand.'

'Indeed. But I grow weary of this conversation. Bring the ring to my house tonight,' Oberon said, pouring himself another glass of brandy. 'I intend having it made into a necklace for my new bride. I shall tell her how I came by it and every time she looks at it, she will think of you. A fitting present, don't you think?'

Robert slowly clenched his fists, aware of an unholy desire to punch Oberon senseless. The man's arrogance was revolting, his certainty that he had won an offence to common decency. But it was his total lack of regard for Sophie's feelings that had Robert longing to throw the existence of the journal in his face and watch him squeal like a stuck pig.

He wouldn't, of course. Adrian Brocknower would never be made to suffer for his honesty. The journal was now in the hands of Robert's lawyer with the instructions that it be kept under lock and key until he returned. That alone enabled him to keep a grip on his emotions. He must for Sophie's sake. To prevent the horror her life would become if she were to marry Oberon.

'I will not give you the ring, Oberon,' Robert said at length. 'And there will be no wedding. You are to release Miss Vallois from her promise and swear never to go near her again.'

After a moment spent gazing at him in astonishment, Oberon threw back his head and laughed. 'My dear Silver, what on earth are you talking about? Of course there will be a wedding. And you will be there to see it. Sitting in the front row with Jane and Nicholas and Lavinia. And once it is over, I intend to get *very* close to my darling wife. I intend to strip the gown from her delicious body and take my time ravishing her—'

'You said more than once,' Robert interrupted, his voice vibrating with anger, 'that everyone had a history. Some histories are good, some contain secrets that are both dark and disturbing. Yours is just such a history, Oberon. And I intend to expose it for all the world to see.'

'Expose me?' Oberon sneered. 'My poor deluded friend, you don't know what you're talking about.'

'Ah, but I do. Because I know what you've been doing. I know about your abominable treatment of Lawrence Welton and your attempts to cripple him by having him pour money into a phoney investment scheme. I also know that what you spend far exceeds your allowance and that you do, in fact, owe a great deal of money. Debts your father knows nothing about. Oh, yes, I've done my own bit of investigating,' Robert said, taking pleasure in watching the colour drain out of Oberon's face. 'And when the world finds out what you've done, you *will* be a broken man.'

'You've taken leave of your senses,' Oberon said, his expression growing uglier by the minute. 'No one will believe you. And you certainly won't find anyone to corroborate your story.'

'I don't need corroboration when I have proof. Proof that is safely in the hands of my lawyer even now.'

For the first time, Oberon faltered, a crack appearing in the smooth façade. 'You're lying! No one knew what I was doing.'

'Unfortunately for you, several people did,' Robert said. 'And records *were* kept. Meticulous records, I might add.'

He knew the moment Oberon began to believe him. It was the same moment the snake reappeared, a desperate creature concerned only with its own survival. 'Who told you?' he hissed. 'Give me his name and we'll talk about my releasing Miss Vallois.'

Robert shook his head. 'I'm afraid it isn't that simple. You see, crimes *have* been committed. The Scottish railway scheme for one. The California land deal for another.'

Oberon's face suddenly went a sickly shade of grey. 'You're bluffing.'

'Are you willing to bet your life on it?'

In an instant, it was over. The cocky, self-assured man was replaced by a quivering coward who knew the cards were stacked against him. Lady luck had turned—and she had turned with a vengeance. 'What do you want?' Oberon growled.

'Write a note. Two lines will suffice,' Robert said, 'agreeing to release Miss Vallois from her promise and guaranteeing that you will never contact her again. Write the same letter to Lord and Lady Longworth. I will deliver them both this evening.'

'And if I refuse?'

'You won't.' Robert got to his feet and signalled for the butler to bring pen and paper. 'You will also place a notice in *The Times*, announcing that the engagement between you and Miss Vallois is over.'

'And if I do all that,' Oberon asked petulantly, 'what is my fate to be?'

'That is for the authorities to decide. I'm sure your father will intervene on your behalf and no doubt he will succeed in getting your sentence reduced. But given what is likely to be revealed about your dealings with others, you may not wish to remain long in London.'

The butler placed parchment and a quill on the table. With a visible display of irritation, Oberon began to write. 'Anything else?'

'Yes. Strike the entry from the betting book,' Robert said. 'The Mistress Wager is now officially and for ever at an end.'

Sophie heard a carriage draw to a halt in the street outside the house just before ten o'clock that evening and went rigid with apprehension. Surely Oberon had not come to gloat. Surely he would have the decency to leave her in peace on this, her final evening as a single woman.

She heard the sharp rap of the brass knocker and then the sound of footsteps as Banyon went to answer the door. Muffled conversation followed, followed by more footsteps, and then still more muffled conversation.

She waited for what seemed an eternity for the drawing-room door to open. Ten minutes later when the mantel clock chimed the hour and the drawing-room door still remained closed, Sophie sank into the nearest chair, relieved beyond measure that the visitor had not come to see her.

How tragic her life had become that she should so desperately fear the thought of callers. That the sound of a carriage should set her nerves on edge. This, truly, was what it was to live in fear. And tomorrow, that fear would take on an entirely new dimension. Tomorrow she would become the wife of Montague Oberon and lose all rights to how she led her life. She would be expected to do as her husband bid. Go where her husband directed. Say what her husband told her to say. Without thought. Without will. Without choice.

In short, her life would become purgatory. It would have to, for Oberon didn't love her. The expression of disgust on his face had been more than enough to convince her of his true sentiments. Lust would remain, as would the need to chastise and control, but there would be nothing of the gentler emotions in their marriage. No affection. No respect. No forgiveness. There would be fear and brutality and loathing—and there was nothing Sophie could do to prevent it. If she ran back to Paris and tried to lose herself in the crowded streets, Oberon would exact his vengeance on those who stayed behind. Her fate was sealed. She *had* to marry him to ensure the safety of the people she loved.

And Robert?

Sophie closed her eyes, feeling the hot sting of tears as she pictured his face. They'd had so little time together, and now even that was over. His memory would become her salvation. When the days stretched long and the weight of her new life pressed down upon her, thoughts of him would be all that carried her through. She would remember the way it felt to be held in his arms, play over and over the sweetness of his kiss.

And when the night came and with it a suffocating darkness that threatened to blot out all hope, she would cling to the memory of him asking her to be his wife. She would remember that, for a few blissful days, she had actually believed it would come true. Until Oberon had returned—and ground her dreams into dust.

The click of the drawing-room door as it opened brought Sophie to her feet. She held her breath and pressed her hands to her stomach, willing the tumultuous butterflies to settle. But it was only Nicholas and Lavinia who came in. Nicholas, who had tried to do so much for her and, in the end, had been able to do nothing. And dear Lavinia, who had become like a second mother. She searched their faces, looking for some indication as to what had happened. 'Someone came?' she ventured.

'Yes, someone came,' Lavinia said quietly. 'A gentleman, bringing with him the most wonderful news.'

'*Wonderful* news?' Sophie glanced at Nicholas, hardly daring to breathe. 'Tell me quickly. What has happened?'

'You are not to marry Oberon,' Nicholas said, holding out a sheet of parchment. 'He has withdrawn his offer.'

'*Withdrawn it?*' Sophie flew across the room and took the letter in hands that shook so badly she could scarcely read the words. There were only two lines—but they said all that mattered. 'I am released,' she whispered. 'Oberon no longer wishes to marry me. And he has given his word that…he will not try to see me again.' She raised her head. 'How has this come to pass? What on earth could have made him change his mind?'

'Can you not guess?' Nicholas asked. And when he moved aside, she saw Robert standing quietly in the doorway.

'Good evening, Miss Vallois. I trust you are well.'

'Robert! That is…Mr Silverton. Yes, I think I am.'

The letter fluttered to the floor. 'In fact...better than I've been for some time. But I am also very confused.'

Robert strolled forwards, his eyes never leaving her face. 'Then I will do my best to clear up the mystery.'

'Lavinia, I believe our presence is required elsewhere,' Nicholas said, stretching his arm towards his wife. 'These two have much to talk about.'

Lavinia was beaming. 'Yes, of course they do.' But before she left, she stopped to give Sophie a quick hug and whisper in her ear, 'I told you your face would give you away.' Then she joined her husband and the two left the room arm in arm.

As the door closed behind them, Sophie turned to face the man she had thought never to see again. 'Why has he released me?'

Robert bent to pick up the fallen piece of parchment. 'Oberon once told me that everyone had secrets, and he was right. But he intended using yours as a weapon against you and I couldn't allow that to happen. So I started asking questions. I needed to uncover the secrets in his past, and if I could find any, to use them against him.'

'And you found some?'

'Oh, yes, and they were far more incriminating than yours. You see, Oberon had several fatal flaws,' Robert said. 'His insatiable appetite for money, his reckless desire for power and his uncontrollable need to gamble. Taken alone, any one of those vices would be enough to destroy a man. But when all three are combined and you add a complete lack of conscience to the mix, disaster is sure to follow. It was only a matter of time before his wrongdoings caught up with him.'

'What did you find out?'

Robert shook his head. 'The details don't matter. Suffice it to say that he committed a crime for which he will be made to pay.'

Sophie arched a brow. 'Lawrence Welton?'

'Amongst others. The list stretches long.'

'What will happen to him now?'

'That is for the courts to decide. There is no getting around the fact that his father is a peer and that he will do everything in his power to clear his son of the charges. But the harm Oberon has done other people is extensive and will not soon be forgotten. I think it unlikely he will wish to linger in London once word of this gets out.'

So it was true. She was not to marry Oberon—and he was never going to bother her again. Relief bubbled up like a wellspring. 'Then it really is over.'

'It is, and you are free to go on with your life. A retraction of the engagement will appear in *The Times*, and your brother and Lord and Lady Longworth need no longer fear exposure of any kind for their past activities.'

Sophie's eyes opened wide. 'You knew about that?'

'I put two and two together—after a rather enlightening conversation with Lord Longworth.' His gaze was both gentle and teasing. 'If I ever find myself nursing a gunshot wound, I'll know who to go to. It seems you and your brother are quite adept when it comes to patching up wounded Englishmen.'

She started to laugh, not sure whether it was from joy or relief. 'I told you I could be of assistance, but you *would* try to put me in my place.'

'So I did.' His own eyes lightened, his expression becoming almost boyish. 'You're quite the woman,

Sophie Vallois. Marrying Oberon to ensure their safety was an incredibly brave, albeit unspeakably foolish, thing to do.'

'How could I have done otherwise?' Sophie asked simply. 'There was so much at stake. Antoine's future. Nicholas and Lavinia's well-being. Your reputation. Perhaps your very *life*. How could I have married you *knowing* that by doing so, I was wilfully putting all of that at risk?'

'For what it's worth, he couldn't have done anything worse to me than force me to watch you marry him,' Robert said. He came so close that she could see the tiny creases fanning out from the corners of his eyes. 'But now it doesn't matter. No one's life is in jeopardy and you are free to marry whomever you please. Although…' he reached for her left hand and raised it to his lips '…I hope your mind is already made up in that regard.'

Sophie raised her free hand to caress his face, loving the texture of his skin, the rough stubble of beard on his chin. She could scarcely bear to think about how close she'd come to losing him. Of what her life would have been like without him. 'It has been made up for some time. And I cannot see it changing now that we have been given a second chance.'

'Ah, Sophie.' Her name was a benediction, and having her in his arms was a sure sign that all was right in his world. 'When will you marry me?'

'Now. Tonight, if it were possible,' she told him, her eyes glowing. 'But I suspect there are those who would object to the lack of notice.'

'Your brother being one,' he said ruefully. 'He would

never forgive me for marrying you without his being here to give you away.'

'Then I shall write to him at once,' Sophie said. 'Apparently Monsieur Larocque is recovering well, and I am told he has taken on another apprentice. As soon as Antoine can arrange to be here, I will become your wife.'

Robert smiled as he lowered his head to nuzzle the soft white skin of her throat. 'Perhaps I shall have Jane write to him as well. Then Nicholas and Lavinia will have *two* weddings to look forward to.'

A soft gasp escaped. 'You would *allow* Jane and Antoine to marry?'

'I think it the only humane thing to do. Jane has been wandering around like a sad little ghost ever since your brother went back to France. How could I enjoy my own happiness if it came at the expense of hers?'

Sophie closed her eyes, loving the warmth of his mouth on her skin though it made it exceedingly difficult to concentrate. 'For what it's worth, Antoine has been miserable too. He is desperately in love with her.'

'Then why did he say nothing to me before he left?'

'Because he felt he had nothing to offer.' Reluctantly, Sophie opened her eyes. 'Jane is a gentleman's daughter, Antoine a farmer's son. What could he give her that would compensate for all he believed she would lose by marrying him?'

'Love,' Robert said simply. 'Love, and the rest will take care of itself. With a little help from me, of course.'

Sophie smiled. 'And what about your other concern? The fact that, like myself, Antoine is French?'

'Ah, Sophie.' Robert pressed his lips to her hair. 'You see a fool standing before you. It wasn't a Frenchman who shot my brother. It was an Englishman working both sides of the war. The *same* man who shot Lord Longworth and left him for dead.'

'Never!'

'He told me as much a few days ago. And for all those years, I carried hatred in my soul for a man who didn't even exist.' Robert looked down at her, searching her face for signs that it was still an issue between them. 'When I think what it nearly cost me—'

'No.' Sophie placed her fingers against his lips. 'This is not the time for regrets. All that matters is that you do not resent Antoine for being French, or for being in love with your sister.'

'How could I resent him when I saw how he felt about her,' Robert said. 'Antoine was the only man who ever really *looked* at Jane. He didn't see her handicap. He saw a beautiful, intelligent woman and he fell in love with her. I couldn't ask for a better husband for my sister.'

'And Antoine could not ask for a better husband for his,' Sophie said softly. 'Thank you, Robert, for everything.'

'It is not your thanks I want, darling girl. Only your love.'

'That you have. But now, I think we should find Nicholas and Lavinia and tell them the wonderful news. It was very good of them to give us this time alone together.'

'I think they knew you were about to receive yet another proposal of marriage. You will marry me, won't you, Sophie?' Robert asked, gently pulling her back into his arms. 'And stay with me always?'

Sophie smiled. To think that one day soon she would say the words that would make this wonderful man her husband. Was it only a few weeks ago that the idea of marriage had seemed so untenable? That the thought of entrusting her heart to a man she'd met in a crowded coaching inn would seem so utterly implausible?

Hard to believe, but it was—and she wouldn't have changed a thing. Because everything she'd gone through had brought her to this moment. To this conclusion. To this man standing before her. 'Yes, I will marry you,' she said without hesitation. 'And I will stay with you for as long as you wish me to stay. For as long as you love me.'

'Then I expect we're going to be together for a very long time.' His eyes grew dark as he bent his head to kiss her. 'And that we are going to be happy for a longer time still.'

\* \* \* \* \*

# MILLS & BOON®

## Want to get more from Mills & Boon?

Here's what's available to you if you join the exclusive **Mills & Boon eBook Club** today:

✦ *Convenience – choose your books each month*
✦ *Exclusive – receive your books a month before anywhere else*
✦ *Flexibility – change your subscription at any time*
✦ *Variety – gain access to eBook-only series*
✦ *Value – subscriptions from just £1.99 a month*

So visit **www.millsandboon.co.uk/esubs** today to be a part of this exclusive eBook Club!

# The World of Mills & Boon

There's a Mills & Boon® series that's perfect for you. There are ten different series to choose from and new titles every month, so whether you're looking for glamorous seduction, Regency rakes, homespun heroes or sizzling erotica, we'll give you plenty of inspiration for your next read.

**By Request**

*Relive the romance with the best of the best*
12 stories every month

*Cherish*™

*Experience the ultimate rush of falling in love.*
12 new stories every month

**INTRIGUE...**

*A seductive combination of danger and desire...*
7 new stories every month

*Desire*™

*Passionate and dramatic love stories*
6 new stories every month

**n o c t u r n e**™

*An exhilarating underworld of dark desires*
3 new stories every month

For exclusive member offers go to
**millsandboon.co.uk/subscribe**

# *Which series will you try next?*

*Awaken the romance of the past...*
6 new stories every month

*The ultimate in romantic medical drama*
6 new stories every month

# MODERN™

*Power, passion and irresistible temptation*
8 new stories every month

MODERN
# tempted™

*True love and temptation!*
4 new stories every month